PENGUIN ⦿ CLASSICS

NORTHLAND STORIES

Jack London—his real name was John Griffith London—had a wild and colorful youth on the waterfront of San Francisco, his native city. Born in 1876, he left school at the age of fourteen and worked in a cannery. By the time he was sixteen he had been both an oyster pirate and a member of the Fish Patrol in San Francisco Bay and he later wrote about his experiences in *The Cruise of the Dazzler* (1902) and *Tales of the Fish Patrol* (1905). In 1893 he joined a sealing cruise which took him as far as Japan. Returning to the United States, he travelled throughout the country. He was determined to become a writer and read voraciously. After a brief period of study at the University of California he joined the gold rush to the Kondike in 1897. He returned to San Francisco the following year and wrote about his experiences. His short stories of the Yukon were published in *Overland Monthly* (1898) and the *Atlantic Monthly* (1899), and in 1900 his first collection, *The Son of the Wolf*, appeared, bringing him national fame. In 1902 he went to London, where he studied the slum conditions of the East End. He wrote about his experiences in *The People of the Abyss* (1903). His life was exciting and eventful. There were sailing voyages to the Caribbean and the South Seas. He reported on the Russo-Japanese War for the Hearst papers and gave lecture tours. A prolific writer, he published an enormous number of stories and novels. Besides several collections of short stories, including *Love of Life* (1907), *Lost Face* (1910), and *On the Makatoa Mat* (1919), he wrote many novels, including *The Call of the Wild* (1903), *The Sea-Wolf* (1904), *The Game* (1905), *White Fang* (1906), *The Iron Heel* (1908), *Martin Eden* (1909), and *The Star Rover* (1915). Jack London died in 1916, at his home in California.

Jonathan Auerbach, professor of English at the University of Maryland, College Park, is the author of *Male Call: Becoming Jack London* and *The Romance of Failure: First-Person Fictions of Poe, Hawthorne, and James*, as well as various articles on American literature and culture.

NORTHLAND STORIES

JACK LONDON

EDITED
WITH AN INTRODUCTION
AND NOTES BY
JONATHAN AUERBACH

PENGUIN BOOKS

To my father—J.A.

PENGUIN BOOKS

Published by the Penguin Group

Penguin Group (USA) Inc., 375 Hudson Street, New York, New York 10014, U.S.A.

Penguin Group (Canada), 90 Eglinton Avenue East, Suite 700, Toronto,
Ontario, Canada M4P 2Y3 (a division of Pearson Penguin Canada Inc.)

Penguin Books Ltd, 80 Strand, London WC2R 0RL, England

Penguin Ireland, 25 St Stephen's Green, Dublin 2, Ireland (a division of Penguin Books Ltd)

Penguin Group (Australia), 250 Camberwell Road, Camberwell,
Victoria 3124, Australia (a division of Pearson Australia Group Pty Ltd)

Penguin Books India Pvt Ltd, 11 Community Centre, Panchsheel Park, New Delhi – 110 017, India

Penguin Group (NZ), cnr Airborne and Rosedale Roads,
Albany, Auckland 1310, New Zealand (a division of Pearson New Zealand Ltd)

Penguin Books (South Africa) (Pty) Ltd, 24 Sturdee Avenue,
Rosebank, Johannesburg 2196, South Africa

Penguin Books Ltd, Registered Offices: 80 Strand, London WC2R 0RL, England

This volume first published in Penguin Books 1997

7   9   10   8   6

Introduction and notes copyright © Jonathan Auerbach, 1997
All rights reserved

LIBRARY OF CONGRESS CATALOGING-IN-PUBLICATION DATA
London, Jack, 1876–1916.
Northland stories / Jack London ; edited with an introduction and
notes by Jonathan Auerbach.
p.   cm. — (Penguin twentieth-century classics)
Includes bibliographical references (p.   ).
ISBN 0 14 01.8996 3 (pbk.)
I. Auerbach, Jonathan, 1954–   .   II. Title.   III. Series.
PS3523.O46A6   1997
813'.52—dc20   96-21720

Printed in the United States of America
Set in Stempel Garamond

CONTENTS

INTRODUCTION

In the summer of 1897 Jack London left San Francisco to seek his fortune in the Klondike, where gold had recently been discovered. Seventy-two years later, in 1969, a group of men set out to retrace the young man's adventures in the Yukon wilderness. Locating the very cabin in which the twenty-two-year-old stayed during the long winter, the expedition authenticated an extraordinary find: a log in a cabin wall still bearing the handwritten scrawl "Jack London. Miner, author, Jan. 27, 1898." By way of this signature, the aspiring writer had symbolically staked a claim to a small piece of the Yukon territory—a claim all the more revealing for its joining together the vocations of gold mining and writing.

Even though Jack London stayed less than a year in the Klondike and discovered no fortune, his trip to the Yukon proved invaluable. Soon after his return to California, he published in yearly succession three collections of Northland stories—*The Son of the Wolf* (1900), *The God of His Fathers* (1901), and *Children of the Frost* (1902), to be quickly followed by his wildly successful novel *The Call of the Wild* (1903). The site of his initial fame as a writer, the Far North remains today in the popular imagination closely linked with the name Jack London. Making his mark in testimony to his twin ambitions of finding Eldorado and becoming an author, the young man who whiled away the cold, dead winter by dreaming of wealth thus proved to be more prophetic than he could ever have hoped or expected.

Yet our childhood memories play tricks on us if we recall only London's fictional Northland filled with the extended adventures of gold miners and their furry counterparts. Most of these early tales detail strenuous toil and pursuit, not digging for gold, activities that spoke profoundly to turn-of-the-century American anxieties about masculinity and racial identity, as I demonstrate shortly. Rather than directly associate London's interest in mining with events rendered in his stories, we therefore need to regard the vocation of prospecting more in terms of London's perceived prospects as a successful man of letters—a business every bit as risky and prone to failure as searching for nuggets of gold.

At the turn of the last century the chances of making it as a professional author in the United States were about as slim as striking it rich in the Yukon. Like gold mining, writing for a living was clearly a long shot, but occasionally offered the talented, diligent, and lucky few quite a sizable income. The explosive growth of publishing in the 1890s triggered a Gold Rush of another sort, helping a number of authors such as Mark Twain and Rudyard Kipling to reach a kind of celebrity status thanks to new methods that mass-marketed, distributed, and promoted books and magazines. But for every best-selling author earning hundreds of thousands of dollars, there were scores of would-be writers who received nothing but rejection slips. The rate of acceptance for mass-circulation magazines such as the *Ladies' Home Journal*, for example, hovered around 4 percent, presenting daunting odds indeed for any literary aspirant setting out to make a name from scratch.

These facts of failure and success were not lost on Jack London, who as early as 1893 was awarded twenty-five dollars in an amateur writing contest sponsored by a local San Francisco newspaper. At the time he was working in a jute mill earning ten cents an hour, so that his prize money for a single short sketch written over a period of a few days represented roughly the equivalent of a month's pay as a wage slave. Having toiled since the age of fifteen at a series of tedious, low-paying jobs—in a cannery, a power plant, and a laundry, in addition to the jute mill—Jack London had decided by 1897 (the year he headed up north) to abandon manual labor in order to try his hand at another kind of occupation, to be a "brain merchant," as he dubbed the work of the writer.

London's experience in the Yukon was crucial for his literary apprenticeship, not because it afforded him much direct raw material for his writing, but rather because it gave him a special sense of place—a figurative terrain that he could imaginatively make his own. As Richard Brodhead has recently pointed out, during the late nineteenth century the important literary mode of regional writing became a crucial way for unknown, disenfranchised American writers such as London to gain access to centers and institutions of publishing otherwise unavailable to them.[1] These writers made up for their lack of cultural clout—traditionally defined in terms of college and business connections, social status, or professional training—by cashing in on their presumed authentic expertise representing particular places and particular ways of life that genteel middle-class readers, armchair tourists as it were, often found especially attractive.

As one such specialized region, the Far North thus enabled Jack London to forge a unique authorial identity for himself. He could construct such a trademark self, London realized, only in conjunction with a trademark locale. In his early letters to friends expressing his professional ambitions, he often called this regional work a brand-new literary "field" awaiting the author's "exploitation." With the key term "field" London connected the space imagined inside the fiction with the space in the writer's market that he hoped to occupy by successfully placing these stories set exclusively in the Klondike.

Beyond the question of access to publishing, literary regionalism afforded aspiring authors other tangible benefits as well. Following the career trajectory of many other young writers, Jack London began his literary apprenticeship by sending out individual short stories, poems, and essays to an array of established and obscure periodicals, hoping to make his reputation by gradually building up a loyal following of magazine readers. Such magazines paid their contributors piecemeal, often by the word, with rates for beginners ranging from as low as one dollar to ten dollars or perhaps twenty dollars per thousand words. Such a system of literary pay and production turned authors into independent entrepreneurs (like miners working in gold fields), each struggling to break into the writers' market.

Recognizing the shaky financial status of magazine work, as well as the ephemeral, fragmentary nature of magazine print,

1. Richard Brodhead, *Cultures of Letters: Scenes of Reading and Writing in Nineteenth-Century America* (Chicago: University of Chicago Press, 1993), pp. 107–76.

London also aspired to publish books—a more enduring, prestigious, and lucrative medium. Regionalism offered writers one crucial means to move from magazines to books by allowing them to conceive of their shorter, discrete productions as potentially part of a greater whole unified by a single sense of place. Needing a steady income to pay his bills, London could take his chances on monthly piecemeal magazine placement and still hope for a second, larger bonus to come: a collected volume; in effect being paid twice for these same stories.

From an aesthetic point of view regional writing could also give authors greater control over their productions. Pieces that were often cut and maimed by magazine editors worrying about length could be restored to their proper condition as parts of a coherent body of work, thereby reinforcing the integrity of the author himself. Consider, for instance, London's first big breakthrough. In August 1899 his long, ambitious Klondike tale "An Odyssey of the North," was accepted by the prestigious *Atlantic Monthly*, which had been publishing regional writing since the Civil War. The magazine offered London the prodigious sum of $120 if he was willing to shorten the story's opening by three thousand words, which he quickly agreed to do. Within a few months his first collection of nine Klondike stories, *The Son of the Wolf: Tales of the Far North*, had been accepted for book publication by the equally prestigious publisher Houghton, Mifflin, with the concluding tale "An Odyssey of the North" returned to its original state.

London's triumph was largely a matter of timing, combined with a shrewd submission strategy. Just as he was beginning to shop around for a book publisher in the summer of 1899, London stopped publishing his Klondike stories in the local San Francisco magazine *Overland Monthly* (once edited by Bret Harte) to try for greater national exposure. More pointedly, the publishing house Houghton, Mifflin actually owned the *Atlantic Monthly*, whose influential editor William B. Parker was so impressed with "An Odyssey of the North" that he recommended London's entire volume when London submitted it to Houghton, Mifflin soon thereafter. Grasping the intimate relationship between a respected magazine and its parent company, London was thus able to parlay their acceptance of his short stories into a book contract.

As the example of "An Odyssey of the North" shows, London's early successes as a writer to a large extent derived from his knack for seizing the opportunities presented by turn-of-the-century publishing's multiple venues. From the very start of his career, London regarded virtually all of his pieces as potential parts of books; in the back of an early notebook recording magazine submissions, rejections, and acceptances, the young writer spent page after page trying to organize previously published works, listed by title and word count, into various groupings—"Hints on Writing," "Economic Essays," "Future Tales," and, of course, "Klondike Tales"—that would each add up to a book. Set in one particular region, London's Yukon material was particularly apt to be construed as a "series," as he himself called this writing. After his Northland story "To the Man on Trail" was accepted by the *Overland Monthly* in December 1898 (mistitled and for the paltry sum of five dollars), the editor, James Howard Bridge, encouraged London to submit more work in the same vein as a kind of package deal. Bridge even began numbering London's story subtitles consecutively as they appeared monthly in order to remind his magazine's readers that London's stories constituted a continuing Northland saga.

Both Bridge and London understood that these stories needed more than just a common setting to make them cohere as a series. Following the practice of other regionalists, particularly popular writers of Westerns, London organized his *Overland* magazine stories around a recurring character, the "Malemute Kid," who would end up appearing in seven out of the nine tales collected in *The Son of the Wolf*. A hardened veteran of the Klondike, the Kid initially served as the presiding moral center of London's fictional Northland. In his various roles as arbiter of disputes, sympathetic auditor, and main actor, the Malemute Kid offered London's magazine readers an exemplary source of manly strength and wisdom. Yet despite Bridge's enthusiasm for the Kid, London in his letters to friends betrayed a certain impatience with his own creation, who bore a perilously close resemblance to stock frontier figures peopling so many dime novel Westerns and detective stories produced during the 1870s, '80s, and '90s. This dime novel mode of publishing was frequently modeled after factory production, with authors anonymously or pseudonymously churning out stories and novels dominated by trademark protagonists such as Deadwood Dick, Old Sleuth, and Nick Carter. In many cases these character types became the legal property of the publishers who hired the writers, and not the writers themselves.

Jack London simply would not allow a fictional protagonist—even one of his own devising—to overshadow his potential fame as a man of letters. Beyond character and setting, he searched for a way to impress upon these Northland tales his unique authorial personality, what he termed (in an 1899 advice essay addressed to other literary aspirants) the writer's "stamp of 'self'." In this respect the instrumental tale bearing such a stamp remains "The White Silence," which appeared second in the *Overland* series, but which London pointedly selected to lead off his first collected volume, *The Son of the Wolf*. Titled "A Northland Episode" when first submitted to *Godey's* on October 4, 1898, the story's far more suggestive revised title derives from a passage midway through the narrative. Recounting the desperate race of the half-starving Malemute Kid, a companion named Mason, and his Indian wife, Ruth, on trail across the frozen wilderness, London pauses to offer a context for their toil: "with the awe, born of the White Silence, the voiceless travelers bent to their work."

In the course of narrating the subsequent sacrifice of one of these three characters for the sake of the other two, London repeats four times this capitalized expression. This recurring signature phrase, "the White Silence," designed to establish the author's strong individual presence (his and his alone) at the same time that it figuratively registers an atmosphere of menace and wonder governing the Northland landscape, also appears at key moments in other stories throughout the collection. The phrase clearly maps a state of mind, not a geography—a mood in which the activity of work speaks louder than words. Here we can see how London's concept of a fictional "field" is more interesting and innovative than a mere "series," looking forward to modernist short story cycles such as Jean Toomer's *Cane* (1923) and Hemingway's *In Our Time* (1925), whose discrete parts are unified by lyrical abstractions beyond specific place or people or plot.

To appreciate more fully how London's Northland tales actually function as a coherent "field" of writing, we need to return to the year 1897. London's brand of regionalism, it turns out, would come to depend on a complex unfolding symbolic genealogy. In June, about a month before leaving for the Yukon, London received a remarkable pair of letters from an itinerant astrologer named W. H. Chaney, whom London had lately suspected of being his real biological father. Bluntly denying his patrimony, Chaney left London with little but to muse on his presumed illegitimacy. London's response to Chaney's denial was to submit for national publication an early batch of stories, among them a curious gothic potboiler entitled "A Thousand Deaths." London later credited this lurid tale with saving his literary career when it was finally accepted for the hefty sum of forty dollars in early 1899. The story concerns a mad scientist who at first fails to recognize his own son, but then repeatedly subjects him to sadistic rounds of lethal torture and miraculous resuscitation, only to be himself vaporized by the son in the end.

This story carries profound implications for London's attempts at self-location as a writer. Cruelly rejected by his ostensible father, London within weeks submitted a fantasy about a son's patricidal revenge and then immediately headed north. Upon his return, he began generic streamlining, focusing on a series of stories all set in the Yukon whose characters are united by virtue of belonging to a single common family. London called this family the "Wolf" clan, identifying his fictional Northland protagonists (including his surrogate the "Malemute Kid" and implicitly himself) collectively as "The Son of the Wolf"—the story which appeared third in the *Overland* sequence, but whose title London chose for his first collected volume. And so began Jack London's lifelong fascination with the figure of the wolf, his personal projection of dominance and power, as well as the intimate nickname by which he would call himself a few years later in affectionate letters to his wife, Charmian, and his best friend, George Sterling.

Trading in the surname "Chaney" for "Wolf," the aspiring author in the field of the Klondike "found myself" (as he fondly liked to recall) by replacing his biological father with an imaginary set of tribal clansmen. By "Wolf" London meant something rather specific, as the seldom reprinted title story makes quite clear. A young but grizzled gold prospector named Scruff Mackenzie leaves his cozy cabin to seek wealth of another sort—a wife and helpmate. He boldly chooses for his bride the daughter of an Indian chief, whose tribal clan, "the Raven," has come to identify these few strange white men invading the Northland as "Sons of the Wolf." Forcibly stealing the royal daughter against the wishes of the natives, Mackenzie warns his vanquished foes to heed "the Law of the Wolf." This law the Indians themselves have associated with "the fighting and destructive principle"—the Devil—as opposed to the "creative principles" governing their tribe.

"Wolf" thus stands for the white race, whose sons are conceived by London as belonging to their own totemic clan which is defined by, even as it is opposed to, Native Americans. While "the Law of the Wolf" in this story explicitly concerns the white man's exacting brand of punishment, more generally, totemic law functions in London's fictional Northland to dictate social relations. These relations depend on racial difference, which is why Mackenzie seeks a red bride, no less than a princess, who also happens to be the sister of Ruth in "The White Silence." The irony is that although the Indians in the tale argue against interracial marriage in order to preserve the purity of their threatened clan, the "Wolf" Mackenzie fears no such impurity. In fact the white man is compelled to take a racial Other as his mate, given the practice of exogamy, which under totemic law prohibits marriage within a single group. The native "Raven" conversely adopt the familiar rhetoric of United States citizens, such as President Teddy Roosevelt, who reacted to the great influx of immigrants and "alien" peoples at the turn of the century by darkly prophesizing racial suicide. By putting this dread of mixed blood in the mouths of Indians, London forced his contemporary readers to question some of their most basic assumptions about race.

Clearly not all of the more than fifty stories London set in the Klondike concern miscegenation. "In a Far Country," for instance, tells the chilling tale of two men of differing social classes cooped up together in a cabin—a difficult "marriage" of another sort anticipating the intense homoerotic strife between men that London would later explore in his novel *The Sea-Wolf* (1904). But from "The Son of the Wolf" and "The White Silence," which introduces us to the pregnant native wife, Ruth, (and her impending half-breed child), to the powerful tales "The League of the Old Men" and "The Story of Jees Uck," miscegenation lies at the very heart of London's early Northland narratives. In "An Odyssey of the North," to cite one notable example, London actually offers two stories of racial intermingling: the tale of the Indian Naass who narrates his obsessive quest to retrieve his intended Indian bride, Unga, stolen from him on his wedding night by a mighty superhuman white man; and the related myth of the Indian's own racial origins which can be traced to a prior primal encounter between white and red, whose fates have been linked, this myth suggests, long before the recent incursion of the likes of the Malemute Kid, Mason, and Mackenzie.

These relations between white men and red women have enormous import for our understanding of London's Northland as a single evolving conceptual field extending beyond individual stories and even beyond individual collections of stories. Although it is intriguing to speculate about his ordering of tales within particular volumes—why "The White Silence" precedes "The Son of the Wolf" in *The Son of the Wolf*, for example—we therefore need to consider how miscegenation (sanctioned by whites but feared by native men) operates more broadly throughout these tales to establish for London an imaginary kinship based on a rediscovered patriarchal order.

London's progressive search for patriarchy takes place in three stages that roughly correspond to his first three volumes of stories. Throughout *The Son of the Wolf* (1900) he represents white men ravishing Indian brides. The next volume, *The God of His Fathers* (1901), focuses on the strength of these red "daughters of the soil" as mates, while simultaneously exploring the role of white women as mothers (but not wives). In his third Northland collection, *Children of the Frost* (1902), London finally directs his attention to tribal elders, the royal fathers who are originally responsible for setting totemic law even as they have become increasingly victimized by the rapacious sons of the Wolf.

Does London's primary identification between white men and the domineering Wolf make him a blatant racist? His interest in giving some voice to the "Raven" who bestow the designation "Wolf" on their more aggressive foes would suggest otherwise. Most recent discussions of turn-of-the-century theories of race assume Anglo-Saxon supremacy was modeled either on conquest and exploitation of the colonized subject, or else, a bit more improbably, on the isolationist's dread of racial contamination altogether. But once we take London's initial representation of "Wolf" and "Raven" clans seriously, his rendering of interracial marriage throughout his Northland suggests a third, more intricate set of possibilities in keeping with early-twentieth-century ethnographers and thinkers such as Sigmund Freud and Émile Durkheim. These writers found in totemism one way to theorize about the religious foundations of secular society. Like these thinkers, albeit less systematically, London discovered how primitivism in general and totemism in particular could help make some sense of the rapid social changes brought about by a bewildering modernity. These changes more immediately and personally for London concerned his own status in the social order as an ambitious working-class Nobody with no cultural capital trying to make a name for himself in publishing—to imagine his place, establish a field of kinship, as an author.

Most commentary on these early Klondike tales has tended to shy away from race altogether to concentrate on London's heroic representations of manhood—virtues such as valor, loyalty, and steadfastness displayed by the Malemute Kid and his comrades. These moral attributes constitute what London calls "the code of the Yukon": how men in the wild and in the absence of civil law interact with one another. Assumed as unchanging universal constants, or a bit more pointedly as prime components of London's literary naturalism, these manly characteristics take on an inert, static quality. But focusing on totemism allows us to historicize such concepts by reading them in relation to the question of race. By so merging race and manhood in relation to totemic law— equating the sons of the Wolf with white *men* who sustain their clan by taking red *women*—London in effect manages to revise, if not completely reinvent, turn-of-the-century notions of manhood as well as race.

A small but especially important clue to understanding this conceptual revision can be found in London's prefatory dedication to *The Son of the Wolf*. Summing up the collection's thematic integrity, this preface serves as the author's sharpest gloss on his own work. The dedication reads: TO THE SONS OF THE WOLF WHO SOUGHT THEIR HERITAGE AND LEFT THEIR BONES AMONG THE SHADOWS OF THE CIRCLE. By linking the ambiguous word "heritage" with the verb "sought," London implies that white manhood is a condition that must be earned, achieved, and won, not passively taken for granted. Like the White Silence, racial categories in the Northland refer primarily to a state of mind. Here London overturns the prevailing belief of many of his contemporaries who assumed that racial difference was grounded in a set of natural, biological givens. For all of his professed adherence to Darwin's theory, London's views on race more closely anticipate Durkheim's. Analyzing totemic kinship as an abstract system of social organization governed by the symbolic logic of religion, Durkheim insisted that clan affiliations in primitive societies need not depend strictly on geographical region or biological bloodlines, as previous ethnographers had supposed.

If London's protagonists become Wolves amidst the White Silence by virtue of their will and hard work, then it stands to reason that the category of "whiteness" would be available to anyone. In this regard the most interesting and resonant recurring Northland character is not the Malemute Kid, but Sitka Charley, an Indian trail guide and letter carrier who (unlike the Kid) continues to show up in London's fiction after the first volume of stories. Charley is a "white" Indian, as London takes some length to explain in the opening paragraph of "The Wisdom of the Trail": "Sitka Charley had achieved the impossible. Other Indians might have known as much of the wisdom of the trail as did he; but he alone knew the white man's wisdom, the honor of the trail, and the law. . . . Being an alien, when he did know he knew it better than the white man himself." While the concluding reference to the native as an "alien" generates a sharp set of ironies of its own, at least London entertains the possibility that an Indian man could in effect convert to whiteness by virtue of fully realizing its higher law. Charley's symbolic status becomes crucial later in the story when he is paired on trail with a Mrs. Eppingwell, one of only two white women in *The Son of the Wolf*. Unwilling or unable to imagine reverse miscegenation—a red man taking a white bride—London links Charley and this (already married) woman at a more abstract conceptual level: What Charley learns to love and respect about Mrs. Eppingwell is her toughness, which in so resembling his own enables him to appreciate "why the sons of such women mastered the land and the sea, and why the sons of his own womankind could not prevail against them."

Introducing this white mother by way of a converted Indian, whose "manhood" is "nourished" by her presence, London's thinking on race takes a considerable turn in "The Wisdom of the Trail." In the absence of any white fathers (the presumed father W. H. Chaney had denied him, after all), London relies on white mothers to help define his sons of the Wolf precisely at the moment a powerful "white" red man has emerged in his fiction to destabilize fixed racial categories. As many feminist theorists have suggested, patriarchy is anxiety-provoking because fathers can remain invisible, in ways that mothers, as birth givers, tangibly cannot; to counteract the authority of a "white" Indian who threatens to undermine the "Wolf" clan's essential foundations, London bypasses the missing father altogether to reanchor racial identity along matrilineal lines.

London codifies this genealogy of mothers in the dedication prefacing *The God of His Fathers*, which reads: TO THE DAUGHTERS OF THE WOLF WHO HAVE BRED AND SUCKLED A RACE OF MEN. Ostensibly a parallel to the dedication prefacing his first volume, this second, curious dedication actually works quite differently. London would seem to have skipped a generation. Although he introduces these women as daughters of the "Wolf" clan (presumably still representing the white race), London immediately shifts to their roles as mothers, so that "a race of men" have in effect become the sons of the daughters of the Wolf. Part of the confusion stems from London's effort in these stories to treat two

very distinct sorts of women at once: Indian wives, who are cele-
brated in tales such as "Where the Trail Forks," "Siwash," and
"Grit of Women" (narrated by Sitka Charley) for their loyalty
and endurance of hardship, and white mothers, who somehow
magically pass on their own strength to their sons.

By such a sharp bifurcation between the roles of mother and
helpmate, London manages to avoid (for the most part) the un-
settling prospect of the half-breed—a possibility which has
loomed large in his Northland since the character of the pregnant
Ruth appeared in "The White Silence." Akin to the mulatto, the
figure of the half-breed threatens to blur racial difference. But in
steering clear of such blurring by keeping the roles of mother and
wife so separated, London creates other problems for himself, ob-
scuring the very distinction between "Raven" and "Wolf" that he
had initially posited in his early Klondike tales.

Comparing these two dedications enables us to see a larger set
of contradictions beginning to riddle Jack London's growing
Northland field. As the second dedication suggests, London is
moving in two directions at once: backward in mythic time
searching for the origins of patriarchy, and forward in historical
time documenting the incursion of whites in the Yukon Territory.
The introduction of Mrs. Eppingwell in the Far North signals a
stage in the colonizing process that inevitably must follow the
appearance of the original "Wolf" Mason, but which also functions for London to explain how these men got there in the first
place. Historians of the Canadian fur trade have noted how the
introduction of white women into the Far North triggered an
increase in racism aimed against native women, who were readily
accepted as mates until white women arrived on the scene.[2] In this
regard there is some historical validity behind London's dedication in *The God of His Fathers* praising white women, whose
strength is linked to the ideology of Anglo-Saxon supremacy.
Such an ideology, or rather theology of race, is depicted most
dramatically in the volume's first (and title) story. But in so re-
fusing to give up native women as wives, emphasizing white

2. See, for instance, Sylvia Van Kirk, *Many Tender Ties: Women in Fur-Trade
Society, 1670–1870* (Norman: University of Oklahoma Press, 1980).

women solely as mothers of the race, London mixes history with myth in his continuing search for the foundations of patriarchy.

In his next collection, *Children of the Frost*, that search would take him past symbolic mothers to return to the missing father. The "Wolf," London discovered, could be understood only directly in relation to those tribal elders whose daughters had been taken as brides. In a letter to his Macmillan publisher, George Brett, London remarked that his ambition in writing this volume of stories was to represent the Indian's point of view. But most of these rarely reprinted tales have a far more specific focus, documenting in effect the tragic destruction of patriarchal law itself at the hands of the white race. These Indian leaders are old and they are dying along with their children, emasculated by liquor ("The Death of Ligoun"), by Christianity ("Keesh, the Son of Keesh"), by the hunger for material goods ("Li Wan, the Fair"), and other gifts bestowed by the white man. Digging deeper and deeper for the sources of patriarchy, London gradually has come up against an all too present history. Even a familiar tale like "The Law of Life," which would seem to offer the purest demonstration of nature's Darwinian logic, takes on a more urgent and immediate cast when set in the context of these other disturbing and violent stories portraying ruined kings.

Such a dark view of defeated manhood compels London to alter his representation of women. While the first two collections of Klondike stories depict native women as items of exchange who assure bonds of totemic kinship among men, here London begins to see these native fathers and daughters as unwilling actors in a larger historical process driven by the expansion of capital into foreign lands. No longer governed by miscegenation, social relations in the Northland have become mainly dictated by commerce, with commodities replacing squaws as fetishized objects of desire for both white and red men. The economy of the totem, based on the principle of exogamy, has turned into the rule of the capitalist State.

The destructive force of commerce had made itself felt in London's Far North since "The Son of the Wolf." But in these earlier tales London is more intent on imaginatively establishing his "Wolf" kinship than in exploring the consequences of his exploitation of a regional field. Only by letting dying patriarchs speak for themselves does London begin to come to terms with his attempted reconstruction of race. In this regard London's crowning achievement remains "The League of the Old Men," one of his greatest and most poignant tales, which he chose to conclude *Children of the Frost*. The main action of the story takes place in a court of law, where Old Imber, an Indian chief, faces punishment for murdering whites. The figurative "Law of the Wolf" is thus rendered as a concrete institution which no longer dispenses the Malemute Kid's informal (but highly moral) brand of frontier justice. In the earlier tale "To the Man on Trail" the Kid and his mates triumph over the official agents of the law. But now the wisdom of the trail has given way to the machinery of a trial. Yet in moving from trail to trial whom does London view as the real criminal?

As the story opens we see how London's Klondike is now under the control of a series of state functionaries—clerks, mounted policemen, governor, presiding judge—all surrogates for the "chief white man" that London has been searching for throughout the Northland and is yet to find. Against the inexorable incursions of the State, Imber and his fellow tribal elders have banded together to form a terrorist union of their own bent on taking the white man down with them. At a key moment in Imber's confession, London interrupts the native's testimony to bring his own art to account. He registers the illiterate Indian's shock at the power of writing as a magical instrument of subjugation, as opposed to the impermanence of Imber's own act of speaking. Not these petty functionaries, not even the authority of the court, hold the secret to the Wolf's domination, but rather the field of writing/reading through which the symbolic Law of the (White) Father makes itself known.

Jack London used to insist to his friends, somewhat notoriously, that he was a white man first and a socialist only second. But his sympathetic rendering of conspiring red revolutionaries in "The League of the Old Men" suggests a more complex and unstable relation between his thinking on race and his politics. Closing out three concentrated collections totaling thirty tales, "The League of the Old Men" culminates London's search for patriarchal order in the Northland. In its ambitious anatomizing of the regulatory function of the State, the story also harkens back to London's earliest public role as "Boy Socialist of Oakland" (in 1895–96), as well as looking forward to his powerful depiction of class warfare in *The Iron Heel* (1908). No wonder London himself once deemed "The League of the Old Men" his favorite story.

After "The League" London would continue to publish other tales set in the Klondike, including "Love of Life" (1905) and his most famous short story of all, "To Build a Fire" (1908). In addition to these well-known tales of survival, this present edition reprints "The Sun-Dog Trail" (first published in 1905)—a brilliant, austere narrative that again takes up the question of writing/reading in its depiction of an obsessive pursuit through ice and snow with no apparent object. By way of such Northland trailing, London explores the relationship between artistic production and interpretation; although the story would seem to have little to do with race, it is noteworthy that this quest narrative is told by Sitka Charley, appearing for the final time in London's fiction. The "white" native's role as an illiterate mailman and trail guide—an entrepreneur for hire—significantly sheds light on London's self-perception as a writer engaged in his own strenuous pursuit of signs.

The pointed illiteracy of the Indians Imber and Charley also gives us a crucial clue as to what would subsequently become of the question of race in London's Northland. Early in Imber's mythic account of the white man's invasion of his tribe's land, he remarks that the first Wolf brought with him an equally strange hairless dog, who begins breeding with the Indians' own wolf-like dogs to produce a new stock of dog, "big-headed, thick-jawed, and short-haired, and helpless" in the wilderness. The miscegenation between "Wolf" and "Raven" clans is thus matched by an analogous miscegenation of their animals, whose offspring bears a striking resemblance to London's most famous creation of all: Buck in *The Call of the Wild* (1903), which London began composing two months after *Children of the Frost* was published. As a mail carrier in the wild, learning how to deliver letters without being able to read them, London's animal protagonist closely follows in the footsteps of Imber and carries on the hard work of

Charley. The dog's link to Northland natives is reinforced by his very name; showing up in a number of these tales, including "Where the Trail Forks" (which ends with a passage about animal interbreeding), the word "buck" at the turn of the century was common slang for an Indian male. As an intelligent beast, not a noble savage, Buck further enables London to treat racial crossing in terms of a naturalist parable of survival. Transforming concepts of race into the concept of species, London at once naturalizes the cultural categories of "white" and "red" at the same time that he literalizes his quest for the status of "Wolf." By the end of *The Call of the Wild*, Buck has actually turned into a wolf—the very creature that London's men in the Northland could only approximate through totemic identification. Working like a dog, Buck lets his author Jack completely realize the "Wolf" in him: to become in effect his own self-sufficient father.

The Call of the Wild remains London's most enduring fiction. Readers over the years have attributed the narrative's power to its lyrical mythopoetic structure—a universal quest-romance celebrating a hero's initiation, courage, education, survival, and eventual apotheosis. Yet situating the novel in relation to London's first three collections of Northland tales, seeing it as a logical extension of London's ongoing, evolving treatment of totemic kinship, may help give us a new perspective on a very familiar text. Perhaps we find *The Call of the Wild* so satisfying, so comforting, because anxieties about race and manhood seem to be completely absent in it—anxieties that London expressed more openly, albeit more uncertainly, throughout his early Klondike tales. Preparing the way for Buck, this Northland field of publication deserves our close and sustained revisiting: the region where Jack London first struck gold, first found himself as a man of letters.

SUGGESTIONS FOR FURTHER READING

EDITIONS

London, Jack. *The Letters of Jack London*. Edited by Earle Labor, Robert C. Leitz III, and I. Milo Shepard. 3 vols. Stanford: Stanford University Press, 1988.

————. *The Complete Stories of Jack London*. Edited by Earle Labor, Robert C. Leitz III, and I. Milo Shepard. 3 vols. Stanford: Stanford University Press, 1993.

BOOKS

Auerbach, Jonathan. *Male Call: Becoming Jack London*. Durham: Duke University Press, 1996.

Cassuto, Leonard, and Jeanne Campbell Reesman, eds. *Rereading Jack London*. Stanford: Stanford University Press, 1996.

Foner, Philip S. *Jack London, American Rebel: A Collection of His Social Writings Together with an Extensive Study of the Man and His Times*. New York: Citadel, 1947.

Hedrick, Joan D. *Solitary Comrade: Jack London and His Work*. Chapel Hill: University of North Carolina Press, 1982.

Johnston, Carolyn. *Jack London—An American Radical?* Westport, Conn.: Greenwood, 1984.

Kingman, Russ. *A Pictorial Life of Jack London*. New York: Crown Publishers, 1979.

Labor, Earle, and Jeanne Campbell Reesman. *Jack London*. Rev. ed. New York: Twayne, 1994.

London, Joan. *Jack London and His Times: An Unconventional Biography*. New York: Doubleday, Doran, 1939; reprint, Seattle: University of Washington Press, 1968.

McClintock, James I. *White Logic: Jack London's Short Stories*. Grand Rapids, Mich.: Wolf House Books, 1975.

Sinclair, Andrew. *Jack: A Biography of Jack London*. New York: Harper & Row, 1977.

Walker, Franklin. *Jack London and the Klondike*. San Marino, Calif.: Huntington Library, 1966.

Watson, Charles N., Jr. *The Novels of Jack London: A Reappraisal*. Madison: University of Wisconsin Press, 1983.

A NOTE ON THE TEXT

This Penguin Twentieth-Century Classics edition of selected Northland stories is based on the first American book editions of Jack London's short story collections. Although many of these stories were initially published in periodicals, London regularly used the opportunity of book publication to restore cuts and changes that had been made previously by magazine editors. With the exception of a few minor typographical errors, which have been silently corrected, the present edition preserves the spelling and punctuation (including open contractions) in the texts of the first editions. For a list of original dates and places of publication for these stories, see Appendix.

NORTHLAND STORIES

The White Silence

"Carmen won't last more than a couple of days." Mason spat out a chunk of ice and surveyed the poor animal ruefully, then put her foot in his mouth and proceeded to bite out the ice which clustered cruelly between the toes.

"I never saw a dog with a highfalutin' name that ever was worth a rap," he said, as he concluded his task and shoved her aside. "They just fade away and die under the responsibility. Did ye ever see one go wrong with a sensible name like Cassiar, Siwash, or Husky? No, sir! Take a look at Shookum here, he's"—

Snap! The lean brute flashed up, the white teeth just missing Mason's throat.

"Ye will, will ye?" A shrewd clout behind the ear with the butt of the dogwhip stretched the animal in the snow, quivering softly, a yellow slaver dripping from its fangs.

"As I was saying, just look at Shookum, here—he's got the spirit. Bet ye he eats Carmen before the week's out."

"I'll bank another proposition against that," replied Malemute Kid, reversing the frozen bread placed before the fire to thaw. "We'll eat Shookum before the trip is over. What d' ye say, Ruth?"

The Indian woman settled the coffee with a piece of ice, glanced from Malemute Kid to her husband, then at the dogs, but vouchsafed no reply. It was such a palpable truism that none was necessary. Two hundred miles of unbroken trail in prospect, with a scant six days' grub for themselves and none for the dogs, could admit no other alternative. The two men and the woman grouped about the fire and began their meagre meal. The dogs lay in their harnesses, for it was a midday halt, and watched each mouthful enviously.

"No more lunches after to-day," said Malemute Kid. "And we've got to keep a close eye on the dogs,—they're getting vicious. They'd just as soon pull a fellow down as not, if they get a chance."

"And I was president of an Epworth once, and taught in the Sunday school." Having irrelevantly delivered himself of this, Mason fell into a dreamy contemplation of his steaming moccasins, but was aroused by Ruth filling his cup. "Thank God, we've got slathers of tea! I've seen it growing, down in Tennessee. What would n't I give for a hot corn pone just now! Never mind, Ruth; you won't starve much longer, nor wear moccasins either."

The woman threw off her gloom at this, and in her eyes welled up a great love for her white lord,—the first white man she had ever seen,—the first man whom she had known to treat a woman as something better than a mere animal or beast of burden.

"Yes, Ruth," continued her husband, having recourse to the macaronic jargon in which it was alone possible for them to understand each other; "wait till we clean up and pull for the Outside. We'll take the White Man's canoe and go to the Salt Water. Yes, bad water, rough water,—great mountains dance up and down all the time. And so big, so far, so far away,—you travel ten sleep, twenty sleep, forty sleep" (he graphically enumerated the days on his fingers), "all the time water, bad water. Then you come to great village, plenty people, just the same mosquitoes next summer. Wigwams oh, so high,—ten, twenty pines. Hi-yu skookum!"

He paused impotently, cast an appealing glance at Malemute Kid, then laboriously placed the twenty pines, end on end, by sign language. Malemute Kid smiled with cheery cynicism; but Ruth's eyes were wide with wonder, and with pleasure; for she half believed he was joking, and such condescension pleased her poor woman's heart.

"And then you step into a—a box, and pouf! up you go." He tossed his empty cup in the air by way of illustration, and as he deftly caught it, cried: "And biff! down you come. Oh, great medicine-men! You go Fort Yukon, I go Arctic City,—twenty-five sleep,—big string, all the time,—I catch him string,—I say, 'Hello, Ruth! How are ye?'—and you say, 'Is that my good husband?'—and I say 'Yes,'—and you say, 'No can bake good bread, no more soda,'—then I say, 'Look in cache, under flour; good-by.' You look and catch plenty soda. All the time you Fort Yukon, me Arctic City. Hi-yu medicine-man!"

Ruth smiled so ingenuously at the fairy story, that both men burst into laughter. A row among the dogs cut short the wonders of the Outside, and by the time the snarling combatants were separated, she had lashed the sleds and all was ready for the trail.

"Mush! Baldy! Hi! Mush on!" Mason worked his whip smartly, and as the dogs whined low in the traces, broke out the sled with the gee-pole. Ruth followed with the second team, leaving Malemute Kid, who had helped her start, to bring up the rear. Strong man, brute that he was, capable of felling an ox at a blow, he could not bear to beat the poor animals, but humored them as a dog-driver rarely does,—nay, almost wept with them in their misery.

"Come, mush on there, you poor sorefooted brutes!" he murmured, after several ineffectual attempts to start the load. But his patience was at last rewarded, and though whimpering with pain, they hastened to join their fellows.

No more conversation; the toil of the trail will not permit such extravagance. And of all deadening labors, that of the Northland trail is the worst. Happy is the man who can weather a day's travel at the price of silence, and that on a beaten track.

And of all heart-breaking labors, that of breaking trail is the worst. At every step the great webbed shoe sinks till the snow is level with the knee. Then up, straight up, the deviation of a fraction of an inch being a certain precursor of disaster, the snowshoe must be lifted till the surface is cleared; then forward, down, and the other foot is raised perpendicularly for the matter of half a yard. He who tries this for the first time, if haply he avoids bringing his shoes in dangerous propinquity and measures not his length on the treacherous footing, will give up exhausted at the end of a hundred yards; he who can keep out of the way of the dogs for a whole day may well crawl into his sleeping-bag with a clear conscience and a pride which passeth all understanding; and he who travels twenty sleeps on the Long Trail is a man whom the gods may envy.

The afternoon wore on, and with the awe, born of the White Silence, the voiceless travelers bent to their work. Nature has many tricks wherewith she convinces man of his finity,—the ceaseless flow of the tides, the fury of the storm, the shock of the earthquake, the long roll of heaven's artillery,—but the most tremendous, the most stupefying of all, is the passive phase of the White Silence. All movement ceases, the sky clears, the heavens are as brass; the slightest whisper seems sacrilege, and man becomes timid, affrighted at the sound of his own voice. Sole speck of life journeying across the ghostly wastes of a dead world, he trembles at his audacity, realizes that his is a maggot's life, nothing more. Strange thoughts arise unsummoned, and the mystery of all things strives for utterance. And the fear of death, of God, of the universe, comes over him,—the hope of the Resurrection and the Life, the yearning for immortality, the vain striving of the imprisoned essence,—it is then, if ever, man walks alone with God.

So wore the day away. The river took a great bend, and Mason headed his team for the cut-off across the narrow neck of land. But the dogs balked at the high bank. Again and again, though Ruth and Malemute Kid were shoving on the sled, they slipped back. Then came the concerted effort. The miserable creatures, weak from hunger, exerted their last strength. Up—up—the sled poised on the top of the bank; but the leader swung the string of dogs behind him to the right, fouling Mason's snowshoes. The result was grievous. Mason was whipped off his feet; one of the dogs fell in the traces; and the sled toppled back, dragging everything to the bottom again.

Slash! the whip fell among the dogs savagely, especially upon the one which had fallen.

"Don't, Mason," entreated Malemute Kid; "the poor devil's on its last legs. Wait and we'll put my team on."

Mason deliberately withheld the whip till the last word had fallen, then out flashed the long lash, completely curling about the offending creature's body. Carmen—for it was Carmen—cowered in the snow, cried piteously, then rolled over on her side.

It was a tragic moment, a pitiful incident of the trail,—a dying dog, two comrades in anger. Ruth glanced solicitously from man to man. But Malemute Kid restrained himself, though there was a world of reproach in his eyes, and bending over the dog, cut the traces. No word was spoken. The teams were double-spanned and the difficulty overcome; the sleds were under way again, the dying dog dragging herself along in the rear. As long as an animal can travel, it is not shot, and this last chance is accorded it,—the crawling into camp, if it can, in the hope of a moose being killed.

Already penitent for his angry action, but too stubborn to make amends, Mason toiled on at the head of the cavalcade, little dreaming that danger hovered in the air. The timber clustered thick in the sheltered bottom, and through this they threaded their way. Fifty feet or more from the trail towered a lofty pine. For generations it had stood there, and for generations destiny had had this one end in view,—perhaps the same had been decreed of Mason.

He stooped to fasten the loosened thong of his moccasin. The sleds came to a halt and the dogs lay down in the snow without a whimper. The stillness was weird; not a breath rustled the frost-encrusted forest; the cold and silence of outer space had chilled the heart and smote the trembling lips of nature. A sigh pulsed through the air,—they did not seem to actually hear it, but rather felt it, like the premonition of movement in a motionless void. Then the great tree, burdened with its weight of years and snow, played its last part in the tragedy of life. He heard the warning crash and attempted to spring up, but almost erect, caught the blow squarely on the shoulder.

The sudden danger, the quick death,—how often had Malemute Kid faced it! The pine needles were still quivering as he gave his commands and sprang into action. Nor did the Indian girl faint or raise her voice in idle wailing, as might many of her white sisters. At his order, she threw her weight on the end of a quickly extemporized handspike, easing the pressure and listening to her husband's groans, while Malemute Kid attacked the tree with his axe. The steel rang merrily as it bit into the frozen trunk, each stroke being accompanied by a forced, audible respiration, the "Huh!" "Huh!" of the woodsman.

At last the Kid laid the pitiable thing that was once a man in the snow. But worse than his comrade's pain was the dumb anguish in the woman's face, the blended look of hopeful, hopeless query. Little was said; those of the Northland are early taught the futility of words and the inestimable value of deeds. With the temperature at sixty-five below zero, a man cannot lie many minutes in the snow and live. So the sled-lashings were cut, and the sufferer, rolled in furs, laid on a couch of boughs. Before him roared a fire, built of the very wood which wrought the mishap. Behind and partially over him was stretched the primitive fly,—a piece of canvas, which caught the radiating heat and threw it back and down upon him,—a trick which men may know who study physics at the fount.

And men who have shared their bed with death know when the call is sounded. Mason was terribly crushed. The most cursory examination revealed it. His right arm, leg, and back, were broken; his limbs were paralyzed from the hips; and the likelihood of internal injuries was large. An occasional moan was his only sign of life.

No hope; nothing to be done. The pitiless night crept slowly by,—Ruth's portion, the despairing stoicism of her race, and Malemute Kid adding new lines to his face of bronze. In fact, Mason suffered least of all, for he spent his time in Eastern Tennessee, in the Great Smoky Mountains, living over the scenes of his childhood. And most pathetic was the melody of his long-forgotten Southern vernacular, as he raved of swimming-holes and coon-hunts and watermelon raids. It was as Greek to Ruth, but the Kid understood and felt,—felt as only one can feel who has been shut out for years from all that civilization means.

Morning brought consciousness to the stricken man, and Malemute Kid bent closer to catch his whispers.

"You remember when we foregathered on the Tanana, four years come next ice-run? I did n't care so much for her then. It was more like she was pretty, and there was a smack of excitement about it, I think. But d' ye know, I've come to think a heap of her. She's been a good wife to me, always at my shoulder in the pinch. And when it comes to trading, you know there is n't her equal. D' ye recollect the time she shot the Moosehorn Rapids to pull you and me off that rock, the bullets whipping the water like hailstones?—and the time of the famine at Nuklukyeto?—or when she raced the ice-run to bring the news? Yes, she's been a good wife to me, better'n that other one. Did n't know I'd been there? Never told you, eh? Well, I tried it once, down in the

States. That's why I'm here. Been raised together, too. I came away to give her a chance for divorce. She got it.

"But that's got nothing to do with Ruth. I had thought of cleaning up and pulling for the Outside next year,—her and I,—but it's too late. Don't send her back to her people, Kid. It's beastly hard for a woman to go back. Think of it!—nearly four years on our bacon and beans and flour and dried fruit, and then to go back to her fish and cariboo. It's not good for her to have tried our ways, to come to know they 're better 'n her people's, and then return to them. Take care of her, Kid,—why don't you,—but no, you always fought shy of them,—and you never told me why you came to this country. Be kind to her, and send her back to the States as soon as you can. But fix it so as she can come back,—liable to get homesick, you know.

"And the youngster—it's drawn us closer, Kid. I only hope it is a boy. Think of it!—flesh of my flesh, Kid. He must n't stop in this country. And if it 's a girl, why she can 't. Sell my furs; they'll fetch at least five thousand, and I've got as much more with the company. And handle my interests with yours. I think that bench claim will show up. See that he gets a good schooling; and Kid, above all, don't let him come back. This country was not made for white men.

"I 'm a gone man, Kid. Three or four sleeps at the best. You've got to go on. You must go on! Remember, it's my wife, it's my boy,—O God! I hope it's a boy! You can't stay by me,—and I charge you, a dying man, to pull on."

"Give me three days," pleaded Malemute Kid. "You may change for the better; something may turn up."

"No."

"Just three days."

"You must pull on."

"Two days."

"It's my wife and my boy, Kid. You would not ask it."

"One day."

"No, no! I charge"—

"Only one day. We can shave it through on the grub, and I might knock over a moose."

"No,—all right; one day, but not a minute more. And Kid, don 't—don 't leave me to face it alone. Just a shot, one pull on the trigger. You understand. Think of it! Think of it! Flesh of my flesh, and I'll never live to see him!

"Send Ruth here. I want to say good-by and tell her that she must think of the boy and not wait till I'm dead. She might refuse to go with you if I did n't. Good-by, old man; good-by.

"Kid! I say—a—sink a hole above the pup, next to the slide. I panned out forty cents on my shovel there.

"And Kid!" he stooped lower to catch the last faint words, the dying man's surrender of his pride. "I'm sorry—for—you know—Carmen."

Leaving the girl crying softly over her man, Malemute Kid slipped into his *parka* and snowshoes, tucked his rifle under his arm, and crept away into the forest. He was no tyro in the stern sorrows of the Northland, but never had he faced so stiff a problem as this. In the abstract, it was a plain, mathematical proposition,—three possible lives as against one doomed one. But now he hesitated. For five years, shoulder to shoulder, on the rivers and trails, in the camps and mines, facing death by field and flood and famine, had they knitted the bonds of their comradeship. So close was the tie, that he had often been conscious of a vague jealousy of Ruth, from the first time she had come between. And now it must be severed by his own hand.

Though he prayed for a moose, just one moose, all game seemed to have deserted the land, and nightfall found the exhausted man crawling into camp, light-handed, heavy-hearted. An uproar from the dogs and shrill cries from Ruth hastened him.

Bursting into the camp, he saw the girl in the midst of the snarling pack, laying about her with an axe. The dogs had broken the iron rule of their masters and were rushing the grub. He joined the issue with his rifle reversed, and the hoary game of natural selection was played out with all the ruthlessness of its primeval environment. Rifle and axe went up and down, hit or missed with monotonous regularity; lithe bodies flashed, with wild eyes and dripping fangs; and man and beast fought for supremacy to the bitterest conclusion. Then the beaten brutes crept to the edge of the firelight, licking their wounds, voicing their misery to the stars.

The whole stock of dried salmon had been devoured, and perhaps five pounds of flour remained to tide them over two hundred miles of wilderness. Ruth returned to her husband, while Malemute Kid cut up the warm body of one of the dogs, the skull of which had been crushed by the axe. Every portion was carefully put away, save the hide and offal, which were cast to his fellows of the moment before.

Morning brought fresh trouble. The animals were turning on each other. Carmen, who still clung to her slender thread of life, was downed by the pack. The lash fell among them unheeded. They cringed and cried under the blows, but refused to scatter till the last wretched bit had disappeared,—bones, hide, hair, everything.

Malemute Kid went about his work, listening to Mason, who was back in Tennessee, delivering tangled discourses and wild exhortations to his brethren of other days.

Taking advantage of neighboring pines, he worked rapidly, and Ruth watched him make a cache similar to those sometimes used by hunters to preserve their meat from the wolverines and dogs. One after the other, he bent the tops of two small pines toward each other and nearly to the ground, making them fast with thongs of moosehide. Then he beat the dogs into submission and harnessed them to two of the sleds, loading the same with everything but the furs which enveloped Mason. These he wrapped and lashed tightly about him, fastening either end of the robes to the bent pines. A single stroke of his hunting-knife would release them and send the body high in the air.

Ruth had received her husband's last wishes and made no struggle. Poor girl, she had learned the lesson of obedience well. From a child, she had bowed, and seen all women bow, to the lords of creation, and it did not seem in the nature of things for woman to resist. The Kid permitted her one outburst of grief, as she kissed her husband,—her own people had no such custom,— then led her to the foremost sled and helped her into her snow-shoes. Blindly, instinctively, she took the gee-pole and whip, and "mushed" the dogs out on the trail. Then he returned to Mason, who had fallen into a coma; and long after she was out of sight, crouched by the fire, waiting, hoping, praying for his comrade to die.

It is not pleasant to be alone with painful thoughts in the White Silence. The silence of gloom is merciful, shrouding one as with protection and breathing a thousand intangible sympathies; but the bright White Silence, clear and cold, under steely skies, is pitiless.

An hour passed,—two hours,—but the man would not die. At high noon, the sun, without raising its rim above the southern horizon, threw a suggestion of fire athwart the heavens, then quickly drew it back. Malemute Kid roused and dragged himself to his comrade's side. He cast one glance about him. The White Silence seemed to sneer, and a great fear came upon him. There was a sharp report; Mason swung into his aerial sepulchre; and Malemute Kid lashed the dogs into a wild gallop as he fled across the snow.

The Son of the Wolf

Man rarely places a proper valuation upon his womankind, at least not until deprived of them. He has no conception of the subtle atmosphere exhaled by the sex feminine so long as he bathes in it; but let it be withdrawn, and an ever-growing void begins to manifest itself in his existence, and he becomes hungry, in a vague sort of way, for a something so indefinite that he cannot characterize it. If his comrades have no more experience than himself, they will shake their heads dubiously and dose him with strong physic. But the hunger will continue and become stronger; he will lose interest in the things of his every-day life and wax morbid; and one day, when the emptiness has become unbearable, a revelation will dawn upon him.

In the Yukon country, when this comes to pass, the man usually provisions a poling-boat, if it be summer, and if winter harnesses his dogs, and heads for the Southland. A few months later, supposing him to be possessed of a faith in the country, he returns with a wife to share with him in that faith, and incidentally in his hardships. This but serves to show the innate selfishness of man. It also brings us to the trouble of "Scruff" Mackenzie, which occurred in the old days, before the country was stampeded and staked by a tidal-wave of *che-cha-quas*, and when the Klondike's only claim to notice was its salmon fisheries.

Scruff Mackenzie bore the ear-marks of a frontier birth and a frontier life. His face was stamped with twenty-five years of incessant struggle with nature in her wildest moods,—the last two, the wildest and hardest of all, having been spent in groping for the gold which lies in the shadow of the Arctic Circle. When the yearning sickness came upon him he was not surprised, for he was a practical man and had seen other men thus stricken. But he showed no sign of his malady, save that he worked harder. All summer he fought mosquitoes and washed the sure-thing bars of the Stuart River for a double grub-stake. Then he floated a raft of house-logs down the Yukon to Forty Mile, and put together as comfortable a cabin as any the camp could boast of. In fact, it showed such cosy promise that many men elected to be his partner and to come and live with him. But he crushed their aspirations with rough speech, peculiar for its strength and brevity, and bought a double supply of grub from the trading-post.

As has been noted, Scruff Mackenzie was a practical man. If he wanted a thing he usually got it, but in doing so, went no farther out of his way than was necessary. Though a son of toil and hardship, he was averse to a journey of six hundred miles on the ice, a second of two thousand miles on the ocean, and still a third thousand miles or so to his last stamping-grounds,—all in the mere quest of a wife. Life was too short. So he rounded up his dogs, lashed a curious freight to his sled, and faced across the divide whose westward slopes were drained by the head-reaches of the Tanana.

He was a sturdy traveler, and his wolf-dogs could work harder and travel farther on less grub than any other team in the Yukon. Three weeks later he strode into a hunting-camp of the Upper Tanana Sticks. They marveled at his temerity; for they had a bad name and had been known to kill white men for as trifling a thing as a sharp axe or a broken rifle. But he went among them single-handed, his bearing being a delicious composite of humility, familiarity, *sang-froid,* and insolence. It required a deft hand and deep knowledge of the barbaric mind effectually to handle such diverse weapons; but he was a past master in the art, knowing when to conciliate and when to threaten with Jove-like wrath.

He first made obeisance to the Chief Thling-Tinneh, presenting him with a couple of pounds of black tea and tobacco, and thereby winning his most cordial regard. Then he mingled with the men and maidens, and that night gave a *potlach.* The snow was beaten down in the form of an oblong, perhaps a hundred feet in length and quarter as many across. Down the centre a long fire was built, while either side was carpeted with spruce boughs. The lodges were forsaken, and the fivescore or so members of the tribe gave tongue to their folk-chants in honor of their guest.

Scruff Mackenzie's two years had taught him the not many hundred words of their vocabulary, and he had likewise conquered their deep gutturals, their Japanese idioms, constructions,

and honorific and agglutinative particles. So he made oration after
their manner, satisfying their instinctive poetry-love with crude
flights of eloquence and metaphorical contortions. After Thling-
Tinneh and the Shaman had responded in kind, he made trifling
presents to the menfolk, joined in their singing, and proved an
expert in their fifty-two-stick gambling game.

And they smoked his tobacco and were pleased. But among
the younger men there was a defiant attitude, a spirit of bragga-
docio, easily understood by the raw insinuations of the toothless
squaws and the giggling of the maidens. They had known few
white men, "Sons of the Wolf," but from those few they had
learned strange lessons.

Nor had Scruff Mackenzie, for all his seeming carelessness,
failed to note these phenomena. In truth, rolled in his sleeping-
furs, he thought it all over, thought seriously, and emptied many
pipes in mapping out a campaign. One maiden only had caught
his fancy,—none other than Zarinska, daughter to the chief. In
features, form, and poise, answering more nearly to the white
man's type of beauty, she was almost an anomaly among her tribal
sisters. He would possess her, make her his wife, and name her
—ah, he would name her Gertrude! Having thus decided, he
rolled over on his side and dropped off to sleep, a true son of his
all-conquering race.

It was slow work and a stiff game; but Scruff Mackenzie ma-
nœuvred cunningly, with an unconcern which served to puzzle
the Sticks. He took great care to impress the men that he was a
sure shot and a mighty hunter, and the camp rang with his plau-
dits when he brought down a moose at six hundred yards. Of a
night he visited in Chief Thling-Tinneh's lodge of moose and cariboo skins, talking big and dispensing tobacco with a lavish hand.
Nor did he fail to likewise honor the Shaman; for he realized the
medicine-man's influence with his people, and was anxious to
make of him an ally. But that worthy was high and mighty, refused to be propitiated, and was unerringly marked down as a
prospective enemy.

Though no opening presented for an interview with Zarinska,
Mackenzie stole many a glance to her, giving fair warning of his
intent. And well she knew, yet coquettishly surrounded herself

with a ring of women whenever the men were away and he had
a chance. But he was in no hurry; besides, he knew she could not
help but think of him, and a few days of such thought would only
better his suit.

At last, one night, when he deemed the time to be ripe, he
abruptly left the chief's smoky dwelling and hastened to a neighboring lodge. As usual, she sat with squaws and maidens about
her, all engaged in sewing moccasins and beadwork. They laughed
at his entrance, and badinage, which linked Zarinska to him, ran
high. But one after the other they were unceremoniously bundled
into the outer snow, whence they hurried to spread the tale
through all the camp.

His cause was well pleaded, in her tongue, for she did not know
his, and at the end of two hours he rose to go.

"So Zarinska will come to the White Man's lodge? Good! I go
now to have talk with thy father, for he may not be so minded.
And I will give him many tokens; but he must not ask too much.
If he say no? Good! Zarinska shall yet come to the White Man's
lodge."

He had already lifted the skin flap to depart, when a low exclamation brought him back to the girl's side. She brought herself
to her knees on the bearskin mat, her face aglow with true Eve-
light, and shyly unbuckled his heavy belt. He looked down, perplexed, suspicious, his ears alert for the slightest sound without.
But her next move disarmed his doubt, and he smiled with pleasure. She took from her sewing-bag a moosehide sheath, brave
with bright beadwork, fantastically designed. She drew his great
hunting-knife, gazed reverently along the keen edge, half tempted
to try it with her thumb, and shot it into place in its new home.
Then she slipped the sheath along the belt to its customary
resting-place, just above the hip.

For all the world, it was like a scene of olden time,—a lady
and her knight. Mackenzie drew her up full height and swept her
red lips with his mustache,—the, to her, foreign caress of the
Wolf. It was a meeting of the stone age and the steel.

There was a thrill of excitement in the air as Scruff Mackenzie,
a bulky bundle under his arm, threw open the flap of Thling-

Tinneh's tent. Children were running about in the open, dragging dry wood to the scene of the *potlach,* a babble of women's voices was growing in intensity, the young men were consulting in sullen groups, while from the Shaman's lodge rose the eerie sounds of an incantation.

The chief was alone with his blear-eyed wife, but a glance sufficed to tell Mackenzie that the news was already old. So he plunged at once into the business, shifting the beaded sheath prominently to the fore as advertisement of the betrothal.

"O Thling-Tinneh, mighty chief of the Sticks and the land of the Tanana, ruler of the salmon and the bear, the moose and the cariboo! The White Man is before thee with a great purpose. Many moons has his lodge been empty, and he is lonely. And his heart has eaten itself in silence, and grown hungry for a woman to sit beside him in his lodge, to meet him from the hunt with warm fire and good food. He has heard strange things, the patter of baby moccasins and the sound of children's voices. And one night a vision came upon him, and he beheld the Raven, who is thy father, the great Raven, who is the father of all the Sticks. And the Raven spake to the lonely White Man, saying: 'Bind thou thy moccasins upon thee, and gird thy snowshoes on, and lash thy sled with food for many sleeps and fine tokens for the Chief Thling-Tinneh. For thou shalt turn thy face to where the midspring sun is wont to sink below the land, and journey to this great chief's hunting-grounds. There thou shalt make big presents, and Thling-Tinneh, who is my son, shall become to thee as a father. In his lodge there is a maiden into whom I breathed the breath of life for thee. This maiden shalt thou take to wife.'

"O Chief, thus spake the great Raven; thus do I lay many presents at thy feet; thus am I come to take thy daughter!"

The old man drew his furs about him with crude consciousness of royalty, but delayed reply while a youngster crept in, delivered a quick message to appear before the council, and was gone.

"O White Man, whom we have named Moose-Killer, also known as the Wolf, and the Son of the Wolf! We know thou comest of a mighty race; we are proud to have thee our *potlach*-guest; but the king-salmon does not mate with the dog-salmon, nor the Raven with the Wolf."

"Not so!" cried Mackenzie. "The daughters of the Raven have I met in the camps of the Wolf,—the squaw of Mortimer, the squaw of Tregidgo, the squaw of Barnaby, who came two ice-runs back, and I have heard of other squaws, though my eyes beheld them not."

"Son, your words are true; but it were evil mating, like the water with the sand, like the snowflake with the sun. But met you one Mason and his squaw? No? He came ten ice-runs ago,—the first of all the Wolves. And with him there was a mighty man, straight as a willow-shoot, and tall; strong as the bald-faced grizzly, with a heart like the full summer moon; his"—

"Oh!" interrupted Mackenzie, recognizing the well-known Northland figure,—"Malemute Kid!"

"The same,—a mighty man. But saw you aught of the squaw? She was full sister to Zarinska."

"Nay, Chief; but I have heard. Mason—far, far to the north, a spruce-tree, heavy with years, crushed out his life beneath. But his love was great, and he had much gold. With this, and her boy, she journeyed countless sleeps toward the winter's noonday sun, and there she yet lives,—no biting frost, no snow, no summer's midnight sun, no winter's noonday night."

A second messenger interrupted with imperative summons from the council. As Mackenzie threw him into the snow, he caught a glimpse of the swaying forms before the council-fire, heard the deep basses of the men in rhythmic chant, and knew the Shaman was fanning the anger of his people. Time pressed. He turned upon the chief.

"Come! I wish thy child. And now. See! here are tobacco, tea, many cups of sugar, warm blankets, handkerchiefs, both good and large; and here, a true rifle, with many bullets and much powder."

"Nay," replied the old man, struggling against the great wealth spread before him. "Even now are my people come together. They will not have this marriage."

"But thou art chief."

"Yet do my young men rage because the Wolves have taken their maidens so that they may not marry."

"Listen, O Thling-Tinneh! Ere the night has passed into the day, the Wolf shall face his dogs to the Mountains of the East and fare forth to the Country of the Yukon. And Zarinska shall break trail for his dogs."

"And ere the night has gained its middle, my young men may fling to the dogs the flesh of the Wolf, and his bones be scattered in the snow till the springtime lay them bare."

It was threat and counter-threat. Mackenzie's bronzed face flushed darkly. He raised his voice. The old squaw, who till now had sat an impassive spectator, made to creep by him for the door. The song of the men broke suddenly, and there was a hubbub of many voices as he whirled the old woman roughly to her couch of skins.

"Again I cry—listen, O Thling-Tinneh! The Wolf dies with teeth fast-locked, and with him there shall sleep ten of thy strongest men,—men who are needed, for the hunting is but begun, and the fishing is not many moons away. And again, of what profit should I die? I know the custom of thy people; thy share of my wealth shall be very small. Grant me thy child, and it shall all be thine. And yet again, my brothers will come, and they are many, and their maws are never filled; and the daughters of the Raven shall bear children in the lodges of the Wolf. My people are greater than thy people. It is destiny. Grant, and all this wealth is thine."

Moccasins were crunching the snow without. Mackenzie threw his rifle to cock, and loosened the twin Colts in his belt.

"Grant, O Chief!"

"And yet will my people say no."

"Grant, and the wealth is thine. Then shall I deal with thy people after."

"The Wolf will have it so. I will take his tokens,—but I would warn him."

Mackenzie passed over the goods, taking care to clog the rifle's ejector, and capping the bargain with a kaleidoscopic silk kerchief. The Shaman and half a dozen young braves entered, but he shouldered boldly among them and passed out.

"Pack!" was his laconic greeting to Zarinska as he passed her lodge and hurried to harness his dogs. A few minutes later he swept into the council at the head of the team, the woman by his side. He took his place at the upper end of the oblong, by the side of the chief. To his left, a step to the rear, he stationed Zarinska,—her proper place. Besides, the time was ripe for mischief, and there was need to guard his back.

On either side, the men crouched to the fire, their voices lifted in a folk-chant out of the forgotten past. Full of strange, halting cadences and haunting recurrences, it was not beautiful. "Fearful" may inadequately express it. At the lower end, under the eye of the Shaman, danced half a score of women. Stern were his reproofs to those who did not wholly abandon themselves to the ecstasy of the rite. Half hidden in their heavy masses of raven hair, all disheveled and falling to their waists, they slowly swayed to and fro, their forms rippling to an ever-changing rhythm.

It was a weird scene; an anachronism. To the south, the nineteenth century was reeling off the few years of its last decade; here flourished man primeval, a shade removed from the prehistoric cave-dweller, a forgotten fragment of the Elder World. The tawny wolf-dogs sat between their skin-clad masters or fought for room, the firelight cast backward from their red eyes and slavered fangs. The woods, in ghostly shroud, slept on unheeding. The White Silence, for the moment driven to the rimming forest, seemed ever crushing inward; the stars danced with great leaps, as is their wont in the time of the Great Cold; while the Spirits of the Pole trailed their robes of glory athwart the heavens.

Scruff Mackenzie dimly realized the wild grandeur of the setting as his eyes ranged down the fur-fringed sides in quest of missing faces. They rested for a moment on a newborn babe, suckling at its mother's naked breast. It was forty below,—seventy and odd degrees of frost. He thought of the tender women of his own race, and smiled grimly. Yet from the loins of some such tender woman had he sprung with a kingly inheritance,—an inheritance which gave to him and his dominance over the land and sea, over the animals and the peoples of all the zones. Single-handed against fivescore, girt by the Arctic winter, far from his own, he felt the prompting of his heritage, the desire to possess, the wild danger-love, the thrill of battle, the power to conquer or to die.

The singing and the dancing ceased, and the Shaman flared up in rude eloquence. Through the sinuosities of their vast mythology, he worked cunningly upon the credulity of his people. The case was strong. Opposing the creative principles as embodied in the Crow and the Raven, he stigmatized Mackenzie as the Wolf, the fighting and the destructive principle. Not only was the combat of these forces spiritual, but men fought, each to his totem. They were the children of Jelchs, the Raven, the Promethean fire-bringer; Mackenzie was the child of the Wolf, or, in other words, the Devil. For them to bring a truce to this perpetual warfare, to marry their daughters to the archenemy, were treason and blasphemy of the highest order. No phrase was harsh, nor figure vile, enough in branding Mackenzie as a sneaking interloper and emissary of Satan. There was a subdued, savage roar in the deep chests of his listeners as he took the swing of his peroration.

"Ay, my brothers, Jelchs is all-powerful! Did he not bring heaven-born fire that we might be warm? Did he not draw the sun, moon, and stars from their holes that we might see? Did he not teach us that we might fight the Spirits of Famine and of Frost? But now Jelchs is angry with his children, and they are grown to a handful, and he will not help. For they have forgotten him, and done evil things, and trod bad trails, and taken his enemies into their lodges to sit by their fires. And the Raven is sorrowful at the wickedness of his children; but when they shall rise up and show they have come back, he will come out of the darkness to aid them. O brothers! the Fire-Bringer has whispered messages to thy Shaman; the same shall ye hear. Let the young men take the young women to their lodges; let them fly at the throat of the Wolf; let them be undying in their enmity! Then shall their women become fruitful, and they shall multiply into a mighty people! And the Raven shall lead great tribes of their fathers and their fathers' fathers from out of the North; and they shall beat back the Wolves till they are as last year's camp-fires; and they shall again come to rule over all the land! 'T is the message of Jelchs, the Raven."

This foreshadowing of the Messiah's coming brought a hoarse howl from the Sticks as they leaped to their feet. Mackenzie slipped the thumbs of his mittens, and waited. There was a clamor for the Fox, not to be stilled till one of the young men stepped forward to speak.

"Brothers! The Shaman has spoken wisely. The Wolves have taken our women, and our men are childless. We are grown to a handful. The Wolves have taken our warm furs, and given for them evil spirits which dwell in bottles, and clothes which come not from the beaver or the lynx, but are made from the grass. And they are not warm, and our men die of strange sicknesses. I, the Fox, have taken no woman to wife; and why? Twice have the maidens which pleased me gone to the camps of the Wolf. Even now have I laid by skins of the beaver, of the moose, of the cari-boo, that I might win favor in the eyes of Thling-Tinneh, that I might marry Zarinska, his daughter. Even now are her snowshoes bound to her feet, ready to break trail for the dogs of the Wolf. Nor do I speak for myself alone. As I have done, so has the Bear. He, too, had fain been the father of her children, and many skins has he cured thereto. I speak for all the young men who know not wives. The Wolves are ever hungry. Always do they take the choice meat at the killing. To the Ravens are left the leavings.

"There is Gugkla!" he cried, brutally pointing out one of the women, who was a cripple. "Her legs are bent like the ribs of a birch canoe. She cannot gather wood nor carry the meat of the hunters. Did the Wolves choose her?"

"Ai! ai!" vociferated his tribesmen.

"There is Moyri, whose eyes are crossed by the Evil Spirit. Even the babes are affrighted when they gaze upon her, and it is said the bald-face gives her the trail. Was she chosen?"

Again the cruel applause rang out.

"And there sits Pischet. She does not hearken to my words. Never has she heard the cry of the chit-chat, the voice of her husband, the babble of her child. She lives in the White Silence. Cared the Wolves aught for her? No! Theirs is the choice of the kill; ours is the leavings.

"Brothers, it shall not be! No more shall the Wolves slink among our camp-fires. The time is come."

A great streamer of fire, the aurora borealis, purple, green, and yellow, shot across the zenith, bridging horizon to horizon. With head thrown back and arms extended, he swayed to his climax.

"Behold! The spirits of our fathers have arisen and great deeds are afoot this night!"

He stepped back, and another young man somewhat diffidently came forward, pushed on by his comrades. He towered a full head above them, his broad chest defiantly bared to the frost. He swung tentatively from one foot to the other. Words halted upon his tongue, and he was ill at ease. His face was horrible to look upon, for it had at one time been half torn away by some terrific blow. At last he struck his breast with his clenched fist, drawing sound as from a drum, and his voice rumbled forth as the surf from an ocean cavern.

"I am the Bear,—the Silver-Tip and the Son of the Silver-Tip! When my voice was yet as a girl's, I slew the lynx, the moose, and the cariboo; when it whistled like the wolverines from under a cache, I crossed the Mountains of the South and slew three of the White Rivers; when it became as the roar of the Chinook, I met the bald-faced grizzly, but gave no trail."

At this he paused, his hand significantly sweeping across his hideous scars.

"I am not as the Fox. My tongue is frozen like the river. I cannot make great talk. My words are few. The Fox says great deeds are afoot this night. Good! Talk flows from his tongue like the freshets of the spring, but he is chary of deeds. This night shall I do battle with the Wolf. I shall slay him, and Zarinska shall sit by my fire. The Bear has spoken."

Though pandemonium raged about him, Scruff Mackenzie held his ground. Aware how useless was the rifle at close quarters, he slipped both holsters to the fore, ready for action, and drew his mittens till his hands were barely shielded by the elbow gauntlets. He knew there was no hope in attack *en masse,* but true to his boast, was prepared to die with teeth fast-locked. But the Bear restrained his comrades, beating back the more impetuous with his terrible fist. As the tumult began to die away, Mackenzie shot a glance in the direction of Zarinska. It was a superb picture. She was leaning forward on her snowshoes, lips apart and nostrils quivering, like a tigress about to spring. Her great black eyes were fixed upon her tribesmen, in fear and in defiance. So extreme the

tension, she had forgotten to breathe. With one hand pressed spasmodically against her breast and the other as tightly gripped about
the dogwhip, she was as turned to stone. Even as he looked, relief
came to her. Her muscles loosened; with a heavy sigh she settled
back, giving him a look of more than love.

Thling-Tinneh was trying to speak, but his people drowned his
voice. Then Mackenzie strode forward. The Fox opened mouth
to a piercing yell, but so savagely did Mackenzie whirl upon him
that he shrank back, his larynx all a-gurgle with suppressed sound.
His discomfiture was greeted with roars of laughter, and served
to soothe his fellows to a listening mood.

"Brothers! The White Man, whom ye have chosen to call the
Wolf, came among you with fair words. He was not like the Innuit; he spoke not lies. He came as a friend, as one who would
be a brother. But your men have had their say, and the time for
soft words is past. First, I will tell you that the Shaman has an
evil tongue and is a false prophet, that the messages he spake are
not those of the Fire-Bringer. His ears are locked to the voice of
the Raven, and out of his own head he weaves cunning fancies,
and he has made fools of you. He has no power. When the dogs
were killed and eaten, and your stomachs were heavy with untan-
ned hide and strips of moccasins; when the old men died, and the
old women died, and the babes at the dry dugs of the mothers
died; when the land was dark, and ye perished as do the salmon
in the fall; ay, when the famine was upon you, did the Shaman
bring reward to your hunters? did the Shaman put meat in your
bellies? Again I say, the Shaman is without power. Thus! I spit
upon his face!"

Though taken aback by the sacrilege, there was no uproar.
Some of the women were even frightened, but among the men
there was an uplifting, as though in preparation or anticipation of
the miracle. All eyes were turned upon the two central figures.
The priest realized the crucial moment, felt his power tottering,
opened his mouth in denunciation, but fled backward before the
truculent advance, upraised fist, and flashing eyes of Mackenzie.
He sneered and resumed.

"Was I stricken dead? Did the lightning burn me? Did the stars fall from the sky and crush me? Pish! I have done with the dog. Now will I tell you of my people, who are the mightiest of all the peoples, who rule in all the lands. At first we hunt as I hunt, alone. After that we hunt in packs; and at last, like the cariboo-run, we sweep across all the land. Those whom we take into our lodges live; those who will not come die. Zarinska is a comely maiden, full and strong, fit to become the mother of Wolves. Though I die, such shall she become; for my brothers are many, and they will follow the scent of my dogs. Listen to the Law of the Wolf: *Whoso taketh the life of one Wolf, the forfeit shall ten of his people pay.* In many lands has the price been paid; in many lands shall it yet be paid.

"Now will I deal with the Fox and the Bear. It seems they have cast eyes upon the maiden. So? Behold, I have bought her! Thling-Tinneh leans upon the rifle; the goods of purchase are by his fire. Yet will I be fair to the young men. To the Fox, whose tongue is dry with many words, will I give of tobacco five long plugs. Thus will his mouth be wetted that he may make much noise in the council. But to the Bear, of whom I am well proud, will I give of blankets two; of flour, twenty cups; of tobacco, double that of the Fox; and if he fare with me over the Mountains of the East, then will I give him a rifle, mate to Thling-Tinneh's. If not? Good! The Wolf is weary of speech. Yet once again will he say the Law: *Whoso taketh the life of one Wolf, the forfeit shall ten of his people pay.*"

Mackenzie smiled as he stepped back to his old position, but at heart he was full of trouble. The night was yet dark. The girl came to his side, and he listened closely as she told of the Bear's battle-tricks with the knife.

The decision was for war. In a trice, scores of moccasins were widening the space of beaten snow by the fire. There was much chatter about the seeming defeat of the Shaman; some averred he had but withheld his power, while others conned past events and agreed with the Wolf. The Bear came to the centre of the battle-ground, a long naked hunting-knife of Russian make in his hand. The Fox called attention to Mackenzie's revolvers; so he stripped his belt, buckling it about Zarinska, into whose hands he also intrusted his rifle. She shook her head that she could not shoot, —small chance had a woman to handle such precious things.

"Then, if danger come by my back, cry aloud, 'My husband!' No; thus, 'My husband!' "

He laughed as she repeated it, pinched her cheek, and reentered the circle. Not only in reach and stature had the Bear the advantage of him, but his blade was longer by a good two inches. Scruff Mackenzie had looked into the eyes of men before, and he knew it was a man who stood against him; yet he quickened to the glint of light on the steel, to the dominant pulse of his race.

Time and again he was forced to the edge of the fire or the deep snow, and time and again, with the foot tactics of the pugilist, he worked back to the centre. Not a voice was lifted in encouragement, while his antagonist was heartened with applause, suggestions, and warnings. But his teeth only shut the tighter as the knives clashed together, and he thrust or eluded with a coolness born of conscious strength. At first he felt compassion for his enemy; but this fled before the primal instinct of life, which in turn gave way to the lust of slaughter. The ten thousand years of culture fell from him, and he was a cave-dweller, doing battle for his female.

Twice he pricked the Bear, getting away unscathed; but the third time caught, and to save himself, free hands closed on fighting hands, and they came together. Then did he realize the tremendous strength of his opponent. His muscles were knotted in painful lumps, and cords and tendons threatened to snap with the strain; yet nearer and nearer came the Russian steel. He tried to break away, but only weakened himself. The fur-clad circle closed in, certain of and anxious to see the final stroke. But with wrestler's trick, swinging partly to the side, he struck at his adversary with his head. Involuntarily the Bear leaned back, disturbing his centre of gravity. Simultaneous with this, Mackenzie tripped properly and threw his whole weight forward, hurling him clear through the circle into the deep snow. The Bear floundered out and came back full tilt.

"O my husband!" Zarinska's voice rang out, vibrant with danger.

To the twang of a bow-string, Mackenzie swept low to the ground, and a bone-barbed arrow passed over him into the breast of the Bear, whose momentum carried him over his crouching foe. The next instant Mackenzie was up and about. The Bear lay motionless, but across the fire was the Shaman, drawing a second arrow.

Mackenzie's knife leaped short in the air. He caught the heavy blade by the point. There was a flash of light as it spanned the fire. Then the Shaman, the hilt alone appearing without his throat, swayed a moment and pitched forward into the glowing embers.

Click! click!—the Fox had possessed himself of Thling-Tinneh's rifle and was vainly trying to throw a shell into place. But he dropped it at the sound of Mackenzie's laughter.

"So the Fox has not learned the way of the plaything? He is yet a woman. Come! Bring it, that I may show thee!"

The Fox hesitated.

"Come, I say!"

He slouched forward like a beaten cur.

"Thus, and thus; so the thing is done." A shell flew into place and the trigger was at cock as Mackenzie brought it to shoulder.

"The Fox has said great deeds were afoot this night, and he spoke true. There have been great deeds, yet least among them were those of the Fox. Is he still intent to take Zarinska to his lodge? Is he minded to tread the trail already broken by the Shaman and the Bear? No? Good!"

Mackenzie turned contemptuously and drew his knife from the priest's throat.

"Are any of the young men so minded? If so, the Wolf will take them by two and three till none are left. No? Good! Thling-Tinneh, I now give thee this rifle a second time. If in the days to come thou shouldst journey to the Country of the Yukon, know thou that there shall always be a place and much food by the fire of the Wolf. The night is now passing into the day. I go, but I may come again. And for the last time, remember the Law of the Wolf!"

He was supernatural in their sight as he rejoined Zarinska. She took her place at the head of the team, and the dogs swung into motion. A few moments later they were swallowed up by the ghostly forest. Till now Mackenzie had waited; he slipped into his snowshoes to follow.

"Has the Wolf forgotten the five long plugs?"

Mackenzie turned upon the Fox angrily; then the humor of it struck him.

"I will give thee one short plug."

"As the Wolf sees fit," meekly responded the Fox, stretching out his hand.

In a Far Country

When a man journeys into a far country, he must be prepared to forget many of the things he has learned, and to acquire such customs as are inherent with existence in the new land; he must abandon the old ideals and the old gods, and oftentimes he must reverse the very codes by which his conduct has hitherto been shaped. To those who have the protean faculty of adaptability, the novelty of such change may even be a source of pleasure; but to those who happen to be hardened to the ruts in which they were created, the pressure of the altered environment is unbearable, and they chafe in body and in spirit under the new restrictions which they do not understand. This chafing is bound to act and react, producing divers evils and leading to various misfortunes. It were better for the man who cannot fit himself to the new groove to return to his own country; if he delay too long, he will surely die.

The man who turns his back upon the comforts of an elder civilization, to face the savage youth, the primordial simplicity of the North, may estimate success at an inverse ratio to the quantity and quality of his hopelessly fixed habits. He will soon discover, if he be a fit candidate, that the material habits are the less important. The exchange of such things as a dainty menu for rough fare, of the stiff leather shoe for the soft, shapeless moccasin, of the feather bed for a couch in the snow, is after all a very easy matter. But his pinch will come in learning properly to shape his mind's attitude toward all things, and especially toward his fellow man. For the courtesies of ordinary life, he must substitute unselfishness, forbearance, and tolerance. Thus, and thus only, can he gain that pearl of great price,—true comradeship. He must not say "Thank you;" he must mean it without opening his mouth, and prove it by responding in kind. In short, he must substitute the deed for the word, the spirit for the letter.

When the world rang with the tale of Arctic gold, and the lure of the North gripped the heartstrings of men, Carter Weatherbee

27

threw up his snug clerkship, turned the half of his savings over to his wife, and with the remainder bought an outfit. There was no romance in his nature,—the bondage of commerce had crushed all that; he was simply tired of the ceaseless grind, and wished to risk great hazards in view of corresponding returns. Like many another fool, disdaining the old trails used by the Northland pioneers for a score of years, he hurried to Edmonton in the spring of the year; and there, unluckily for his soul's welfare, he allied himself with a party of men.

There was nothing unusual about this party, except its plans. Even its goal, like that of all other parties, was the Klondike. But the route it had mapped out to attain that goal took away the breath of the hardiest native, born and bred to the vicissitudes of the Northwest. Even Jacques Baptiste, born of a Chippewa woman and a renegade *voyageur* (having raised his first whimpers in a deerskin lodge north of the sixty-fifth parallel, and had the same hushed by blissful sucks of raw tallow), was surprised. Though he sold his services to them and agreed to travel even to the never-opening ice, he shook his head ominously whenever his advice was asked.

Percy Cuthfert's evil star must have been in the ascendant, for he, too, joined this company of argonauts. He was an ordinary man, with a bank account as deep as his culture, which is saying a good deal. He had no reason to embark on such a venture,— no reason in the world, save that he suffered from an abnormal development of sentimentality. He mistook this for the true spirit of romance and adventure. Many another man has done the like, and made as fatal a mistake.

The first break-up of spring found the party following the ice-run of Elk River. It was an imposing fleet, for the outfit was large, and they were accompanied by a disreputable contingent of half-breed *voyageurs* with their women and children. Day in and day out, they labored with the bateaux and canoes, fought mosquitoes and other kindred pests, or sweated and swore at the portages. Severe toil like this lays a man naked to the very roots of his soul, and ere Lake Athabasca was lost in the south, each member of the party had hoisted his true colors.

The two shirks and chronic grumblers were Carter Weatherbee

and Percy Cuthfert. The whole party complained less of its aches and pains than did either of them. Not once did they volunteer for the thousand and one petty duties of the camp. A bucket of water to be brought, an extra armful of wood to be chopped, the dishes to be washed and wiped, a search to be made through the outfit for some suddenly indispensable article,—and these two effete scions of civilization discovered sprains or blisters requiring instant attention. They were the first to turn in at night, with a score of tasks yet undone; the last to turn out in the morning, when the start should be in readiness before the breakfast was begun. They were the first to fall to at meal-time, the last to have a hand in the cooking; the first to dive for a slim delicacy, the last to discover they had added to their own another man's share. If they toiled at the oars, they slyly cut the water at each stroke and allowed the boat's momentum to float up the blade. They thought nobody noticed; but their comrades swore under their breaths and grew to hate them, while Jacques Baptiste sneered openly and damned them from morning till night. But Jacques Baptiste was no gentleman.

At the Great Slave, Hudson Bay dogs were purchased, and the fleet sank to the guards with its added burden of dried fish and pemmican. Then canoe and bateau answered to the swift current of the Mackenzie, and they plunged into the Great Barren Ground. Every likely-looking "feeder" was prospected, but the elusive "pay-dirt" danced ever to the north. At the Great Bear, overcome by the common dread of the Unknown Lands, their *voyageurs* began to desert, and Fort of Good Hope saw the last and bravest bending to the tow-lines as they bucked the current down which they had so treacherously glided. Jacques Baptiste alone remained. Had he not sworn to travel even to the never-opening ice?

The lying charts, compiled in main from hearsay, were now constantly consulted. And they felt the need of hurry, for the sun had already passed its northern solstice and was leading the winter south again. Skirting the shores of the bay, where the Mackenzie disembogues into the Arctic Ocean, they entered the mouth of the Little Peel River. Then began the arduous up-stream toil, and the two Incapables fared worse than ever. Tow-line and pole, paddle and tump-line, rapids and portages,—such tortures served to give the one a deep disgust for great hazards, and printed for the other a fiery text on the true romance of adventure. One day they waxed mutinous, and being vilely cursed by Jacques Baptiste, turned, as worms sometimes will. But the half-breed thrashed the twain, and sent them, bruised and bleeding, about their work. It was the first time either had been man-handled.

Abandoning their river craft at the headwaters of the Little Peel, they consumed the rest of the summer in the great portage over the Mackenzie watershed to the West Rat. This little stream fed the Porcupine, which in turn joined the Yukon where that mighty highway of the North countermarches on the Arctic Circle. But they had lost in the race with winter, and one day they tied their rafts to the thick eddy-ice and hurried their goods ashore. That night the river jammed and broke several times; the following morning it had fallen asleep for good.

"We can't be more 'n four hundred miles from the Yukon," concluded Sloper, multiplying his thumb nails by the scale of the map. The council, in which the two Incapables had whined to excellent disadvantage, was drawing to a close.

"Hudson Bay Post, long time ago. No use um now." Jacques Baptiste's father had made the trip for the Fur Company in the old days, incidentally marking the trail with a couple of frozen toes.

"Sufferin' cracky!" cried another of the party. "No whites?"

"Nary white," Sloper sententiously affirmed; "but it's only five hundred more up the Yukon to Dawson. Call it a rough thousand from here."

Weatherbee and Cuthfert groaned in chorus.

"How long 'll that take, Baptiste?"

The half-breed figured for a moment. "Workum like hell, no man play out, ten—twenty—forty—fifty days. Um babies come" (designating the Incapables), "no can tell. Mebbe when hell freeze over; mebbe not then."

The manufacture of snowshoes and moccasins ceased. Somebody called the name of an absent member, who came out of an ancient cabin at the edge of the camp-fire and joined them. The cabin was one of the many mysteries which lurk in the vast recesses of the North. Built when and by whom, no man could tell. Two graves in the open, piled high with stones, perhaps contained the secret of those early wanderers. But whose hand had piled the stones?

The moment had come. Jacques Baptiste paused in the fitting of a harness and pinned the struggling dog in the snow. The cook made mute protest for delay, threw a handful of bacon into a noisy pot of beans, then came to attention. Sloper rose to his feet. His body was a ludicrous contrast to the healthy physiques of the Incapables. Yellow and weak, fleeing from a South American fever-hole, he had not broken his flight across the zones, and was still able to toil with men. His weight was probably ninety pounds, with the heavy hunting-knife thrown in, and his grizzled hair told of a prime which had ceased to be. The fresh young muscles of either Weatherbee or Cuthfert were equal to ten times the endeavor of his; yet he could walk them into the earth in a day's journey. And all this day he had whipped his stronger comrades into venturing a thousand miles of the stiffest hardship man can conceive. He was the incarnation of the unrest of his race, and the old Teutonic stubbornness, dashed with the quick grasp and action of the Yankee, held the flesh in the bondage of the spirit.

"All those in favor of going on with the dogs as soon as the ice sets, say ay."

"Ay!" rang out eight voices,—voices destined to string a trail of oaths along many a hundred miles of pain.

"Contrary minded?"

"No!" For the first time the Incapables were united without some compromise of personal interests.

"And what are you going to do about it?" Weatherbee added belligerently.

"Majority rule! Majority rule!" clamored the rest of the party.

"I know the expedition is liable to fall through if you don 't come," Sloper replied sweetly; "but I guess, if we try real hard, we can manage to do without you. What do you say, boys?"

The sentiment was cheered to the echo.

"But I say, you know," Cuthfert ventured apprehensively; "what's a chap like me to do?"

"Ain 't you coming with us?"

"No-o."

"Then do as you damn well please. We won't have nothing to say."

"Kind o' calkilate yuh might settle it with that canoodlin' pardner of yourn," suggested a heavy-going Westerner from the Dakotas, at the same time pointing out Weatherbee. "He 'll be shore to ask yuh what yur a-goin' to do when it comes to cookin' an' gatherin' the wood."

"Then we'll consider it all arranged," concluded Sloper. "We'll pull out to-morrow, if we camp within five miles,—just to get everything in running order and remember if we've forgotten anything."

The sleds groaned by on their steel-shod runners, and the dogs strained low in the harnesses in which they were born to die. Jacques Baptiste paused by the side of Sloper to get a last glimpse of the cabin. The smoke curled up pathetically from the Yukon stove-pipe. The two Incapables were watching them from the doorway.

Sloper laid his hand on the other's shoulder.

"Jacques Baptiste, did you ever hear of the Kilkenny cats?"

The half-breed shook his head.

"Well, my friend and good comrade, the Kilkenny cats fought till neither hide, nor hair, nor yowl, was left. You understand?—till nothing was left. Very good. Now, these two men don 't like work. They won 't work. We know that. They'll be all alone in that cabin all winter,—a mighty long, dark winter. Kilkenny cats,—well?"

The Frenchman in Baptiste shrugged his shoulders, but the Indian in him was silent. Nevertheless, it was an eloquent shrug, pregnant with prophecy.

Things prospered in the little cabin at first. The rough badinage of their comrades had made Weatherbee and Cuthfert conscious

of the mutual responsibility which had devolved upon them; besides, there was not so much work after all for two healthy men.
And the removal of the cruel whip-hand, or in other words the
bulldozing half-breed, had brought with it a joyous reaction. At
first, each strove to outdo the other, and they performed petty
tasks with an unction which would have opened the eyes of their
comrades who were now wearing out bodies and souls on the
Long Trail.

All care was banished. The forest, which shouldered in upon
them from three sides, was an inexhaustible woodyard. A few
yards from their door slept the Porcupine, and a hole through its
winter robe formed a bubbling spring of water, crystal clear and
painfully cold. But they soon grew to find fault with even that.
The hole would persist in freezing up, and thus gave them many
a miserable hour of ice-chopping. The unknown builders of the
cabin had extended the side-logs so as to support a cache at the
rear. In this was stored the bulk of the party's provisions. Food
there was, without stint, for three times the men who were fated
to live upon it. But the most of it was of the kind which built up
brawn and sinew, but did not tickle the palate. True, there was
sugar in plenty for two ordinary men; but these two were little
else than children. They early discovered the virtues of hot water
judiciously saturated with sugar, and they prodigally swam their
flapjacks and soaked their crusts in the rich, white syrup. Then
coffee and tea, and especially the dried fruits, made disastrous
inroads upon it. The first words they had were over the sugar
question. And it is a really serious thing when two men, wholly
dependent upon each other for company, begin to quarrel.

Weatherbee loved to discourse blatantly on politics, while
Cuthfert, who had been prone to clip his coupons and let the
commonwealth jog on as best it might, either ignored the subject or delivered himself of startling epigrams. But the clerk was
too obtuse to appreciate the clever shaping of thought, and this
waste of ammunition irritated Cuthfert. He had been used to
blinding people by his brilliancy, and it worked him quite a hardship, this loss of an audience. He felt personally aggrieved and un-
consciously held his mutton-head companion responsible for it.

Save existence, they had nothing in common,—came in touch

on no single point. Weatherbee was a clerk who had known naught but clerking all his life; Cuthfert was a master of arts, a dabbler in oils, and had written not a little. The one was a lower-class man who considered himself a gentleman, and the other was a gentleman who knew himself to be such. From this it may be remarked that a man can be a gentleman without possessing the first instinct of true comradeship. The clerk was as sensuous as the other was æsthetic, and his love adventures, told at great length and chiefly coined from his imagination, affected the super-sensitive master of arts in the same way as so many whiffs of sewer gas. He deemed the clerk a filthy, uncultured brute, whose place was in the muck with the swine, and told him so; and he was reciprocally informed that he was a milk-and-water sissy and a cad. Weatherbee could not have defined "cad" for his life; but it satisfied its purpose, which after all seems the main point in life.

Weatherbee flatted every third note and sang such songs as "The Boston Burglar" and "The Handsome Cabin Boy," for hours at a time, while Cuthfert wept with rage, till he could stand it no longer and fled into the outer cold. But there was no escape. The intense frost could not be endured for long at a time, and the little cabin crowded them—beds, stove, table, and all—into a space of ten by twelve. The very presence of either became a personal affront to the other, and they lapsed into sullen silences which increased in length and strength as the days went by. Occasionally, the flash of an eye or the curl of a lip got the better of them, though they strove to wholly ignore each other during these mute periods. And a great wonder sprang up in the breast of each, as to how God had ever come to create the other.

With little to do, time became an intolerable burden to them. This naturally made them still lazier. They sank into a physical lethargy which there was no escaping, and which made them rebel at the performance of the smallest chore. One morning when it was his turn to cook the common breakfast, Weatherbee rolled out of his blankets, and to the snoring of his companion, lighted first the slush-lamp and then the fire. The kettles were frozen hard, and there was no water in the cabin with which to wash. But he did not mind that. Waiting for it to thaw, he sliced the bacon and plunged into the hateful task of bread-making. Cuthfert had been slyly watching through his half-closed lids. Consequently there was a scene, in which they fervently blessed each other, and agreed, thenceforth, that each do his own cooking. A week later, Cuthfert neglected his morning ablutions, but none the less complacently ate the meal which he had cooked. Weatherbee grinned. After that the foolish custom of washing passed out of their lives.

As the sugar-pile and other little luxuries dwindled, they began to be afraid they were not getting their proper shares, and in order that they might not be robbed, they fell to gorging themselves. The luxuries suffered in this gluttonous contest, as did also the men. In the absence of fresh vegetables and exercise, their blood became impoverished, and a loathsome, purplish rash crept over their bodies. Yet they refused to heed the warning. Next, their muscles and joints began to swell, the flesh turning black, while their mouths, gums, and lips took on the color of rich cream. Instead of being drawn together by their misery, each gloated over the other's symptoms as the scurvy took its course.

They lost all regard for personal appearance, and for that matter, common decency. The cabin became a pigpen, and never once were the beds made or fresh pine boughs laid underneath. Yet they could not keep to their blankets, as they would have wished; for the frost was inexorable, and the fire box consumed much fuel. The hair of their heads and faces grew long and shaggy, while their garments would have disgusted a ragpicker. But they did not care. They were sick, and there was no one to see; besides, it was very painful to move about.

To all this was added a new trouble,—the Fear of the North. This Fear was the joint child of the Great Cold and the Great Silence, and was born in the darkness of December, when the sun dipped below the southern horizon for good. It affected them according to their natures. Weatherbee fell prey to the grosser superstitions, and did his best to resurrect the spirits which slept in the forgotten graves. It was a fascinating thing, and in his dreams they came to him from out of the cold, and snuggled into his blankets, and told him of their toils and troubles ere they died. He shrank away from the clammy contact as they drew closer and twined their frozen limbs about him, and when they whis-

pered in his ear of things to come, the cabin rang with his frightened shrieks. Cuthfert did not understand,—for they no longer
spoke,—and when thus awakened he invariably grabbed for his
revolver. Then he would sit up in bed, shivering nervously, with
the weapon trained on the unconscious dreamer. Cuthfert deemed
the man going mad, and so came to fear for his life.

His own malady assumed a less concrete form. The mysterious
artisan who had laid the cabin, log by log, had pegged a wind-
vane to the ridge-pole. Cuthfert noticed it always pointed south,
and one day, irritated by its steadfastness of purpose, he turned
it toward the east. He watched eagerly, but never a breath came
by to disturb it. Then he turned the vane to the north, swearing
never again to touch it till the wind did blow. But the air frightened him with its unearthly calm, and he often rose in the middle
of the night to see if the vane had veered,—ten degrees would
have satisfied him. But no, it poised above him as unchangeable
as fate. His imagination ran riot, till it became to him a fetich.
Sometimes he followed the path it pointed across the dismal do-
minions, and allowed his soul to become saturated with the Fear.
He dwelt upon the unseen and the unknown till the burden of
eternity appeared to be crushing him. Everything in the Northland had that crushing effect,—the absence of life and motion; the
darkness; the infinite peace of the brooding land; the ghastly silence, which made the echo of each heart-beat a sacrilege; the
solemn forest which seemed to guard an awful, inexpressible
something, which neither word nor thought could compass.

The world he had so recently left, with its busy nations and
great enterprises, seemed very far away. Recollections occasionally obtruded,—recollections of marts and galleries and crowded
thoroughfares, of evening dress and social functions, of good men
and dear women he had known,—but they were dim memories
of a life he had lived long centuries agone, on some other planet.
This phantasm was the Reality. Standing beneath the wind-vane,
his eyes fixed on the polar skies, he could not bring himself to
realize that the Southland really existed, that at that very moment
it was a-roar with life and action. There was no Southland, no
men being born of women, no giving and taking in marriage. Be-

yond his bleak sky-line there stretched vast solitudes, and beyond these still vaster solitudes. There were no lands of sunshine, heavy with the perfume of flowers. Such things were only old dreams of paradise. The sunlands of the West and the spicelands of the East, the smiling Arcadias and blissful Islands of the Blest,—ha! ha! His laughter split the void and shocked him with its unwonted sound. There was no sun. This was the Universe, dead and cold and dark, and he its only citizen. Weatherbee? At such moments Weatherbee did not count. He was a Caliban, a monstrous phantom, fettered to him for untold ages, the penalty of some forgotten crime.

He lived with Death among the dead, emasculated by the sense of his own insignificance, crushed by the passive mastery of the slumbering ages. The magnitude of all things appalled him. Everything partook of the superlative save himself,—the perfect cessation of wind and motion, the immensity of the snow-covered wilderness, the height of the sky and the depth of the silence. That wind-vane,—if it would only move. If a thunderbolt would fall, or the forest flare up in flame. The rolling up of the heavens as a scroll, the crash of Doom—anything, anything! But no, nothing moved; the Silence crowded in, and the Fear of the North laid icy fingers on his heart.

Once, like another Crusoe, by the edge of the river he came upon a track,—the faint tracery of a snowshoe rabbit on the delicate snow-crust. It was a revelation. There was life in the Northland. He would follow it, look upon it, gloat over it. He forgot his swollen muscles, plunging through the deep snow in an ecstasy of anticipation. The forest swallowed him up, and the brief midday twilight vanished; but he pursued his quest till exhausted nature asserted itself and laid him helpless in the snow. There he groaned and cursed his folly, and knew the track to be the fancy of his brain; and late that night he dragged himself into the cabin on hands and knees, his cheeks frozen and a strange numbness about his feet. Weatherbee grinned malevolently, but made no offer to help him. He thrust needles into his toes and thawed them out by the stove. A week later mortification set in.

But the clerk had his own troubles. The dead men came out of their graves more frequently now, and rarely left him, waking or sleeping. He grew to wait and dread their coming, never passing the twin cairns without a shudder. One night they came to him in his sleep and led him forth to an appointed task. Frightened into inarticulate horror, he awoke between the heaps of stones and fled wildly to the cabin. But he had lain there for some time, for his feet and cheeks were also frozen.

Sometimes he became frantic at their insistent presence, and danced about the cabin, cutting the empty air with an axe, and smashing everything within reach. During these ghostly encounters, Cuthfert huddled into his blankets and followed the madman about with a cocked revolver, ready to shoot him if he came too near. But, recovering from one of these spells, the clerk noticed the weapon trained upon him. His suspicions were aroused, and thenceforth he, too, lived in fear of his life. They watched each other closely after that, and faced about in startled fright whenever either passed behind the other's back. This apprehensiveness became a mania which controlled them even in their sleep. Through mutual fear they tacitly let the slush-lamp burn all night, and saw to a plentiful supply of bacon-grease before retiring. The slightest movement on the part of one was sufficient to arouse the other, and many a still watch their gazes countered as they shook beneath their blankets with fingers on the trigger-guards.

What with the Fear of the North, the mental strain, and the ravages of the disease, they lost all semblance of humanity, taking on the appearance of wild beasts, hunted and desperate. Their cheeks and noses, as an aftermath of the freezing, had turned black. Their frozen toes had begun to drop away at the first and second joints. Every movement brought pain, but the fire box was insatiable, wringing a ransom of torture from their miserable bodies. Day in, day out, it demanded its food,—a veritable pound of flesh,—and they dragged themselves into the forest to chop wood on their knees. Once, crawling thus in search of dry sticks, unknown to each other they entered a thicket from opposite sides. Suddenly, without warning, two peering death's-heads confronted each other. Suffering had so transformed them that recognition was impossible. They sprang to their feet, shrieking with terror, and dashed away on their mangled stumps; and falling at the cabin door, they clawed and scratched like demons till they discovered their mistake.

Occasionally they lapsed normal, and during one of these sane intervals, the chief bone of contention, the sugar, had been divided equally between them. They guarded their separate sacks, stored up in the cache, with jealous eyes; for there were but a few cupfuls left, and they were totally devoid of faith in each other. But one day Cuthfert made a mistake. Hardly able to move, sick with pain, with his head swimming and eyes blinded, he crept into the cache, sugar canister in hand, and mistook Weatherbee's sack for his own.

January had been born but a few days when this occurred. The sun had some time since passed its lowest southern declination, and at meridian now threw flaunting streaks of yellow light upon the northern sky. On the day following his mistake with the sugar-bag, Cuthfert found himself feeling better, both in body and in spirit. As noontime drew near and the day brightened, he dragged himself outside to feast on the evanescent glow, which was to him an earnest of the sun's future intentions. Weatherbee was also feeling somewhat better, and crawled out beside him. They propped themselves in the snow beneath the moveless wind-vane, and waited.

The stillness of death was about them. In other climes, when nature falls into such moods, there is a subdued air of expectancy, a waiting for some small voice to take up the broken strain. Not so in the North. The two men had lived seeming æons in this ghostly peace. They could remember no song of the past; they could conjure no song of the future. This unearthly calm had always been,—the tranquil silence of eternity.

Their eyes were fixed upon the north. Unseen, behind their backs, behind the towering mountains to the south, the sun swept toward the zenith of another sky than theirs. Sole spectators of the mighty canvas, they watched the false dawn slowly grow. A faint flame began to glow and smoulder. It deepened in intensity, ringing the changes of reddish-yellow, purple, and saffron. So bright did it become that Cuthfert thought the sun must surely be behind it,—a miracle, the sun rising in the north! Suddenly, without warning and without fading, the canvas was swept clean. There was no color in the sky. The light had gone out of the day. They caught their breaths in half-sobs. But lo! the air was a-glint with particles of scintillating frost, and there, to the north, the wind-vane lay in vague outline on the snow. A shadow! A shadow! It was exactly midday. They jerked their heads hurriedly to the south. A golden rim peeped over the mountain's snowy shoulder, smiled upon them an instant, then dipped from sight again.

There were tears in their eyes as they sought each other. A strange softening came over them. They felt irresistibly drawn toward each other. The sun was coming back again. It would be with them to-morrow, and the next day, and the next. And it would stay longer every visit, and a time would come when it would ride their heaven day and night, never once dropping below the sky-line. There would be no night. The ice-locked winter would be broken; the winds would blow and the forests answer; the land would bathe in the blessed sunshine, and life renew. Hand in hand, they would quit this horrid dream and journey back to the Southland. They lurched blindly forward, and their hands met,—their poor maimed hands, swollen and distorted beneath their mittens.

But the promise was destined to remain unfulfilled. The Northland is the Northland, and men work out their souls by strange rules, which other men, who have not journeyed into far countries, cannot come to understand.

An hour later, Cuthfert put a pan of bread into the oven, and fell to speculating on what the surgeons could do with his feet when he got back. Home did not seem so very far away now. Weatherbee was rummaging in the cache. Of a sudden, he raised a whirlwind of blasphemy, which in turn ceased with startling abruptness. The other man had robbed his sugar-sack. Still, things might have happened differently, had not the two dead men come out from under the stones and hushed the hot words in his throat. They led him quite gently from the cache, which he forgot to close. That consummation was reached; that something they had whispered to him in his dreams was about to happen. They guided him gently, very gently, to the woodpile, where they put the axe in his hands. Then they helped him shove open the cabin door, and he felt sure they shut it after him,—at least he heard it slam and the latch fall sharply into place. And he knew they were waiting just without, waiting for him to do his task.

"Carter! I say, Carter!"

Percy Cuthfert was frightened at the look on the clerk's face, and he made haste to put the table between them.

Carter Weatherbee followed, without haste and without enthusiasm. There was neither pity nor passion in his face, but rather the patient, stolid look of one who has certain work to do and goes about it methodically.

"I say, what 's the matter?"

The clerk dodged back, cutting off his retreat to the door, but never opening his mouth.

"I say, Carter, I say; let 's talk. There 's a good chap."

The master of arts was thinking rapidly, now, shaping a skillful flank movement on the bed where his Smith & Wesson lay. Keeping his eyes on the madman, he rolled backward on the bunk, at the same time clutching the pistol.

"Carter!"

The powder flashed full in Weatherbee's face, but he swung his weapon and leaped forward. The axe bit deeply at the base of the spine, and Percy Cuthfert felt all consciousness of his lower limbs leave him. Then the clerk fell heavily upon him, clutching him by the throat with feeble fingers. The sharp bite of the axe had caused Cuthfert to drop the pistol, and as his lungs panted for release, he fumbled aimlessly for it among the blankets. Then he remembered. He slid a hand up the clerk's belt to the sheath-knife; and they drew very close to each other in that last clinch.

Percy Cuthfert felt his strength leave him. The lower portion of his body was useless. The inert weight of Weatherbee crushed him,—crushed him and pinned him there like a bear under a trap. The cabin became filled with a familiar odor, and he knew the bread to be burning. Yet what did it matter? He would never need it. And there were all of six cupfuls of sugar in the cache,—if he had foreseen this he would not have been so saving the last several days. Would the wind-vane ever move? It might even be veering now. Why not? Had he not seen the sun to-day? He would go and see. No; it was impossible to move. He had not thought the clerk so heavy a man.

How quickly the cabin cooled! The fire must be out. The cold was forcing in. It must be below zero already, and the ice creeping up the inside of the door. He could not see it, but his past experience enabled him to gauge its progress by the cabin's temperature. The lower hinge must be white ere now. Would the tale of this ever reach the world? How would his friends take it? They would read it over their coffee, most likely, and talk it over at the clubs. He could see them very clearly. "Poor Old Cuthfert," they murmured; "not such a bad sort of a chap, after all." He smiled at their eulogies, and passed on in search of a Turkish bath. It was the same old crowd upon the streets. Strange, they did not notice his moosehide moccasins and tattered German socks! He would take a cab. And after the bath a shave would not be bad. No; he would eat first. Steak, and potatoes, and green things,—how fresh it all was! And what was that? Squares of honey, streaming liquid amber! But why did they bring so much? Ha! ha! he could never eat it all. Shine! Why certainly. He put his foot on the box. The bootblack looked curiously up at him, and he remembered his moosehide moccasins and went away hastily.

Hark! The wind-vane must be surely spinning. No; a mere singing in his ears. That was all,—a mere singing. The ice must have passed the latch by now. More likely the upper hinge was covered. Between the moss-chinked roof-poles, little points of frost began to appear. How slowly they grew! No; not so slowly. There was a new one, and there another. Two—three—four; they were coming too fast to count. There were two growing together. And there, a third had joined them. Why, there were no more spots. They had run together and formed a sheet.

Well, he would have company. If Gabriel ever broke the silence of the North, they would stand together, hand in hand, before the great White Throne. And God would judge them, God would judge them!

Then Percy Cuthfert closed his eyes and dropped off to sleep.

To the Man on Trail

"Dump it in."

"But I say, Kid, is n't that going it a little too strong? Whiskey and alcohol's bad enough; but when it comes to brandy and pepper-sauce and"—

"Dump it in. Who 's making this punch, anyway?" And Malemute Kid smiled benignantly through the clouds of steam. "By the time you 've been in this country as long as I have, my son, and lived on rabbit-tracks and salmon-belly, you'll learn that Christmas comes only once per annum. And a Christmas without punch is sinking a hole to bedrock with nary a pay-streak."

"Stack up on that fer a high cyard," approved Big Jim Belden, who had come down from his claim on Mazy May to spend Christmas, and who, as every one knew, had been living the two months past on straight moose-meat. "Hain't fergot the *hooch* we-uns made on the Tanana, hev yeh?"

"Well, I guess yes. Boys, it would have done your hearts good to see that whole tribe fighting drunk—and all because of a glorious ferment of sugar and sour dough. That was before your time," Malemute Kid said as he turned to Stanley Prince, a young mining expert who had been in two years. "No white women in the country then, and Mason wanted to get married. Ruth's father was chief of the Tananas, and objected, like the rest of the tribe. Stiff? Why, I used my last pound of sugar; finest work in that line I ever did in my life. You should have seen the chase, down the river and across the portage."

"But the squaw?" asked Louis Savoy, the tall French-Canadian, becoming interested; for he had heard of this wild deed, when at Forty Mile the preceding winter.

Then Malemute Kid, who was a born raconteur, told the unvarnished tale of the Northland Lochinvar. More than one rough adventurer of the North felt his heartstrings draw closer, and experienced vague yearnings for the sunnier pastures of the Southland, where life promised something more than a barren struggle with cold and death.

"We struck the Yukon just behind the first ice-run," he concluded, "and the tribe only a quarter of an hour behind. But that saved us; for the second run broke the jam above and shut them out. When they finally got into Nuklukyeto, the whole Post was ready for them. And as to the foregathering, ask Father Roubeau here: he performed the ceremony."

The Jesuit took the pipe from his lips, but could only express his gratification with patriarchal smiles, while Protestant and Catholic vigorously applauded.

"By gar!" ejaculated Louis Savoy, who seemed overcome by the romance of it. "La petite squaw; mon Mason brav. By gar!"

Then, as the first tin cups of punch went round, Bettles the Unquenchable sprang to his feet and struck up his favorite drinking song:—

> *"There's Henry Ward Beecher*
> *And Sunday-school teachers,*
> *All drink of the sassafras root;*
> *But you bet all the same,*
> *If it had its right name,*
> *It 's the juice of the forbidden fruit."*

> *"Oh the juice of the forbidden fruit,"*

roared out the Bacchanalian chorus,—

> *"Oh the juice of the forbidden fruit;*
> *But you bet all the same,*
> *If it had its right name,*
> *It 's the juice of the forbidden fruit."*

Malemute Kid's frightful concoction did its work; the men of the camps and trails unbent in its genial glow, and jest and song and tales of past adventure went round the board. Aliens from a dozen lands, they toasted each and all. It was the Englishman, Prince, who pledged "Uncle Sam, the precocious infant of the New World;" the Yankee, Bettles, who drank to "The Queen,

God bless her;" and together, Savoy and Meyers, the German trader, clanged their cups to Alsace and Lorraine.

Then Malemute Kid arose, cup in hand, and glanced at the greased-paper window, where the frost stood full three inches thick. "A health to the man on trail this night; may his grub hold out; may his dogs keep their legs; may his matches never miss fire."

Crack! Crack!—they heard the familiar music of the dogwhip, the whining howl of the Malemutes, and the crunch of a sled as it drew up to the cabin. Conversation languished while they waited the issue.

"An old-timer; cares for his dogs and then himself," whispered Malemute Kid to Prince, as they listened to the snapping jaws and the wolfish snarls and yelps of pain which proclaimed to their practiced ears that the stranger was beating back their dogs while he fed his own.

Then came the expected knock, sharp and confident, and the stranger entered. Dazzled by the light, he hesitated a moment at the door, giving to all a chance for scrutiny. He was a striking personage, and a most picturesque one, in his Arctic dress of wool and fur. Standing six foot two or three, with proportionate breadth of shoulders and depth of chest, his smooth-shaven face nipped by the cold to a gleaming pink, his long lashes and eyebrows white with ice, and the ear and neck flaps of his great wolfskin cap loosely raised, he seemed, of a verity, the Frost King, just stepped in out of the night. Clasped outside his mackinaw jacket, a beaded belt held two large Colt's revolvers and a hunting-knife, while he carried, in addition to the inevitable dogwhip, a smokeless rifle of the largest bore and latest pattern. As he came forward, for all his step was firm and elastic, they could see that fatigue bore heavily upon him.

An awkward silence had fallen, but his hearty "What cheer, my lads?" put them quickly at ease, and the next instant Malemute Kid and he had gripped hands. Though they had never met, each had heard of the other, and the recognition was mutual. A sweeping introduction and a mug of punch were forced upon him before he could explain his errand.

"How long since that basket-sled, with three men and eight dogs, passed?" he asked.

"An even two days ahead. Are you after them?"

"Yes; my team. Run them off under my very nose, the cusses. I've gained two days on them already,—pick them up on the next run."

"Reckon they'll show spunk?" asked Belden, in order to keep up the conversation, for Malemute Kid already had the coffee-pot on and was busily frying bacon and moose-meat.

The stranger significantly tapped his revolvers.

"When 'd yeh leave Dawson?"

"Twelve o'clock."

"Last night?"—as a matter of course.

"To-day."

A murmur of surprise passed round the circle. And well it might; for it was just midnight, and seventy-five miles of rough river trail was not to be sneered at for a twelve hours' run.

The talk soon became impersonal, however, harking back to the trails of childhood. As the young stranger ate of the rude fare, Malemute Kid attentively studied his face. Nor was he long in deciding that it was fair, honest, and open, and that he liked it. Still youthful, the lines had been firmly traced by toil and hardship. Though genial in conversation, and mild when at rest, the blue eyes gave promise of the hard steel-glitter which comes when called into action, especially against odds. The heavy jaw and square-cut chin demonstrated rugged pertinacity and indomitability. Nor, though the attributes of the lion were there, was there wanting the certain softness, the hint of womanliness, which bespoke the emotional nature.

"So thet's how me an' the ol' woman got spliced," said Belden, concluding the exciting tale of his courtship. " 'Here we be, dad,' sez she. 'An' may yeh be damned,' sez he to her, an' then to me, 'Jim, yeh—yeh git outen them good duds o' yourn; I want a right peart slice o' thet forty acre ploughed 'fore dinner.' An' then he turns on her an' sez, 'An' yeh, Sal; yeh sail inter them dishes.' An' then he sort o' sniffled an' kissed her. An' I was thet happy,— but he seen me an' roars out, 'Yeh, Jim!' An' yeh bet I dusted fer the barn."

"Any kids waiting for you back in the States?" asked the stranger.

"Nope; Sal died 'fore any come. Thet's why I'm here." Belden abstractedly began to light his pipe, which had failed to go out, and then brightened up with, "How 'bout yerself, stranger,—married man?"

For reply, he opened his watch, slipped it from the thong which served for a chain, and passed it over. Belden pricked up the slush-lamp, surveyed the inside of the case critically, and swearing admiringly to himself, handed it over to Louis Savoy. With numerous "By gars!" he finally surrendered it to Prince, and they noticed that his hands trembled and his eyes took on a peculiar softness. And so it passed from horny hand to horny hand—the pasted photograph of a woman, the clinging kind that such men fancy, with a babe at the breast. Those who had not yet seen the wonder were keen with curiosity; those who had, became silent and retrospective. They could face the pinch of famine, the grip of scurvy, or the quick death by field or flood; but the pictured semblance of a stranger woman and child made women and children of them all.

"Never have seen the youngster yet,—he's a boy, she says, and two years old," said the stranger as he received the treasure back. A lingering moment he gazed upon it, then snapped the case and turned away, but not quick enough to hide the restrained rush of tears.

Malemute Kid led him to a bunk and bade him turn in.

"Call me at four, sharp. Don't fail me," were his last words, and a moment later he was breathing in the heaviness of exhausted sleep.

"By Jove! he 's a plucky chap," commented Prince. "Three hours' sleep after seventy-five miles with the dogs, and then the trail again. Who is he, Kid?"

"Jack Westondale. Been in going on three years, with nothing but the name of working like a horse, and any amount of bad luck to his credit. I never knew him, but Sitka Charley told me about him."

"It seems hard that a man with a sweet young wife like his

should be putting in his years in this God-forsaken hole, where every year counts two on the outside."

"The trouble with him is clean grit and stubbornness. He's cleaned up twice with a stake, but lost it both times."

Here the conversation was broken off by an uproar from Bettles, for the effect had begun to wear away. And soon the bleak years of monotonous grub and deadening toil were being forgotten in rough merriment. Malemute Kid alone seemed unable to lose himself, and cast many an anxious look at his watch. Once he put on his mittens and beaver-skin cap, and leaving the cabin, fell to rummaging about in the cache.

Nor could he wait the hour designated; for he was fifteen minutes ahead of time in rousing his guest. The young giant had stiffened badly, and brisk rubbing was necessary to bring him to his feet. He tottered painfully out of the cabin, to find his dogs harnessed and everything ready for the start. The company wished him good luck and a short chase, while Father Roubeau, hurriedly blessing him, led the stampede for the cabin; and small wonder, for it is not good to face seventy-four degrees below zero with naked ears and hands.

Malemute Kid saw him to the main trail, and there, gripping his hand heartily, gave him advice.

"You 'll find a hundred pounds of salmon-eggs on the sled," he said. "The dogs will go as far on that as with one hundred and fifty of fish, and you can't get dog-food at Pelly, as you probably expected." The stranger started, and his eyes flashed, but he did not interrupt. "You can't get an ounce of food for dog or man till you reach Five Fingers, and that's a stiff two hundred miles. Watch out for open water on the Thirty Mile River, and be sure you take the big cut-off above Le Barge."

"How did you know it? Surely the news can 't be ahead of me already?"

"I don't know it; and what's more, I don't want to know it. But you never owned that team you 're chasing. Sitka Charley sold it to them last spring. But he sized you up to me as square once, and I believe him. I've seen your face; I like it. And I've seen—why, damn you, hit the high places for salt water and that wife of yours, and"—Here the Kid unmittened and jerked out his sack.

"No; I don't need it," and the tears froze on his cheeks as he convulsively gripped Malemute Kid's hand.

"Then don't spare the dogs; cut them out of the traces as fast as they drop; buy them, and think they're cheap at ten dollars a pound. You can get them at Five Fingers, Little Salmon, and the Hootalinqua. And watch out for wet feet," was his parting advice. "Keep a-traveling up to twenty-five, but if it gets below that, build a fire and change your socks."

Fifteen minutes had barely elapsed when the jingle of bells announced new arrivals. The door opened, and a mounted policeman of the Northwest Territory entered, followed by two half-breed dog-drivers. Like Westondale, they were heavily armed and showed signs of fatigue. The half-breeds had been born to the trail, and bore it easily; but the young policeman was badly exhausted. Still, the dogged obstinacy of his race held him to the pace he had set, and would hold him till he dropped in his tracks.

"When did Westondale pull out?" he asked. "He stopped here, did n't he?" This was supererogatory, for the tracks told their own tale too well.

Malemute Kid had caught Belden's eye, and he, scenting the wind, replied evasively, "A right peart while back."

"Come, my man; speak up," the policeman admonished.

"Yeh seem to want him right smart. Hez he ben gittin' cantankerous down Dawson way?"

"Held up Harry McFarland's for forty thousand; exchanged it at the P. C. store for a check on Seattle; and who's to stop the cashing of it if we don't overtake him? When did he pull out?"

Every eye suppressed its excitement, for Malemute Kid had given the cue, and the young officer encountered wooden faces on every hand.

Striding over to Prince, he put the question to him. Though it hurt him, gazing into the frank, earnest face of his fellow countryman, he replied inconsequentially on the state of the trail.

Then he espied Father Roubeau, who could not lie. "A quarter of an hour ago," the priest answered; "but he had four hours' rest for himself and dogs."

"Fifteen minutes' start, and he's fresh! My God!" The poor fellow staggered back, half fainting from exhaustion and disappointment, murmuring something about the run from Dawson in ten hours and the dogs being played out.

Malemute Kid forced a mug of punch upon him; then he turned for the door, ordering the dog-drivers to follow. But the warmth and promise of rest were too tempting, and they objected strenuously. The Kid was conversant with their French patois, and followed it anxiously.

They swore that the dogs were gone up; that Siwash and Babette would have to be shot before the first mile was covered; that the rest were almost as bad; and that it would be better for all hands to rest up.

"Lend me five dogs?" he asked, turning to Malemute Kid.

But the Kid shook his head.

"I'll sign a check on Captain Constantine for five thousand,— here's my papers,—I'm authorized to draw at my own discretion."

Again the silent refusal.

"Then I'll requisition them in the name of the Queen."

Smiling incredulously, the Kid glanced at his well-stocked arsenal, and the Englishman, realizing his impotency, turned for the door. But the dog-drivers still objecting, he whirled upon them fiercely, calling them women and curs. The swart face of the older half-breed flushed angrily, as he drew himself up and promised in good, round terms that he would travel his leader off his legs, and would then be delighted to plant him in the snow.

The young officer—and it required his whole will—walked steadily to the door, exhibiting a freshness he did not possess. But they all knew and appreciated his proud effort; nor could he veil the twinges of agony that shot across his face. Covered with frost, the dogs were curled up in the snow, and it was almost impossible to get them to their feet. The poor brutes whined under the stinging lash, for the dog-drivers were angry and cruel; nor till Babette, the leader, was cut from the traces, could they break out the sled and get under way.

TO THE MAN ON TRAIL

"A dirty scoundrel and a liar!" "By gar! him no good!" "A thief!" "Worse than an Indian!" It was evident that they were angry—first, at the way they had been deceived; and second, at the outraged ethics of the Northland, where honesty, above all, was man's prime jewel. "An' we gave the cuss a hand, after knowin' what he 'd did." All eyes were turned accusingly upon Malemute Kid, who rose from the corner where he had been making Babette comfortable, and silently emptied the bowl for a final round of punch.

"It's a cold night, boys,—a bitter cold night," was the irrelevant commencement of his defense. "You've all traveled trail, and know what that stands for. Don't jump a dog when he's down. You've only heard one side. A whiter man than Jack Westondale never ate from the same pot nor stretched blanket with you or me. Last fall he gave his whole clean-up, forty thousand, to Joe Castrell, to buy in on Dominion. To-day he 'd be a millionaire. But while he stayed behind at Circle City, taking care of his partner with the scurvy, what does Castrell do? Goes into Mc-Farland's, jumps the limit, and drops the whole sack. Found him dead in the snow the next day. And poor Jack laying his plans to go out this winter to his wife and the boy he 's never seen. You 'll notice he took exactly what his partner lost,—forty thousand. Well, he 's gone out; and what are you going to do about it?"

The Kid glanced round the circle of his judges, noted the softening of their faces, then raised his mug aloft. "So a health to the man on trail this night; may his grub hold out; may his dogs keep their legs; may his matches never miss fire. God prosper him; good luck go with him; and"—

"Confusion to the Mounted Police!" cried Bettles, to the crash of the empty cups.

The Wisdom of the Trail

Sitka Charley had achieved the impossible. Other Indians might have known as much of the wisdom of the trail as did he; but he alone knew the white man's wisdom, the honor of the trail, and the law. But these things had not come to him in a day. The aboriginal mind is slow to generalize, and many facts, repeated often, are required to compass an understanding. Sitka Charley, from boyhood, had been thrown continually with white men, and as a man he had elected to cast his fortunes with them, expatriating himself, once and for all, from his own people. Even then, respecting, almost venerating their power, and pondering over it, he had yet to divine its secret essence—the honor and the law. And it was only by the cumulative evidence of years that he had finally come to understand. Being an alien, when he did know he knew it better than the white man himself; being an Indian, he had achieved the impossible.

And of these things had been bred a certain contempt for his own people,—a contempt which he had made it a custom to conceal, but which now burst forth in a polyglot whirlwind of curses upon the heads of Kah-Chucte and Gowhee. They cringed before him like a brace of snarling wolf-dogs, too cowardly to spring, too wolfish to cover their fangs. They were not handsome creatures. Neither was Sitka Charley. All three were frightful-looking. There was no flesh to their faces; their cheek bones were massed with hideous scabs which had cracked and frozen alternately under the intense frost; while their eyes burned luridly with the light which is born of desperation and hunger. Men so situated, beyond the pale of the honor and the law, are not to be trusted. Sitka Charley knew this; and this was why he had forced them to abandon their rifles with the rest of the camp outfit ten days before. His rifle and Captain Eppingwell's were the only ones that remained.

"Come, get a fire started," he commanded, drawing out the

precious match box with its attendant strips of dry birch bark.

The two Indians fell sullenly to the task of gathering dead branches and underwood. They were weak, and paused often, catching themselves, in the act of stooping, with giddy motions, or staggering to the centre of operations with their knees shaking like castanets. After each trip they rested for a moment, as though sick and deadly weary. At times their eyes took on the patient stoicism of dumb suffering; and again the ego seemed almost bursting forth with its wild cry, "I, I, I want to exist!"—the dominant note of the whole living universe.

A light breath of air blew from the south, nipping the exposed portions of their bodies and driving the frost, in needles of fire, through fur and flesh to the bones. So, when the fire had grown lusty and thawed a damp circle in the snow about it, Sitka Charley forced his reluctant comrades to lend a hand in pitching a fly. It was a primitive affair,—merely a blanket, stretched parallel with the fire and to windward of it, at an angle of perhaps forty-five degrees. This shut out the chill wind, and threw the heat backward and down upon those who were to huddle in its shelter. Then a layer of green spruce boughs was spread, that their bodies might not come in contact with the snow. When this task was completed, Kah-Chucte and Gowhee proceeded to take care of their feet. Their ice-bound moccasins were sadly worn by much travel, and the sharp ice of the river jams had cut them to rags. Their Siwash socks were similarly conditioned, and when these had been thawed and removed, the dead-white tips of the toes, in the various stages of mortification, told their simple tale of the trail.

Leaving the two to the drying of their footgear, Sitka Charley turned back over the course he had come. He, too, had a mighty longing to sit by the fire and tend his complaining flesh, but the honor and the law forbade. He toiled painfully over the frozen field, each step a protest, every muscle in revolt. Several times, where the open water between the jams had recently crusted, he was forced to miserably accelerate his movements as the fragile footing swayed and threatened beneath him. In such places death was quick and easy; but it was not his desire to endure no more.

His deepening anxiety vanished as two Indians dragged into

view round a bend in the river. They staggered and panted like men under heavy burdens; yet the packs on their backs were a matter of but few pounds. He questioned them eagerly, and their replies seemed to relieve him. He hurried on. Next came two white men, supporting between them a woman. They also behaved as though drunken, and their limbs shook with weakness. But the woman leaned lightly upon them, choosing to carry herself forward with her own strength. At sight of her, a flash of joy cast its fleeting light across Sitka Charley's face. He cherished a very great regard for Mrs. Eppingwell. He had seen many white women, but this was the first to travel the trail with him. When Captain Eppingwell proposed the hazardous undertaking and made him an offer for his services, he had shaken his head gravely; for it was an unknown journey through the dismal vastnesses of the Northland, and he knew it to be of the kind that try to the uttermost the souls of men. But when he learned that the Captain's wife was to accompany them, he had refused flatly to have anything further to do with it. Had it been a woman of his own race he would have harbored no objections; but these women of the Southland—no, no, they were too soft, too tender, for such enterprises.

Sitka Charley did not know this kind of woman. Five minutes before, he did not even dream of taking charge of the expedition; but when she came to him with her wonderful smile and her straight clean English, and talked to the point, without pleading or persuading, he had incontinently yielded. Had there been a softness and appeal to mercy in the eyes, a tremble to the voice, a taking advantage of sex, he would have stiffened to steel; instead her clear-searching eyes and clear-ringing voice, her utter frankness and tacit assumption of equality, had robbed him of his reason. He felt, then, that this was a new breed of woman; and ere they had been trail-mates for many days, he knew why the sons of such women mastered the land and the sea, and why the sons of his own womankind could not prevail against them. *Tender and soft!* Day after day he watched her, muscle-weary, exhausted, indomitable, and the words beat in upon him in a perennial refrain. *Tender and soft!* He knew her feet had been born to easy paths and sunny lands, strangers to the moccasined pain of the North, unkissed by the chill lips of the frost, and he watched and marveled at them twinkling ever through the weary day.

She had always a smile and a word of cheer, from which not even the meanest packer was excluded. As the way grew darker she seemed to stiffen and gather greater strength, and when Kah-Chucte and Gowhee, who had bragged that they knew every land-mark of the way as a child did the skin-bales of the tepee, acknowledged that they knew not where they were, it was she who raised a forgiving voice amid the curses of the men. She had sung to them that night, till they felt the weariness fall from them and were ready to face the future with fresh hope. And when the food failed and each scant stint was measured jealously, she it was who rebelled against the machinations of her husband and Sitka Charley, and demanded and received a share neither greater nor less than that of the others.

Sitka Charley was proud to know this woman. A new richess, a greater breadth, had come into his life with her presence. Hitherto he had been his own mentor, had turned to right or left at no man's beck; he had moulded himself according to his own dictates, nourished his manhood regardless of all save his own opinion. For the first time he had felt a call from without for the best that was in him. Just a glance of appreciation from the clear-searching eyes, a word of thanks from the clear-ringing voice, just a slight wreathing of the lips in the wonderful smile, and he walked with the gods for hours to come. It was a new stimulant to his manhood; for the first time he thrilled with a conscious pride in his wisdom of the trail; and between the twain they ever lifted the sinking hearts of their comrades.

The faces of the two men and the woman brightened as they saw him, for after all he was the staff they leaned upon. But Sitka Charley, rigid as was his wont, concealing pain and pleasure impartially beneath an iron exterior, asked them the welfare of the rest, told the distance to the fire, and continued on the back-trip. Next he met a single Indian, unburdened, limping, lips compressed, and eyes set with the pain of a foot in which the quick fought a losing battle with the dead. All possible care had been taken of him, but in the last extremity the weak and unfortunate must perish, and Sitka Charley deemed his days to be few. The man could not keep up for long, so he gave him rough cheering words. After that came two more Indians, to whom he had allotted the task of helping along Joe, the third white man of the party. They had deserted him. Sitka Charley saw at a glance the lurking spring in their bodies, and knew they had at last cast off his mastery. So he was not taken unawares when he ordered them back in quest of their abandoned charge, and saw the gleam of the hunting-knives that they drew from the sheaths. A pitiful spectacle, three weak men lifting their puny strength in the face of the mighty vastness; but the two recoiled under the fierce rifle-blows of the one, and returned like beaten dogs to the leash. Two hours later, with Joe reeling between them and Sitka Charley bringing up the rear, they came to the fire, where the remainder of the expedition crouched in the shelter of the fly.

"A few words, my comrades, before we sleep," Sitka Charley said, after they had devoured their slim rations of unleavened bread. He was speaking to the Indians, in their own tongue, having already given the import to the whites. "A few words, my comrades, for your own good, that ye may yet perchance live. I shall give you the law; on his own head be the death of him that breaks it. We have passed the Hills of Silence, and we now travel the head-reaches of the Stuart. It may be one sleep, it may be several, it may be many sleeps, but in time we shall come among the Men of the Yukon, who have much grub. It were well that we look to the law. To-day, Kah-Chucte and Gowhee, whom I commanded to break trail, forgot they were men, and like frightened children ran away. True, they forgot; so let us forget. But hereafter let them remember. If it should happen they do not"— He touched his rifle carelessly, grimly. "To-morrow they shall carry the flour and see that the white man Joe lies not down by the trail. The cups of flour are counted; should so much as an ounce be wanting at nightfall—Do ye understand? To-day there were others that forgot. Moose-Head and Three-Salmon left the white man Joe to lie in the snow. Let them forget no more. With the light of day shall they go forth and break trail. Ye have heard the law. Look well, lest ye break it."

Sitka Charley found it beyond him to keep the line close up. From Moose-Head and Three-Salmon, who broke trail in advance, to Kah-Chucte, Gowhee, and Joe, it straggled out over a mile. Each staggered, fell, or rested, as he saw fit. The line of march was a progression through a chain of irregular halts. Each drew upon the last remnant of his strength and stumbled onward till it was expended, but in some miraculous way there was always another last remnant. Each time a man fell, it was with the firm belief that he would rise no more; yet he did rise, and again, and again. The flesh yielded, the will conquered; but each triumph was a tragedy. The Indian with the frozen foot, no longer erect, crawled forward on hand and knee. He rarely rested, for he knew the penalty exacted by the frost. Even Mrs. Eppingwell's lips were at last set in a stony smile, and her eyes, seeing, saw not. Often, she stopped, pressing a mittened hand to her heart, gasping and dizzy.

Joe, the white man, had passed beyond the stage of suffering. He no longer begged to be let alone, prayed to die; but was soothed and content under the anodyne of delirium. Kah-Chucte and Gowhee dragged him on roughly, venting upon him many a savage glance or blow. To them it was the acme of injustice. Their hearts were bitter with hate, heavy with fear. Why should they cumber their strength with his weakness? To do so, meant death; not to do so—and they remembered the law of Sitka Charley, and the rifle.

Joe fell with greater frequency as the daylight waned, and so hard was he to raise that they dropped farther and farther behind. Sometimes all three pitched into the snow, so weak had the Indians become. Yet on their backs was life, and strength, and warmth. Within the flour-sacks were all the potentialities of existence. They could not but think of this, and it was not strange, that which came to pass. They had fallen by the side of a great timber-jam where a thousand cords of firewood waited the match. Near by was an air hole through the ice. Kah-Chucte looked on the wood and the water, as did Gowhee; then they looked on each other. Never a word was spoken. Gowhee struck a fire; Kah-

Chucte filled a tin cup with water and heated it; Joe babbled of things in another land, in a tongue they did not understand. They mixed flour with the warm water till it was a thin paste, and of this they drank many cups. They did not offer any to Joe; but he did not mind. He did not mind anything, not even his moccasins, which scorched and smoked among the coals.

A crystal mist of snow fell about them, softly, caressingly, wrapping them in clinging robes of white. And their feet would have yet trod many trails had not destiny brushed the clouds aside and cleared the air. Nay, ten minutes' delay would have been salvation. Sitka Charley, looking back, saw the pillared smoke of their fire, and guessed. And he looked ahead at those who were faithful, and at Mrs. Eppingwell.

"So, my good comrades, ye have again forgotten that you were men? Good. Very good. There will be fewer bellies to feed."

Sitka Charley retied the flour as he spoke, strapping the pack to the one on his own back. He kicked Joe till the pain broke through the poor devil's bliss and brought him doddering to his feet. Then he shoved him out upon the trail and started him on his way. The two Indians attempted to slip off.

"Hold, Gowhee! And thou, too, Kah-Chucte! Hath the flour given such strength to thy legs that they may outrun the swift-winged lead? Think not to cheat the law. Be men for the last time, and be content that ye die full-stomached. Come, step up, back to the timber, shoulder to shoulder. Come!"

The two men obeyed, quietly, without fear; for it is the future which presses upon the man, not the present.

"Thou, Gowhee, hast a wife and children and a deer-skin lodge in the Chippewyan. What is thy will in the matter?"

"Give thou her of the goods which are mine by the word of the Captain—the blankets, the beads, the tobacco, the box which makes strange sounds after the manner of the white men. Say that I did die on the trail, but say not how."

"And thou, Kah-Chucte, who hast nor wife nor child?"

"Mine is a sister, the wife of the Factor at Koshim. He beats her, and she is not happy. Give thou her the goods which are mine by the contract, and tell her it were well she go back to her own people. Shouldst thou meet the man, and be so minded, it were a good deed that he should die. He beats her, and she is afraid."

"Are ye content to die by the law?"

"We are."

"Then good-by, my good comrades. May ye sit by the well-filled pot, in warm lodges, ere the day is done."

As he spoke, he raised his rifle, and many echoes broke the silence. Hardly had they died away, when other rifles spoke in the distance. Sitka Charley started. There had been more than one shot, yet there was but one other rifle in the party. He gave a fleeting glance at the men who lay so quietly, smiled viciously at the wisdom of the trail, and hurried on to meet the Men of the Yukon.

An Odyssey of the North

I

The sleds were singing their eternal lament to the creaking of the harnesses and the tinkling bells of the leaders; but the men and dogs were tired and made no sound. The trail was heavy with new-fallen snow, and they had come far, and the runners, burdened with flint-like quarters of frozen moose, clung tenaciously to the unpacked surface and held back with a stubbornness almost human. Darkness was coming on, but there was no camp to pitch that night. The snow fell gently through the pulseless air, not in flakes, but in tiny frost crystals of delicate design. It was very warm,—barely ten below zero,—and the men did not mind. Meyers and Bettles had raised their earflaps, while Malemute Kid had even taken off his mittens.

The dogs had been fagged out early in the afternoon, but they now began to show new vigor. Among the more astute there was a certain restlessness,—an impatience at the restraint of the traces, an indecisive quickness of movement, a sniffing of snouts and pricking of ears. These became incensed at their more phlegmatic brothers, urging them on with numerous sly nips on their hinderquarters. Those, thus chidden, also contracted and helped spread the contagion. At last, the leader of the foremost sled uttered a sharp whine of satisfaction, crouching lower in the snow and throwing himself against the collar. The rest followed suit. There was an ingathering of back-bands, a tightening of traces; the sleds leaped forward, and the men clung to the gee-poles, violently accelerating the uplift of their feet that they might escape going under the runners. The weariness of the day fell from them, and they whooped encouragement to the dogs. The animals responded with joyous yelps. They were swinging through the gathering darkness at a rattling gallop.

"Gee! Gee!" the men cried, each in turn, as their sleds abruptly left the main-trail, heeling over on single runners like luggers on the wind.

Then came a hundred yards' dash to the lighted parchment window, which told its own story of the home cabin, the roaring Yukon stove, and the steaming pots of tea. But the home cabin had been invaded. Three-score huskies chorused defiance, and as many furry forms precipitated themselves upon the dogs which drew the first sled. The door was flung open, and a man, clad in the scarlet tunic of the Northwest Police, waded knee-deep among the furious brutes, calmly and impartially dispensing soothing justice with the butt end of a dog-whip. After that, the men shook hands; and in this wise was Malemute Kid welcomed to his own cabin by a stranger.

Stanley Prince, who should have welcomed him, and who was responsible for the Yukon stove and hot tea aforementioned, was busy with his guests. There were a dozen or so of them, as nondescript a crowd as ever served the Queen in the enforcement of her laws or the delivery of her mails. They were of many breeds, but their common life had formed of them a certain type,—a lean and wiry type, with trail-hardened muscles, and sun-browned faces, and untroubled souls which gazed frankly forth, clear-eyed and steady. They drove the dogs of the Queen, wrought fear in the hearts of her enemies, ate of her meagre fare, and were happy. They had seen life, and done deeds, and lived romances; but they did not know it.

And they were very much at home. Two of them were sprawled upon Malemute Kid's bunk, singing chansons which their French forbears sang in the days when first they entered the Northwest-land and mated with its Indian women. Bettles' bunk had suffered a similar invasion, and three or four lusty *voyageurs* worked their toes among its blankets as they listened to the tale of one who had served on the boat brigade with Wolseley when he fought his way to Khartoum. And when he tired, a cowboy told of courts and kings and lords and ladies he had seen when Buffalo Bill toured the capitals of Europe. In a corner, two half-breeds, ancient comrades in a lost campaign, mended harnesses and talked of the days when the Northwest flamed with insurrection and Louis Reil was king.

Rough jests and rougher jokes went up and down, and great hazards by trail and river were spoken of in the light of commonplaces, only to be recalled by virtue of some grain of humor or ludicrous happening. Prince was led away by these uncrowned heroes who had seen history made, who regarded the great and the romantic as but the ordinary and the incidental in the routine of life. He passed his precious tobacco among them with lavish disregard, and rusty chains of reminiscence were loosened, and forgotten odysseys resurrected for his especial benefit.

When conversation dropped and the travelers filled the last pipes and unlashed their tight-rolled sleeping-furs, Prince fell back upon his comrade for further information.

"Well, you know what the cowboy is," Malemute Kid answered, beginning to unlace his moccasins; "and it's not hard to guess the British blood in his bed-partner. As for the rest, they're all children of the *coureurs du bois,* mingled with God knows how many other bloods. The two turning in by the door are the regulation 'breeds' or *bois brules.* That lad with the worsted breech scarf—notice his eyebrows and the turn of his jaw— shows a Scotchman wept in his mother's smoky tepee. And that handsome-looking fellow putting the capote under his head is a French half-breed,—you heard him talking; he does n't like the two Indians turning in next to him. You see, when the 'breeds' rose under Reil the full-bloods kept the peace, and they've not lost much love for one another since."

"But I say, what's that glum-looking fellow by the stove? I'll swear he can't talk English. He has n't opened his mouth all night."

"You're wrong. He knows English well enough. Did you follow his eyes when he listened? I did. But he's neither kith nor kin to the others. When they talked their own patois you could see he did n't understand. I've been wondering myself what he is. Let's find out."

"Fire a couple of sticks into the stove!" Malemute Kid commanded, raising his voice and looking squarely at the man in question.

He obeyed at once.

"Had discipline knocked into him somewhere," Prince commented in a low tone.

Malemute Kid nodded, took off his socks, and picked his way among the recumbent men to the stove. There he hung his damp footgear among a score or so of mates.

"When do you expect to get to Dawson?" he asked tentatively.

The man studied him a moment before replying. "They say seventy-five mile. So? Maybe two days."

The very slightest accent was perceptible, while there was no awkward hesitancy or groping for words.

"Been in the country before?"

"No."

"Northwest Territory?"

"Yes."

"Born there?"

"No."

"Well, where the devil were you born? You 're none of these." Malemute Kid swept his hand over the dog-drivers, even including the two policemen who had turned into Prince's bunk. "Where did you come from? I've seen faces like yours before, though I can 't remember just where."

"I know you," he irrelevantly replied, at once turning the drift of Malemute Kid's questions.

"Where? Ever see me?"

"No; your partner, him priest, Pastilik, long time ago. Him ask me if I see you, Malemute Kid. Him give me grub. I no stop long. You hear him speak 'bout me?"

"Oh! you're the fellow that traded the otter skins for the dogs?"

The man nodded, knocked out his pipe, and signified his disinclination for conversation by rolling up in his furs. Malemute Kid blew out the slush-lamp and crawled under the blankets with Prince.

"Well, what is he?"

"Don't know—turned me off, somehow, and then shut up like a clam. But he 's a fellow to whet your curiosity. I 've heard of him. All the Coast wondered about him eight years ago. Sort of mysterious, you know. He came down out of the North, in the dead of winter, many a thousand miles from here, skirting Bering Sea and traveling as though the devil were after him. No one ever learned where he came from, but he must have come far. He was badly travel-worn when he got food from the Swedish missionary on Golovin Bay and asked the way south. We heard of this afterward. Then he abandoned the shore-line, heading right across Norton Sound. Terrible weather, snowstorms and high winds, but he pulled through where a thousand other men would have died, missing St. Michael's and making the land at Pastilik. He'd lost all but two dogs, and was nearly gone with starvation.

"He was so anxious to go on that Father Roubeau fitted him out with grub; but he could n't let him have any dogs, for he was only waiting my arrival to go on a trip himself. Mr. Ulysses knew too much to start on without animals, and fretted around for several days. He had on his sled a bunch of beautifully cured otter skins, sea-otters, you know, worth their weight in gold. There was also at Pastilik an old Shylock of a Russian trader, who had dogs to kill. Well, they did n't dicker very long, but when the Strange One headed south again, it was in the rear of a spanking dog-team. Mr. Shylock, by the way, had the otter skins. I saw them, and they were magnificent. We figured it up and found the dogs brought him at least five hundred apiece. And it was n't as if the Strange One did n't know the value of sea-otter; he was an Indian of some sort, and what little he talked showed he 'd been among white men.

"After the ice passed out of the Sea, word came up from Nunivak Island that he'd gone in there for grub. Then he dropped from sight, and this is the first heard of him in eight years. Now where did he come from? and what was he doing there? and why did he come from there? He 's Indian, he's been nobody knows where, and he's had discipline, which is unusual for an Indian. Another mystery of the North for you to solve, Prince."

"Thanks, awfully; but I've got too many on hand as it is," he replied.

Malemute Kid was already breathing heavily; but the young mining engineer gazed straight up through the thick darkness, waiting for the strange orgasm which stirred his blood to die away. And when he did sleep, his brain worked on, and for the nonce he, too, wandered through the white unknown, struggled with the dogs on endless trails, and saw men live, and toil, and die like men.

The next morning, hours before daylight, the dog-drivers and policemen pulled out for Dawson. But the powers that saw to her Majesty's interests, and ruled the destinies of her lesser creatures, gave the mailmen little rest; for a week later they appeared at Stuart River, heavily burdened with letters for Salt Water. However, their dogs had been replaced by fresh ones; but then, they were dogs.

The men had expected some sort of a layover in which to rest up; besides, this Klondike was a new section of the Northland, and they had wished to see a little something of the Golden City where dust flowed like water, and dance halls rang with never ending revelry. But they dried their socks and smoked their evening pipes with much the same gusto as on their former visit, though one or two bold spirits speculated on desertion and the possibility of crossing the unexplored Rockies to the east, and thence, by the Mackenzie Valley, of gaining their old stamping-grounds in the Chippewyan Country. Two or three even decided to return to their homes by that route when their terms of service had expired, and they began to lay plans forthwith, looking forward to the hazardous undertaking in much the same way a city-bred man would to a day's holiday in the woods.

He of the Otter Skins seemed very restless, though he took little interest in the discussion, and at last he drew Malemute Kid to one side and talked for some time in low tones. Prince cast curious eyes in their direction, and the mystery deepened when they put on caps and mittens, and went outside. When they returned, Malemute Kid placed his gold-scales on the table, weighed out the matter of sixty ounces, and transferred them to the Strange One's sack. Then the chief of the dog-drivers joined the conclave, and certain business was transacted with him. The next day the gang went on up river, but He of the Otter Skins took several pounds of grub and turned his steps back toward Dawson.

—

"Did n't know what to make of it," said Malemute Kid in response to Prince's queries; "but the poor beggar wanted to be quit of the service for some reason or other—at least it seemed a most important one to him, though he would n't let on what. You see, it's just like the army; he signed for two years, and the only way to get free was to buy himself out. He could n't desert and then stay here, and he was just wild to remain in the country. Made up his mind when he got to Dawson, he said; but no one knew him, had n't a cent, and I was the only one he 'd spoken two words with. So he talked it over with the Lieutenant-Governor, and made arrangements in case he could get the money from me—loan, you know. Said he 'd pay back in the year, and if I wanted, would put me onto something rich. Never 'd seen it, but knew it was rich.

"And talk! why, when he got me outside he was ready to weep. Begged and pleaded; got down in the snow to me till I hauled him out of it. Palavered around like a crazy man. Swore he's worked to this very end for years and years, and could n't bear to be disappointed now. Asked him what end, but he would n't say. Said they might keep him on the other half of the trail and he would n't get to Dawson in two years, and then it would be too late. Never saw a man take on so in my life. And when I said I'd let him have it, had to yank him out of the snow again. Told him to consider it in the light of a grub-stake. Think he 'd have it? No, sir! Swore he 'd give me all he found, make me rich beyond the dreams of avarice, and all such stuff. Now a man who puts his life and time against a grub-stake ordinarily finds it hard enough to turn over half of what he finds. Something behind all this, Prince; just you make a note of it. We'll hear of him if he stays in the country"—

"And if he does n't?"

"Then my good nature gets a shock, and I 'm sixty some odd ounces out."

The cold weather had come on with the long nights, and the sun had begun to play his ancient game of peekaboo along the southern snow-line ere aught was heard of Malemute Kid's grub-stake. And then, one bleak morning in early January, a heavily laden dog-train pulled into his cabin below Stuart River. He of the Otter Skins was there, and with him walked a man such as the gods have almost forgotten how to fashion. Men never talked of luck and pluck and five-hundred-dollar dirt without bringing in the name of Axel Gunderson; nor could tales of nerve or strength or daring pass up and down the camp-fire without the summoning of his presence. And when the conversation flagged, it blazed anew at mention of the woman who shared his fortunes.

As has been noted, in the making of Axel Gunderson the gods had remembered their old-time cunning, and cast him after the manner of men who were born when the world was young. Full seven feet he towered in his picturesque costume which marked a king of Eldorado. His chest, neck, and limbs were those of a giant. To bear his three hundred pounds of bone and muscle, his snowshoes were greater by a generous yard than those of other men. Rough-hewn, with rugged brow and massive jaw and un-flinching eyes of palest blue, his face told the tale of one who knew but the law of might. Of the yellow of ripe corn silk, his frost-incrusted hair swept like day across the night, and fell far down his coat of bearskin. A vague tradition of the sea seemed to cling about him, as he swung down the narrow trail in advance of the dogs; and he brought the butt of his dog-whip against Malemute Kid's door as a Norse sea rover, on southern foray, might thunder for admittance at the castle gate.

Prince bared his womanly arms and kneaded sour-dough bread, casting, as he did so, many a glance at the three guests,— three guests the like of which might never come under a man's roof in a lifetime. The Strange One, whom Malemute Kid had surnamed Ulysses, still fascinated him; but his interest chiefly gravitated between Axel Gunderson and Axel Gunderson's wife. She felt the day's journey, for she had softened in comfortable cabins during the many days since her husband mastered the wealth of frozen pay-streaks, and she was tired. She rested against his great breast like a slender flower against a wall, replying lazily to Malemute Kid's good-natured banter, and stirring Prince's blood strangely with an occasional sweep of her deep, dark eyes. For Prince was a man, and healthy, and had seen few women in many months. And she was older than he, and an Indian besides.

But she was different from all native wives he had met: she had traveled,—had been in his country among others, he gathered from the conversation; and she knew most of the things the women of his own race knew, and much more that it was not in the nature of things for them to know. She could make a meal of sun-dried fish or a bed in the snow; yet she teased them with tantalizing details of many-course dinners, and caused strange internal dissensions to arise at the mention of various quondam dishes which they had well-nigh forgotten. She knew the ways of the moose, the bear, and the little blue fox, and of the wild amphibians of the Northern seas; she was skilled in the lore of the woods and the streams, and the tale writ by man and bird and beast upon the delicate snow crust was to her an open book; yet Prince caught the appreciative twinkle in her eye as she read the Rules of the Camp. These rules had been fathered by the Unquenchable Bettles at a time when his blood ran high, and were remarkable for the terse simplicity of their humor. Prince always turned them to the wall before the arrival of ladies; but who could suspect that this native wife—Well, it was too late now.

This, then, was the wife of Axel Gunderson, a woman whose name and fame had traveled with her husband's, hand in hand, through all the Northland. At table, Malemute Kid baited her with the assurance of an old friend, and Prince shook off the shyness of first acquaintance and joined in. But she held her own in the unequal contest, while her husband, slower in wit, ventured naught but applause. And he was very proud of her; his every look and action revealed the magnitude of the place she occupied in his life. He of the Otter Skins ate in silence, forgotten in the merry battle; and long ere the others were done he pushed back from the table and went out among the dogs. Yet all too soon his fellow travelers drew on their mittens and *parkas*, and followed him.

There had been no snow for many days, and the sleds slipped along the hard-packed Yukon trail as easily as if it had been glare ice. Ulysses led the first sled; with the second came Prince and Axel Gunderson's wife; while Malemute Kid and the yellow-haired giant brought up the third.

"It's only a 'hunch,' Kid," he said; "but I think it's straight.

He's never been there, but he tells a good story, and shows a map I heard of when I was in the Kootenay country, years ago. I 'd like to have you go along; but he 's a strange one, and swore point-blank to throw it up if any one was brought in. But when I come back you'll get first tip, and I'll stake you next to me, and give you a half share in the town site besides.

"No! no!" he cried, as the other strove to interrupt. "I'm running this, and before I'm done it'll need two heads. If it 's all right, why it'll be a second Cripple Creek, man; do you hear?—a second Cripple Creek! It's quartz, you know, not placer; and if we work it right we'll corral the whole thing,—millions upon millions. I 've heard of the place before, and so have you. We 'll build a town— thousands of workmen—good waterways—steamship lines—big carrying trade—light-draught steamers for head-reaches—survey a railroad, perhaps—sawmills—electric-light plant—do our own banking—commercial company—syndicate—Say! just you hold your hush till I get back!"

The sleds came to a halt where the trail crossed the mouth of Stuart River. An unbroken sea of frost, its wide expanse stretched away into the unknown east. The snowshoes were withdrawn from the lashings of the sleds. Axel Gunderson shook hands and stepped to the fore, his great webbed shoes sinking a fair half yard into the feathery surface and packing the snow so the dogs should not wallow. His wife fell in behind the last sled, betraying long practice in the art of handling the awkward footgear. The stillness was broken with cheery farewells; the dogs whined; and He of the Otter Skins talked with his whip to a recalcitrant wheeler.

An hour later, the train had taken on the likeness of a black pencil crawling in a long, straight line across a mighty sheet of foolscap.

II

One night, many weeks later, Malemute Kid and Prince fell to solving chess problems from the torn page of an ancient magazine. The Kid had just returned from his Bonanza properties, and was resting up preparatory to a long moose hunt. Prince too had been on creek and trail nearly all winter, and had grown hungry for a blissful week of cabin life.

"Interpose the black knight, and force the king. No, that won't do. See, the next move"—

"Why advance the pawn two squares? Bound to take it in transit, and with the bishop out of the way"—

"But hold on! That leaves a hole, and"—

"No; it's protected. Go ahead! You 'll see it works."

It was very interesting. Somebody knocked at the door a second time before Malemute Kid said, "Come in." The door swung open. Something staggered in. Prince caught one square look, and sprang to his feet. The horror in his eyes caused Malemute Kid to whirl about; and he too was startled, though he had seen bad things before. The thing tottered blindly toward them. Prince edged away till he reached the nail from which hung his Smith & Wesson.

"My God! what is it?" he whispered to Malemute Kid.

"Don't know. Looks like a case of freezing and no grub," replied the Kid, sliding away in the opposite direction. "Watch out! It may be mad," he warned, coming back from closing the door.

The thing advanced to the table. The bright flame of the slush-lamp caught its eye. It was amused, and gave voice to eldritch cackles which betokened mirth. Then, suddenly, he—for it was a man—swayed back, with a hitch to his skin trousers, and began to sing a chanty, such as men lift when they swing around the capstan circle and the sea snorts in their ears:—

> "Yan-kee ship come down de ri-ib-er,
>   Pull! my bully boys! Pull!
> D'yeh want—to know de captain ru-uns her?
>   Pull! my bully boys! Pull!
> Jon-a-than Jones ob South Caho-li-in-a,
>   Pull! my bully"—

He broke off abruptly, tottered with a wolfish snarl to the meat-shelf, and before they could intercept was tearing with his teeth at a chunk of raw bacon. The struggle was fierce between him and Malemute Kid; but his mad strength left him as suddenly as it had come, and he weakly surrendered the spoil. Between them they got him upon a stool, where he sprawled with half his body across the table. A small dose of whiskey strengthened him, so that he could dip a spoon into the sugar caddy which Malemute Kid placed before him. After his appetite had been somewhat cloyed, Prince, shuddering as he did so, passed him a mug of weak beef tea.

The creature's eyes were alight with a sombre frenzy, which blazed and waned with every mouthful. There was very little skin to the face. The face, for that matter, sunken and emaciated, bore very little likeness to human countenance. Frost after frost had bitten deeply, each depositing its stratum of scab upon the half-healed scar that went before. This dry, hard surface was of a bloody-black color, serrated by grievous cracks wherein the raw red flesh peeped forth. His skin garments were dirty and in tatters, and the fur of one side was singed and burned away, showing where he had lain upon his fire.

Malemute Kid pointed to where the suntanned hide had been cut away, strip by strip,—the grim signature of famine.

"Who—are—you?" slowly and distinctly enunciated the Kid.

The man paid no heed.

"Where do you come from?"

"Yan-kee ship come down de ri-ib-er," was the quavering response.

"Do n't doubt the beggar came down the river," the Kid said, shaking him in an endeavor to start a more lucid flow of talk.

But the man shrieked at the contact, clapping a hand to his side in evident pain. He rose slowly to his feet, half leaning on the table.

"She laughed at me—so—with the hate in her eye; and she—would—not—come."

His voice died away, and he was sinking back when Malemute Kid gripped him by the wrist, and shouted, "Who? Who would not come?"

"She, Unga. She laughed, and struck at me, so, and so. And then"—

"Yes?"

"And then"—

"And then what?"

"And then he lay very still, in the snow, a long time. He is—still in—the—snow."

The two men looked at each other helplessly.

"Who is in the snow?"

"She, Unga. She looked at me with the hate in her eye, and then"—

"Yes, yes."

"And then she took the knife, so; and once, twice—she was weak. I traveled very slow. And there is much gold in that place, very much gold."

"Where is Unga?" For all Malemute Kid knew, she might be dying a mile away. He shook the man savagely, repeating again and again, "Where is Unga? Who is Unga?"

"She—is—in—the—snow."

"Go on!" The Kid was pressing his wrist cruelly.

"So—I—would—be—in—the   snow—but—I—had—a—debt—to—pay. It—was—heavy—I—had—a—debt—to—pay—a—debt—to—pay—I—had"— The faltering monosyllables ceased, as he fumbled in his pouch and drew forth a buckskin sack. "A—debt—to—pay—five—pounds—of—gold—grub—stake—Mal—e—mute—Kid—I"— The exhausted head dropped upon the table; nor could Malemute Kid rouse it again.

"It 's Ulysses," he said quietly, tossing the bag of dust on the table. "Guess it's all day with Axel Gunderson and the woman. Come on, let 's get him between the blankets. He's Indian; he'll pull through, and tell a tale besides."

As they cut his garments from him, near his right breast could be seen two unhealed, hard-lipped knife thrusts.

III

"I will talk of the things which were, in my own way; but you will understand. I will begin at the beginning, and tell of myself and the woman, and, after that, of the man."

He of the Otter Skins drew over to the stove as do men who have been deprived of fire and are afraid the Promethean gift may vanish at any moment. Malemute Kid pricked up the slush-lamp, and placed it so its light might fall upon the face of the narrator. Prince slid his body over the edge of the bunk and joined them.

"I am Naass, a chief, and the son of a chief, born between a sunset and a rising, on the dark seas, in my father's oomiak. All of a night the men toiled at the paddles, and the women cast out the waves which threw in upon us, and we fought with the storm. The salt spray froze upon my mother's breast till her breath passed with the passing of the tide. But I,—I raised my voice with the wind and the storm, and lived.

"We dwelt in Akatan"—

"Where?" asked Malemute Kid.

"Akatan, which is in the Aleutians; Akatan, beyond Chignik, beyond Kardalak, beyond Unimak. As I say, we dwelt in Akatan, which lies in the midst of the sea on the edge of the world. We farmed the salt seas for the fish, the seal, and the otter; and our homes shouldered about one another on the rocky strip between the rim of the forest and the yellow beach where our kayaks lay. We were not many, and the world was very small. There were strange lands to the east,—islands like Akatan; so we thought all the world was islands, and did not mind.

"I was different from my people. In the sands of the beach were the crooked timbers and wave-warped planks of a boat such as my people never built; and I remember on the point of the island which overlooked the ocean three ways there stood a pine tree which never grew there, smooth and straight and tall. It is said the two men came to that spot, turn about, through many days, and watched with the passing of the light. These two men came from out of the sea in the boat which lay in pieces on the beach. And they were white like you, and weak as the little children when the seal have gone away and the hunters come home empty. I know of these things from the old men and the old women, who got them from their fathers and mothers before them. These strange white men did not take kindly to our ways at first, but they grew strong, what of the fish and the oil, and fierce. And they built them each his own house, and took the pick of our women, and in time children came. Thus he was born who was to become the father of my father's father.

"As I said, I was different from my people, for I carried the strong, strange blood of this white man who came out of the sea. It is said we had other laws in the days before these men; but they were fierce and quarrelsome, and fought with our men till there were no more left who dared to fight. Then they made themselves chiefs, and took away our old laws and gave us new ones, insomuch that the man was the son of his father, and not his mother, as our way had been. They also ruled that the son, firstborn, should have all things which were his father's before him, and that the brothers and sisters should shift for themselves. And they gave us other laws. They showed us new ways in the catching of fish and the killing of bear which were thick in the woods; and they taught us to lay by bigger stores for the time of famine. And these things were good.

"But when they had become chiefs, and there were no more men to face their anger, they fought, these strange white men, each with the other. And the one whose blood I carry drove his seal spear the length of an arm through the other's body. Their children took up the fight, and their children's children; and there was great hatred between them, and black doings, even to my time, so that in each family but one lived to pass down the blood of them that went before. Of my blood I was alone; of the other man's there was but a girl, Unga, who lived with her mother. Her father and my father did not come back from the fishing one night; but afterward they washed up to the beach on the big tides, and they held very close to each other.

"The people wondered, because of the hatred between the houses, and the old men shook their heads and said the fight would go on when children were born to her and children to me. They told me this as a boy, till I came to believe, and to look upon Unga as a foe, who was to be the mother of children which were to fight with mine. I thought of these things day by day, and when I grew to a stripling I came to ask why this should be so. And they answered, 'We do not know, but that in such way your fathers did.' And I marveled that those which were to come should fight the battles of those that were gone, and in it I could see no right. But the people said it must be, and I was only a stripling.

"And they said I must hurry, that my blood might be the

older and grow strong before hers. This was easy, for I was head man, and the people looked up to me because of the deeds and the laws of my fathers, and the wealth which was mine. Any maiden would come to me, but I found none to my liking. And the old men and the mothers of maidens told me to hurry, for even then were the hunters bidding high to the mother of Unga; and should her children grow strong before mine, mine would surely die.

"Nor did I find a maiden till one night coming back from the fishing. The sunlight was lying, so, low and full in the eyes, the wind free, and the kayaks racing with the white seas. Of a sudden the kayak of Unga came driving past me, and she looked upon me, so, with her black hair flying like a cloud of night and the spray wet on her cheek. As I say, the sunlight was full in the eyes, and I was a stripling; but somehow it was all clear, and I knew it to be the call of kind to kind. As she whipped ahead she looked back within the space of two strokes,—looked as only the woman Unga could look,—and again I knew it as the call of kind. The people shouted as we ripped past the lazy oomiaks and left them far behind. But she was quick at the paddle, and my heart was like the belly of a sail, and I did not gain. The wind freshened, the sea whitened, and, leaping like the seals on the windward breech, we roared down the golden pathway of the sun."

Naass was crouched half out of his stool, in the attitude of one driving a paddle, as he ran the race anew. Somewhere across the stove he beheld the tossing kayak and the flying hair of Unga. The voice of the wind was in his ears, and its salt beat fresh upon his nostrils.

"But she made the shore, and ran up the sand, laughing, to the house of her mother. And a great thought came to me that night,—a thought worthy of him that was chief over all the people of Akatan. So, when the moon was up, I went down to the house of her mother, and looked upon the goods of Yash-Noosh, which were piled by the door,—the goods of Yash-Noosh, a strong hunter who had it in mind to be the father of the children of Unga. Other young men had piled their goods there, and taken them away again; and each young man had made a pile greater than the one before.

"And I laughed to the moon and the stars, and went to my own house where my wealth was stored. And many trips I made, till my pile was greater by the fingers of one hand than the pile of Yash-Noosh. There were fish, dried in the sun and smoked; and forty hides of the hair seal, and half as many of the fur, and each hide was tied at the mouth and big-bellied with oil; and ten skins of bear which I killed in the woods when they came out in the spring. And there were beads and blankets and scarlet cloths, such as I got in trade from the people who lived to the east, and who got them in trade from the people who lived still beyond in the east. And I looked upon the pile of Yash-Noosh and laughed; for I was head man in Akatan, and my wealth was greater than the wealth of all my young men, and my fathers had done deeds, and given laws, and put their names for all time in the mouths of the people.

"So, when the morning came, I went down to the beach, casting out of the corner of my eye at the house of the mother of Unga. My offer yet stood untouched. And the women smiled, and said sly things one to the other. I wondered, for never had such a price been offered; and that night I added more to the pile, and put beside it a kayak of well-tanned skins which never yet had swam in the sea. But in the day it was yet there, open to the laughter of all men. The mother of Unga was crafty, and I grew angry at the shame in which I stood before my people. So that night I added till it became a great pile, and I hauled up my oomiak, which was of the value of twenty kayaks. And in the morning there was no pile.

"Then made I preparation for the wedding, and the people that lived even to the east came for the food of the feast and the *potlach* token. Unga was older than I by the age of four suns in the way we reckoned the years. I was only a stripling; but then I was a chief, and the son of a chief, and it did not matter.

"But a ship shoved her sails above the floor of the ocean, and grew larger with the breath of the wind. From her scuppers she ran clear water, and the men were in haste and worked hard at the pumps. On the bow stood a mighty man, watching the depth of the water and giving commands with a voice of thunder. His eyes were of the pale blue of the deep waters, and his head was maned like that of a sea lion. And his hair was yellow, like the straw of a southern harvest or the manila rope-yarns which sailormen plait.

"Of late years we had seen ships from afar, but this was the first to come to the beach of Akatan. The feast was broken, and the women and children fled to the houses, while we men strung our bows and waited with spears in hand. But when the ship's forefoot smelt the beach the strange men took no notice of us, being busy with their own work. With the falling of the tide they careened the schooner and patched a great hole in her bottom. So the women crept back, and the feast went on.

"When the tide rose, the sea wanderers kedged the schooner to deep water, and then came among us. They bore presents and were friendly; so I made room for them, and out of the largeness of my heart gave them tokens such as I gave all the guests; for it was my wedding day, and I was head man in Akatan. And he with the mane of the sea lion was there, so tall and strong that one looked to see the earth shake with the fall of his feet. He looked much and straight at Unga, with his arms folded, so, and stayed till the sun went away and the stars came out. Then he went down to his ship. After that I took Unga by the hand and led her to my own house. And there was singing and great laughter, and the women said sly things, after the manner of women at such times. But we did not care. Then the people left us alone and went home.

"The last noise had not died away, when the chief of the sea wanderers came in by the door. And he had with him black bottles, from which we drank and made merry. You see, I was only a stripling, and had lived all my days on the edge of the world. So my blood became as fire, and my heart as light as the froth that flies from the surf to the cliff. Unga sat silent among the skins in the corner, her eyes wide, for she seemed to fear. And he with the mane of the sea lion looked upon her straight and long. Then his men came in with bundles of goods, and he piled before me wealth such as was not in all Akatan. There were guns, both large and small, and powder and shot and shell, and bright axes and knives of steel, and cunning tools, and strange things the like of which I had never seen. When he showed me by sign that it was all mine, I thought him a great man to be so free; but he showed me also that Unga was to go away with him in his ship. Do you understand?—that Unga was to go away with him in his ship. The blood of my fathers flamed hot on the sudden, and I made to drive him through with my spear. But the spirit of the bottles had stolen the life from my arm, and he took me by the neck, so, and knocked my head against the wall of the house. And I was made weak like a newborn child, and my legs would no more stand under me. Unga screamed, and she laid hold of the things of the house with her hands, till they fell all about us as he dragged her to the door. Then he took her in his great arms, and when she tore at his yellow hair laughed with a sound like that of the big bull seal in the rut.

"I crawled to the beach and called upon my people; but they were afraid. Only Yash-Noosh was a man, and they struck him on the head with an oar, till he lay with his face in the sand and did not move. And they raised the sails to the sound of their songs, and the ship went away on the wind.

"The people said it was good, for there would be no more war of the bloods in Akatan; but I said never a word, waiting till the time of the full moon, when I put fish and oil in my kayak, and went away to the east. I saw many islands and many people, and I, who had lived on the edge, saw that the world was very large. I talked by signs; but they had not seen a schooner nor a man with the mane of a sea lion, and they pointed always to the east. And I slept in queer places, and ate odd things, and met strange faces. Many laughed, for they thought me light of head; but sometimes old men turned my face to the light and blessed me, and the eyes of the young women grew soft as they asked me of the strange ship, and Unga, and the men of the sea.

"And in this manner, through rough seas and great storms, I came to Unalaska. There were two schooners there, but neither was the one I sought. So I passed on to the east, with the world growing ever larger, and in the Island of Unamok there was no word of the ship, nor in Kadiak, nor in Atognak. And so I came one day to a rocky land, where men dug great holes in the mountain. And there was a schooner, but not my schooner, and men loaded upon it the rocks which they dug. This I thought childish, for all the world was made of rocks; but they gave me food and set me to work. When the schooner was deep in the water, the captain gave me money and told me to go; but I asked which way he went, and he pointed south. I made signs that I would go with him; and he laughed at first, but then, being short of men, took me to help work the ship. So I came to talk after their manner, and to heave on ropes, and to reef the stiff sails in sudden squalls, and to take my turn at the wheel. But it was not strange, for the blood of my fathers was the blood of the men of the sea.

"I had thought it an easy task to find him I sought, once I got among his own people; and when we raised the land one day, and passed between a gateway of the sea to a port, I looked for perhaps as many schooners as there were fingers to my hands. But the ships lay against the wharves for miles, packed like so many little fish; and when I went among them to ask for a man with the mane of a sea lion, they laughed, and answered me in the tongues of many peoples. And I found that they hailed from the uttermost parts of the earth.

"And I went into the city to look upon the face of every man. But they were like the cod when they run thick on the banks, and I could not count them. And the noise smote upon me till I could not hear, and my head was dizzy with much movement. So I went on and on, through the lands which sang in the warm sunshine; where the harvests lay rich on the plains; and where great cities were fat with men that lived like women, with false words in their mouths and their hearts black with the lust of gold. And all the while my people of Akatan hunted and fished, and were happy in the thought that the world was small.

"But the look in the eyes of Unga coming home from the fishing was with me always, and I knew I would find her when the time was met. She walked down quiet lanes in the dusk of the evening, or led me chases across the thick fields wet with the morning dew, and there was a promise in her eyes such as only the woman Unga could give.

"So I wandered through a thousand cities. Some were gentle and gave me food, and others laughed, and still others cursed; but I kept my tongue between my teeth, and went strange ways and saw strange sights. Sometimes, I, who was a chief and the son of a chief, toiled for men,—men rough of speech and hard as iron, who wrung gold from the sweat and sorrow of their fellow men. Yet no word did I get of my quest, till I came back to the sea like a homing seal to the rookeries. But this was at another port, in another country which lay to the north. And there I heard dim tales of the yellow-haired sea wanderer, and I learned that he was a hunter of seals, and that even then he was abroad on the ocean.

"So I shipped on a seal schooner with the lazy Siwashes, and followed his trackless trail to the north where the hunt was then warm. And we were away weary months, and spoke many of the fleet, and heard much of the wild doings of him I sought; but never once did we raise him above the sea. We went north, even to the Pribyloffs, and killed the seals in herds on the beach, and brought their warm bodies aboard till our scuppers ran grease and blood and no man could stand upon the deck. Then were we chased by a ship of slow steam, which fired upon us with great guns. But we put on sail till the sea was over our decks and washed them clean, and lost ourselves in a fog.

"It is said, at this time, while we fled with fear at our hearts, that the yellow-haired sea wanderer put into the Pribyloffs, right to the factory, and while the part of his men held the servants of the company, the rest loaded ten thousand green skins from the salt-houses. I say it is said, but I believe; for in the voyages I made on the coast with never a meeting, the northern seas rang with his wildness and daring, till the three nations which have lands there sought him with their ships. And I heard of Unga, for the captains sang loud in her praise, and she was always with him. She had learned the ways of his people, they said, and was happy. But I knew better,—knew that her heart harked back to her own people by the yellow beach of Akatan.

"So, after a long time, I went back to the port which is by a gateway of the sea, and there I learned that he had gone across the girth of the great ocean to hunt for the seal to the east of the warm land which runs south from the Russian Seas. And I, who was become a sailorman, shipped with men of his own race, and went after him in the hunt of the seal. And there were few ships off that new land; but we hung on the flank of the seal pack and harried it north through all the spring of the year. And when the cows were heavy with pup and crossed the Russian line, our men grumbled and were afraid. For there was much fog, and every day men were lost in the boats. They would not work, so the captain turned the ship back toward the way it came. But I knew the yellow-haired sea wanderer was unafraid, and would hang by the pack, even to the Russian Isles, where few men go. So I took a boat, in the black of night, when the lookout dozed on the fok's'lehead, and went alone to the warm, long land. And I journeyed south to meet the men by Yeddo Bay, who are wild and unafraid. And the Yoshiwara girls were small, and bright like steel, and good to look upon; but I could not stop, for I knew that Unga rolled on the tossing floor by the rookeries of the north.

"The men by Yeddo Bay had met from the ends of the earth, and had neither gods nor homes, sailing under the flag of the Japanese. And with them I went to the rich beaches of Copper Island, where our salt-piles became high with skins. And in that silent sea we saw no man till we were ready to come away. Then, one day, the fog lifted on the edge of a heavy wind, and there jammed down upon us a schooner, with close in her wake the cloudy funnels of a Russian man-of-war. We fled away on the beam of the wind, with the schooner jamming still closer and plunging ahead three feet to our two. And upon her poop was the man with the mane of the sea lion, pressing the rails under with the canvas and laughing in his strength of life. And Unga was there,—I knew her on the moment,—but he sent her below when the cannons began to talk across the sea. As I say, with three feet to our two, till we saw the rudder lift green at every jump,—and I swinging on to the wheel and cursing, with my back to the Russian shot. For we knew he had it in mind to run before us, that he might get away while we were caught. And they knocked our masts out of us till we dragged into the wind like a wounded gull; but he went on over the edge of the sky-line,—he and Unga.

"What could we? The fresh hides spoke for themselves. So they took us to a Russian port, and after that to a lone country, where they set us to work in the mines to dig salt. And some died, and—and some did not die."

Naass swept the blanket from his shoulders, disclosing the

gnarled and twisted flesh, marked with the unmistakable striations of the knout. Prince hastily covered him, for it was not nice to look upon.

"We were there a weary time; and sometimes men got away to the south, but they always came back. So, when we who hailed from Yeddo Bay rose in the night and took the guns from the guards, we went to the north. And the land was very large, with plains, soggy with water, and great forests. And the cold came, with much snow on the ground, and no man knew the way. Weary months we journeyed through the endless forest,—I do not remember, now, for there was little food and often we lay down to die. But at last we came to the cold sea, and but three were left to look upon it. One had shipped from Yeddo as captain, and he knew in his head the lay of the great lands, and of the place where men may cross from one to the other on the ice. And he led us,—I do not know, it was so long,—till there were but two. When we came to that place we found five of the strange people which live in that country, and they had dogs and skins, and we were very poor. We fought in the snow till they died, and the captain died, and the dogs and skins were mine. Then I crossed on the ice, which was broken, and once I drifted till a gale from the west put me upon the shore. And after that, Golovin Bay, Pastilik, and the priest. Then south, south, to the warm sunlands where first I wandered.

"But the sea was no longer fruitful, and those who went upon it after the seal went to little profit and great risk. The fleets scattered, and the captains and the men had no word of those I sought. So I turned away from the ocean which never rests, and went among the lands, where the trees, the houses, and the mountains sit always in one place and do not move. I journeyed far, and came to learn many things, even to the way of reading and writing from books. It was well I should do this, for it came upon me that Unga must know these things, and that some day, when the time was met—we—you understand, when the time was met.

"So I drifted, like those little fish which raise a sail to the wind, but cannot steer. But my eyes and my ears were open always, and I went among men who traveled much, for I knew they had but to see those I sought, to remember. At last there came a man, fresh from the mountains, with pieces of rock in which the free gold stood to the size of peas, and he had heard, he had met, he knew them. They were rich, he said, and lived in the place where they drew the gold from the ground.

"It was in a wild country, and very far away; but in time I came to the camp, hidden between the mountains, where men worked night and day, out of the sight of the sun. Yet the time was not come. I listened to the talk of the people. He had gone away,—they had gone away,—to England, it was said, in the matter of bringing men with much money together to form companies. I saw the house they had lived in; more like a palace, such as one sees in the old countries. In the nighttime I crept in through a window that I might see in what manner he treated her. I went from room to room, and in such way thought kings and queens must live, it was all so very good. And they all said he treated her like a queen, and many marveled as to what breed of woman she was; for there was other blood in her veins, and she was different from the women of Akatan, and no one knew her for what she was. Ay, she was a queen; but I was a chief, and the son of a chief, and I had paid for her an untold price of skin and boat and bead.

"But why so many words? I was a sailorman, and knew the way of the ships on the seas. I followed to England, and then to other countries. Sometimes I heard of them by word of mouth, sometimes I read of them in the papers; yet never once could I come by them, for they had much money, and traveled fast, while I was a poor man. Then came trouble upon them, and their wealth slipped away, one day, like a curl of smoke. The papers were full of it at the time; but after that nothing was said, and I knew they had gone back where more gold could be got from the ground.

"They had dropped out of the world, being now poor; and so I wandered from camp to camp, even north to the Kootenay Country, where I picked up the cold scent. They had come and gone, some said this way, and some that, and still others that they had gone to the Country of the Yukon. And I went this way, and I went that, ever journeying from place to place, till it seemed I must grow weary of the world which was so large. But in the Kootenay I traveled a bad trail, and a long trail, with a 'breed' of the Northwest, who saw fit to die when the famine pinched. He had been to the Yukon by an unknown way over the mountains, and when he knew his time was near gave me the map and the secret of a place where he swore by his gods there was much gold.

"After that all the world began to flock into the north. I was a poor man; I sold myself to be a driver of dogs. The rest you know. I met him and her in Dawson. She did not know me, for I was only a stripling, and her life had been large, so she had no time to remember the one who had paid for her an untold price.

"So? You bought me from my term of service. I went back to bring things about in my own way; for I had waited long, and now that I had my hand upon him was in no hurry. As I say, I had it in mind to do my own way; for I read back in my life, through all I had seen and suffered, and remembered the cold and hunger of the endless forest by the Russian Seas. As you know, I led him into the east,—him and Unga,—into the east where many have gone and few returned. I led them to the spot where the bones and the curses of men lie with the gold which they may not have.

"The way was long and the trail unpacked. Our dogs were many and ate much; nor could our sleds carry till the break of spring. We must come back before the river ran free. So here and there we cached grub, that our sleds might be lightened and there be no chance of famine on the back trip. At the McQuestion there were three men, and near them we built a cache, as also did we at the Mayo, where was a hunting-camp of a dozen Pellys which had crossed the divide from the south. After that, as we went on into the east, we saw no men; only the sleeping river, the moveless forest, and the White Silence of the North. As I say, the way was long and the trail unpacked. Sometimes, in a day's toil, we made no more than eight miles, or ten, and at night we slept like dead men. And never once did they dream that I was Naass, head man of Akatan, the righter of wrongs.

"We now made smaller caches, and in the nighttime it was a small matter to go back on the trail we had broken, and change them in such way that one might deem the wolverines the thieves. Again, there be places where there is a fall to the river, and the water is unruly, and the ice makes above and is eaten away beneath. In such a spot the sled I drove broke through, and the dogs; and to him and Unga it was ill luck, but no more. And there was much grub on that sled, and the dogs the strongest. But he laughed, for he was strong of life, and gave the dogs that were left little grub till we cut them from the harnesses, one by one, and fed them to their mates. We would go home light, he said, traveling and eating from cache to cache, with neither dogs nor sleds; which was true, for our grub was very short, and the last dog died in the traces the night we came to the gold and the bones and the curses of men.

"To reach that place,—and the map spoke true,—in the heart of the great mountains, we cut ice steps against the wall of a divide. One looked for a valley beyond, but there was no valley; the snow spread away, level as the great harvest plains, and here and there about us mighty mountains shoved their white heads among the stars. And midway on that strange plain which should have been a valley, the earth and the snow fell away, straight down toward the heart of the world. Had we not been sailormen our heads would have swung round with the sight; but we stood on the dizzy edge that we might see a way to get down. And on one side, and one side only, the wall had fallen away till it was like the slope of the decks in a topsail breeze. I do not know why this thing should be so, but it was so. 'It is the mouth of hell,' he said; 'let us go down.' And we went down.

"And on the bottom there was a cabin, built by some man, of logs which he had cast down from above. It was a very old cabin; for men had died there alone at different times, and on pieces of birch bark which were there we read their last words and their curses. One had died of scurvy; another's partner had robbed him of his last grub and powder and stolen away; a third had been mauled by a bald-face grizzly; a fourth had hunted for game and starved,—and so it went, and they had been loath to leave the gold, and had died by the side of it in one way or another. And the worthless gold they had gathered yellowed the floor of the cabin like in a dream.

"But his soul was steady, and his head clear, this man I had led thus far. 'We have nothing to eat,' he said, 'and we will only look upon this gold, and see whence it comes and how much there be. Then we will go away quick, before it gets into our eyes and steals away our judgment. And in this way we may return in the end, with more grub, and possess it all.' So we looked upon the great vein, which cut the wall of the pit as a true vein should; and we measured it, and traced it from above and below, and drove the stakes of the claims and blazed the trees in token of our rights. Then, our knees shaking with lack of food, and a sickness in our bellies, and our hearts chugging close to our mouths, we climbed the mighty wall for the last time and turned our faces to the back trip.

"The last stretch we dragged Unga between us, and we fell often, but in the end we made the cache. And lo, there was no grub. It was well done, for he thought it the wolverines, and damned them and his gods in the one breath. But Unga was brave, and smiled, and put her hand in his, till I turned away that I might hold myself. 'We will rest by the fire,' she said, 'till morning, and we will gather strength from our moccasins.' So we cut the tops of our moccasins in strips, and boiled them half of the night, that we might chew them and swallow them. And in the morning we talked of our chance. The next cache was five days' journey; we could not make it. We must find game.

" 'We will go forth and hunt,' he said.

" 'Yes,' said I, 'we will go forth and hunt.'

"And he ruled that Unga stay by the fire and save her strength. And we went forth, he in quest of the moose, and I to the cache I had changed. But I ate little, so they might not see in me much strength. And in the night he fell many times as he drew into camp. And I too made to suffer great weakness, stumbling over my snowshoes as though each step might be my last. And we gathered strength from our moccasins.

"He was a great man. His soul lifted his body to the last; nor did he cry aloud, save for the sake of Unga. On the second day I followed him, that I might not miss the end. And he lay down to rest often. That night he was near gone; but in the morning he swore weakly and went forth again. He was like a drunken man, and I looked many times for him to give up; but his was the strength of the strong, and his soul the soul of a giant, for he lifted his body through all the weary day. And he shot two ptarmigan, but would not eat them. He needed no fire; they meant life; but his thought was for Unga, and he turned toward camp. He no longer walked, but crawled on hand and knee through the snow. I came to him, and read death in his eyes. Even then it was not too late to eat of the ptarmigan. He cast away his rifle, and carried the birds in his mouth like a dog. I walked by his side, upright. And he looked at me during the moments he rested, and wondered that I was so strong. I could see it, though he no longer spoke; and when his lips moved, they moved without sound. As I say, he was a great man, and my heart spoke for softness; but I read back in my life, and remembered the cold and hunger of the endless forest by the Russian Seas. Besides, Unga was mine, and I had paid for her an untold price of skin and boat and bead.

"And in this manner we came through the white forest, with the silence heavy upon us like a damp sea mist. And the ghosts of the past were in the air and all about us; and I saw the yellow beach of Akatan, and the kayaks racing home from the fishing, and the houses on the rim of the forest. And the men who had made themselves chiefs were there, the lawgivers whose blood I bore, and whose blood I had wedded in Unga. Ay, and Yash-Noosh walked with me, the wet sand in his hair, and his war spear, broken as he fell upon it, still in his hand. And I knew the time was met, and saw in the eyes of Unga the promise.

"As I say, we came thus through the forest, till the smell of the camp smoke was in our nostrils. And I bent above him, and tore the ptarmigan from his teeth. He turned on his side and rested, the wonder mounting in his eyes, and the hand which was under slipping slow toward the knife at his hip. But I took it from him, smiling close in his face. Even then he did not understand. So I made to drink from black bottles, and to build high upon the snow a pile of goods, and to live again the things which happened on the night of my marriage. I spoke no word, but he understood. Yet was he unafraid. There was a sneer to his lips, and cold anger, and he gathered new strength with the knowledge. It was not far, but the snow was deep, and he dragged himself very slow. Once, he lay so long, I turned him over and gazed into his eyes. And sometimes he looked forth, and sometimes death. And when I loosed him he struggled on again. In this way we came to the fire. Unga was at his side on the instant. His lips moved, without sound; then he pointed at me, that Unga might understand. And after that he lay in the snow, very still, for a long while. Even now is he there in the snow.

"I said no word till I had cooked the ptarmigan. Then I spoke to her, in her own tongue, which she had not heard in many years. She straightened herself, so, and her eyes were wonder-wide, and she asked who I was, and where I had learned that speech.

" 'I am Naass,' I said.

" 'You?' she said. 'You?' And she crept close that she might look upon me.

" 'Yes,' I answered; 'I am Naass, head man of Akatan, the last of the blood, as you are the last of the blood.'

"And she laughed. By all the things I have seen and the deeds I have done, may I never hear such a laugh again. It put the chill to my soul, sitting there in the White Silence, alone with death and this woman who laughed.

" 'Come!' I said, for I thought she wandered. 'Eat of the food and let us be gone. It is a far fetch from here to Akatan.'

"But she shoved her face in his yellow mane, and laughed till it seemed the heavens must fall about our ears. I had thought she would be overjoyed at the sight of me, and eager to go back to the memory of old times; but this seemed a strange form to take.

" 'Come!' I cried, taking her strong by the hand. 'The way is long and dark. Let us hurry!'

" 'Where?' she asked, sitting up, and ceasing from her strange mirth.

" 'To Akatan,' I answered, intent on the light to grow on her face at the thought. But it became like his, with a sneer to the lips, and cold anger.

" 'Yes,' she said; 'we will go, hand in hand, to Akatan, you and I. And we will live in the dirty huts, and eat of the fish and oil, and bring forth a spawn,—a spawn to be proud of all the days of our life. We will forget the world and be happy, very happy. It is good, most good. Come! Let us hurry. Let us go back to Akatan.'

"And she ran her hand through his yellow hair, and smiled in a way which was not good. And there was no promise in her eyes.

"I sat silent, and marveled at the strangeness of woman. I went back to the night when he dragged her from me, and she screamed and tore at his hair,—at his hair which now she played with and would not leave. Then I remembered the price and the long years of waiting; and I gripped her close, and dragged her away as he had done. And she held back, even as on that night, and fought like a she-cat for its whelp. And when the fire was between us and the man, I loosed her, and she sat and listened. And I told her of all that lay between, of all that had happened me on strange seas, of all that I had done in strange lands; of my weary quest, and the hungry years, and the promise which had been mine from the first. Ay, I told all, even to what had passed that day between the man and me, and in the days yet young. And as I spoke I saw the promise grow in her eyes, full and large like the break of dawn. And I read pity there, the tenderness of woman, the love, the heart and the soul of Unga. And I was a stripling again, for the look was the look of Unga as she ran up the beach, laughing, to the home of her mother. The stern unrest was gone, and the hunger, and the weary waiting. The time was met. I felt the call of her breast, and it seemed there I must pillow my head and forget. She opened her arms to me, and I came against her. Then, sudden, the hate flamed in her eye, her hand was at my hip. And once, twice, she passed the knife.

"'Dog!' she sneered, as she flung me into the snow. 'Swine!' And then she laughed till the silence cracked, and went back to her dead.

"As I say, once she passed the knife, and twice; but she was weak with hunger, and it was not meant that I should die. Yet was I minded to stay in that place, and to close my eyes in the last long sleep with those whose lives had crossed with mine and led my feet on unknown trails. But there lay a debt upon me which would not let me rest.

"And the way was long, the cold bitter, and there was little grub. The Pellys had found no moose, and had robbed my cache. And so had the three white men; but they lay thin and dead in their cabin as I passed. After that I do not remember, till I came here, and found food and fire,—much fire."

As he finished, he crouched closely, even jealously, over the stove. For a long while the slush-lamp shadows played tragedies upon the wall.

"But Unga!" cried Prince, the vision still strong upon him.

"Unga? She would not eat of the ptarmigan. She lay with her arms about his neck, her face deep in his yellow hair. I drew the fire close, that she might not feel the frost; but she crept to the other side. And I built a fire there; yet it was little good, for she would not eat. And in this manner they still lie up there in the snow."

"And you?" asked Malemute Kid.

"I do not know; but Akatan is small, and I have little wish to go back and live on the edge of the world. Yet is there small use in life. I can go to Constantine, and he will put irons upon me, and one day they will tie a piece of rope, so, and I will sleep good. Yet—no; I do not know."

"But, Kid," protested Prince, "this is murder!"

"Hush!" commanded Malemute Kid. "There be things greater than our wisdom, beyond our justice. The right and the wrong of this we cannot say, and it is not for us to judge."

Naass drew yet closer to the fire. There was a great silence, and in each man's eyes many pictures came and went.

The God of His Fathers

I

On every hand stretched the forest primeval,—the home of noisy comedy and silent tragedy. Here the struggle for survival continued to wage with all its ancient brutality. Briton and Russian were still to overlap in the Land of the Rainbow's End—and this was the very heart of it—nor had Yankee gold yet purchased its vast domain. The wolf-pack still clung to the flank of the cariboo-herd, singling out the weak and the big with calf, and pulling them down as remorselessly as were it a thousand, thousand generations into the past. The sparse aborigines still acknowledged the rule of their chiefs and medicine men, drove out bad spirits, burned their witches, fought their neighbors, and ate their enemies with a relish which spoke well of their bellies. But it was at the moment when the stone age was drawing to a close. Already, over unknown trails and chartless wildernesses, were the harbingers of the steel arriving,—fair-faced, blue-eyed, indomitable men, incarnations of the unrest of their race. By accident or design, single-handed and in twos and threes, they came from no one knew whither, and fought, or died, or passed on, no one knew whence. The priests raged against them, the chiefs called forth their fighting men, and stone clashed with steel; but to little purpose. Like water seeping from some mighty reservoir, they trickled through the dark forests and mountain passes, threading the highways in bark canoes, or with their moccasined feet breaking trail for the wolf-dogs. They came of a great breed, and their mothers were many; but the fur-clad denizens of the Northland had this yet to learn. So many an unsung wanderer fought his last and died under the cold fire of the aurora, as did his brothers in burning sands and reeking jungles, and as they shall continue to do till in the fulness of time the destiny of their race be achieved.

It was near twelve. Along the northern horizon a rosy glow, fading to the west and deepening to the east, marked the unseen dip of the midnight sun. The gloaming and the dawn were so commingled that there was no night,—simply a wedding of day with day, a scarcely perceptible blending of two circles of the sun. A kildee timidly chirped good-night; the full, rich throat of a robin proclaimed good-morrow. From an island on the breast of the Yukon a colony of wild fowl voiced its interminable wrongs, while a loon laughed mockingly back across a still stretch of river.

In the foreground, against the bank of a lazy eddy, birch-bark canoes were lined two and three deep. Ivory-bladed spears, bone-barbed arrows, buckskin-thonged bows, and simple basket-woven traps bespoke the fact that in the muddy current of the river the salmon-run was on. In the background, from the tangle of skin tents and drying frames, rose the voices of the fisher folk. Bucks skylarked with bucks or flirted with the maidens, while the older squaws, shut out from this by virtue of having fulfilled the end of their existence in reproduction, gossiped as they braided rope from the green roots of trailing vines. At their feet their naked progeny played and squabbled, or rolled in the muck with the tawny wolf-dogs.

To one side of the encampment, and conspicuously apart from it, stood a second camp of two tents. But it was a white man's camp. If nothing else, the choice of position at least bore convincing evidence of this. In case of offence, it commanded the Indian quarters a hundred yards away; of defence, a rise to the ground and the cleared intervening space; and last, of defeat, the swift slope of a score of yards to the canoes below. From one of the tents came the petulant cry of a sick child and the crooning song of a mother. In the open, over the smouldering embers of a fire, two men held talk.

"Eh? I love the church like a good son. *Bien!* So great a love that my days have been spent in fleeing away from her, and my nights in dreaming dreams of reckoning. Look you!" The half-breed's voice rose to an angry snarl. "I am Red River born. My father was white—as white as you. But you are Yankee, and he was British bred, and a gentleman's son. And my mother was the daughter of a chief, and I was a man. Ay, and one had to look the second time to see what manner of blood ran in my veins; for I lived with the whites, and was one of them, and my father's heart beat in me. It happened there was a maiden—white—who looked on me with kind eyes. Her father had much land and many horses; also he was a big man among his people, and his blood was the blood of the French. He said the girl knew not her own mind, and talked overmuch with her, and became wroth that such things should be.

"But she knew her mind, for we came quick before the priest. And quicker had come her father, with lying words, false promises, I know not what; so that the priest stiffened his neck and would not make us that we might live one with the other. As at the beginning it was the church which would not bless my birth, so now it was the church which refused me marriage and put the blood of men upon my hands. *Bien!* Thus have I cause to love the church. So I struck the priest on his woman's mouth, and we took swift horses, the girl and I, to Fort Pierre, where was a minister of good heart. But hot on our trail was her father, and brothers, and other men he had gathered to him. And we fought, our horses on the run, till I emptied three saddles and the rest drew off and went on to Fort Pierre. Then we took east, the girl and I, to the hills and forests, and we lived one with the other, and we were not married,—the work of the good church which I love like a son.

"But mark you, for this is the strangeness of woman, the way of which no man may understand. One of the saddles I emptied was that of her father's, and the hoofs of those who came behind had pounded him into the earth. This we saw, the girl and I, and this I had forgot had she not remembered. And in the quiet of the evening, after the day's hunt were done, it came between us, and in the silence of the night when we lay beneath the stars and should have been one. It was there always. She never spoke, but it sat by our fire and held us ever apart. She tried to put it aside, but at such times it would rise up till I could read it in the look of her eyes, in the very in-take of her breath.

"So in the end she bore me a child, a woman-child, and died. Then I went among my mother's people, that it might nurse at a warm breast and live. But my hands were wet with the blood of men, look you, because of the church, wet with the blood of men. And the Riders of the North came for me, but my mother's brother, who was then chief in his own right, hid me and gave me horses and food. And we went away, my woman-child and I, even to the Hudson Bay Country, where white men were few and the questions they asked not many. And I worked for the company as a hunter, as a guide, as a driver of dogs, till my woman-child was become a woman, tall, and slender, and fair to the eye.

"You know the winter, long and lonely, breeding evil thoughts and bad deeds. The Chief Factor was a hard man, and bold. And he was not such that a woman would delight in looking upon. But he cast eyes upon my woman-child who was become a woman. Mother of God! he sent me away on a long trip with the dogs, that he might—you understand, he was a hard man and without heart. She was most white, and her soul was white, and a good woman, and—well, she died.

"It was bitter cold the night of my return, and I had been away months, and the dogs were limping sore when I came to the fort. The Indians and breeds looked on me in silence, and I felt the fear of I knew not what, but I said nothing till the dogs were fed and I had eaten as a man with work before him should. Then I spoke up, demanding the word, and they shrank from me, afraid of my anger and what I should do; but the story came out, the pitiful story, word for word and act for act, and they marvelled that I should be so quiet.

"When they had done I went to the Factor's house, calmer than now in the telling of it. He had been afraid and called upon the breeds to help him; but they were not pleased with the deed, and had left him to lie on the bed he had made. So he had fled to the house of the priest. Thither I followed. But when I was come to that place, the priest stood in my way, and spoke soft words, and said a man in anger should go neither to the right nor left, but straight to God. I asked by the right of a father's wrath that he give me past, but he said only over his body, and besought with me to pray. Look you, it was the church, always the church; for I passed over his body and sent the Factor to meet my woman-child before his god, which is a bad god, and the god of the white men.

"Then was there hue and cry, for word was sent to the station below, and I came away. Through the Land of the Great Slave, down the Valley of the Mackenzie to the never-opening ice, over the White Rockies, past the Great Curve of the Yukon, even to this place did I come. And from that day to this, yours is the first face of my father's people I have looked upon. May it be the last! These people, which are my people, are a simple folk, and I have been raised to honor among them. My word is their law, and their priests but do my bidding, else would I not suffer them. When I speak for them I speak for myself. We ask to be let alone. We do not want your kind. If we permit you to sit by our fires, after you will come your church, your priests, and your gods. And know this, for each white man who comes to my village, him will I make deny his god. You are the first, and I give you grace. So it were well you go, and go quickly."

"I am not responsible for my brothers," the second man spoke up, filling his pipe in a meditative manner. Hay Stockard was at times as thoughtful of speech as he was wanton of action; but only at times.

"But I know your breed," responded the other. "Your brothers are many, and it is you and yours who break the trail for them to follow. In time they shall come to possess the land, but not in my time. Already, have I heard, are they on the head-reaches of the Great River, and far away below are the Russians."

Hay Stockard lifted his head with a quick start. This was startling geographical information. The Hudson Bay post at Fort Yukon had other notions concerning the course of the river, believing it to flow into the Arctic.

"Then the Yukon empties into Bering Sea?" he asked.

"I do not know, but below there are Russians, many Russians. Which is neither here nor there. You may go on and see for yourself; you may go back to your brothers; but up the Koyukuk you shall not go while the priests and fighting men do my bidding. Thus do I command, I, Baptiste the Red, whose word is law and who am head man over this people."

"And should I not go down to the Russians, or back to my brothers?"

"Then shall you go swift-footed before your god, which is a bad god, and the god of the white men."

The red sun shot up above the northern skyline, dripping and bloody. Baptiste the Red came to his feet, nodded curtly, and went back to his camp amid the crimson shadows and the singing of the robins.

Hay Stockard finished his pipe by the fire, picturing in smoke and coal the unknown upper reaches of the Koyukuk, the strange stream which ended here its arctic travels and merged its waters with the muddy Yukon flood. Somewhere up there, if the dying words of a shipwrecked sailorman who had made the fearful overland journey were to be believed, and if the vial of golden grains in his pouch attested anything,—somewhere up there, in that home of winter, stood the Treasure House of the North. And as keeper of the gate, Baptiste the Red, English half-breed and renegade, barred the way.

"Bah!" He kicked the embers apart and rose to his full height, arms lazily outstretched, facing the flushing north with careless soul.

II

Hay Stockard swore, harshly, in the rugged monosyllables of his mother tongue. His wife lifted her gaze from the pots and pans, and followed his in a keen scrutiny of the river. She was a woman of the Teslin Country, wise in the ways of her husband's vernacular when it grew intensive. From the slipping of a snowshoe thong to the forefront of sudden death, she could gauge occasion by the pitch and volume of his blasphemy. So she knew the present occasion merited attention. A long canoe, with paddles flashing back the rays of the westering sun, was crossing the current from above and urging in for the eddy. Hay Stockard watched it intently. Three men rose and dipped, rose and dipped, in rhythmical precision; but a red bandanna, wrapped about the head of one, caught and held his eye.

"Bill!" he called. "Oh, Bill!"

A shambling, loose-jointed giant rolled out of one of the tents, yawning and rubbing the sleep from his eyes. Then he sighted the strange canoe and was wide awake on the instant.

"By the jumping Methuselah! That damned sky-pilot!"

Hay Stockard nodded his head bitterly, half-reached for his rifle, then shrugged his shoulders.

"Pot-shot him," Bill suggested, "and settle the thing out of hand. He 'll spoil us sure if we don't." But the other declined this drastic measure and turned away, at the same time bidding the woman return to her work, and calling Bill back from the bank. The two Indians in the canoe moored it on the edge of the eddy, while its white occupant, conspicuous by his gorgeous head-gear, came up the bank.

"Like Paul of Tarsus, I give you greeting. Peace be unto you and grace before the Lord."

His advances were met sullenly, and without speech.

"To you, Hay Stockard, blasphemer and Philistine, greeting. In your heart is the lust of Mammon, in your mind cunning devils, in your tent this woman whom you live with in adultery; yet of these divers sins, even here in the wilderness, I, Sturges Owen, apostle to the Lord, bid you to repent and cast from you your iniquities."

"Save your cant! Save your cant!" Hay Stockard broke in testily. "You 'll need all you 've got, and more, for Red Baptiste over yonder."

He waved his hand toward the Indian camp, where the half-breed was looking steadily across, striving to make out the new-comers. Sturges Owen, disseminator of light and apostle to the Lord, stepped to the edge of the steep and commanded his men to bring up the camp outfit. Stockard followed him.

"Look here," he demanded, plucking the missionary by the shoulder and twirling him about. "Do you value your hide?"

"My life is in the Lord's keeping, and I do but work in His vineyard," he replied solemnly.

"Oh, stow that! Are you looking for a job of martyrship?"

"If He so wills."

"Well, you 'll find it right here, but I 'm going to give you some advice first. Take it or leave it. If you stop here, you 'll be cut off in the midst of your labors. And not you alone, but your men, Bill, my wife—"

"Who is a daughter of Belial and hearkeneth not to the true Gospel."

"And myself. Not only do you bring trouble upon yourself, but upon us. I was frozen in with you last winter, as you will well recollect, and I know you for a good man and a fool. If you think it your duty to strive with the heathen, well and good; but do exercise some wit in the way you go about it. This man, Red Baptiste, is no Indian. He comes of our common stock, is as bull-necked as I ever dared be, and as wild a fanatic the one way as you are the other. When you two come together, hell 'll be to pay, and I don't care to be mixed up in it. Understand? So take my advice and go away. If you go down-stream, you 'll fall in with the Russians. There 's bound to be Greek priests among them, and they 'll see you safe through to Bering Sea,—that 's where the Yukon empties,—and from there it won't be hard to get back to civilization. Take my word for it and get out of here as fast as God 'll let you."

"He who carries the Lord in his heart and the Gospel in his hand hath no fear of the machinations of man or devil," the missionary answered stoutly. "I will see this man and wrestle with him. One backslider returned to the fold is a greater victory than a thousand heathen. He who is strong for evil can be as mighty for good, witness Saul when he journeyed up to Damascus to bring Christian captives to Jerusalem. And the voice of the Saviour came to him, crying, 'Saul, Saul, why persecutest thou me?' And therewith Paul arrayed himself on the side of the Lord, and thereafter was most mighty in the saving of souls. And even as thou, Paul of Tarsus, even so do I work in the vineyard of the Lord, bearing trials and tribulations, scoffs and sneers, stripes and punishments, for His dear sake."

"Bring up the little bag with the tea and a kettle of water," he called the next instant to his boatmen; "not forgetting the haunch of cariboo and the mixing-pan."

When his men, converts by his own hand, had gained the bank, the trio fell to their knees, hands and backs burdened with camp equipage, and offered up thanks for their passage through the wilderness and their safe arrival. Hay Stockard looked upon the function with sneering disapproval, the romance and solemnity of it lost to his matter-of-fact soul. Baptiste the Red, still gazing across, recognized the familiar postures, and remembered the girl who had shared his star-roofed couch in the hills and forests, and the woman-child who lay somewhere by bleak Hudson's Bay.

III

"Confound it, Baptiste, could n't think of it. Not for a moment. Grant that this man is a fool and of small use in the nature of things, but still, you know, I can't give him up."

Hay Stockard paused, striving to put into speech the rude ethics of his heart.

"He 's worried me, Baptiste, in the past and now, and caused me all manner of troubles; but can't you see, he 's my own breed—white—and—and—why, I could n't buy my life with his, not if he was a nigger."

"So be it," Baptiste the Red made answer. "I have given you grace and choice. I shall come presently, with my priests and fighting men, and either shall I kill you, or you deny your god. Give up the priest to my pleasure, and you shall depart in peace. Otherwise your trail ends here. My people are against you to the babies. Even now have the children stolen away your canoes." He pointed down to the river. Naked boys had slipped down the water from the point above, cast loose the canoes, and by then had worked them into the current. When they had drifted out of rifle-shot they clambered over the sides and paddled ashore.

"Give me the priest, and you may have them back again. Come! Speak your mind, but without haste."

Stockard shook his head. His glance dropped to the woman of the Teslin Country with his boy at her breast, and he would have wavered had he not lifted his eyes to the men before him.

"I am not afraid," Sturges Owen spoke up. "The Lord bears me in his right hand, and alone am I ready to go into the camp of the unbeliever. It is not too late. Faith may move mountains. Even in the eleventh hour may I win his soul to the true righteousness."

"Trip the beggar up and make him fast," Bill whispered hoarsely in the ear of his leader, while the missionary kept the floor and wrestled with the heathen. "Make him hostage, and bore him if they get ugly."

"No," Stockard answered. "I gave him my word that he could speak with us unmolested. Rules of warfare, Bill; rules of warfare. He's been on the square, given us warning, and all that, and— why, damn it, man, I can't break my word!"

"He 'll keep his, never fear."

"Don't doubt it, but I won't let a half-breed outdo me in fair dealing. Why not do what he wants,—give him the missionary and be done with it?"

"N-no," Bill hesitated doubtfully.

"Shoe pinches, eh?"

Bill flushed a little and dropped the discussion. Baptiste the Red was still waiting the final decision. Stockard went up to him.

"It 's this way, Baptiste. I came to your village minded to go up the Koyukuk. I intended no wrong. My heart was clean of evil. It is still clean. Along comes this priest, as you call him. I did n't bring him here. He 'd have come whether I was here or not. But now that he is here, being of my people, I 've got to stand by him. And I 'm going to. Further, it will be no child's play. When you have done, your village will be silent and empty, your people wasted as after a famine. True, we will be gone; like-wise the pick of your fighting men—"

"But those who remain shall be in peace, nor shall the word of strange gods and the tongues of strange priests be buzzing in their ears."

Both men shrugged their shoulders and turned away, the half-breed going back to his own camp. The missionary called his two men to him, and they fell into prayer. Stockard and Bill attacked the few standing pines with their axes, felling them into convenient breastworks. The child had fallen asleep, so the woman placed it on a heap of furs and lent a hand in fortifying the camp. Three sides were thus defended, the steep declivity at the rear precluding attack from that direction. When these arrangements had been completed, the two men stalked into the open, clearing away, here and there, the scattered underbrush. From the opposing camp came the booming of war-drums and the voices of the priests stirring the people to anger.

"Worst of it is they 'll come in rushes," Bill complained as they walked back with shouldered axes.

"And wait till midnight, when the light gets dim for shooting."

"Can't start the ball a-rolling too early, then." Bill exchanged the axe for a rifle, and took a careful rest. One of the medicine-men, towering above his tribesmen, stood out distinctly. Bill drew a bead on him.

"All ready?" he asked.

Stockard opened the ammunition box, placed the woman where she could reload in safety, and gave the word. The medicine-man dropped. For a moment there was silence, then a wild howl went up and a flight of bone arrows fell short.

"I'd like to take a look at the beggar," Bill remarked, throwing a fresh shell into place. "I'll swear I drilled him clean between the eyes."

"Did n't work." Stockard shook his head gloomily. Baptiste had evidently quelled the more warlike of his followers, and instead of precipitating an attack in the bright light of day, the shot had caused a hasty exodus, the Indians drawing out of the village beyond the zone of fire.

In the full tide of his proselyting fervor, borne along by the hand of God, Sturges Owen would have ventured alone into the camp of the unbeliever, equally prepared for miracle or martyrdom; but in the waiting which ensued, the fever of conviction died away gradually, as the natural man asserted itself. Physical fear replaced spiritual hope; the love of life, the love of God. It was no new experience. He could feel his weakness coming on, and knew it of old time. He had struggled against it and been overcome by it before. He remembered when the other men had driven their paddles like mad in the van of a roaring ice-flood, how, at the critical moment, in a panic of worldly terror, he had dropped his paddle and besought wildly with his God for pity. And there were other times. The recollection was not pleasant. It brought shame to him that his spirit should be so weak and his flesh so strong. But the love of life! the love of life! He could not strip it from him. Because of it had his dim ancestors perpetuated their line; because of it was he destined to perpetuate his. His courage, if courage it might be called, was bred of fanaticism. The courage of Stockard and Bill was the adherence to deep-rooted ideals. Not that the love of life was less, but the love of race tradition more; not that they were unafraid to die, but that they were brave enough not to live at the price of shame.

The missionary rose, for the moment swayed by the mood of sacrifice. He half crawled over the barricade to proceed to the other camp, but sank back, a trembling mass, wailing: "As the spirit moves! As the spirit moves! Who am I that I should set aside the judgments of God? Before the foundations of the world were all things written in the book of life. Worm that I am, shall I erase the page or any portion thereof? As God wills, so shall the spirit move!"

Bill reached over, plucked him to his feet, and shook him, fiercely, silently. Then he dropped the bundle of quivering nerves and turned his attention to the two converts. But they showed little fright and a cheerful alacrity in preparing for the coming passage at arms.

Stockard, who had been talking in undertones with the Teslin woman, now turned to the missionary.

"Fetch him over here," he commanded of Bill.

"Now," he ordered, when Sturges Owen had been duly deposited before him, "make us man and wife, and be lively about it." Then he added apologetically to Bill: "No telling how it 's to end, so I just thought I 'd get my affairs straightened up."

The woman obeyed the behest of her white lord. To her the ceremony was meaningless. By her lights she was his wife, and had been from the day they first foregathered. The converts served as witnesses. Bill stood over the missionary, prompting him when he stumbled. Stockard put the responses in the woman's mouth, and when the time came, for want of better, ringed her finger with thumb and forefinger of his own.

"Kiss the bride!" Bill thundered, and Sturges Owen was too weak to disobey.

"Now baptize the child!"

"Neat and tidy," Bill commented.

"Gathering the proper outfit for a new trail," the father explained, taking the boy from the mother's arms. "I was grub-staked, once, into the Cascades, and had everything in the kit except salt. Never shall forget it. And if the woman and the kid cross the divide to-night they might as well be prepared for potluck. A long shot, Bill, between ourselves, but nothing lost if it misses."

A cup of water served the purpose, and the child was laid away in a secure corner of the barricade. The men built the fire, and the evening meal was cooked.

The sun hurried round to the north, sinking closer to the horizon. The heavens in that quarter grew red and bloody. The shadows lengthened, the light dimmed, and in the sombre recesses of the forest life slowly died away. Even the wild fowl in the river softened their raucous chatter and feigned the nightly farce of going to bed. Only the tribesmen increased their clamor, wardrums booming and voices raised in savage folk songs. But as the sun dipped they ceased their tumult. The rounded hush of midnight was complete. Stockard rose to his knees and peered over the logs. Once the child wailed in pain and disconcerted him. The mother bent over it, but it slept again. The silence was interminable, profound. Then, of a sudden, the robins burst into full-throated song. The night had passed.

A flood of dark figures boiled across the open. Arrows whistled and bow-thongs sang. The shrill-tongued rifles answered back. A spear, and a mighty cast, transfixed the Teslin woman as she hovered above the child. A spent arrow, diving between the logs, lodged in the missionary's arm.

There was no stopping the rush. The middle distance was cumbered with bodies, but the rest surged on, breaking against and over the barricade like an ocean wave. Sturges Owen fled to the tent, while the men were swept from their feet, buried beneath the human tide. Hay Stockard alone regained the surface, flinging the tribesmen aside like yelping curs. He had managed to seize an axe. A dark hand grasped the child by a naked foot, and drew it from beneath its mother. At arm's length its puny body circled through the air, dashing to death against the logs. Stockard clove the man to the chin and fell to clearing space. The ring of savage faces closed in, raining upon him spear-thrusts and bone-barbed arrows. The sun shot up, and they swayed back and forth in the crimson shadows. Twice, with his axe blocked by too deep a blow, they rushed him; but each time he flung them clear. They fell underfoot and he trampled dead and dying, the way slippery with blood. And still the day brightened and the robins sang. Then they drew back from him in awe, and he leaned breathless upon his axe.

"Blood of my soul!" cried Baptiste the Red. "But thou art a man. Deny thy god, and thou shalt yet live."

Stockard swore his refusal, feebly but with grace.

"Behold! A woman!" Sturges Owen had been brought before the half-breed.

Beyond a scratch on the arm, he was uninjured, but his eyes roved about him in an ecstasy of fear. The heroic figure of the blasphemer, bristling with wounds and arrows, leaning defiantly upon his axe, indifferent, indomitable, superb, caught his wavering vision. And he felt a great envy of the man who could go down serenely to the dark gates of death. Surely Christ, and not he, Sturges Owen, had been moulded in such manner. And why not he? He felt dimly the curse of ancestry, the feebleness of spirit which had come down to him out of the past, and he felt an anger at the creative force, symbolize it as he would, which had formed him, its servant, so weakly. For even a stronger man, this anger and the stress of circumstance were sufficient to breed apostasy, and for Sturges Owen it was inevitable. In the fear of man's anger he would dare the wrath of God. He had been raised up to serve the Lord only that he might be cast down. He had been given faith without the strength of faith; he had been given spirit without the power of spirit. It was unjust.

"Where now is thy god?" the half-breed demanded.

"I do not know." He stood straight and rigid, like a child repeating a catechism.

"Hast thou then a god at all?"

"I had."

"And now?"

"No."

Hay Stockard swept the blood from his eyes and laughed. The missionary looked at him curiously, as in a dream. A feeling of infinite distance came over him, as though of a great remove. In that which had transpired, and which was to transpire, he had no part. He was a spectator—at a distance, yes, at a distance. The words of Baptiste came to him faintly:—

"Very good. See that this man go free, and that no harm befall him. Let him depart in peace. Give him a canoe and food. Set his face toward the Russians, that he may tell their priests of Baptiste the Red, in whose country there is no god."

They led him to the edge of the steep, where they paused to witness the final tragedy. The half-breed turned to Hay Stockard.

"There is no god," he prompted.

The man laughed in reply. One of the young men poised a war-spear for the cast.

"Hast thou a god?"

"Ay, the God of my fathers."

He shifted the axe for a better grip. Baptiste the Red gave the sign, and the spear hurtled full against his breast. Sturges Owen saw the ivory head stand out beyond his back, saw the man sway, laughing, and snap the shaft short as he fell upon it. Then he went down to the river, that he might carry to the Russians the message of Baptiste the Red, in whose country there was no god.

Siwash

"If I was a man—" Her words were in themselves indecisive, but the withering contempt which flashed from her black eyes was not lost upon the men-folk in the tent.

Tommy, the English sailor, squirmed, but chivalrous old Dick Humphries, Cornish fisherman and erstwhile American salmon capitalist, beamed upon her benevolently as ever. He bore women too large a portion of his rough heart to mind them, as he said, when they were in the doldrums, or when their limited vision would not permit them to see all around a thing. So they said nothing, these two men who had taken the half-frozen woman into their tent three days back, and who had warmed her, and fed her, and rescued her goods from the Indian packers. This latter had necessitated the payment of numerous dollars, to say nothing of a demonstration in force—Dick Humphries squinting along the sights of a Winchester while Tommy apportioned their wages among them at his own appraisement. It had been a little thing in itself, but it meant much to a woman playing a desperate single-hand in the equally desperate Klondike rush of '97. Men were occupied with their own pressing needs, nor did they approve of women playing, single-handed, the odds of the arctic winter.

"If I was a man, I know what I would do." Thus reiterated Molly, she of the flashing eyes, and therein spoke the cumulative grit of five American-born generations.

In the succeeding silence, Tommy thrust a pan of biscuits into the Yukon stove and piled on fresh fuel. A reddish flood pounded along under his sun-tanned skin, and as he stooped, the skin of his neck was scarlet. Dick palmed a three-cornered sail needle through a set of broken pack straps, his good nature in nowise disturbed by the feminine cataclysm which was threatening to burst in the storm-beaten tent.

"And if you was a man?" he asked, his voice vibrant with kindness. The three-cornered needle jammed in the damp leather, and he suspended work for the moment.

"I 'd be a man. I 'd put the straps on my back and light out. I would n't lay in camp here, with the Yukon like to freeze most any day, and the goods not half over the portage. And you—you are men, and you sit here, holding your hands, afraid of a little wind and wet. I tell you straight, Yankee-men are made of different stuff. They 'd be hitting the trail for Dawson if they had to wade through hell-fire. And you, you—I wish I was a man."

"I 'm very glad, my dear, that you 're not." Dick Humphries threw the bight of the sail twine over the point of the needle and drew it clear with a couple of deft turns and a jerk.

A snort of the gale dealt the tent a broad-handed slap as it hurtled past, and the sleet rat-tat-tatted with snappy spite against the thin canvas. The smoke, smothered in its exit, drove back through the fire-box door, carrying with it the pungent odor of green spruce.

"Good Gawd! Why can't a woman listen to reason?" Tommy lifted his head from the denser depths and turned upon her a pair of smoke-outraged eyes.

"And why can't a man show his manhood?"

Tommy sprang to his feet with an oath which would have shocked a woman of lesser heart, ripped loose the sturdy reef-knots and flung back the flaps of the tent.

The trio peered out. It was not a heartening spectacle. A few water-soaked tents formed the miserable foreground, from which the streaming ground sloped to a foaming gorge. Down this ramped a mountain torrent. Here and there, dwarf spruce, rooting and grovelling in the shallow alluvium, marked the proximity of the timber line. Beyond, on the opposing slope, the vague outlines of a glacier loomed dead-white through the driving rain. Even as they looked, its massive front crumbled into the valley, on the breast of some subterranean vomit, and it lifted its hoarse thunder above the screeching voice of the storm. Involuntarily, Molly shrank back.

"Look, woman! Look with all your eyes! Three miles in the teeth of the gale to Crater Lake, across two glaciers, along the slippery rimrock, knee-deep in a howling river! Look, I say, you Yankee woman! Look! There 's your Yankee-men!" Tommy pointed a passionate hand in the direction of the struggling tents.

"Yankees, the last mother's son of them. Are they on trail? Is there one of them with the straps to his back? And you would teach us men our work? Look, I say!"

Another tremendous section of the glacier rumbled earthward. The wind whipped in at the open doorway, bulging out the sides of the tent till it swayed like a huge bladder at its guy ropes. The smoke swirled about them, and the sleet drove sharply into their flesh. Tommy pulled the flaps together hastily, and returned to his tearful task at the fire-box. Dick Humphries threw the mended pack straps into a corner and lighted his pipe. Even Molly was for the moment persuaded.

"There 's my clothes," she half-whimpered, the feminine for the moment prevailing. "They 're right at the top of the cache, and they 'll be ruined! I tell you, ruined!"

"There, there," Dick interposed, when the last quavering syllable had wailed itself out. "Don't let that worry you, little woman. I 'm old enough to be your father's brother, and I 've a daughter older than you, and I 'll tog you out in fripperies when we get to Dawson if it takes my last dollar."

"When we get to Dawson!" The scorn had come back to her throat with a sudden surge. "You 'll rot on the way, first. You 'll drown in a mudhole. You—you—Britishers!"

The last word, explosive, intensive, had strained the limits of her vituperation. If that would not stir these men, what could? Tommy's neck ran red again, but he kept his tongue between his teeth. Dick's eyes mellowed. He had the advantage over Tommy, for he had once had a white woman for a wife.

The blood of five American-born generations is, under certain circumstances, an uncomfortable heritage; and among these circumstances might be enumerated that of being quartered with next of kin. These men were Britons. On sea and land her ancestry and the generations thereof had thrashed them and theirs. On sea and land they would continue to do so. The traditions of her race clamored for vindication. She was but a woman of the present, but in her bubbled the whole mighty past. It was not alone Molly Travis who pulled on gum boots, mackintosh, and straps; for the phantom hands of ten thousand forbears drew tight the buckles, just so as they squared her jaw and set her eyes with determination. She, Molly Travis, intended to shame these Britishers; they, the innumerable shades, were asserting the dominance of the common race.

The men-folk did not interfere. Once Dick suggested that she take his oilskins, as her mackintosh was worth no more than paper in such a storm. But she sniffed her independence so sharply that he communed with his pipe till she tied the flaps on the outside and slushed away on the flooded trail.

"Think she 'll make it?" Dick's face belied the indifference of his voice.

"Make it? If she stands the pressure till she gets to the cache, what of the cold and misery, she 'll be stark, raving mad. Stand it? She 'll be dumb-crazed. You know it yourself, Dick. You 've wind-jammed round the Horn. You know what it is to lay out on a topsail yard in the thick of it, bucking sleet and snow and frozen canvas till you 're ready to just let go and cry like a baby. Clothes? She won 't be able to tell a bundle of skirts from a gold pan or a teakettle."

"Kind of think we were wrong in letting her go, then?"

"Not a bit of it. So help me, Dick, she 'd 'a' made this tent a hell for the rest of the trip if we had n't. Trouble with her she 's got too much spirit. This 'll tone it down a bit."

"Yes," Dick admitted, "she 's too ambitious. But then Molly's all right. A cussed little fool to tackle a trip like this, but a plucky sight better than those pick-me-up-and-carry-me kind of women. She 's the stock that carried you and me, Tommy, and you 've got to make allowance for the spirit. Takes a woman to breed a man. You can't suck manhood from the dugs of a creature whose only claim to womanhood is her petticoats. Takes a she-cat, not a cow, to mother a tiger."

"And when they 're unreasonable we 've got to put up with it, eh?"

"The proposition. A sharp sheath-knife cuts deeper on a slip than a dull one; but that 's no reason for to hack the edge off over a capstan bar."

"All right, if you say so, but when it comes to woman, I guess I 'll take mine with a little less edge."

"What do you know about it?" Dick demanded.

"Some." Tommy reached over for a pair of Molly's wet stockings and stretched them across his knees to dry.

Dick, eying him querulously, went fishing in her hand satchel, then hitched up to the front of the stove with divers articles of damp clothing spread likewise to the heat.

"Thought you said you never were married?" he asked.

"Did I? No more was I—that is—yes, by Gawd! I was. And as good a woman as ever cooked grub for a man."

"Slipped her moorings?" Dick symbolized infinity with a wave of his hand.

"Ay."

"Childbirth," he added, after a moment's pause.

The beans bubbled rowdily on the front lid, and he pushed the pot back to a cooler surface. After that he investigated the biscuits, tested them with a splinter of wood, and placed them aside under cover of a damp cloth. Dick, after the manner of his kind, stifled his interest and waited silently.

"A different woman to Molly. Siwash."

Dick nodded his understanding.

"Not so proud and wilful, but stick by a fellow through thick and thin. Sling a paddle with the next and starve as contentedly as Job. Go for'ard when the sloop's nose was more often under than not, and take in sail like a man. Went prospecting once, up Teslin way, past Surprise Lake and the Little Yellow-Head. Grub gave out, and we ate the dogs. Dogs gave out, and we ate harnesses, moccasins, and furs. Never a whimper; never a pick-me-up-and-carry-me. Before we went she said look out for grub, but when it happened, never a I-told-you-so. 'Never mind, Tommy,' she 'd say, day after day, that weak she could bare lift a snow-shoe and her feet raw with the work. 'Never mind. I 'd sooner be flat-bellied of hunger and be your woman, Tommy, than have a *potlach* every day and be Chief George's *klooch*.' George was chief of the Chilcoots, you know, and wanted her bad.

"Great days, those. Was a likely chap myself when I struck the coast. Jumped a whaler, the *Pole Star*, at Unalaska, and worked my way down to Sitka on an otter hunter. Picked up with Happy Jack there—know him?"

"Had charge of my traps for me," Dick answered, "down on

the Columbia. Pretty wild, was n't he, with a warm place in his heart for whiskey and women?"

"The very chap. Went trading with him for a couple of seasons—*hooch*, and blankets, and such stuff. Then got a sloop of my own, and not to cut him out, came down Juneau way. That 's where I met Killisnoo; I called her Tilly for short. Met her at a squaw dance down on the beach. Chief George had finished the year's trade with the Sticks over the Passes, and was down from Dyea with half his tribe. No end of Siwashes at the dance, and I the only white. No one knew me, barring a few of the bucks I 'd met over Sitka way, but I 'd got most of their histories from Happy Jack.

"Everybody talking Chinook, not guessing that I could spit it better than most; and principally two girls who 'd run away from Haine's Mission up the Lynn Canal. They were trim creatures, good to the eye, and I kind of thought of casting that way; but they were fresh as fresh-caught cod. Too much edge, you see. Being a new-comer, they started to twist me, not knowing I gathered in every word of Chinook they uttered.

"I never let on, but set to dancing with Tilly, and the more we danced the more our hearts warmed to each other. 'Looking for a woman,' one of the girls says, and the other tosses her head and answers, 'Small chance he 'll get one when the women are looking for men.' And the bucks and squaws standing around began to grin and giggle and repeat what had been said. 'Quite a pretty boy,' says the first one. I 'll not deny I was rather smooth-faced and youngish, but I 'd been a man amongst men many 's the day, and it rankled me. 'Dancing with Chief George's girl,' pipes the second. 'First thing George 'll give him the flat of a paddle and send him about his business.' Chief George had been looking pretty black up to now, but at this he laughed and slapped his knees. He was a husky beggar and would have used the paddle too.

" 'Who 's the girls?' I asked Tilly, as we went ripping down the centre in a reel. And as soon as she told me their names I remembered all about them from Happy Jack. Had their pedigree down fine—several things he 'd told me that not even their own tribe knew. But I held my hush, and went on courting Tilly, they a-casting sharp remarks and everybody roaring. 'Bide a wee, Tommy,' I says to myself; 'bide a wee.'

"And bide I did, till the dance was ripe to break up, and Chief George had brought a paddle all ready for me. Everybody was on the lookout for mischief when we stopped; but I marched, easy as you please, slap into the thick of them. The Mission girls cut me up something clever, and for all I was angry I had to set my teeth to keep from laughing. I turned upon them suddenly.

" 'Are you done?' I asked.

"You should have seen them when they heard me spitting Chinook. Then I broke loose. I told them all about themselves, and their people before them; their fathers, mothers, sisters, brothers —everybody, everything. Each mean trick they 'd played; every scrape they 'd got into; every shame that 'd fallen them. And I burned them without fear or favor. All hands crowded round. Never had they heard a white man sling their lingo as I did. Everybody was laughing save the Mission girls. Even Chief George forgot the paddle, or at least he was swallowing too much respect to dare to use it.

"But the girls. 'Oh, do n't, Tommy,' they cried, the tears running down their cheeks. 'Please don't. We 'll be good. Sure, Tommy, sure.' But I knew them well, and I scorched them on every tender spot. Nor did I slack away till they came down on their knees, begging and pleading with me to keep quiet. Then I shot a glance at Chief George; but he did not know whether to have at me or not, and passed it off by laughing hollowly.

"So be. When I passed the parting with Tilly that night I gave her the word that I was going to be around for a week or so, and that I wanted to see more of her. Not thick-skinned, her kind, when it came to showing like and dislike, and she looked her pleasure for the honest girl she was. Ay, a striking lass, and I did n't wonder that Chief George was taken with her.

"Everything my way. Took the wind from his sails on the first leg. I was for getting her aboard and sailing down Wrangel way till it blew over, leaving him to whistle; but I was n't to get her that easy. Seems she was living with an uncle of hers—guardian, the way such things go—and seems he was nigh to shuffling off with consumption or some sort of lung trouble. He was good and bad by turns, and she would n't leave him till it was over with. Went up to the tepee just before I left, to speculate on how long it 'd be; but the old beggar had promised her to Chief George, and when he clapped eyes on me his anger brought on a hemorrhage.

"'Come and take me, Tommy,' she says when we bid goodby on the beach. 'Ay,' I answers; 'when you give the word.' And I kissed her, white-man-fashion and lover-fashion, till she was all of a tremble like a quaking aspen, and I was so beside myself I 'd half a mind to go up and give the uncle a lift over the divide.

"So I went down Wrangel way, past St. Mary's and even to the Queen Charlottes, trading, running whiskey, turning the sloop to most anything. Winter was on, stiff and crisp, and I was back to Juneau, when the word came. 'Come,' the beggar says who brought the news. 'Killisnoo say, "Come now."' 'What 's the row?' I asks. 'Chief George,' says he. '*Potlach*. Killisnoo, makum *klooch*.'

"Ay, it was bitter—the Taku howling down out of the north, the salt water freezing quick as it struck the deck, and the old sloop and I hammering into the teeth of it for a hundred miles to Dyea. Had a Douglass Islander for crew when I started, but midway up he was washed over from the bows. Jibed all over and crossed the course three times, but never a sign of him."

"Doubled up with the cold most likely," Dick suggested, putting a pause into the narrative while he hung one of Molly's skirts up to dry, "and went down like a pot of lead."

"My idea. So I finished the course alone, half-dead when I made Dyea in the dark of the evening. The tide favored, and I ran the sloop plump to the bank, in the shelter of the river. Could n't go an inch further, for the fresh water was frozen solid. Halyards and blocks were that iced up I did n't dare lower mainsail or jib. First I broached a pint of the cargo raw, and then, leaving all standing, ready for the start, and with a blanket around me, headed across the flat to the camp. No mistaking, it was a grand layout. The Chilcats had come in a body—dogs, babies, and canoes—to say nothing of the Dog-Ears, the Little Salmons, and the Missions. Full half a thousand of them to celebrate Tilly's wedding, and never a white man in a score of miles.

"Nobody took note of me, the blanket over my head and hiding my face, and I waded knee deep through the dogs and youngsters till I was well up to the front. The show was being pulled off in a big open place among the trees, with great fires burning and the snow moccasin-packed as hard as Portland cement. Next me was Tilly, beaded and scarlet-clothed galore, and against her Chief George and his head men. The shaman was being helped out by the big medicines from the other tribes, and it shivered my spine up and down, the deviltries they cut. I caught myself wondering if the folks in Liverpool could only see me now; and I thought of yellow-haired Gussie, whose brother I licked after my first voyage, just because he was not for having a sailor-man courting his sister. And with Gussie in my eyes I looked at Tilly. A rum old world, thinks I, with man a-stepping in trails the mother little dreamed of when he lay at suck.

"So be. When the noise was loudest, walrus hides booming and priests a-singing, I says, 'Are you ready?' Gawd! Not a start, not a shot of the eyes my way, not the twitch of a muscle. 'I knew,' she answers, slow and steady as a calm spring tide. 'Where?' 'The high bank at the edge of the ice,' I whispers back. 'Jump out when I give the word.'

"Did I say there was no end of huskies? Well, there was no end. Here, there, everywhere, they were scattered about,—tame wolves and nothing less. When the strain runs thin they breed them in the bush with the wild, and they 're bitter fighters. Right at the toe of my moccasin lay a big brute, and by the heel another. I doubled the first one's tail, quick, till it snapped in my grip. As his jaws clipped together where my hand should have been, I threw the second one by the scruff straight into his mouth. 'Go!' I cried to Tilly.

"You know how they fight. In the wink of an eye there was a raging hundred of them, top and bottom, ripping and tearing each other, kids and squaws tumbling which way, and the camp gone wild. Tilly 'd slipped away, so I followed. But when I looked over my shoulder at the skirt of the crowd, the devil laid me by the heart, and I dropped the blanket and went back.

"By then the dogs 'd been knocked apart and the crowd was untangling itself. Nobody was in proper place, so they did n't note that Tilly 'd gone. 'Hello,' I says, gripping Chief George by the hand. 'May your potlach-smoke rise often, and the Sticks bring many furs with the spring.'

"Lord love me, Dick, but he was joyed to see me,—him with the upper hand and wedding Tilly. Chance to puff big over me. The tale that I was hot after her had spread through the camps, and my presence did him proud. All hands knew me, without my blanket, and set to grinning and giggling. It was rich, but I made it richer by playing unbeknowing.

" 'What 's the row?' I asks. 'Who 's getting married now?'

" 'Chief George,' the shaman says, ducking his reverence to him.

" 'Thought he had two *klooches*.'

" 'Him takum more,—three,' with another duck.

" 'Oh!' And I turned away as though it did n't interest me.

"But this would n't do, and everybody begins singing out, 'Killisnoo! Killisnoo!'

" 'Killisnoo what?' I asked.

" 'Killisnoo, *klooch*, Chief George,' they blathered. 'Killisnoo, *klooch*.'

"I jumped and looked at Chief George. He nodded his head and threw out his chest.

" 'She 'll be no *klooch* of yours,' I says solemnly. 'No *klooch* of yours,' I repeats, while his face went black and his hand began dropping to his hunting-knife.

" 'Look!' I cries, striking an attitude. 'Big medicine. You watch my smoke.'

"I pulled off my mittens, rolled back my sleeves, and made half-a-dozen passes in the air.

" 'Killisnoo!' I shouts. 'Killisnoo! Killisnoo!'

"I was making medicine, and they began to scare. Every eye was on me; no time to find out that Tilly was n't there. Then I called Killisnoo three times again, and waited; and three times more. All for mystery and to make them nervous. Chief George could n't guess what I was up to, and wanted to put a stop to the foolery; but the shamans said to wait, and that they 'd see me and go me one better, or words to that effect. Besides, he was a superstitious cuss, and I fancy a bit afraid of the white man's magic.

"Then I called Killisnoo, long and soft like the howl of a wolf, till the women were all a-tremble and the bucks looking serious.

" 'Look!' I sprang for'ard, pointing my finger into a bunch of squaws—easier to deceive women than men, you know. 'Look!' And I raised it aloft as though following the flight of a bird. Up, up, straight overhead, making to follow it with my eyes till it disappeared in the sky.

" 'Killisnoo,' I said, looking at Chief George and pointing upward again. 'Killisnoo.'

"So help me, Dick, the gammon worked. Half of them, at least, saw Tilly disappear in the air. They 'd drunk my whiskey at Juneau and seen stranger sights, I 'll warrant. Why should I not do this thing, I, who sold bad spirits corked in bottles? Some of the women shrieked. Everybody fell to whispering in bunches. I folded my arms and held my head high, and they drew further away from me. The time was ripe to go. 'Grab him,' Chief George cries. Three or four of them came at me, but I whirled, quick, made a couple of passes like to send them after Tilly, and pointed up. Touch me? Not for the kingdoms of the earth. Chief George harangued them, but he could n't get them to lift a leg. Then he made to take me himself; but I repeated the mummery and his grit went out through his fingers.

" 'Let your shamans work wonders the like of which I have done this night,' I says. 'Let them call Killisnoo down out of the sky whither I have sent her.' But the priests knew their limits. 'May your *klooches* bear you sons as the spawn of the salmon,' I says, turning to go; 'and may your totem pole stand long in the land, and the smoke of your camp rise always.'

"But if the beggars could have seen me hitting the high places for the sloop as soon as I was clear of them, they 'd thought my own medicine had got after me. Tilly 'd kept warm by chopping the ice away, and was all ready to cast off. Gawd! how we ran before it, the Taku howling after us and the freezing seas sweeping over at every clip. With everything battened down, me a-steering and Tilly chopping ice, we held on half the night, till I plumped the sloop ashore on Porcupine Island, and we shivered it out on the beach; blankets wet, and Tilly drying the matches on her breast.

"So I think I know something about it. Seven years, Dick, man and wife, in rough sailing and smooth. And then she died, in the heart of the winter, died in childbirth, up there on the Chilcat Station. She held my hand to the last, the ice creeping up inside the door and spreading thick on the gut of the window. Outside, the lone howl of the wolf and the Silence; inside, death and the Silence. You 've never heard the Silence yet, Dick, and Gawd grant you do n't ever have to hear it when you sit by the side of death. Hear it? Ay, till the breath whistles like a siren, and the heart booms, booms, booms, like the surf on the shore.

"Siwash, Dick, but a woman. White, Dick, white, clear through. Towards the last she says, 'Keep my feather bed, Tommy, keep it always.' And I agreed. Then she opened her eyes, full with the pain. 'I 've been a good woman to you, Tommy, and because of that I want you to promise—to promise'—the words seemed to stick in her throat—'that when you marry, the woman be white. No more Siwash, Tommy. I know. Plenty white women down to Juneau now. I know. Your people call you "squaw-man," your women turn their heads to the one side on the street, and you do not go to their cabins like other men. Why? Your wife Siwash. Is it not so? And this is not good. Wherefore I die. Promise me. Kiss me in token of your promise.'

"I kissed her, and she dozed off, whispering, 'It is good.' At the end, that near gone my ear was at her lips, she roused for the last time. 'Remember, Tommy; remember my feather bed.' Then she died, in childbirth, up there on the Chilcat Station."

The tent heeled over and half flattened before the gale. Dick refilled his pipe, while Tommy drew the tea and set it aside against Molly's return.

And she of the flashing eyes and Yankee blood? Blinded, falling, crawling on hand and knee, the wind thrust back in her throat by the wind, she was heading for the tent. On her shoulders a bulky pack caught the full fury of the storm. She plucked feebly at the knotted flaps, but it was Tommy and Dick who cast them loose. Then she set her soul for the last effort, staggered in, and fell exhausted on the floor.

Tommy unbuckled the straps and took the pack from her. As he lifted it there was a clanging of pots and pans. Dick, pouring out a mug of whiskey, paused long enough to pass the wink across her body. Tommy winked back. His lips pursed the monosyllable, "clothes," but Dick shook his head reprovingly.

"Here, little woman," he said, after she had drunk the whiskey and straightened up a bit. "Here 's some dry togs. Climb into them. We 're going out to extra-peg the tent. After that, give us the call, and we 'll come in and have dinner. Sing out when you 're ready."

"So help me, Dick, that 's knocked the edge off her for the rest of this trip," Tommy spluttered as they crouched to the lee of the tent.

"But it 's the edge is her saving grace," Dick replied, ducking his head to a volley of sleet that drove around a corner of the canvas. "The edge that you and I 've got, Tommy, and the edge of our mothers before us."

Grit of Women

A wolfish head, wistful-eyed and frost-rimed, thrust aside the tent-flaps.

"Hi! Chook! Siwash! Chook, you limb of Satan!" chorused the protesting inmates. Bettles rapped the dog sharply with a tin plate, and it withdrew hastily. Louis Savoy refastened the flaps, kicked a frying-pan over against the bottom, and warmed his hands. It was very cold without. Forty-eight hours gone, the spirit thermometer had burst at sixty-eight below, and since that time it had grown steadily and bitterly colder. There was no telling when the snap would end. And it is poor policy, unless the gods will it, to venture far from a stove at such times, or to increase the quantity of cold atmosphere one must breathe. Men sometimes do it, and sometimes they chill their lungs. This leads up to a dry, hacking cough, noticeably irritable when bacon is being fried. After that, somewhere along in the spring or summer, a hole is burned in the frozen muck. Into this a man's carcass is dumped, covered over with moss, and left with the assurance that it will rise on the crack of Doom, wholly and frigidly intact. For those of little faith, sceptical of material integration on that fateful day, no fitter country than the Klondike can be recommended to die in. But it is not to be inferred from this that it is a fit country for living purposes.

It was very cold without, but it was not over-warm within. The only article which might be designated furniture was the stove, and for this the men were frank in displaying their preference. Upon half of the floor pine boughs had been cast; above this were spread the sleeping-furs, beneath lay the winter's snowfall. The remainder of the floor was moccasin-packed snow, littered with pots and pans and the general *impedimenta* of an Arctic camp. The stove was red and roaring hot, but only a bare three feet away lay a block of ice, as sharp-edged and dry as when first quarried from the creek bottom. The pressure of the outside cold forced the inner heat upward. Just above the stove, where the pipe penetrated the roof, was a tiny circle of dry canvas; next, with the pipe always as centre, a circle of steaming canvas; next a damp and moisture-exuding ring; and finally, the rest of the tent, side-walls and top, coated with a half-inch of dry, white, crystal-encrusted frost.

"*Oh!* Oн! OH!" A young fellow, lying asleep in the furs, bearded and wan and weary, raised a moan of pain, and without waking increased the pitch and intensity of his anguish. His body half-lifted from the blankets, and quivered and shrank spasmodi-cally, as though drawing away from a bed of nettles.

"Roll 'm over!" ordered Bettles. "He 's crampin'."

And thereat, with pitiless good-will, he was pitched upon and rolled and thumped and pounded by half-a-dozen willing com-rades.

"Damn the trail," he muttered softly, as he threw off the robes and sat up. "I 've run across country, played quarter three seasons hand-running, and hardened myself in all manner of ways; and then I pilgrim it into this God-forsaken land and find myself an effeminate Athenian without the simplest rudiments of man-hood!" He hunched up to the fire and rolled a cigarette. "Oh, I 'm not whining. I can take my medicine all right, all right; but I 'm just decently ashamed of myself, that 's all. Here I am, on top of a dirty thirty miles, as knocked up and stiff and sore as a pink-tea degenerate after a five-mile walk on a country turnpike. Bah! It makes me sick! Got a match?"

"Don't git the tantrums, youngster." Bettles passed over the required fire-stick and waxed patriarchal. "Ye 've gotter 'low some for the breakin'-in. Sufferin' cracky! don't I recollect the first time I hit the trail! Stiff? I 've seen the time it 'd take me ten minutes to git my mouth from the waterhole an' come to my feet—every jint crackin' an' kickin' fit to kill. Cramp? In sech knots it 'd take the camp half a day to untangle me. You 're all right, for a cub, an' ye 've the true sperrit. Come this day year, you 'll walk all us old bucks into the ground any time. An' best in your favor, you hain't got that streak of fat in your make-up which has sent many a husky man to the bosom of Abraham afore his right and proper time."

"Streak of fat?"

"Yep. Comes along of bulk. 'T ain't the big men as is the best when it comes to the trail."

"Never heard of it."

"Never heered of it, eh? Well, it 's a dead straight, open-an'-shut fact, an' no gittin' round. Bulk 's all well enough for a mighty big effort, but 'thout stayin' powers it ain't worth a continental whoop; an' stayin' powers an' bulk ain't runnin' mates. Takes the small, wiry fellows when it comes to gittin' right down an' hangin' on like a lean-jowled dog to a bone. Why, hell's fire, the big men they ain't in it!"

"By gar!" broke in Louis Savoy, "dat is no, vot you call, josh! I know one mans, so vaire beeg like ze buffalo. Wit him, on ze Sulphur Creek stampede, go one small mans, Lon McFane. You know dat Lon McFane, dat leetle Irisher wit ze red hair and ze grin. An' dey walk an' walk an' walk, all ze day long an' ze night long. And beeg mans, him become vaire tired, an' lay down mooch in ze snow. And leetle mans keek beeg mans, an' him cry like, vot you call—ah! vot you call ze kid. And leetle mans keek an' keek an' keek, an' bime by, long time, long way, keek beeg mans into my cabin. Tree days 'fore him crawl out my blankets. Nevaire I see beeg squaw like him. No nevaire. Him haf vot you call ze streak of fat. You bet."

"But there was Axel Gunderson," Prince spoke up. The great Scandinavian, with the tragic events which shadowed his passing, had made a deep mark on the mining engineer. "He lies up there, somewhere." He swept his hand in the vague direction of the mysterious east.

"Biggest man that ever turned his heels to Salt Water or run a moose down with sheer grit," supplemented Bettles; "but he 's the prove-the-rule exception. Look at his woman, Unga,—tip the scales at a hundred an' ten, clean meat an' nary ounce to spare. She 'd bank grit 'gainst his for all there was in him, an' see him, an' go him better if it was possible. Nothing over the earth, or in it, or under it, she would n't 'a' done."

"But she loved him," objected the engineer.

" 'T ain't that. It—"

"Look you, brothers," broke in Sitka Charley from his seat on the grub-box. "Ye have spoken of the streak of fat that runs in

big men's muscles, of the grit of women and the love, and ye have
spoken fair; but I have in mind things which happened when the
land was young and the fires of men apart as the stars. It was then
I had concern with a big man, and a streak of fat, and a woman.
And the woman was small; but her heart was greater than the
beef-heart of the man, and she had grit. And we traveled a weary
trail, even to the Salt Water, and the cold was bitter, the snow
deep, the hunger great. And the woman's love was a mighty
love—no more can man say than this."

He paused, and with the hatchet broke pieces of ice from the
large chunk beside him. These he threw into the gold pan on the
stove, where the drinking-water thawed. The men drew up closer,
and he of the cramps sought greater comfort vainly for his stiffened body.

"Brothers, my blood is red with Siwash, but my heart is white.
To the faults of my fathers I owe the one, to the virtues of my
friends the other. A great truth came to me when I was yet a boy.
I learned that to your kind and you was given the earth; that the
Siwash could not withstand you, and like the caribou and the bear,
must perish in the cold. So I came into the warm and sat among
you, by your fires, and behold, I became one of you. I have seen
much in my time. I have known strange things, and bucked big,
on big trails, with men of many breeds. And because of these
things, I measure deeds after your manner, and judge men, and
think thoughts. Wherefore, when I speak harshly of one of your
own kind, I know you will not take it amiss; and when I speak
high of one of my father's people, you will not take it upon you
to say, 'Sitka Charley is Siwash, and there is a crooked light in
his eyes and small honor to his tongue.' Is it not so?"

Deep down in throat, the circle vouchsafed its assent.

"The woman was Passuk. I got her in fair trade from her
people, who were of the Coast and whose Chilcat totem stood at
the head of a salt arm of the sea. My heart did not go out to the
woman, nor did I take stock of her looks. For she scarce took her
eyes from the ground, and she was timid and afraid, as girls will
be when cast into a stranger's arms whom they have never seen
before. As I say, there was no place in my heart for her to creep,
for I had a great journey in mind, and stood in need of one to

feed my dogs and to lift a paddle with me through the long river days. One blanket would cover the twain; so I chose Passuk.

"Have I not said I was a servant to the Government? If not, it is well that ye know. So I was taken on a warship, sleds and dogs and evaporated foods, and with me came Passuk. And we went north, to the winter ice-rim of Bering Sea, where we were landed,—myself, and Passuk, and the dogs. I was also given moneys of the Government, for I was its servant, and charts of lands which the eyes of man had never dwelt upon, and messages. These messages were sealed, and protected shrewdly from the weather, and I was to deliver them to the whale-ships of the Arctic, ice-bound by the great Mackenzie. Never was there so great a river, forgetting only our own Yukon, the Mother of all Rivers.

"All of which is neither here nor there, for my story deals not with the whale-ships, nor the berg-bound winter I spent by the Mackenzie. Afterward, in the spring, when the days lengthened and there was a crust to the snow, we came south, Passuk and I, to the Country of the Yukon. A weary journey, but the sun pointed out the way of our feet. It was a naked land then, as I have said, and we worked up the current, with pole and paddle, till we came to Forty Mile. Good it was to see white faces once again, so we put into the bank. And that winter was a hard winter. The darkness and the cold drew down upon us, and with them the famine. To each man the agent of the Company gave forty pounds of flour and twenty of bacon. There were no beans. And the dogs howled always, and there were flat bellies and deep-lined faces, and strong men became weak, and weak men died. There was also much scurvy.

"Then came we together in the store one night, and the empty shelves made us feel our own emptiness the more. We talked low, by the light of the fire, for the candles had been set aside for those who might yet gasp in the spring. Discussion was held, and it was said that a man must go forth to the Salt Water and tell to the world our misery. At this all eyes turned to me, for it was understood that I was a great traveler. 'It is seven hundred miles,' said I, 'to Haines Mission by the sea, and every inch of it snowshoe work. Give me the pick of your dogs and the best of your grub, and I will go. And with me shall go Passuk.'

"To this they were agreed. But there arose one, Long Jeff, a Yankee-man, big-boned and big-muscled. Also his talk was big. He, too, was a mighty traveler, he said, born to the snowshoe and bred up on buffalo milk. He would go with me, in case I fell by the trail, that he might carry the word on to the Mission. I was young, and I knew not Yankee-men. How was I to know that big talk betokened the streak of fat, or that Yankee-men who did great things kept their teeth together? So we took the pick of the dogs and the best of the grub, and struck the trail, we three,— Passuk, Long Jeff, and I.

"Well, ye have broken virgin snow, labored at the gee-pole, and are not unused to the packed river-jams; so I will talk little of the toil, save that on some days we made ten miles, and on others thirty, but more often ten. And the best of the grub was not good, while we went on stint from the start. Likewise the pick of the dogs was poor, and we were hard put to keep them on their legs. At the White River our three sleds became two sleds, and we had only come two hundred miles. But we lost nothing; the dogs that left the traces went into the bellies of those that remained.

"Not a greeting, not a curl of smoke, till we made Pelly. Here I had counted on grub; and here I had counted on leaving Long Jeff, who was whining and trail-sore. But the factor's lungs were wheezing, his eyes bright, his cache nigh empty; and he showed us the empty cache of the missionary, also his grave with the rocks piled high to keep off the dogs. There was a bunch of Indians there, but babies and old men there were none, and it was clear that few would see the spring.

"So we pulled on, light-stomached and heavy-hearted, with half a thousand miles of snow and silence between us and Haines Mission by the sea. The darkness was at its worst, and at midday the sun could not clear the sky-line to the south. But the ice-jams were smaller, the going better; so I pushed the dogs hard and traveled late and early. As I said at Forty Mile, every inch of it was snowshoe work. And the shoes made great sores on our feet, which cracked and scabbed but would not heal. And every day these sores grew more grievous, till in the morning, when we girded on the shoes, Long Jeff cried like a child. I put him at the fore of the light sled to break trail, but he slipped off the shoes for comfort. Because of this the trail was not packed, his moccasins made great holes, and into these holes the dogs wallowed. The bones of the dogs were ready to break through their hides, and this was not good for them. So I spoke hard words to the man, and he promised, and broke his word. Then I beat him with the dogwhip, and after that the dogs wallowed no more. He was a child, what of the pain and the streak of fat.

"But Passuk. While the man lay by the fire and wept, she cooked, and in the morning helped lash the sleds, and in the evening to unlash them. And she saved the dogs. Ever was she to the fore, lifting the webbed shoes and making the way easy. Passuk —how shall I say?—I took it for granted that she should do these things, and thought no more about it. For my mind was busy with other matters, and besides, I was young in years and knew little of woman. It was only on looking back that I came to understand.

"And the man became worthless. The dogs had little strength in them, but he stole rides on the sled when he lagged behind. Passuk said she would take the one sled, so the man had nothing to do. In the morning I gave him his fair share of grub and started him on the trail alone. Then the woman and I broke camp, packed the sleds, and harnessed the dogs. By midday, when the sun mocked us, we would overtake the man, with the tears frozen on his cheeks, and pass him. In the night we made camp, set aside his fair share of grub, and spread his furs. Also we made a big fire, that he might see. And hours afterward he would come limping in, and eat his grub with moans and groans, and sleep. He was not sick, this man. He was only trail-sore and tired, and weak with hunger. But Passuk and I were trail-sore and tired, and weak with hunger; and we did all the work and he did none. But he had the streak of fat of which our brother Bettles has spoken. Further, we gave the man always his fair share of grub.

"Then one day we met two ghosts journeying through the Silence. They were a man and a boy, and they were white. The ice had opened on Lake Le Barge, and through it had gone their main outfit. One blanket each carried about his shoulders. At night they built a fire and crouched over it till morning. They had a little flour. This they stirred in warm water and drank. The man showed me eight cups of flour—all they had, and Pelly, stricken with famine, two hundred miles away. They said, also, that there was an Indian behind; that they had whacked fair, but that he could not keep up. I did not believe they had whacked fair, else would the Indian have kept up. But I could give them no grub. They strove to steal a dog—the fattest, which was very thin—but I shoved my pistol in their faces and told them begone. And they went away, like drunken men, through the Silence toward Pelly.

"I had three dogs now, and one sled, and the dogs were only bones and hair. When there is little wood, the fire burns low and the cabin grows cold. So with us. With little grub the frost bites sharp, and our faces were black and frozen till our own mothers would not have known us. And our feet were very sore. In the morning, when I hit the trail, I sweated to keep down the cry when the pain of the snowshoes smote me. Passuk never opened her lips, but stepped to the fore to break the way. The man howled.

"The Thirty Mile was swift, and the current ate away the ice from beneath, and there were many air-holes and cracks, and much open water. One day we came upon the man, resting, for he had gone ahead, as was his wont, in the morning. But between us was open water. This he had passed around by taking to the rim-ice where it was too narrow for a sled. So we found an ice-bridge. Passuk weighed little, and went first, with a long pole crosswise in her hands in chance she broke through. But she was light, and her shoes large, and she passed over. Then she called the dogs. But they had neither poles nor shoes, and they broke through and were swept under by the water. I held tight to the sled from behind, till the traces broke and the dogs went on down under the ice. There was little meat to them, but I had counted on them for a week's grub, and they were gone.

"The next morning I divided all the grub, which was little, into three portions. And I told Long Jeff that he could keep up with us, or not, as he saw fit; for we were going to travel light and fast. But he raised his voice and cried over his sore feet and his troubles, and said harsh things against comradeship. Passuk's feet were sore, and my feet were sore—ay, sorer than his, for we had worked with the dogs; also, we looked to see. Long Jeff swore he would die before he hit the trail again; so Passuk took a fur robe, and I a cooking pot and an axe, and we made ready to go. But she looked on the man's portion, and said, 'It is wrong to waste good food on a baby. He is better dead.' I shook my head and said no—that a comrade once was a comrade always. Then she spoke of the men of Forty Mile; that they were many men and good; and that they looked to me for grub in the spring. But when I still said no, she snatched the pistol from my belt, quick, and as our brother Bettles has spoken, Long Jeff went to the bosom of Abraham before his time. I chided Passuk for this; but she showed no sorrow, nor was she sorrowful. And in my heart I knew she was right."

Sitka Charley paused and threw pieces of ice into the gold pan on the stove. The men were silent, and their backs chilled to the sobbing cries of the dogs as they gave tongue to their misery in the outer cold.

"And day by day we passed in the snow the sleeping-places of the two ghosts—Passuk and I—and we knew we would be glad for such ere we made Salt Water. Then we came to the Indian, like another ghost, with his face set toward Pelly. They had not whacked up fair, the man and the boy, he said, and he had had no flour for three days. Each night he boiled pieces of his moccasins in a cup, and ate them. He did not have much moccasins left. And he was a Coast Indian, and told us these things through Passuk, who talked his tongue. He was a stranger in the Yukon, and he knew not the way, but his face was set to Pelly. How far was it? Two sleeps? ten? a hundred?—he did not know, but he was going to Pelly. It was too far to turn back; he could only keep on.

"He did not ask for grub, for he could see we, too, were hard put. Passuk looked at the man, and at me, as though she were of two minds, like a mother partridge whose young are in trouble. So I turned to her and said, 'This man has been dealt unfair. Shall I give him of our grub a portion?' I saw her eyes light, as with quick pleasure; but she looked long at the man and at me, and her mouth drew close and hard, and she said, 'No. The Salt Water is afar off, and Death lies in wait. Better it is that he take this stranger man and let my man Charley pass.' So the man went away in the Silence toward Pelly. That night she wept. Never had I seen her weep before. Nor was it the smoke of the fire, for the wood was dry wood. So I marveled at her sorrow, and thought her woman's heart had grown soft at the darkness of the trail and the pain.

"Life is a strange thing. Much have I thought on it, and pondered long, yet daily the strangeness of it grows not less, but more. Why this longing for Life? It is a game which no man wins. To live is to toil hard, and to suffer sore, till Old Age creeps heavily upon us and we throw down our hands on the cold ashes of dead fires. It is hard to live. In pain the babe sucks his first breath, in pain the old man gasps his last, and all his days are full of trouble and sorrow; yet he goes down to the open arms of Death, stumbling, falling, with head turned backward, fighting to the last. And Death is kind. It is only Life, and the things of Life that hurt. Yet we love Life, and we hate Death. It is very strange.

"We spoke little, Passuk and I, in the days which came. In the night we lay in the snow like dead people, and in the morning we went on our way, walking like dead people. And all things were dead. There were no ptarmigan, no squirrels, no snowshoe rabbits,—nothing. The river made no sound beneath its white robes. The sap was frozen in the forest. And it became cold, as now; and in the night the stars drew near and large, and leaped and danced; and in the day the sun-dogs mocked us till we saw many suns, and all the air flashed and sparkled, and the snow was diamond dust. And there was no heat, no sound, only the bitter cold and the Silence. As I say, we walked like dead people, as in a dream, and we kept no count of time. Only our faces were set to Salt Water, our souls strained for Salt Water, and our feet carried us toward Salt Water. We camped by the Tahkeena, and knew it not. Our eyes looked upon the White Horse, but we saw it not. Our feet trod the portage of the Canyon, but they felt it not. We felt nothing. And we fell often by the way, but we fell, always, with our faces toward Salt Water.

"Our last grub went, and we had shared fair, Passuk and I, but she fell more often, and at Caribou Crossing her strength left her. And in the morning we lay beneath the one robe and did not take the trail. It was in my mind to stay there and meet Death hand-in-hand with Passuk; for I had grown old, and had learned the love of woman. Also, it was eighty miles to Haines Mission, and the great Chilcoot, far above the timber-line, reared his storm-swept head between. But Passuk spoke to me, low, with my ear against her lips that I might hear. And now, because she need not fear my anger, she spoke her heart, and told me of her love, and of many things which I did not understand.

"And she said: 'You are my man, Charley, and I have been a good woman to you. And in all the days I have made your fire, and cooked your food, and fed your dogs, and lifted paddle or broken trail, I have not complained. Nor did I say that there was more warmth in the lodge of my father, or that there was more grub on the Chilcat. When you have spoken, I have listened. When you have ordered, I have obeyed. Is it not so, Charley?'

"And I said: 'Ay, it is so.'

"And she said: 'When first you came to the Chilcat, nor looked upon me, but bought me as a man buys a dog, and took me away, my heart was hard against you and filled with bitterness and fear. But that was long ago. For you were kind to me, Charley, as a good man is kind to his dog. Your heart was cold, and there was no room for me; yet you dealt me fair and your ways were just. And I was with you when you did bold deeds and led great ventures, and I measured you against the men of other breeds, and I saw you stood among them full of honor, and your word was wise, your tongue true. And I grew proud of you, till it came that you filled all my heart, and all my thought was of you. You were as the midsummer sun, when its golden trail runs in a circle and never leaves the sky. And whatever way I cast my eyes I beheld the sun. But your heart was ever cold, Charley, and there was no room.'

"And I said: 'It is so. It was cold, and there was no room. But that is past. Now my heart is like the snowfall in the spring, when the sun has come back. There is a great thaw and a bending, a sound of running waters, and a budding and sprouting of green things. And there is drumming of partridges, and songs of robins, and great music, for the winter is broken, Passuk, and I have learned the love of woman.'

"She smiled and moved for me to draw her closer. And she said, 'I am glad.' After that she lay quiet for a long time, breathing softly, her head upon my breast. Then she whispered: 'The trail ends here, and I am tired. But first I would speak of other things. In the long ago, when I was a girl on the Chilcat, I played alone among the skin bales of my father's lodge; for the men were away on the hunt, and the women and boys were dragging in the meat. It was in the spring, and I was alone. A great brown bear, just awake from his winter's sleep, hungry, his fur hanging to the bones in flaps of leanness, shoved his head within the lodge and said, "Oof!" My brother came running back with the first sled of meat. And he fought the bear with burning sticks from the fire, and the dogs in their harnesses, with the sled behind them, fell upon the bear. There was a great battle and much noise. They rolled in the fire, the skin bales were scattered, the lodge overthrown. But in the end the bear lay dead, with the fingers of my brother in his mouth and the marks of his claws upon my brother's face. Did you mark the Indian by the Pelly trail, his mitten which had no thumb, his hand which he warmed by our fire? He was my brother. And I said he should have no grub. And he went away in the Silence without grub.'

"This, my brothers, was the love of Passuk, who died in the snow, by the Caribou Crossing. It was a mighty love, for she denied her brother for the man who led her away on weary trails to a bitter end. And, further, such was this woman's love, she denied herself. Ere her eyes closed for the last time she took my hand and slipped it under her squirrel-skin *parka* to her waist. I felt there a well-filled pouch, and learned the secret of her lost strength. Day by day we had shared fair, to the last least bit; and day by day but half her share had she eaten. The other half had gone into the well-filled pouch.

"And she said: 'This is the end of the trail for Passuk; but your trail, Charley, leads on and on, over the great Chilcoot, down to Haines Mission and the sea. And it leads on and on, by the light of many suns, over unknown lands and strange waters, and it is full of years and honors and great glories. It leads you to the lodges of many women, and good women, but it will never lead you to a greater love than the love of Passuk.'

"And I knew the woman spoke true. But a madness came upon me, and I threw the well-filled pouch from me, and swore that my trail had reached an end, till her tired eyes grew soft with tears, and she said: 'Among men has Sitka Charley walked in honor, and ever has his word been true. Does he forget that honor now, and talk vain words by the Caribou Crossing? Does he remember no more the men of Forty Mile, who gave him of their grub the best, of their dogs the pick? Ever has Passuk been proud of her man. Let him lift himself up, gird on his snowshoes, and begone, that she may still keep her pride.'

"And when she grew cold in my arms I arose, and sought out the well-filled pouch, and girt on my snowshoes, and staggered along the trail; for there was a weakness in my knees, and my head was dizzy, and in my ears there was a roaring, and a flashing of fire upon my eyes. The forgotten trails of boyhood came back to me. I sat by the full pots of the *potlach* feast, and raised my voice in song, and danced to the chanting of the men and maidens and the booming of the walrus drums. And Passuk held my hand and walked by my side. When I laid down to sleep, she waked me. When I stumbled and fell, she raised me. When I wandered in the deep snow, she led me back to the trail. And in this wise, like a man bereft of reason, who sees strange visions and whose thoughts are light with wine, I came to Haines Mission by the sea."

Sitka Charley threw back the tent-flaps. It was midday. To the south, just clearing the bleak Henderson Divide, poised the cold-disked sun. On either hand the sun-dogs blazed. The air was a gossamer of glittering frost. In the foreground, beside the trail, a wolf-dog, bristling with frost, thrust a long snout heavenward and mourned.

Where the Trail Forks

"Must I, then, must I, then, now leave this town—
And you, my love, stay here?"
—SCHWABIAN FOLK-SONG.

The singer, clean-faced and cheery-eyed, bent over and added water to a pot of simmering beans, and then, rising, a stick of firewood in hand, drove back the circling dogs from the grub-box and cooking-gear. He was blue of eye, and his long hair was golden, and it was a pleasure to look upon his lusty freshness. A new moon was thrusting a dim horn above the white line of close-packed snow-capped pines which ringed the camp and segregated it from all the world. Overhead, so clear it was and cold, the stars danced with quick, pulsating movements. To the southeast an evanescent greenish glow heralded the opening revels of the aurora borealis. Two men, in the immediate foreground, lay upon the bearskin which was their bed. Between the skin and naked snow was a six-inch layer of pine boughs. The blankets were rolled back. For shelter, there was a fly at their backs,—a sheet of canvas stretched between two trees and angling at forty-five degrees. This caught the radiating heat from the fire and flung it down upon the skin. Another man sat on a sled, drawn close to the blaze, mending moccasins. To the right, a heap of frozen gravel and a rude windlass denoted where they toiled each day in dismal groping for the pay-streak. To the left, four pairs of snowshoes stood erect, showing the mode of travel which obtained when the stamped snow of the camp was left behind.

That Schwabian folk-song sounded strangely pathetic under the cold northern stars, and did not do the men good who lounged about the fire after the toil of the day. It put a dull ache into their hearts, and a yearning which was akin to belly-hunger, and sent their souls questing southward across the divides to the sun-lands.

"For the love of God, Sigmund, shut up!" expostulated one of the men. His hands were clenched painfully, but he hid them from sight in the folds of the bearskin upon which he lay.

"And what for, Dave Wertz?" Sigmund demanded. "Why shall I not sing when the heart is glad?"

"Because you 've got no call to, that 's why. Look about you, man, and think of the grub we 've been defiling our bodies with for the last twelvemonth, and the way we 've lived and worked like beasts!"

Thus abjured, Sigmund, the golden-haired, surveyed it all, and the frost-rimmed wolf-dogs and the vapor breaths of the men. "And why shall not the heart be glad?" he laughed. "It is good; it is all good. As for the grub—" He doubled up his arm and caressed the swelling biceps. "And if we have lived and worked like beasts, have we not been paid like kings? Twenty dollars to the pan the streak is running, and we know it to be eight feet thick. It is another Klondike—and we know it—Jim Hawes there, by your elbow, knows it and complains not. And there 's Hitchcock! He sews moccasins like an old woman, and waits against the time. Only you can't wait and work until the wash-up in the spring. Then we shall all be rich, rich as kings, only you cannot wait. You want to go back to the States. So do I, and I was born there, but I can wait, when each day the gold in the pan shows up yellow as butter in the churning. But you want your good time, and, like a child, you cry for it now. Bah! Why shall I not sing:

> "In a year, in a year, when the grapes are ripe,
>   I shall stay no more away.
> Then if you still are true, my love,
>   It will be our wedding day.
> In a year, in a year, when my time is past,
>   Then I 'll live in your love for aye.
> Then if you still are true, my love,
>   It will be our wedding day."

The dogs, bristling and growling, drew in closer to the firelight. There was a monotonous crunch-crunch of webbed shoes, and between each crunch the dragging forward of the heel of the shoe like the sound of sifting sugar. Sigmund broke off from his song to hurl oaths and firewood at the animals. Then the light was parted by a fur-clad figure, and an Indian girl slipped out of the webs, threw back the hood of her squirrel-skin *parka,* and stood in their midst. Sigmund and the men on the bearskin greeted her as "Sipsu," with the customary "Hello," but Hitchcock made room on the sled that she might sit beside him.

"And how goes it, Sipsu?" he asked, talking, after her fashion, in broken English and bastard Chinook. "Is the hunger still mighty in the camp? and has the witch doctor yet found the cause wherefore game is scarce and no moose in the land?"

"Yes; even so. There is little game, and we prepare to eat the dogs. Also has the witch doctor found the cause of all this evil, and tomorrow will he make sacrifice and cleanse the camp."

"And what does the sacrifice chance to be?—a new-born babe or some poor devil of a squaw, old and shaky, who is a care to the tribe and better out of the way?"

"It chanced not that wise; for the need was great, and he chose none other than the chief's daughter; none other than I, Sipsu."

"Hell!" The word rose slowly to Hitchcock's lips, and brimmed over full and deep, in a way which bespoke wonder and consideration.

"Wherefore we stand by a forking of the trail, you and I," she went on calmly, "and I have come that we may look once more upon each other, and once more only."

She was born of primitive stock, and primitive had been her traditions and her days; so she regarded life stoically, and human sacrifice as part of the natural order. The powers which ruled the daylight and the dark, the flood and the frost, the bursting of the bud and the withering of the leaf, were angry and in need of propitiation. This they exacted in many ways,—death in the bad water, through the treacherous ice-crust, by the grip of the grizzly, or a wasting sickness which fell upon a man in his own lodge till he coughed, and the life of his lungs went out through his mouth and nostrils. Likewise did the powers receive sacrifice. It was all one. And the witch doctor was versed in the thoughts of the powers and chose unerringly. It was very natural. Death came by many ways, yet was it all one after all,—a manifestation of the all-powerful and inscrutable.

But Hitchcock came of a later world-breed. His traditions were less concrete and without reverence, and he said, "Not so, Sipsu. You are young, and yet in the full joy of life. The witch doctor is a fool, and his choice is evil. This thing shall not be."

She smiled and answered, "Life is not kind, and for many reasons. First, it made of us twain the one white and the other red, which is bad. Then it crossed our trails, and now it parts them again; and we can do nothing. Once before, when the gods were angry, did your brothers come to the camp. They were three, big men and white, and they said the thing shall not be. But they died quickly, and the thing was."

Hitchcock nodded that he heard, half-turned, and lifted his voice. "Look here, you fellows! There 's a lot of foolery going on over to the camp, and they 're getting ready to murder Sipsu. What d' ye say?"

Wertz looked at Hawes, and Hawes looked back, but neither spoke. Sigmund dropped his head, and petted the shepherd dog between his knees. He had brought Shep in with him from the outside, and thought a great deal of the animal. In fact, a certain girl, who was much in his thoughts, and whose picture in the little locket on his breast often inspired him to sing, had given him the dog and her blessing when they kissed good-by and he started on his Northland quest.

"What d' ye say?" Hitchcock repeated.

"Mebbe it 's not so serious," Hawes answered with deliberation. "Most likely it 's only a girl's story."

"That is n't the point!" Hitchcock felt a hot flush of anger sweep over him at their evident reluctance. "The question is, if it is so, are we going to stand it? What are we going to do?"

"I don't see any call to interfere," spoke up Wertz. "If it is so, it is so, and that 's all there is about it. It 's a way these people have of doing. It 's their religion, and it 's no concern of ours. Our concern is to get the dust and then get out of this God-forsaken land. 'T is n't fit for naught else but beasts? And what are these black devils but beasts? Besides, it 'd be damn poor policy."

"That 's what I say," chimed in Hawes.

"Here we are, four of us, three hundred miles from the Yukon or a white face. And what can we do against half-a-hundred

Indians? If we quarrel with them, we have to vamose; if we fight, we are wiped out. Further, we 've struck pay, and, by God! I, for one, am going to stick by it!"

"Ditto here," supplemented Wertz.

Hitchcock turned impatiently to Sigmund, who was softly singing,—

> *"In a year, in a year, when the grapes are ripe,*
> *I shall stay no more away."*

"Well, it 's this way, Hitchcock," he finally said, "I 'm in the same boat with the rest. If three-score bucks have made up their mind to kill the girl, why, we can't help it. One rush, and we 'd be wiped off the landscape. And what good 'd that be? They 'd still have the girl. There 's no use in going against the customs of a people except you 're in force."

"But we are in force!" Hitchcock broke in.

"Four whites are a match for a hundred times as many reds. And think of the girl!"

Sigmund stroked the dog meditatively. "But I do think of the girl. And her eyes are blue like summer skies, and laughing like summer seas, and her hair is yellow, like mine, and braided in ropes the size of a big man's arms. She 's waiting for me, out there, in a better land. And she 's waited long, and now my pile 's in sight I 'm not going to throw it away."

"And shamed I would be to look into the girl's blue eyes and remember the black ones of the girl whose blood was on my hands," Hitchcock sneered; for he was born to honor and championship, and to do the thing for the thing's sake, nor stop to weigh or measure.

Sigmund shook his head. "You can't make me mad, Hitchcock, nor do mad things because of your madness. It 's a cold business proposition and a question of facts. I did n't come to this country for my health, and, further, it 's impossible for us to raise a hand. If it is so, it is too bad for the girl, that 's all. It 's a way of her people, and it just happens we 're on the spot this one time. They 've done the same for a thousand-thousand years, and they 're

going to do it now, and they 'll go on doing it for all time to
come. Besides, they 're not our kind. Nor 's the girl. No, I take
my stand with Wertz and Hawes, and—"

But the dogs snarled and drew in, and he broke off, listening
to the crunch-crunch of many snowshoes. Indian after Indian
stalked into the firelight, tall and grim, fur-clad and silent, their
shadows dancing grotesquely on the snow. One, the witch doctor,
spoke gutturally to Sipsu. His face was daubed with savage paint
blotches, and over his shoulders was drawn a wolfskin, the gleaming teeth and cruel snout surmounting his head. No other word
was spoken. The prospectors held the peace. Sipsu arose and
slipped into her snowshoes.

"Good-by, O my man," she said to Hitchcock. But the man
who had sat beside her on the sled gave no sign, nor lifted his
head as they filed away into the white forest.

Unlike many men, his faculty of adaptation, while large, had
never suggested the expediency of an alliance with the women of
the Northland. His broad cosmopolitanism had never impelled
toward covenanting in marriage with the daughters of the soil. If
it had, his philosophy of life would not have stood between. But
it simply had not. Sipsu? He had pleasured in camp-fire chats with
her, not as a man who knew himself to be man and she woman,
but as a man might with a child, and as a man of his make certainly
would if for no other reason than to vary the tedium of a bleak
existence. That was all. But there was a certain chivalric thrill of
warm blood in him, despite his Yankee ancestry and New England upbringing, and he was so made that the commercial aspect
of life often seemed meaningless and bore contradiction to his
deeper impulses.

So he sat silent, with head bowed forward, an organic force,
greater than himself, as great as his race, at work within him.
Wertz and Hawes looked askance at him from time to time, a
faint but perceptible trepidation in their manner. Sigmund also
felt this. Hitchcock was strong, and his strength had been impressed upon them in the course of many an event in their pre-
carious life. So they stood in a certain definite awe and curiosity
as to what his conduct would be when he moved to action.

But his silence was long, and the fire nigh out, when Wertz stretched his arms and yawned, and thought he 'd go to bed. Then Hitchcock stood up his full height.

"May God damn your souls to the deepest hells, you chicken-hearted cowards! I 'm done with you!" He said it calmly enough, but his strength spoke in every syllable, and every intonation was advertisement of intention. "Come on," he continued, "whack up, and in whatever way suits you best. I own a quarter-interest in the claims; our contracts show that. There 're twenty-five or thirty ounces in the sack from the test pans. Fetch out the scales. We 'll divide that now. And you, Sigmund, measure me my quarter-share of the grub and set it apart. Four of the dogs are mine, and I want four more. I 'll trade you my share in the camp outfit and mining-gear for the dogs. And I 'll throw in my six or seven ounces and the spare 45-90 with the ammunition. What d' ye say?"

The three men drew apart and conferred. When they returned, Sigmund acted as spokesman. "We 'll whack up fair with you, Hitchcock. In everything you 'll get your quarter-share, neither more nor less; and you can take it or leave it. But we want the dogs as bad as you do, so you get four, and that 's all. If you don't want to take your share of the outfit and gear, why, that 's your lookout. If you want it, you can have it; if you don't, leave it."

"The letter of the law," Hitchcock sneered.

"But go ahead. I 'm willing. And hurry up. I can't get out of this camp and away from its vermin any too quick."

The division was effected without further comment. He lashed his meagre belongings upon one of the sleds, rounded in his four dogs, and harnessed up. His portion of outfit and gear he did not touch, though he threw onto the sled half a dozen dog harnesses, and challenged them with his eyes to interfere. But they shrugged their shoulders and watched him disappear in the forest.

A man crawled upon his belly through the snow. On every hand loomed the moose-hide lodges of the camp. Here and there a miserable dog howled or snarled abuse upon his neighbor. Once, one of them approached the creeping man, but the man became motionless. The dog came closer and sniffed, and came yet closer, till its nose touched the strange object which had not been there when darkness fell. Then Hitchcock, for it was Hitchcock, up-reared suddenly, shooting an unmittened hand out to the brute's shaggy throat. And the dog knew its death in that clutch, and when the man moved on, was left broken-necked under the stars. In this manner Hitchcock made the chief's lodge. For long he lay in the snow without, listening to the voices of the occupants and striving to locate Sipsu. Evidently there were many in the tent, and from the sounds they were in high excitement.

At last he heard the girl's voice, and crawled around so that only the moose-hide divided them. Then burrowing in the snow, he slowly wormed his head and shoulders underneath. When the warm inner air smote his face, he stopped and waited, his legs and the greater part of his body still on the outside. He could see nothing, nor did he dare lift his head. On one side of him was a skin bale. He could smell it, though he carefully felt to be certain. On the other side his face barely touched a furry garment which he knew clothed a body. This must be Sipsu. Though he wished she would speak again, he resolved to risk it.

He could hear the chief and the witch doctor talking high, and in a far corner some hungry child whimpering to sleep. Squirming over on his side, he carefully raised his head, still just touching the furry garment. He listened to the breathing. It was a woman's breathing; he would chance it.

He pressed against her side softly but firmly, and felt her start at the contact. Again he waited, till a questioning hand slipped down upon his head and paused among the curls. The next instant the hand turned his face gently upward, and he was gazing into Sipsu's eyes.

She was quite collected. Changing her position casually, she threw an elbow well over on the skin bale, rested her body upon it, and arranged her *parka*. In this way he was completely con-cealed. Then, and still most casually, she reclined across him, so that he could breathe between her arm and breast, and when she lowered her head her ear pressed lightly against his lips.

"When the time suits, go thou," he whispered, "out of the lodge and across the snow, down the wind to the bunch of jack-

pine in the curve of the creek. There wilt thou find my dogs and
my sled, packed for the trail. This night we go down to the Yukon; and since we go fast, lay thou hands upon what dogs come
nigh thee, by the scruff of the neck, and drag them to the sled in
the curve of the creek."

Sipsu shook her head in dissent; but her eyes glistened with
gladness, and she was proud that this man had shown toward her
such favor. But she, like the women of all her race, was born to
obey the will masculine, and when Hitchcock repeated "Go!" he
did it with authority, and though she made no answer he knew
that his will was law.

"And never mind harness for the dogs," he added, preparing
to go. "I shall wait. But waste no time. The day chaseth the night
alway, nor does it linger for man's pleasure."

Half an hour later, stamping his feet and swinging his arms by
the sled, he saw her coming, a surly dog in either hand. At the
approach of these his own animals waxed truculent, and he favored them with the butt of his whip till they quieted. He had
approached the camp up the wind, and sound was the thing to be
most feared in making his presence known.

"Put them into the sled," he ordered when she had got the
harness on the two dogs. "I want my leaders to the fore."

But when she had done this, the displaced animals pitched
upon the aliens. Though Hitchcock plunged among them with
clubbed rifle, a riot of sound went up and across the sleeping
camp.

"Now we shall have dogs, and in plenty," he remarked grimly,
slipping an axe from the sled lashings. "Do thou harness which-
ever I fling thee, and betweenwhiles protect the team."

He stepped a space in advance and waited between two pines.
The dogs of the camp were disturbing the night with their jangle,
and he watched for their coming. A dark spot, growing rapidly,
took form upon the dim white expanse of snow. It was a forerunner of the pack, leaping cleanly, and, after the wolf fashion,
singing direction to its brothers. Hitchcock stood in the shadow.
As it sprang past, he reached out, gripped its forelegs in mid-
career, and sent it whirling earthward. Then he struck it a well-
judged blow beneath the ear, and flung it to Sipsu. And while

she clapped on the harness, he, with his axe, held the passage between the trees, till a shaggy flood of white teeth and glistening eyes surged and crested just beyond reach. Sipsu worked rapidly. When she had finished, he leaped forward, seized and stunned a second, and flung it to her. This he repeated thrice again, and when the sled team stood snarling in a string of ten, he called, "Enough!"

But at this instant a young buck, the forerunner of the tribe, and swift of limb, wading through the dogs and cuffing right and left, attempted the passage. The butt of Hitchcock's rifle drove him to his knees, whence he toppled over sideways. The witch doctor, running lustily, saw the blow fall.

Hitchcock called to Sipsu to pull out. At her shrill "Chook!" the maddened brutes shot straight ahead, and the sled, bounding mightily, just missed unseating her. The powers were evidently angry with the witch doctor, for at this moment they plunged him upon the trail. The lead-dog fouled his snowshoes and tripped him up, and the nine succeeding dogs trod him under foot and the sled bumped over him. But he was quick to his feet, and the night might have turned out differently had not Sipsu struck backward with the long dog-whip and smitten him a blinding blow across the eyes. Hitchcock, hurrying to overtake her, collided against him as he swayed with pain in the middle of the trail. Thus it was, when this primitive theologian got back to the chief's lodge, that his wisdom had been increased in so far as concerns the efficacy of the white man's fist. So, when he orated then and there in the council, he was wroth against all white men.

"Tumble out, you loafers! Tumble out! Grub 'll be ready before you get into your footgear!"

Dave Wertz threw off the bearskin, sat up, and yawned.

Hawes stretched, discovered a lame muscle in his arm, and rubbed it sleepily. "Wonder where Hitchcock bunked last night?" he queried, reaching for his moccasins. They were stiff, and he walked gingerly in his socks to the fire to thaw them out. "It 's a blessing he 's gone," he added, "though he was a mighty good worker."

"Yep. Too masterful. That was his trouble. Too bad for Sipsu. Think he cared for her much?"

"Don't think so. Just principle. That 's all. He thought it was n't right—and, of course, it was n't,—but that was no reason for us to interfere and get hustled over the divide before our time."

"Principle is principle, and it 's good in its place, but it 's best left to home when you go to Alaska. Eh?" Wertz had joined his mate, and both were working pliability into their frozen moccasins. "Think we ought to have taken a hand?"

Sigmund shook his head. He was very busy. A scud of chocolate-colored foam was rising in the coffee-pot, and the bacon needed turning. Also, he was thinking about the girl with laughing eyes like summer seas, and he was humming softly.

His mates chuckled to each other and ceased talking. Though it was past seven, daybreak was still three hours distant. The aurora borealis had passed out of the sky, and the camp was an oasis of light in the midst of deep darkness. And in this light the forms of the three men were sharply defined. Emboldened by the silence, Sigmund raised his voice and opened the last stanza of the old song:—

"In a year, in a year, when the grapes are ripe—"

Then the night was split with a rattling volley of rifle-shots. Hawes sighed, made an effort to straighten himself, and collapsed. Wertz went over on an elbow with drooping head. He choked a little, and a dark stream flowed from his mouth. And Sigmund, the Golden-Haired, his throat a-gurgle with the song, threw up his arms and pitched across the fire.

The witch doctor's eyes were well blackened, and his temper none of the best; for he quarrelled with the chief over the possession of Wertz's rifle, and took more than his share of the part-sack of beans. Also he appropriated the bearskin, and caused grumbling among the tribesmen. And finally, he tried to kill Sigmund's dog, which the girl had given him, but the dog ran away, while he fell into the shaft and dislocated his shoulder on the bucket. When the camp was well looted they went back to their own lodges, and there was a great rejoicing among the women. Further, a band of moose strayed over the south divide and fell before the hunters, so the witch doctor attained yet greater honor, and the people whispered among themselves that he spoke in council with the gods.

But later, when all were gone, the shepherd dog crept back to the deserted camp, and all the night long and a day it wailed the dead. After that it disappeared, though the years were not many before the Indian hunters noted a change in the breed of timber wolves, and there were dashes of bright color and variegated markings such as no wolf bore before.

The Law of Life

Old Koskoosh listened greedily. Though his sight had long since faded, his hearing was still acute, and the slightest sound penetrated to the glimmering intelligence which yet abode behind the withered forehead, but which no longer gazed forth upon the things of the world. Ah! that was Sit-cum-to-ha, shrilly anathematizing the dogs as she cuffed and beat them into the harnesses. Sit-cum-to-ha was his daughter's daughter, but she was too busy to waste a thought upon her broken grandfather, sitting alone there in the snow, forlorn and helpless. Camp must be broken. The long trail waited while the short day refused to linger. Life called her, and the duties of life, not death. And he was very close to death now.

The thought made the old man panicky for the moment, and he stretched forth a palsied hand which wandered tremblingly over the small heap of dry wood beside him. Reassured that it was indeed there, his hand returned to the shelter of his mangy furs, and he again fell to listening. The sulky crackling of half-frozen hides told him that the chief's moose-skin lodge had been struck, and even then was being rammed and jammed into portable compass. The chief was his son, stalwart and strong, head man of the tribesmen, and a mighty hunter. As the women toiled with the camp luggage, his voice rose, chiding them for their slowness. Old Koskoosh strained his ears. It was the last time he would hear that voice. There went Geehow's lodge! And Tusken's! Seven, eight, nine; only the shaman's could be still standing. There! They were at work upon it now. He could hear the shaman grunt as he piled it on the sled. A child whimpered, and a woman soothed it with soft, crooning gutturals. Little Koo-tee, the old man thought, a fretful child, and not overstrong. It would die soon, perhaps, and they would burn a hole through the frozen tundra and pile rocks above to keep the wolverines away. Well, what did it matter? A few years at best, and as many an empty belly as a full one. And in the end, Death waited, ever-hungry and hungriest of them all.

What was that? Oh, the men lashing the sleds and drawing tight the thongs. He listened, who would listen no more. The whip-lashes snarled and bit among the dogs. Hear them whine! How they hated the work and the trail! They were off! Sled after sled churned slowly away into the silence. They were gone. They had passed out of his life, and he faced the last bitter hour alone. No. The snow crunched beneath a moccasin; a man stood beside him; upon his head a hand rested gently. His son was good to do this thing. He remembered other old men whose sons had not waited after the tribe. But his son had. He wandered away into the past, till the young man's voice brought him back.

"Is it well with you?" he asked.

And the old man answered, "It is well."

"There be wood beside you," the younger man continued, "and the fire burns bright. The morning is gray, and the cold has broken. It will snow presently. Even now is it snowing."

"Ay, even now is it snowing."

"The tribesmen hurry. Their bales are heavy, and their bellies flat with lack of feasting. The trail is long and they travel fast. I go now. It is well?"

"It is well. I am as a last year's leaf, clinging lightly to the stem. The first breath that blows, and I fall. My voice is become like an old woman's. My eyes no longer show me the way of my feet, and my feet are heavy, and I am tired. It is well."

He bowed his head in content till the last noise of the complaining snow had died away, and he knew his son was beyond recall. Then his hand crept out in haste to the wood. It alone stood between him and the eternity that yawned in upon him. At last the measure of his life was a handful of fagots. One by one they would go to feed the fire, and just so, step by step, death would creep upon him. When the last stick had surrendered up its heat, the frost would begin to gather strength. First his feet would yield, then his hands; and the numbness would travel, slowly, from the extremities to the body. His head would fall forward upon his knees, and he would rest. It was easy. All men must die.

He did not complain. It was the way of life, and it was just. He had been born close to the earth, close to the earth had he lived, and the law thereof was not new to him. It was the law of all flesh. Nature was not kindly to the flesh. She had no concern for that concrete thing called the individual. Her interest lay in the species, the race. This was the deepest abstraction old Koskoosh's barbaric mind was capable of, but he grasped it firmly. He saw it exemplified in all life. The rise of the sap, the bursting greenness of the willow bud, the fall of the yellow leaf—in this alone was told the whole history. But one task did Nature set the individual. Did he not perform it, he died. Did he perform it, it was all the same, he died. Nature did not care; there were plenty who were obedient, and it was only the obedience in this matter, not the obedient, which lived and lived always. The tribe of Koskoosh was very old. The old men he had known when a boy, had known old men before them. Therefore it was true that the tribe lived, that it stood for the obedience of all its members, way down into the forgotten past, whose very resting-places were unremembered. They did not count; they were episodes. They had passed away like clouds from a summer sky. He also was an episode, and would pass away. Nature did not care. To life she set one task, gave one law. To perpetuate was the task of life, its law was death. A maiden was a good creature to look upon, full-breasted and strong, with spring to her step and light in her eyes. But her task was yet before her. The light in her eyes brightened, her step quickened, she was now bold with the young men, now timid, and she gave them of her own unrest. And ever she grew fairer and yet fairer to look upon, till some hunter, able no longer to withhold himself, took her to his lodge to cook and toil for him and to become the mother of his children. And with the coming of her offspring her looks left her. Her limbs dragged and shuffled, her eyes dimmed and bleared, and only the little children found joy against the withered cheek of the old squaw by the fire. Her task was done. But a little while, on the first pinch of famine or the first long trail, and she would be left, even as he had been left, in the snow, with a little pile of wood. Such was the law.

He placed a stick carefully upon the fire and resumed his meditations. It was the same everywhere, with all things. The mosquitoes vanished with the first frost. The little tree-squirrel crawled away to die. When age settled upon the rabbit it became slow and heavy, and could no longer outfoot its enemies. Even the big bald-face grew clumsy and blind and quarrelsome, in the end to be dragged down by a handful of yelping huskies. He remembered how he had abandoned his own father on an upper reach of the Klondike one winter, the winter before the missionary came with his talk-books and his box of medicines. Many a time had Koskoosh smacked his lips over the recollection of that box, though now his mouth refused to moisten. The "painkiller" had been especially good. But the missionary was a bother after all, for he brought no meat into the camp, and he ate heartily, and the hunters grumbled. But he chilled his lungs on the divide by the Mayo, and the dogs afterwards nosed the stones away and fought over his bones.

Koskoosh placed another stick on the fire and harked back deeper into the past. There was the time of the Great Famine, when the old men crouched empty-bellied to the fire, and let fall from their lips dim traditions of the ancient day when the Yukon ran wide open for three winters, and then lay frozen for three summers. He had lost his mother in that famine. In the summer the salmon run had failed, and the tribe looked forward to the winter and the coming of the caribou. Then the winter came, but with it there were no caribou. Never had the like been known, not even in the lives of the old men. But the caribou did not come, and it was the seventh year, and the rabbits had not replenished, and the dogs were naught but bundles of bones. And through the long darkness the children wailed and died, and the women, and the old men; and not one in ten of the tribe lived to meet the sun when it came back in the spring. That *was* a famine!

But he had seen times of plenty, too, when the meat spoiled on their hands, and the dogs were fat and worthless with overeating—times when they let the game go unkilled, and the women were fertile, and the lodges were cluttered with sprawling men-children and women-children. Then it was the men became high-stomached, and revived ancient quarrels, and crossed the divides to the south to kill the Pellys, and to the west that they might sit by the dead fires of the Tananas. He remembered, when a boy, during a time of plenty, when he saw a moose pulled down by the wolves. Zing-ha lay with him in the snow and watched—Zing-ha, who later became the craftiest of hunters, and who, in the end, fell through an air-hole on the Yukon. They found him, a month afterward, just as he had crawled halfway out and frozen stiff to the ice.

But the moose. Zing-ha and he had gone out that day to play at hunting after the manner of their fathers. On the bed of the creek they struck the fresh track of a moose, and with it the tracks of many wolves. "An old one," Zing-ha, who was quicker at reading the sign, said—"an old one who cannot keep up with the herd. The wolves have cut him out from his brothers, and they will never leave him." And it was so. It was their way. By day and by night, never resting, snarling on his heels, snapping at his nose, they would stay by him to the end. How Zing-ha and he felt the blood-lust quicken! The finish would be a sight to see!

Eager-footed, they took the trail, and even he, Koskoosh, slow of sight and an unversed tracker, could have followed it blind, it was so wide. Hot were they on the heels of the chase, reading the grim tragedy, fresh-written, at every step. Now they came to where the moose had made a stand. Thrice the length of a grown man's body, in every direction, had the snow been stamped about and uptossed. In the midst were the deep impressions of the splay-hoofed game, and all about, everywhere, were the lighter foot-marks of the wolves. Some, while their brothers harried the kill, had lain to one side and rested. The full-stretched impress of their bodies in the snow was as perfect as though made the moment before. One wolf had been caught in a wild lunge of the maddened victim and trampled to death. A few bones, well picked, bore witness.

Again, they ceased the uplift of their snowshoes at a second stand. Here the great animal had fought desperately. Twice had he been dragged down, as the snow attested, and twice had he shaken his assailants clear and gained footing once more. He had done his task long since, but none the less was life dear to him. Zing-ha said it was a strange thing, a moose once down to get free again; but this one certainly had. The shaman would see signs and wonders in this when they told him.

And yet again, they come to where the moose had made to mount the bank and gain the timber. But his foes had laid on from behind, till he reared and fell back upon them, crushing two deep into the snow. It was plain the kill was at hand, for their brothers had left them untouched. Two more stands were hurried past, brief in time-length and very close together. The trail was red now, and the clean stride of the great beast had grown short and slovenly. Then they heard the first sounds of the battle—not the full-throated chorus of the chase, but the short, snappy bark which spoke of close quarters and teeth to flesh. Crawling up the wind, Zing-ha bellied it through the snow, and with him crept he, Koskoosh, who was to be chief of the tribesmen in the years to come. Together they shoved aside the under branches of a young spruce and peered forth. It was the end they saw.

The picture, like all of youth's impressions, was still strong with him, and his dim eyes watched the end played out as vividly as in that far-off time. Koskoosh marvelled at this, for in the days which followed, when he was a leader of men and a head of councillors, he had done great deeds and made his name a curse in the mouths of the Pellys, to say naught of the strange white man he had killed, knife to knife, in open fight.

For long he pondered on the days of his youth, till the fire died down and the frost bit deeper. He replenished it with two sticks this time, and gauged his grip on life by what remained. If Sit-cum-to-ha had only remembered her grandfather, and gathered a larger armful, his hours would have been longer. It would have been easy. But she was ever a careless child, and honored not her ancestors from the time the Beaver, son of the son of Zing-ha, first cast eyes upon her. Well, what mattered it? Had he not done likewise in his own quick youth? For a while he listened to the silence. Perhaps the heart of his son might soften, and he would come back with the dogs to take his old father on with the tribe to where the caribou ran thick and the fat hung heavy upon them.

He strained his ears, his restless brain for the moment stilled. Not a stir, nothing. He alone took breath in the midst of the great silence. It was very lonely. Hark! What was that? A chill passed over his body. The familiar, long-drawn howl broke the void, and it was close at hand. Then on his darkened eyes was projected the vision of the moose—the old bull moose—the torn flanks and bloody sides, the riddled mane, and the great branching horns, down low and tossing to the last. He saw the flashing forms of gray, the gleaming eyes, the lolling tongues, the slavered fangs. And he saw the inexorable circle close in till it became a dark point in the midst of the stamped snow.

A cold muzzle thrust against his cheek, and at its touch his soul leaped back to the present. His hand shot into the fire and dragged out a burning faggot. Overcome for the nonce by his hereditary fear of man, the brute retreated, raising a prolonged call to his brothers; and greedily they answered, till a ring of crouching, jaw-slobbered gray was stretched round about. The old man listened to the drawing in of this circle. He waved his brand wildly, and sniffs turned to snarls; but the panting brutes refused to scatter. Now one wormed his chest forward, dragging his haunches after, now a second, now a third; but never a one drew back. Why should he cling to life? he asked, and dropped the blazing stick into the snow. It sizzled and went out. The circle grunted uneasily, but held its own. Again he saw the last stand of the old bull moose, and Koskoosh dropped his head wearily upon his knees. What did it matter after all? Was it not the law of life?

Keesh, the Son of Keesh

"Thus will I give six blankets, warm and double; six files, large and hard; six Hudson Bay knives, keen-edged and long; two canoes, the work of Mogum, The Maker of Things; ten dogs, heavy-shouldered and strong in the harness; and three guns—the trigger of one be broken, but it is a good gun and can doubtless be mended."

Keesh paused and swept his eyes over the circle of intent faces. It was the time of the Great Fishing, and he was bidding to Gnob for Su-Su his daughter. The place was the St. George Mission by the Yukon, and the tribes had gathered for many a hundred miles. From north, south, east, and west they had come, even from Tozikakat and far Tana-naw.

"And further, O Gnob, thou art chief of the Tana-naw; and I, Keesh, the son of Keesh, am chief of the Thlunget. Wherefore, when my seed springs from the loins of thy daughter, there shall be a friendship between the tribes, a great friendship, and Tana-naw and Thlunget shall be brothers of the blood in the time to come. What I have said I will do, that will I do. And how is it with you, O Gnob, in this matter?"

Gnob nodded his head gravely, his gnarled and age-twisted face inscrutably masking the soul that dwelt behind. His narrow eyes burned like twin coals through their narrow slits, as he piped in a high-cracked voice, "But that is not all."

"What more?" Keesh demanded. "Have I not offered full measure? Was there ever yet a Tana-naw maiden who fetched so great a price? Then name her!"

An open snicker passed round the circle, and Keesh knew that he stood in shame before these people.

"Nay, nay, good Keesh, thou dost not understand." Gnob made a soft, stroking gesture. "The price is fair. It is a good price. Nor do I question the broken trigger. But that is not all. What of the man?"

"Ay, what of the man?" the circle snarled.

"It is said," Gnob's shrill voice piped, "it is said that Keesh does not walk in the way of his fathers. It is said that he has wandered into the dark, after strange gods, and that he is become afraid."

The face of Keesh went dark. "It is a lie!" he thundered. "Keesh is afraid of no man!"

"It is said," old Gnob piped on, "that he has harkened to the speech of the white man up at the Big House, and that he bends head to the white man's god, and, moreover, that blood is displeasing to the white man's god."

Keesh dropped his eyes, and his hands clenched passionately. The savage circle laughed derisively, and in the ear of Gnob whispered Madwan, the shaman, high-priest of the tribe and maker of medicine.

The shaman poked among the shadows on the rim of the firelight and roused up a slender young boy, whom he brought face to face with Keesh; and in the hand of Keesh he thrust a knife.

Gnob leaned forward. "Keesh! O Keesh! Darest thou to kill a man? Behold! This be Kitz-noo, a slave. Strike, O Keesh, strike with the strength of thy arm!"

The boy trembled and waited the stroke. Keesh looked at him, and thoughts of Mr. Brown's higher morality floated through his mind, and strong upon him was a vision of the leaping flames of Mr. Brown's particular brand of hell-fire. The knife fell to the ground, and the boy sighed and went out beyond the firelight with shaking knees. At the feet of Gnob sprawled a wolf-dog, which bared its gleaming teeth and prepared to spring after the boy. But the shaman ground his foot into the brute's body, and so doing, gave Gnob an idea.

"And then, O Keesh, what wouldst thou do, should a man do this thing to you?"—as he spoke, Gnob held a ribbon of salmon to White Fang, and when the animal attempted to take it, smote him sharply on the nose with a stick. "And afterward, O Keesh, wouldst thou do thus?"—White Fang was cringing back on his belly and fawning to the hand of Gnob.

"Listen!"—leaning on the arm of Madwan, Gnob had risen to his feet. "I am very old, and because I am very old I will tell thee things. Thy father, Keesh, was a mighty man. And he did love the song of the bowstring in battle, and these eyes have beheld him cast a spear till the head stood out beyond a man's body. But thou art unlike. Since thou left the Raven to worship the Wolf, thou art become afraid of blood, and thou makest thy people afraid. This is not good. For behold, when I was a boy, even as Kitznoo there, there was no white man in all the land. But they came, one by one, these white men, till now they are many. And they are a restless breed, never content to rest by the fire with a full belly and let the morrow bring its own meat. A curse was laid upon them, it would seem, and they must work it out in toil and hardship."

Keesh was startled. A recollection of a hazy story told by Mr. Brown of one Adam, of old time, came to him, and it seemed that Mr. Brown had spoken true.

"So they lay hands upon all they behold, these white men, and they go everywhere and behold all things. And ever do more follow in their steps, so that if nothing be done they will come to possess all the land and there will be no room for the tribes of the Raven. Wherefore it is meet that we fight with them till none are left. Then will we hold the passes and the land, and perhaps our children and our children's children shall flourish and grow fat. There is a great struggle to come, when Wolf and Raven shall grapple; but Keesh will not fight, nor will he let his people fight. So it is not well that he should take to him my daughter. Thus have I spoken, I, Gnob, chief of the Tana-naw."

"But the white men are good and great," Keesh made answer. "The white men have taught us many things. The white men have given us blankets and knives and guns, such as we have never made and never could make. I remember in what manner we lived before they came. I was unborn then, but I have it from my father. When we went on the hunt we must creep so close to the moose that a spear-cast would cover the distance. To-day we use the white man's rifle, and farther away than can a child's cry be heard. We ate fish and meat and berries—there was nothing else to eat —and we ate without salt. How many be there among you who care to go back to the fish and meat without salt?"

It would have sunk home, had not Madwan leaped to his feet ere silence could come. "And first a question to thee, Keesh. The white man up at the Big House tells you that it is wrong to kill. Yet do we not know that the white men kill? Have we forgotten the great fight on the Koyokuk? or the great fight at Nuklukyeto, where three white men killed twenty of the Tozikakats? Do you think we no longer remember the three men of the Tana-naw that the white man Macklewrath killed? Tell me, O Keesh, why does the Shaman Brown teach you that it is wrong to fight, when all his brothers fight?"

"Nay, nay, there is no need to answer," Gnob piped, while Keesh struggled with the paradox. "It is very simple. The Good Man Brown would hold the Raven tight whilst his brothers pluck the feathers." He raised his voice. "But so long as there is one Tana-naw to strike a blow, or one maiden to bear a man-child, the Raven shall not be plucked!"

Gnob turned to a husky young man across the fire. "And what sayest thou, Makamuk, who art brother to Su-Su?"

Makamuk came to his feet. A long face-scar lifted his upper lip into a perpetual grin which belied the glowing ferocity of his eyes. "This day," he began with cunning irrelevance, "I came by the Trader Macklewrath's cabin. And in the door I saw a child laughing at the sun. And the child looked at me with the Trader Macklewrath's eyes, and it was frightened. The mother ran to it and quieted it. The mother was Ziska, the Thlunget woman."

A snarl of rage rose up and drowned his voice, which he stilled by turning dramatically upon Keesh with outstretched arm and accusing finger.

"So? You give your women away, you Thlunget, and come to the Tana-naw for more? But we have need of our women, Keesh; for we must breed men, many men, against the day when the Raven grapples with the Wolf."

Through the storm of applause, Gnob's voice shrilled clear. "And thou, Nossabok, who art her favorite brother?"

The young fellow was slender and graceful, with the strong aquiline nose and high brows of his type; but from some nervous affliction the lid of one eye drooped at odd times in a suggestive wink. Even as he arose it so drooped and rested a moment against his cheek. But it was not greeted with the accustomed laughter.

Every face was grave. "I, too, passed by the Trader Macklewrath's cabin," he rippled in soft, girlish tones, wherein there was much of youth and much of his sister. "And I saw Indians with the sweat running into their eyes and their knees shaking with weariness—I say, I saw Indians groaning under the logs for the store which the Trader Macklewrath is to build. And with my eyes I saw them chopping wood to keep the Shaman Brown's Big House warm through the frost of the long nights. This be squaw work. Never shall the Tana-naw do the like. We shall be blood brothers to men, not squaws; and the Thlunget be squaws."

A deep silence fell, and all eyes centred on Keesh. He looked about him carefully, deliberately, full into the face of each grown man. "So," he said passionlessly. And "So," he repeated. Then turned on his heel without further word and passed out into the darkness.

Wading among sprawling babies and bristling wolf-dogs, he threaded the great camp, and on its outskirts came upon a woman at work by the light of a fire. With strings of bark stripped from the long roots of creeping vines, she was braiding rope for the Fishing. For some time, without speech, he watched her deft hands bringing law and order out of the unruly mass of curling fibres. She was good to look upon, swaying there to her task, strong-limbed, deep-chested, and with hips made for motherhood. And the bronze of her face was golden in the flickering light, her hair blue-black, her eyes jet.

"O Su-Su," he spoke finally, "thou hast looked upon me kindly in the days that have gone and in the days yet young—"

"I looked kindly upon thee for that thou wert chief of the Thlunget," she answered quickly, "and because thou wert big and strong."

"Ay—"

"But that was in the old days of the Fishing," she hastened to add, "before the Shaman Brown came and taught thee ill things and led thy feet on strange trails."

"But I would tell thee the—"

She held up one hand in a gesture which reminded him of her father. "Nay, I know already the speech that stirs in thy throat,

O Keesh, and I make answer now. It so happeneth that the fish of the water and the beasts of the forest bring forth after their kind. And this is good. Likewise it happeneth to women. It is for them to bring forth their kind, and even the maiden, while she is yet a maiden, feels the pang of the birth, and the pain of the breast, and the small hands at the neck. And when such feeling is strong, then does each maiden look about her with secret eyes for the man—for the man who shall be fit to father her kind. So have I felt. So did I feel when I looked upon thee and found thee big and strong, a hunter and fighter of beasts and men, well able to win meat when I should eat for two, well able to keep danger afar off when my helplessness drew nigh. But that was before the day the Shaman Brown came into the land and taught thee—"

"But it is not right, Su-Su. I have it on good word—"

"It is not right to kill. I know what thou wouldst say. Then breed thou after thy kind, the kind that does not kill; but come not on such quest among the Tana-naw. For it is said in the time to come, that the Raven shall grapple with the Wolf. I do not know, for this be the affair of men; but I do know that it is for me to bring forth men against that time."

"Su-Su," Keesh broke in, "thou must hear me—"

"A *man* would beat me with a stick and make me hear," she sneered. "But thou . . . here!" She thrust a bunch of bark into his hand. "I cannot give thee myself, but this, yes. It looks fittest in thy hands. It is squaw work, so braid away."

He flung it from him, the angry blood pounding a muddy path under his bronze.

"One thing more," she went on. "There be an old custom which thy father and mine were not strangers to. When a man falls in battle, his scalp is carried away in token. Very good. But thou, who have forsworn the Raven, must do more. Thou must bring me, not scalps, but heads, two heads, and then will I give thee, not bark, but a brave-beaded belt, and sheath, and long Russian knife. Then will I look kindly upon thee once again, and all will be well."

"So," the man pondered. "So." Then he turned and passed out through the light.

"Nay, O Keesh!" she called after him. "Not two heads, but three at least!"

But Keesh remained true to his conversion, lived uprightly, and made his tribespeople obey the gospel as propounded by the Rev. Jackson Brown. Through all the time of the Fishing he gave no heed to the Tana-naw, nor took notice of the sly things which were said, nor of the laughter of the women of the many tribes. After the Fishing, Gnob and his people, with great store of salmon, sun-dried and smoke-cured, departed for the Hunting on the head reaches of the Tana-naw. Keesh watched them go, but did not fail in his attendance at Mission service, where he prayed regularly and led the singing with his deep bass voice.

The Rev. Jackson Brown delighted in that deep bass voice, and because of his sterling qualities deemed him the most promising convert. Macklewrath doubted this. He did not believe in the efficacy of the conversion of the heathen, and he was not slow in speaking his mind. But Mr. Brown was a large man, in his way, and he argued it out with such convincingness, all of one long fall night, that the trader, driven from position after position, finally announced in desperation, "Knock out my brains with apples, Brown, if I don't become a convert myself, if Keesh holds fast, true blue, for two years!" Mr. Brown never lost an opportunity, so he clinched the matter on the spot with a virile hand-grip, and thenceforth the conduct of Keesh was to determine the ultimate abiding-place of Macklewrath's soul.

But there came news one day, after the winter's rime had settled down over the land sufficiently for travel. A Tana-naw man arrived at the St. George Mission in quest of ammunition and bringing information that Su-Su had set eyes on Nee-Koo, a nervy young hunter who had bid brilliantly for her by old Gnob's fire. It was at about this time that the Rev. Jackson Brown came upon Keesh by the wood-trail which leads down to the river. Keesh had his best dogs in the harness, and shoved under the sled-lashings was his largest and finest pair of snow-shoes.

"Where goest thou, O Keesh? Hunting?" Mr. Brown asked, falling into the Indian manner.

Keesh looked him steadily in the eyes for a full minute, then started up his dogs. Then again, turning his deliberate gaze upon the missionary, he answered, "No; I go to hell."

In an open space, striving to burrow into the snow as though for shelter from the appalling desolateness, huddled three dreary lodges. Ringed all about, a dozen paces away, was the sombre forest. Overhead there was no keen, blue sky of naked space, but a vague, misty curtain, pregnant with snow, which had drawn between. There was no wind, no sound, nothing but the snow and silence. Nor was there even the general stir of life about the camp; for the hunting party had run upon the flank of the caribou herd and the kill had been large. Thus, after the period of fasting had come the plenitude of feasting, and thus, in broad daylight, they slept heavily under their roofs of moosehide.

By a fire, before one of the lodges, five pairs of snow-shoes stood on end in their element, and by the fire sat Su-Su. The hood of her squirrel-skin parka was about her hair, and well drawn up around her throat; but her hands were unmittened and nimbly at work with needle and sinew, completing the last fantastic design on a belt of leather faced with bright scarlet cloth. A dog, somewhere at the rear of one of the lodges, raised a short, sharp bark, then ceased as abruptly as it had begun. Once, her father, in the lodge at her back, gurgled and grunted in his sleep. "Bad dreams," she smiled to herself. "He grows old, and that last joint was too much."

She placed the last bead, knotted the sinew, and replenished the fire. Then, after gazing long into the flames, she lifted her head to the harsh *crunch-crunch* of a moccasined foot against the flinty snow granules. Keesh was at her side, bending slightly forward to a load which he bore upon his back. This was wrapped loosely in a soft-tanned moosehide, and he dropped it carelessly into the snow and sat down. They looked at each other long and without speech.

"It is a far fetch, O Keesh," she said at last, "a far fetch from St. George Mission by the Yukon."

"Ay," he made answer, absently, his eyes fixed keenly upon the belt and taking note of its girth. "But where is the knife?" he demanded.

"Here." She drew it from inside her parka and flashed its naked length in the firelight. "It is a good knife."

"Give it me!" he commanded.

"Nay, O Keesh," she laughed. "It may be that thou wast not born to wear it."

"Give it me!" he reiterated, without change of tone. "I was so born."

But her eyes, glancing coquettishly past him to the moosehide, saw the snow about it slowly reddening. "It is blood, Keesh?" she asked.

"Ay, it is blood. But give me the belt and the long Russian knife."

She felt suddenly afraid, but thrilled when he took the belt roughly from her, thrilled to the roughness. She looked at him softly, and was aware of a pain at the breast and of small hands clutching her throat.

"It was made for a smaller man," he remarked grimly, drawing in his abdomen and clasping the buckle at the first hole.

Su-Su smiled, and her eyes were yet softer. Again she felt the soft hands at her throat. He was good to look upon, and the belt was indeed small, made for a smaller man; but what did it matter? She could make many belts.

"But the blood?" she asked, urged on by a hope new-born and growing. "The blood, Keesh? Is it . . . are they . . . heads?"

"Ay."

"They must be very fresh, else would the blood be frozen."

"Ay, it is not cold, and they be fresh, quite fresh."

"Oh, Keesh!" Her face was warm and bright. "And for me?"

"Ay; for thee."

He took hold of a corner of the hide, flirted it open, and rolled the heads out before her.

"Three," he whispered savagely; "nay, four at least."

But she sat transfixed. There they lay—the soft-featured Nee-Koo; the gnarled old face of Gnob; Makamuk, grinning at her with his lifted upper lip; and lastly, Nossabok, his eyelid, up to its old trick, drooped on his girlish cheek in a suggestive wink. There they lay, the firelight flashing upon and playing over them, and from each of them a widening circle dyed the snow to scarlet.

Thawed by the fire, the white crust gave way beneath the head of Gnob, which rolled over like a thing alive, spun around, and came to rest at her feet. But she did not move. Keesh, too, sat motionless, his eyes unblinking, centred steadfastly upon her.

Once, in the forest, an overburdened pine dropped its load of snow, and the echoes reverberated hollowly down the gorge; but neither stirred. The short day had been waning fast, and darkness was wrapping round the camp when White Fang trotted up toward the fire. He paused to reconnoitre, but not being driven back, came closer. His nose shot swiftly to the side, nostrils a-tremble and bristles rising along the spine; and straight and true, he followed the sudden scent to his master's head. He sniffed it gingerly at first and licked the forehead with his red lolling tongue. Then he sat abruptly down, pointed his nose up at the first faint star, and raised the long wolf-howl.

This brought Su-Su to herself. She glanced across at Keesh, who had unsheathed the Russian knife and was watching her intently. His face was firm and set, and in it she read the law. Slipping back the hood of her parka, she bared her neck and rose to her feet. There she paused and took a long look about her, at the rimming forest, at the faint stars in the sky, at the camp, at the snow-shoes in the snow—a last long comprehensive look at life. A light breeze stirred her hair from the side, and for the space of one deep breath she turned her head and followed it around until she met it full-faced.

Then she thought of her children, ever to be unborn, and she walked over to Keesh and said, "I am ready."

The Death of Ligoun

Blood for blood, rank for rank.
—THLINKET CODE.

"Hear now the death of Ligoun—"

The speaker ceased, or rather suspended utterance, and gazed upon me with an eye of understanding. I held the bottle between our eyes and the fire, indicated with my thumb the depth of the draught, and shoved it over to him; for was he not Palitlum, the Drinker? Many tales had he told me, and long had I waited for this scriptless scribe to speak of the things concerning Ligoun; for he, of all men living, knew these things best.

He tilted back his head with a grunt that slid swiftly into a gurgle, and the shadow of a man's torso, monstrous beneath a huge inverted bottle, wavered and danced on the frown of the cliff at our backs. Palitlum released his lips from the glass with a caressing suck and glanced regretfully up into the ghostly vault of the sky where played the wan white light of the summer borealis.

"It be strange," he said; "cold like water and hot like fire. To the drinker it giveth strength, and from the drinker it taketh away strength. It maketh old men young, and young men old. To the man who is weary it leadeth him to get up and go onward, and to the man unweary it burdeneth him into sleep. My brother was possessed of the heart of a rabbit, yet did he drink of it, and forthwith slay four of his enemies. My father was like a great wolf, showing his teeth to all men, yet did he drink of it and was shot through the back, running swiftly away. It be most strange."

"It is 'Three Star,' and a better than what they poison their bellies with down there," I answered, sweeping my hand, as it were, over the yawning chasm of blackness and down to where the beach fires glinted far below—tiny jets of flame which gave proportion and reality to the night.

Palitlum sighed and shook his head. "Wherefore I am here with thee."

And here he embraced the bottle and me in a look which told more eloquently than speech of his shameless thirst.

"Nay," I said, snuggling the bottle in between my knees. "Speak now of Ligoun. Of the 'Three Star' we will hold speech hereafter."

"There be plenty, and I am not wearied," he pleaded brazenly. "But the feel of it on my lips, and I will speak great words of Ligoun and his last days."

"From the drinker it taketh away strength," I mocked, "and to the man unweary it burdeneth him into sleep."

"Thou art wise," he rejoined, without anger and pridelessly. "Like all of thy brothers, thou art wise. Waking or sleeping, the 'Three Star' be with thee, yet never have I known thee to drink overlong or overmuch. And the while you gather to you the gold that hides in our mountains and the fish that swim in our seas; and Palitlum, and the brothers of Palitlum, dig the gold for thee and net the fish, and are glad to be made glad when out of thy wisdom thou deemest it fit that the 'Three Star' should wet our lips."

"I was minded to hear of Ligoun," I said impatiently. "The night grows short, and we have a sore journey to-morrow."

I yawned and made as though to rise, but Palitlum betrayed a quick anxiety, and with abruptness began:—

"It was Ligoun's desire, in his old age, that peace should be among the tribes. As a young man he had been first of the fighting men and chief over the war-chiefs of the Islands and the Passes. All his days had been full of fighting. More marks he boasted of bone and lead and iron than any other man. Three wives he had, and for each wife two sons; and the sons, eldest born and last and all, died by his side in battle. Restless as the bald-face, he ranged wide and far—north to Unalaska and the Shallow Sea; south to the Queen Charlottes, ay, even did he go with the Kakes, it is told, to far Puget Sound, and slay thy brothers in their sheltered houses.

"But, as I say, in his old age he looked for peace among the tribes. Not that he was become afraid, or overfond of the corner by the fire and the well-filled pot. For he slew with the shrewdness and blood-hunger of the fiercest, drew in his belly to famine with the youngest, and with the stoutest faced the bitter seas and stinging trail. But because of his many deeds, and in punishment, a warship carried him away, even to thy country, O Hair-Face and Boston Man; and the years were many ere he came back, and I was grown to something more than a boy and something less than a young man. And Ligoun, being childless in his old age, made much of me, and grown wise, gave me of his wisdom.

" 'It be good to fight, O Palitlum,' said he. Nay, O Hair-Face, for I was unknown as Palitlum in those days, being called Olo, the Ever-Hungry. The drink was to come after. 'It be good to fight,' spake Ligoun, 'but it be foolish. In the Boston Man Country, as I saw with mine eyes, they are not given to fighting one with another, and they be strong. Wherefore, of their strength, they come against us of the Islands and Passes, and we are as camp smoke and sea mist before them. Wherefore I say it be good to fight, most good, but it be likewise foolish.'

"And because of this, though first always of the fighting men, Ligoun's voice was loudest, ever, for peace. And when he was very old, being greatest of chiefs and richest of men, he gave a potlatch. Never was there such a potlatch. Five hundred canoes were lined against the river bank, and in each canoe there came not less than ten of men and women. Eight tribes were there; from the first and oldest man to the last and youngest babe were they there. And then there were men from far-distant tribes, great travellers and seekers who had heard of the potlatch of Ligoun. And for the length of seven days they filled their bellies with his meat and drink. Eight thousand blankets did he give to them, as I well know, for who but I kept the tally and apportioned according to degree and rank? And in the end Ligoun was a poor man; but his name was on all men's lips, and other chiefs gritted their teeth in envy that he should be so great.

"And so, because there was weight to his words, he counselled peace; and he journeyed to every potlatch and feast and tribal gathering that he might counsel peace. And so it came that we journeyed together, Ligoun and I, to the great feast given by Niblack, who was chief over the river Indians of the Skoot, which is not far from the Stickeen. This was in the last days, and Ligoun was very old and very close to death. He coughed of cold weather and camp smoke, and often the red blood ran from out his mouth till we looked for him to die.

" 'Nay,' he said once at such time; 'it were better that I should die when the blood leaps to the knife, and there is a clash of steel and smell of powder, and men crying aloud what of the cold iron and quick lead.' So, it be plain, O Hair-Face, that his heart was yet strong for battle.

"It is very far from the Chilcat to the Skoot, and we were many days in the canoes. And the while the men bent to the paddles, I sat at the feet of Ligoun and received the Law. Of small need for me to say the Law, O Hair-Face, for it be known to me that in this thou art well skilled. Yet do I speak of the Law of blood for blood, and rank for rank. Also did Ligoun go deeper into the matter, saying:—

" 'But know this, O Olo, that there be little honor in the killing of a man less than thee. Kill always the man who is greater, and thy honor shall be according to his greatness. But if, of two men, thou killest the lesser, then is shame thine, for which the very squaws will lift their lips at thee. As I say, peace be good; but remember, O Olo, if kill thou must, that thou killest by the Law.'

"It is a way of the Thlinket-folk," Palitlum vouchsafed half apologetically.

And I remembered the gun-fighters and bad men of my own Western land, and was not perplexed at the way of the Thlinket-folk.

"In time," Palitlum continued, "we came to Chief Niblack and the Skoots. It was a feast great almost as the potlatch of Ligoun. There were we of the Chilcat, and the Sitkas, and the Stickeens who are neighbors to the Skoots, and the Wrangels and the Hoonahs. There were Sundowns and Tahkos from Port Houghton, and their neighbors the Awks from Douglass Channel; the Naass River people, and the Tongas from north of Dixon, and the Kakes who come from the island called Kupreanoff. Then there were Siwashes from Vancouver, Cassiars from the Gold Mountains, Teslin men, and even Sticks from the Yukon Country.

"It was a mighty gathering. But first of all, there was to be a meeting of the chiefs with Niblack, and a drowning of all enmities in quass. The Russians it was who showed us the way of making quass, for so my father told me,—my father, who got it from his father before him. But to this quass had Niblack added many things, such as sugar, flour, dried apples, and hops, so that it was a man's drink, strong and good. Not so good as 'Three Star,' O Hair-Face, yet good.

"This quass-feast was for the chiefs, and the chiefs only, and there was a score of them. But Ligoun being very old and very great, it was given that I walk with him that he might lean upon my shoulder and that I might ease him down when he took his seat and raise him up when he arose. At the door of Niblack's house, which was of logs and very big, each chief, as was the custom, laid down his spear or rifle and his knife. For as thou knowest, O Hair-Face, strong drink quickens, and old hates flame up, and head and hand are swift to act. But I noted that Ligoun had brought two knives, the one he left outside the door, the other slipped under his blanket, snug to the grip. The other chiefs did likewise, and I was troubled for what was to come.

"The chiefs were ranged, sitting, in a big circle about the room. I stood at Ligoun's elbow. In the middle was the barrel of quass, and by it a slave to serve the drink. First, Niblack made oration, with much show of friendship and many fine words. Then he gave a sign, and the slave dipped a gourd full of quass and passed it to Ligoun, as was fit, for his was the highest rank.

"Ligoun drank it, to the last drop, and I gave him my strength to get on his feet so that he, too, might make oration. He had kind speech for the many tribes, noted the greatness of Niblack to give such a feast, counselled for peace as was his custom, and at the end said that the quass was very good.

"Then Niblack drank, being next of rank to Ligoun, and after him one chief and another in degree and order. And each spoke friendly words and said that the quass was good, till all had drunk. Did I say all? Nay, not all, O Hair-Face. For last of them was one, a lean and cat-like man, young of face, with a quick and daring eye, who drank darkly, and spat forth upon the ground, and spoke no word.

"To not say that the quass was good were insult; to spit forth upon the ground were worse than insult. And this very thing did he do. He was known for a chief over the Sticks of the Yukon, and further naught was known of him.

"As I say, it was an insult. But mark this, O Hair-Face: it was

an insult, not to Niblack the feast-giver, but to the man chiefest
of rank who sat among those of the circle. And that man was
Ligoun. There was no sound. All eyes were upon him to see what
he might do. He made no movement. His withered lips trembled
not into speech; nor did a nostril quiver, nor an eyelid droop. But
I saw that he looked wan and gray, as I have seen old men look
of bitter mornings when famine pressed, and the women wailed
and the children whimpered, and there was no meat nor sign of
meat. And as the old men looked, so looked Ligoun.

"There was no sound. It were as a circle of the dead, but that
each chief felt beneath his blanket to make sure, and that each
chief glanced to his neighbor, right and left, with a measuring eye.
I was a stripling; the things I had seen were few; yet I knew it to
be the moment one meets but once in all a lifetime.

"The Stick rose up, with every eye upon him, and crossed the
room till he stood before Ligoun.

" 'I am Opitsah, the Knife,' he said.

"But Ligoun said naught, nor looked at him, but gazed unblinking at the ground.

" 'You are Ligoun,' Opitsah said. 'You have killed many men.
I am still alive.'

"And still Ligoun said naught, though he made the sign to me
and with my strength arose and stood upright on his two feet.
He was as an old pine, naked and gray, but still a-shoulder to the
frost and storm. His eyes were unblinking, and as he had not
heard Opitsah, so it seemed he did not see him.

"And Opitsah was mad with anger, and danced stiff-legged
before him, as men do when they wish to give another shame.
And Opitsah sang a song of his own greatness and the greatness
of his people, filled with bad words for the Chilcats and for Ligoun. And as he danced and sang, Opitsah threw off his blanket
and with his knife drew bright circles before the face of Ligoun.
And the song he sang was the Song of the Knife.

"And there was no other sound, only the singing of Opitsah,
and the circle of chiefs that were as dead, save that the flash of
the knife seemed to draw smouldering fire from their eyes. And
Ligoun, also, was very still. Yet did he know his death, and was
unafraid. And the knife sang closer and yet closer to his face, but

his eyes were unblinking and he swayed not to right or left, or this way or that.

"And Opitsah drove in the knife, so, twice on the forehead of Ligoun, and the red blood leaped after it. And then it was that Ligoun gave me the sign to bear up under him with my youth that he might walk. And he laughed with a great scorn, full in the face of Opitsah, the Knife. And he brushed Opitsah to the side, as one brushes to the side a low-hanging branch on the trail and passes on.

"And I knew and understood, for there was but shame in the killing of Opitsah before the faces of a score of greater chiefs. I remembered the Law, and knew Ligoun had it in mind to kill by the Law. And who, chiefest of rank but himself, was there but Niblack? And toward Niblack, leaning on my arm, he walked. And to his other arm, clinging and striking, was Opitsah, too small to soil with his blood the hands of so great a man. And though the knife of Opitsah bit in again and again, Ligoun noted it not, nor winced. And in this fashion we three went our way across the room, Niblack sitting in his blanket and fearful of our coming.

"And now old hates flamed up and forgotten grudges were remembered. Lamuk, a Kake, had had a brother drowned in the bad water of the Stickeen, and the Stickeens had not paid in blankets for their bad water, as was the custom to pay. So Lamuk drove straight with his long knife to the heart of Klok-Kutz the Stickeen. And Katchahook remembered a quarrel of the Naass River people with the Tongas of north of Dixon, and the chief of the Tongas he slew with a pistol which made much noise. And the blood-hunger gripped all the men who sat in the circle, and chief slew chief, or was slain, as chance might be. Also did they stab and shoot at Ligoun, for whoso killed him won great honor and would be unforgotten for the deed. And they were about him like wolves about a moose, only they were so many they were in their own way, and they slew one another to make room. And there was great confusion.

"But Ligoun went slowly, without haste, as though many years were yet before him. It seemed that he was certain he would make his kill, in his own way, ere they could slay him. And as I say, he went slowly, and knives bit into him, and he was red with blood. And though none sought after me, who was a mere stripling, yet did the knives find me, and the hot bullets burn me. And still Ligoun leaned his weight on my youth, and Opitsah struck at him, and we three went forward. And when we stood by Niblack, he was afraid, and covered his head with his blanket. The Skoots were ever cowards.

"And Goolzug and Kadishan, the one a fish-eater and the other a meat-killer, closed together for the honor of their tribes. And they raged madly about, and in their battling swung against the knees of Opitsah, who was overthrown and trampled upon. And a knife, singing through the air, smote Skulpin, of the Sitkas, in the throat, and he flung his arms out blindly, reeling, and dragged me down in his fall.

"And from the ground I beheld Ligoun bend over Niblack, and uncover the blanket from his head, and turn up his face to the light. And Ligoun was in no haste. Being blinded with his own blood, he swept it out of his eyes with the back of his hand, so he might see and be sure. And when he was sure that the upturned face was the face of Niblack, he drew the knife across his throat as one draws a knife across the throat of a trembling deer. And then Ligoun stood erect, singing his death-song and swaying gently to and fro. And Skulpin, who had dragged me down, shot with a pistol from where he lay, and Ligoun toppled and fell, as an old pine topples and falls in the teeth of the wind."

Palitlum ceased. His eyes, smouldering moodily, were bent upon the fire, and his cheek was dark with blood.

"And thou, Palitlum?" I demanded. "And thou?"

"I? I did remember the Law, and I slew Opitsah the Knife, which was well. And I drew Ligoun's own knife from the throat of Niblack, and slew Skulpin, who had dragged me down. For I was a stripling, and I could slay any man and it were honor. And further, Ligoun being dead, there was no need for my youth, and I laid about me with his knife, choosing the chiefest of rank that yet remained."

Palitlum fumbled under his shirt and drew forth a beaded sheath, and from the sheath, a knife. It was a knife home-wrought and crudely fashioned from a whip-saw file; a knife such as one may find possessed by old men in a hundred Alaskan villages.

"The knife of Ligoun?" I said, and Palitlum nodded.

"And for the knife of Ligoun," I said, "will I give thee ten bottles of 'Three Star.' "

But Palitlum looked at me slowly. "Hair-Face, I am weak as water, and easy as a woman. I have soiled my belly with quass, and hooch, and 'Three Star.' My eyes are blunted, my ears have lost their keenness, and my strength has gone into fat. And I am without honor in these days, and am called Palitlum, the Drinker. Yet honor was mine at the potlatch of Niblack, on the Skoot, and the memory of it, and the memory of Ligoun, be dear to me. Nay, didst thou turn the sea itself into 'Three Star' and say that it were all mine for the knife, yet would I keep the knife. I am Palitlum, the Drinker, but I was once Olo, the Ever-Hungry, who bore up Ligoun with his youth!"

"Thou art a great man, Palitlum," I said, "and I honor thee."

Palitlum reached out his hand.

"The 'Three Star' between thy knees be mine for the tale I have told," he said.

And as I looked on the frown of the cliff at our backs, I saw the shadow of a man's torso, monstrous beneath a huge inverted bottle.

Li Wan, the Fair

"The sun sinks, Canim, and the heat of the day is gone!"

So called Li Wan to the man whose head was hidden beneath the squirrel-skin robe, but she called softly, as though divided between the duty of waking him and the fear of him awake. For she was afraid of this big husband of hers, who was like unto none of the men she had known.

The moose-meat sizzled uneasily, and she moved the frying-pan to one side of the red embers. As she did so she glanced warily at the two Hudson Bay dogs dripping eager slaver from their scarlet tongues and following her every movement. They were huge, hairy fellows, crouched to leeward in the thin smoke-wake of the fire to escape the swarming myriads of mosquitoes. As Li Wan gazed down the steep to where the Klondike flung its swollen flood between the hills, one of the dogs bellied its way forward like a worm, and with a deft, catlike stroke of the paw dipped a chunk of hot meat out of the pan to the ground. But Li Wan caught him from out the tail of her eye, and he sprang back with a snap and a snarl as she rapped him over the nose with a stick of firewood.

"Nay, Olo," she laughed, recovering the meat without removing her eye from him. "Thou art ever hungry, and for that thy nose leads thee into endless troubles."

But the mate of Olo joined him, and together they defied the woman. The hair on their backs and shoulders bristled in recurrent waves of anger, and the thin lips writhed and lifted into ugly wrinkles, exposing the flesh-tearing fangs, cruel and menacing. Their very noses serrulated and shook in brute passion, and they snarled as the wolves snarl, with all the hatred and malignity of the breed impelling them to spring upon the woman and drag her down.

"And thou, too, Bash, fierce as thy master and never at peace with the hand that feeds thee! This is not thy quarrel, so that be thine! and that!"

As she cried, she drove at them with the firewood, but they avoided the blows and refused to retreat. They separated and approached her from either side, crouching low and snarling. Li Wan had struggled with the wolf-dog for mastery from the time she toddled among the skin-bales of the teepee, and she knew a crisis was at hand. Bash had halted, his muscles stiff and tense for the spring; Olo was yet creeping into striking distance.

Grasping two blazing sticks by the charred ends, she faced the brutes. The one held back, but Bash sprang, and she met him in mid-air with the flaming weapon. There were sharp yelps of pain and swift odors of burning hair and flesh as he rolled in the dirt and the woman ground the fiery embers into his mouth. Snapping wildly, he flung himself sidewise out of her reach and in a frenzy of fear scrambled for safety. Olo, on the other side, had begun his retreat, when Li Wan reminded him of her primacy by hurling a heavy stick of wood into his ribs. Then the pair retreated under a rain of firewood, and on the edge of the camp fell to licking their wounds and whimpering by turns and snarling.

Li Wan blew the ashes off the meat and sat down again. Her heart had not gone up a beat, and the incident was already old, for this was the routine of life. Canim had not stirred during the disorder, but instead had set up a lusty snoring.

"Come, Canim!" she called. "The heat of the day is gone, and the trail waits for our feet."

The squirrel-skin robe was agitated and cast aside by a brown arm. Then the man's eyelids fluttered and drooped again.

"His pack is heavy," she thought, "and he is tired with the work of the morning."

A mosquito stung her on the neck, and she daubed the unprotected spot with wet clay from a ball she had convenient to hand. All morning, toiling up the divide and enveloped in a cloud of the pests, the man and woman had plastered themselves with the sticky mud, which, drying in the sun, covered their faces with masks of clay. These masks, broken in divers places by the movement of the facial muscles, had constantly to be renewed, so that the deposit was irregular of depth and peculiar of aspect.

Li Wan shook Canim gently but with persistence till he roused and sat up. His first glance was to the sun, and after consulting the celestial timepiece he hunched over to the fire and fell-to ravenously on the meat. He was a large Indian fully six feet in height, deep-chested and heavy-muscled, and his eyes were keener and vested with greater mental vigor than the average of his kind. The lines of will had marked his face deeply, and this, coupled with a sternness and primitiveness, advertised a native indomitability, unswerving of purpose, and prone, when thwarted, to sullen cruelty.

"To-morrow, Li Wan, we shall feast." He sucked a marrow-bone clean and threw it to the dogs. "We shall have *flapjacks* fried in *bacon grease*, and *sugar*, which is more toothsome—"

"*Flapjacks?*" she questioned, mouthing the word curiously.

"Ay," Canim answered with superiority; "and I shall teach you new ways of cookery. Of these things I speak you are ignorant, and of many more things besides. You have lived your days in a little corner of the earth and know nothing. But I,"—he straightened himself and looked at her pridefully,—"I am a great traveller, and have been all places, even among the white people, and I am versed in their ways, and in the ways of many peoples. I am not a tree, born to stand in one place always and know not what there be over the next hill; for I am Canim, the Canoe, made to go here and there and to journey and quest up and down the length and breadth of the world."

She bowed her head humbly. "It is true. I have eaten fish and meat and berries all my days and lived in a little corner of the earth. Nor did I dream the world was so large until you stole me from my people and I cooked and carried for you on the endless trails." She looked up at him suddenly. "Tell me, Canim, does this trail ever end?"

"Nay," he answered. "My trail is like the world; it never ends. My trail *is* the world, and I have travelled it since the time my legs could carry me, and I shall travel it until I die. My father and my mother may be dead, but it is long since I looked upon them, and I do not care. My tribe is like your tribe. It stays in the one place—which is far from here,—but I care naught for my tribe, for I am Canim, the Canoe!"

"And must I, Li Wan, who am weary, travel always your trail until I die?"

"You, Li Wan, are my wife, and the wife travels the husband's trail wheresoever it goes. It is the law. And were it not the law, yet would it be the law of Canim, who is lawgiver unto himself and his."

She bowed her head again, for she knew no other law than that man was the master of woman.

"Be not in haste," Canim cautioned her, as she began to strap the meagre camp outfit to her pack. "The sun is yet hot, and the trail leads down and the footing is good."

She dropped her work obediently and resumed her seat.

Canim regarded her with speculative interest. "You do not squat on your hams like other women," he remarked.

"No," she answered. "It never came easy. It tires me, and I cannot take my rest that way."

"And why is it your feet point not straight before you?"

"I do not know, save that they are unlike the feet of other women."

A satisfied light crept into his eyes, but otherwise he gave no sign.

"Like other women, your hair is black; but have you ever noticed that it is soft and fine, softer and finer than the hair of other women?"

"I have noticed," she answered shortly, for she was not pleased at such cold analysis of her sex-deficiencies.

"It is a year, now, since I took you from your people," he went on, "and you are nigh as shy and afraid of me as when first I looked upon you. How does this thing be?"

Li Wan shook her head. "I am afraid of you, Canim, you are so big and strange. And further, before you looked upon me even, I was afraid of all the young men. I do not know . . . I cannot say . . . only it seemed, somehow, as though I should not be for them, as though . . ."

"Ay," he encouraged, impatient at her faltering.

"As though they were not my kind."

"Not your kind?" he demanded slowly. "Then what is your kind?"

"I do not know, I . . . ." She shook her head in a bewildered manner. "I cannot put into words the way I felt. It was strangeness in me. I was unlike other maidens, who sought the young men slyly. I could not care for the young men that way. It would have been a great wrong, it seemed, and an ill deed."

"What is the first thing you remember?" Canim asked with abrupt irrelevance.

"Pow-Wah-Kaan, my mother."

"And naught else before Pow-Wah-Kaan?"

"Naught else."

But Canim, holding her eyes with his, searched her secret soul and saw it waver.

"Think, and think hard, Li Wan!" he threatened.

She stammered, and her eyes were piteous and pleading, but his will dominated her and wrung from her lips the reluctant speech.

"But it was only dreams, Canim, ill dreams of childhood, shadows of things not real, visions such as the dogs, sleeping in the sun-warmth, behold and whine out against."

"Tell me," he commanded, "of the things before Pow-Wah-Kaan, your mother."

"They are forgotten memories," she protested. "As a child I dreamed awake, with my eyes open to the day, and when I spoke of the strange things I saw I was laughed at, and the other children were afraid and drew away from me. And when I spoke of the things I saw to Pow-Wah-Kaan, she chided me and said they were evil; also she beat me. It was a sickness, I believe, like the falling-sickness that comes to old men; and in time I grew better and dreamed no more. And now . . . I cannot remember"—she brought her hand in a confused manner to her forehead—"they are there, somewhere, but I cannot find them, only . . ."

"Only," Canim repeated, holding her.

"Only one thing. But you will laugh at its foolishness, it is so unreal."

"Nay, Li Wan. Dreams are dreams. They may be memories of other lives we have lived. I was once a moose. I firmly believe I was once a moose, what of the things I have seen in dreams, and heard."

Strive as he would to hide it, a growing anxiety was manifest, but Li Wan, groping after the words with which to paint the picture, took no heed.

"I see a snow-tramped space among the trees," she began, "and across the snow the sign of a man where he has dragged himself heavily on hand and knee. And I see, too, the man in the snow, and it seems I am very close to him when I look. He is unlike real men, for he has hair on his face, much hair, and the hair of his face and head is yellow like the summer coat of the weasel. His eyes are closed, but they open and search about. They are blue like the sky, and look into mine and search no more. And his hand moves, slow, as from weakness, and I feel . . ."

"Ay," Canim whispered hoarsely. "You feel—?"

"No! no!" she cried in haste. "I feel nothing. Did I say 'feel'? I did not mean it. It could not be that I should mean it. I see, and I see only, and that is all I see—a man in the snow, with eyes like the sky, and hair like the weasel. I have seen it many times, and always it is the same—a man in the snow—"

"And do you see yourself?" he asked, leaning forward and regarding her intently. "Do you ever see yourself and the man in the snow?"

"Why should I see myself? Am I not real?"

His muscles relaxed and he sank back, an exultant satisfaction in his eyes which he turned from her so that she might not see.

"I will tell you, Li Wan," he spoke decisively; "you were a little bird in some life before, a little moose-bird, when you saw this thing, and the memory of it is with you yet. It is not strange. I was once a moose, and my father's father afterward became a bear—so said the shaman, and the shaman cannot lie. Thus, on the Trail of the Gods we pass from life to life, and the gods know only and understand. Dreams and the shadows of dreams be memories, nothing more, and the dog, whining asleep in the sun-warmth, doubtless sees and remembers things gone before. Bash, there, was a warrior once. I do firmly believe he was once a warrior."

Canim tossed a bone to the brute and got upon his feet. "Come, let us begone. The sun is yet hot, but it will get no cooler."

"And these white people, what are they like?" Li Wan made bold to ask.

"Like you and me," he answered, "only they are less dark of skin. You will be among them ere the day is dead."

Canim lashed the sleeping-robe to his one-hundred-and-fifty-pound pack, smeared his face with wet clay, and sat down to rest till Li Wan had finished loading the dogs. Olo cringed at sight of the club in her hand, and gave no trouble when the bundle of forty pounds and odd was strapped upon him. But Bash was aggrieved and truculent, and could not forbear to whimper and snarl as he was forced to receive the burden. He bristled his back and bared his teeth as she drew the straps tight, the while throwing all the malignancy of his nature into the glances shot at her sideways and backward. And Canim chuckled and said, "Did I not say he was once a very great warrior?"

"These furs will bring a price," he remarked as he adjusted his head-strap and lifted his pack clear of the ground. "A big price. The white men pay well for such goods, for they have no time to hunt and are soft to the cold. Soon shall we feast, Li Wan, as you have feasted never in all the lives you have lived before."

She grunted acknowledgment and gratitude for her lord's condescension, slipped into the harness, and bent forward to the load.

"The next time I am born, I would be born a white man," he added, and swung off down the trail which dived into the gorge at his feet.

The dogs followed close at his heels, and Li Wan brought up the rear. But her thoughts were far away, across the Ice Mountains to the east, to the little corner of the earth where her childhood had been lived. Ever as a child, she remembered, she had been looked upon as strange, as one with an affliction. Truly she had dreamed awake and been scolded and beaten for the remarkable visions she saw, till, after a time, she had outgrown them. But not utterly. Though they troubled her no more waking, they came to her in her sleep, grown woman that she was, and many a night of nightmare was hers, filled with fluttering shapes, vague and meaningless. The talk with Canim had excited her, and down all the twisted slant of the divide she harked back to the mocking fantasies of her dreams.

"Let us take breath," Canim said, when they had tapped midway the bed of the main creek.

He rested his pack on a jutting rock, slipped the head-strap, and sat down. Li Wan joined him, and the dogs sprawled panting on the ground beside them. At their feet rippled the glacial drip of the hills, but it was muddy and discolored, as if soiled by some commotion of the earth.

"Why is this?" Li Wan asked.

"Because of the white men who work in the ground. Listen!" He held up his hand, and they heard the ring of pick and shovel, and the sound of men's voices. "They are made mad by *gold*, and work without ceasing that they may find it. *Gold?* It is yellow and comes from the ground, and is considered of great value. It is also a measure of price."

But Li Wan's roving eyes had called her attention from him. A few yards below and partly screened by a clump of young spruce, the tiered logs of a cabin rose to meet its overhanging roof of dirt. A thrill ran through her, and all her dream-phantoms roused up and stirred about uneasily.

"Canim," she whispered in an agony of apprehension. "Canim, what is that?"

"The white man's teepee, in which he eats and sleeps."

She eyed it wistfully, grasping its virtues at a glance and thrilling again at the unaccountable sensations it aroused. "It must be very warm in time of frost," she said aloud, though she felt that she must make strange sounds with her lips.

She felt impelled to utter them, but did not, and the next instant Canim said, "It is called a *cabin*."

Her heart gave a great leap. The sounds! the very sounds! She looked about her in sudden awe. How should she know that strange word before ever she heard it? What could be the matter? And then with a shock, half of fear and half of delight, she realized that for the first time in her life there had been sanity and significance in the promptings of her dreams.

"*Cabin*," she repeated to herself. "*Cabin*." An incoherent flood of dream-stuff welled up and up till her head was dizzy and her heart seemed bursting. Shadows, and looming bulks of things, and unintelligible associations fluttered and whirled about, and she strove vainly with her consciousness to grasp and hold them. For she felt that there, in that welter of memories, was the key of the mystery; could she but grasp and hold it, all would be clear and plain—

O Canim! O Pow-Wah-Kaan! O shades and shadows, what was that?

She turned to Canim, speechless and trembling, the dream-stuff in mad, overwhelming riot. She was sick and fainting, and could only listen to the ravishing sounds which proceeded from the cabin in a wonderful rhythm.

"Hum, *fiddle*," Canim vouchsafed.

But she did not hear him, for in the ecstasy she was experiencing, it seemed at last that all things were coming clear. Now! now! she thought. A sudden moisture swept into her eyes, and the tears trickled down her cheeks. The mystery was unlocking, but the faintness was overpowering her. If only she could hold herself long enough! If only—but the landscape bent and crumpled up, and the hills swayed back and forth across the sky as she sprang upright and screamed, "*Daddy! Daddy!*" Then the sun reeled, and darkness smote her, and she pitched forward limp and headlong among the rocks.

Canim looked to see if her neck had been broken by the heavy pack, grunted his satisfaction, and threw water upon her from the creek. She came to slowly, with choking sobs, and sat up.

"It is not good, the hot sun on the head," he ventured.

And she answered, "No, it is not good, and the pack bore upon me hard."

"We shall camp early, so that you may sleep long and win strength," he said gently. "And if we go now, we shall be the quicker to bed."

Li Wan said nothing, but tottered to her feet in obedience and stirred up the dogs. She took the swing of his pace mechanically, and followed him past the cabin, scarce daring to breathe. But no sounds issued forth, though the door was open and smoke curling upward from the sheet-iron stovepipe.

They came upon a man in the bend of the creek, white of skin and blue of eye, and for a moment Li Wan saw the other man in the snow. But she saw dimly, for she was weak and tired from what she had undergone. Still, she looked at him curiously, and stopped with Canim to watch him at his work. He was washing gravel in a large pan, with a circular, tilting movement; and as they looked, giving a deft flirt, he flashed up the yellow gold in a broad streak across the bottom of the pan.

"Very rich, this creek," Canim told her, as they went on. "Sometime I will find such a creek, and then I shall be a big man."

Cabins and men grew more plentiful, till they came to where the main portion of the creek was spread out before them. It was the scene of a vast devastation. Everywhere the earth was torn and rent as though by a Titan's struggles. Where there were no up-thrown mounds of gravel, great holes and trenches yawned, and chasms where the thick rime of the earth had been peeled to bed-rock. There was no worn channel for the creek, and its waters, dammed up, diverted, flying through the air on giddy flumes, trickling into sinks and low places, and raised by huge water-wheels, were used and used again a thousand times. The hills had been stripped of their trees, and their raw sides gored and per-forated by great timber-slides and prospect holes. And over all, like a monstrous race of ants, was flung an army of men—mud-covered, dirty, dishevelled men, who crawled in and out of the holes of their digging, crept like big bugs along the flumes, and toiled and sweated at the gravel-heaps which they kept in constant unrest—men, as far as the eye could see, even to the rims of the hilltops, digging, tearing, and scouring the face of nature.

Li Wan was appalled at the tremendous upheaval. "Truly, these men are mad," she said to Canim.

"Small wonder. The gold they dig after is a great thing," he replied. "It is the greatest thing in the world."

For hours they threaded the chaos of greed, Canim eagerly intent, Li Wan weak and listless. She knew she had been on the verge of disclosure, and she felt that she was still on the verge of disclosure, but the nervous strain she had undergone had tired her, and she passively waited for the thing, she knew not what, to happen. From every hand her senses snatched up and conveyed to her innumerable impressions, each of which became a dull ex-citation to her jaded imagination. Somewhere within her, respon-sive notes were answering to the things without, forgotten and undreamed-of correspondences were being renewed; and she was aware of it in an incurious way, and her soul was troubled, but she was not equal to the mental exultation necessary to transmute and understand. So she plodded wearily on at the heels of her lord, content to wait for that which she knew, somewhere, somehow, must happen.

After undergoing the mad bondage of man, the creek finally returned to its ancient ways, all soiled and smirched from its toil, and coiled lazily among the broad flats and timbered spaces where the valley widened to its mouth. Here the "pay" ran out, and men were loth to loiter with the lure yet beyond. And here, as Li Wan paused to prod Olo with her staff, she heard the mellow silver of a woman's laughter.

Before a cabin sat a woman, fair of skin and rosy as a child, dimpling with glee at the words of another woman in the doorway. But the woman who sat shook about her great masses of dark, wet hair which yielded up its dampness to the warm caresses of the sun.

For an instant Li Wan stood transfixed. Then she was aware of a blinding flash, and a snap, as though something gave way; and the woman before the cabin vanished, and the cabin and the tall spruce timber, and the jagged sky-line, and Li Wan saw another woman, in the shine of another sun, brushing great masses of black hair, and singing as she brushed. And Li Wan heard the words of the song, and understood, and was a child again. She was smitten with a vision, wherein all the troublesome dreams merged and became one, and shapes and shadows took up their accustomed round, and all was clear and plain and real. Many pictures jostled past, strange scenes, and trees, and flowers, and people; and she saw them and knew them all.

"When you were a little bird, a little moose-bird," Canim said, his eyes upon her and burning into her.

"When I was a little moose-bird," she whispered, so faint and low he scarcely heard. And she knew she lied, as she bent her head to the strap and took the swing of the trail.

And such was the strangeness of it, the real now became unreal. The mile tramp and the pitching of camp by the edge of the stream seemed like a passage in a nightmare. She cooked the meat, fed the dogs, and unlashed the packs as in a dream, and it was not until Canim began to sketch his next wandering that she became herself again.

"The Klondike runs into the Yukon," he was saying; "a mighty river, mightier than the Mackenzie, of which you know. So we go, you and I, down to Fort o' Yukon. With dogs, in time of winter, it is twenty sleeps. Then we follow the Yukon away into the west—one hundred sleeps, two hundred—I have never heard. It is very far. And then we come to the sea. You know nothing of the sea, so let me tell you. As the lake is to the island, so the sea is to the land; all the rivers run to it, and it is without end. I have seen it at Hudson Bay; I have yet to see it in Alaska. And then we may take a great canoe upon the sea, you and I, Li Wan, or we may follow the land into the south many a hundred sleeps. And after that I do not know, save that I am Canim, the Canoe, wanderer and far-journeyer over the earth!"

She sat and listened, and fear ate into her heart as she pondered over this plunge into the illimitable wilderness. "It is a weary way," was all she said, head bowed on knee in resignation.

Then it was a splendid thought came to her, and at the wonder of it she was all aglow. She went down to the stream and washed the dried clay from her face. When the ripples died away, she stared long at her mirrored features; but sun and weatherbeat had done their work, and, what of roughness and bronze, her skin was not soft and dimpled as a child's. But the thought was still splendid and the glow unabated as she crept in beside her husband under the sleeping-robe.

She lay awake, staring up at the blue of the sky and waiting for Canim to sink into the first deep sleep. When this came about, she wormed slowly and carefully away, tucked the robe around him, and stood up. At her second step, Bash growled savagely. She whispered persuasively to him and glanced at the man. Canim was snoring profoundly. Then she turned, and with swift, noiseless feet sped up the back trail.

Mrs. Evelyn Van Wyck was just preparing for bed. Bored by the duties put upon her by society, her wealth, and widowed blessedness, she had journeyed into the Northland and gone to housekeeping in a cosy cabin on the edge of the diggings. Here, aided and abetted by her friend and companion, Myrtle Giddings, she played at living close to the soil, and cultivated the primitive with refined abandon.

She strove to get away from the generations of culture and parlor selection, and sought the earth-grip her ancestors had forfeited. Likewise she induced mental states which she fondly believed to approximate those of the stone-folk, and just now, as she put up her hair for the pillow, she was indulging her fancy with a palæolithic wooing. The details consisted principally of cave-dwellings and cracked marrow-bones, intersprinkled with fierce carnivora, hairy mammoths, and combats with rude flaked knives of flint; but the sensations were delicious. And as Evelyn Van Wyck fled through the sombre forest aisles before the too arduous advances of her slant-browed, skin-clad wooer, the door of the cabin opened, without the courtesy of a knock, and a skin-clad woman, savage and primitive, came in.

"Mercy!"

With a leap that would have done credit to a cave-woman, Miss Giddings landed in safety behind the table. But Mrs. Van Wyck held her ground. She noticed that the intruder was laboring under a strong excitement, and cast a swift glance backward to assure herself that the way was clear to the bunk, where the big Colt's revolver lay beneath a pillow.

"Greeting, O Woman of the Wondrous Hair," said Li Wan.

But she said it in her own tongue, the tongue spoken in but a little corner of the earth, and the women did not understand.

"Shall I go for help?" Miss Giddings quavered.

"The poor creature is harmless, I think," Mrs. Van Wyck replied. "And just look at her skin-clothes, ragged and trail-worn and all that. They are certainly unique. I shall buy them for my collection. Get my sack, Myrtle, please, and set up the scales."

Li Wan followed the shaping of the lips, but the words were unintelligible, and then, and for the first time, she realized, in a moment of suspense and indecision, that there was no medium of communication between them.

And at the passion of her dumbness she cried out, with arms stretched wide apart, "O Woman, thou art sister of mine!"

The tears coursed down her cheeks as she yearned toward them, and the break in her voice carried the sorrow she could not utter. But Miss Giddings was trembling, and even Mrs. Van Wyck was disturbed.

"I would live as you live. Thy ways are my ways, and our ways be one. My husband is Canim, the Canoe, and he is big and strange, and I am afraid. His trail is all the world and never ends, and I am weary. My mother was like you, and her hair was as thine, and her eyes. And life was soft to me then, and the sun warm."

She knelt humbly, and bent her head at Mrs. Van Wyck's feet. But Mrs. Van Wyck drew away, frightened at her vehemence.

Li Wan stood up, panting for speech. Her dumb lips could not articulate her overmastering consciousness of kind.

"Trade? you trade?" Mrs. Van Wyck questioned, slipping, after the fashion of the superior peoples, into pigeon tongue.

She touched Li Wan's ragged skins to indicate her choice, and poured several hundreds of gold into the blower. She stirred the dust about and trickled its yellow lustre temptingly through her fingers. But Li Wan saw only the fingers, milk-white and shapely, tapering daintily to the rosy, jewel-like nails. She placed her own hand alongside, all work-worn and calloused, and wept.

Mrs. Van Wyck misunderstood. "Gold," she encouraged. "Good gold! You trade? You changee for changee?" And she laid her hand again on Li Wan's skin garments.

"How much? You sell? How much?" she persisted, running her hand against the way of the hair so that she might make sure of the sinew-thread seam.

But Li Wan was deaf as well, and the woman's speech was without significance. Dismay at her failure sat upon her. How could she identify herself with these women? For she knew they were of the one breed, blood-sisters among men and the women of men. Her eyes roved wildly about the interior, taking in the soft draperies hanging around, the feminine garments, the oval mirror, and the dainty toilet accessories beneath. And the things haunted her, for she had seen like things before; and as she looked at them her lips involuntarily formed sounds which her throat trembled to utter. Then a thought flashed upon her, and she steadied herself. She must be calm. She must control herself, for there must be no misunderstanding this time, or else,—and she shook with a storm of suppressed tears and steadied herself again.

She put her hand on the table. "*Table*," she clearly and distinctly enunciated. "*Table*," she repeated.

She looked at Mrs. Van Wyck, who nodded approbation. Li Wan exulted, but brought her will to bear and held herself steady. "*Stove*," she went on. "*Stove*."

And at every nod of Mrs. Van Wyck, Li Wan's excitement mounted. Now stumbling and halting, and again in feverish haste, as the recrudescence of forgotten words was fast or slow, she moved about the cabin, naming article after article. And when she paused finally, it was in triumph, with body erect and head thrown back, expectant, waiting.

"Cat," Mrs. Van Wyck, laughing, spelled out in kindergarten fashion. "I—see—the—cat—catch—the—rat."

Li Wan nodded her head seriously. They were beginning to understand her at last, these women. The blood flushed darkly under her bronze at the thought, and she smiled and nodded her head still more vigorously.

Mrs. Van Wyck turned to her companion. "Received a smattering of mission education somewhere, I fancy, and has come to show it off."

"Of course," Miss Giddings tittered. "Little fool! We shall lose our sleep with her vanity."

"All the same I want that jacket. If it *is* old, the workmanship is good—a most excellent specimen." She returned to her visitor. "Changee for changee? You! Changee for changee? How much? Eh? How much, you?"

"Perhaps she 'd prefer a dress or something," Miss Giddings suggested.

Mrs. Van Wyck went up to Li Wan and made signs that she would exchange her wrapper for the jacket. And to further the transaction, she took Li Wan's hand and placed it amid the lace and ribbons of the flowing bosom, and rubbed the fingers back and forth so they might feel the texture. But the jewelled butterfly which loosely held the fold in place was insecurely fastened, and the front of the gown slipped to the side, exposing a firm white breast, which had never known the lip-clasp of a child.

Mrs. Van Wyck coolly repaired the mischief; but Li Wan uttered a loud cry, and ripped and tore at her skin-shirt till her own breast showed firm and white as Evelyn Van Wyck's. Murmuring inarticulately and making swift signs, she strove to establish the kinship.

"A half-breed," Mrs. Van Wyck commented. "I thought so from her hair."

Miss Giddings made a fastidious gesture. "Proud of her father's white skin. It 's beastly! Do give her something, Evelyn, and make her go."

But the other woman sighed. "Poor creature, I wish I could do something for her."

A heavy foot crunched the gravel without. Then the cabin door swung wide, and Canim stalked in. Miss Giddings saw a vision of sudden death, and screamed; but Mrs. Van Wyck faced him composedly.

"What do you want?" she demanded.

"How do?" Canim answered suavely and directly, pointing at the same time to Li Wan. "Um my wife."

He reached out for her, but she waved him back.

"Speak, Canim! Tell them that I am—"

"Daughter of Pow-Wah-Kaan? Nay, of what is it to them that they should care? Better should I tell them thou art an ill wife, given to creeping from thy husband's bed when sleep is heavy in his eyes."

Again he reached out for her, but she fled away from him to Mrs. Van Wyck, at whose feet she made frenzied appeal, and whose knees she tried to clasp. But the lady stepped back and gave permission with her eyes to Canim. He gripped Li Wan under the shoulders and raised her to her feet. She fought with him, in a madness of despair, till his chest was heaving with the exertion, and they had reeled about over half the room.

"Let me go, Canim," she sobbed.

But he twisted her wrist till she ceased to struggle. "The memories of the little moose-bird are overstrong and make trouble," he began.

"I know! I know!" she broke in. "I see the man in the snow, and as never before I see him crawl on hand and knee. And I, who am a little child, am carried on his back. And this is before Pow-Wah-Kaan and the time I came to live in a little corner of the earth."

"You know," he answered, forcing her toward the door; "but you will go with me down the Yukon and forget."

"Never shall I forget! So long as my skin is white shall I remember!" She clutched frantically at the door-post and looked a last appeal to Mrs. Evelyn Van Wyck.

"Then will I teach thee to forget, I, Canim, the Canoe!"

As he spoke he pulled her fingers clear and passed out with her upon the trail.

The League of the Old Men

At the Barracks a man was being tried for his life. He was an old man, a native from the Whitefish River, which empties into the Yukon below Lake Le Barge. All Dawson was wrought up over the affair, and likewise the Yukon-dwellers for a thousand miles up and down. It has been the custom of the land-robbing and sea-robbing Anglo-Saxon to give the law to conquered peoples, and ofttimes this law is harsh. But in the case of Imber the law for once seemed inadequate and weak. In the mathematical nature of things, equity did not reside in the punishment to be accorded him. The punishment was a foregone conclusion, there could be no doubt of that; and though it was capital, Imber had but one life, while the tale against him was one of scores.

In fact, the blood of so many was upon his hands that the killings attributed to him did not permit of precise enumeration. Smoking a pipe by the trailside or lounging around the stove, men made rough estimates of the numbers that had perished at his hand. They had been whites, all of them, these poor murdered people, and they had been slain singly, in pairs, and in parties. And so purposeless and wanton had been these killings, that they had long been a mystery to the mounted police, even in the time of the captains, and later, when the creeks realized, and a governor came from the Dominion to make the land pay for its prosperity.

But more mysterious still was the coming of Imber to Dawson to give himself up. It was in the late spring, when the Yukon was growling and writhing under its ice, that the old Indian climbed painfully up the bank from the river trail and stood blinking on the main street. Men who had witnessed his advent, noted that he was weak and tottery, and that he staggered over to a heap of cabin-logs and sat down. He sat there a full day, staring straight before him at the unceasing tide of white men that flooded past. Many a head jerked curiously to the side to meet his stare, and more than one remark was dropped anent the old Siwash with so strange a look upon his face. No end of men remembered afterward that they had been struck by his extraordinary figure, and forever afterward prided themselves upon their swift discernment of the unusual.

But it remained for Dickensen, Little Dickensen, to be the hero of the occasion. Little Dickensen had come into the land with great dreams and a pocketful of cash; but with the cash the dreams vanished, and to earn his passage back to the States he had accepted a clerical position with the brokerage firm of Holbrook and Mason. Across the street from the office of Holbrook and Mason was the heap of cabin-logs upon which Imber sat. Dickensen looked out of the window at him before he went to lunch; and when he came back from lunch he looked out of the window, and the old Siwash was still there.

Dickensen continued to look out of the window, and he, too, forever afterward prided himself upon his swiftness of discernment. He was a romantic little chap, and he likened the immobile old heathen to the genius of the Siwash race, gazing calm-eyed upon the hosts of the invading Saxon. The hours swept along, but Imber did not vary his posture, did not by a hair's-breadth move a muscle; and Dickensen remembered the man who once sat upright on a sled in the main street where men passed to and fro. They thought the man was resting, but later, when they touched him, they found him stiff and cold, frozen to death in the midst of the busy street. To undouble him, that he might fit into a coffin, they had been forced to lug him to a fire and thaw him out a bit. Dickensen shivered at the recollection.

Later on, Dickensen went out on the sidewalk to smoke a cigar and cool off; and a little later Emily Travis happened along. Emily Travis was dainty and delicate and rare, and whether in London or Klondike she gowned herself as befitted the daughter of a millionnaire mining engineer. Little Dickensen deposited his cigar on an outside window ledge where he could find it again, and lifted his hat.

They chatted for ten minutes or so, when Emily Travis, glancing past Dickensen's shoulder, gave a startled little scream. Dickensen turned about to see, and was startled, too. Imber had crossed the street and was standing there, a gaunt and hungry-looking shadow, his gaze riveted upon the girl.

"What do you want?" Little Dickensen demanded, tremulously plucky.

Imber grunted and stalked up to Emily Travis. He looked her over, keenly and carefully, every square inch of her. Especially did he appear interested in her silky brown hair, and in the color of her cheek, faintly sprayed and soft, like the downy bloom of a butterfly wing. He walked around her, surveying her with the calculating eye of a man who studies the lines upon which a horse or a boat is builded. In the course of his circuit the pink shell of her ear came between his eye and the westering sun, and he stopped to contemplate its rosy transparency. Then he returned to her face and looked long and intently into her blue eyes. He grunted and laid a hand on her arm midway between the shoulder and elbow. With his other hand he lifted her forearm and doubled it back. Disgust and wonder showed in his face, and he dropped her arm with a contemptuous grunt. Then he muttered a few guttural syllables, turned his back upon her, and addressed himself to Dickensen.

Dickensen could not understand his speech, and Emily Travis laughed. Imber turned from one to the other, frowning, but both shook their heads. He was about to go away, when she called out:

"Oh, Jimmy! Come here!"

Jimmy came from the other side of the street. He was a big, hulking Indian clad in approved white-man style, with an Eldorado king's sombrero on his head. He talked with Imber, haltingly, with throaty spasms. Jimmy was a Sitkan, possessed of no more than a passing knowledge of the interior dialects.

"Him Whitefish man," he said to Emily Travis. "Me savve um talk no very much. Him want to look see chief white man."

"The Governor," suggested Dickensen.

Jimmy talked some more with the Whitefish man, and his face went grave and puzzled.

"I t'ink um want Cap'n Alexander," he explained. "Him say um kill white man, white woman, white boy, plenty kill um white people. Him want to die."

"Insane, I guess," said Dickensen.

"What you call dat?" queried Jimmy.

Dickensen thrust a finger figuratively inside his head and imparted a rotary motion thereto.

"Mebbe so, mebbe so," said Jimmy, returning to Imber, who still demanded the chief man of the white men.

A mounted policeman (unmounted for Klondike service) joined the group and heard Imber's wish repeated. He was a stalwart young fellow, broad-shouldered, deep-chested, legs cleanly built and stretched wide apart, and tall though Imber was, he towered above him by half a head. His eyes were cool, and gray, and steady, and he carried himself with the peculiar confidence of power that is bred of blood and tradition. His splendid masculinity was emphasized by his excessive boyishness,—he was a mere lad,—and his smooth cheek promised a blush as willingly as the cheek of a maid.

Imber was drawn to him at once. The fire leaped into his eyes at sight of a sabre slash that scarred his cheek. He ran a withered hand down the young fellow's leg and caressed the swelling thew. He smote the broad chest with his knuckles, and pressed and prodded the thick muscle-pads that covered the shoulders like a cuirass. The group had been added to by curious passers-by—husky miners, mountaineers, and frontiersmen, sons of the long-legged and broad-shouldered generations. Imber glanced from one to another, then he spoke aloud in the Whitefish tongue.

"What did he say?" asked Dickensen.

"Him say um all the same one man, dat p'liceman," Jimmy interpreted.

Little Dickensen was little, and what of Miss Travis, he felt sorry for having asked the question.

The policeman was sorry for him and stepped into the breach. "I fancy there may be something in his story. I'll take him up to the captain for examination. Tell him to come along with me, Jimmy."

Jimmy indulged in more throaty spasms, and Imber grunted and looked satisfied.

"But ask him what he said, Jimmy, and what he meant when he took hold of my arm."

So spoke Emily Travis, and Jimmy put the question and received the answer.

"Him say you no afraid," said Jimmy.

Emily Travis looked pleased.

"Him say you no *skookum*, no strong, all the same very soft like little baby. Him break you, in um two hands, to little pieces. Him t'ink much funny, very strange, how you can be mother of men so big, so strong, like dat p'liceman."

Emily Travers kept her eyes up and unfaltering, but her cheeks were sprayed with scarlet. Little Dickensen blushed and was quite embarrassed. The policeman's face blazed with his boy's blood.

"Come along, you," he said gruffly, setting his shoulder to the crowd and forcing a way.

Thus it was that Imber found his way to the Barracks, where he made full and voluntary confession, and from the precincts of which he never emerged.

Imber looked very tired. The fatigue of hopelessness and age was in his face. His shoulders drooped depressingly, and his eyes were lack-lustre. His mop of hair should have been white, but sun and weatherbeat had burned and bitten it so that it hung limp and lifeless and colorless. He took no interest in what went on around him. The courtroom was jammed with the men of the creeks and trails, and there was an ominous note in the rumble and grumble of their low-pitched voices, which came to his ears like the growl of the sea from deep caverns.

He sat close by a window, and his apathetic eyes rested now and again on the dreary scene without. The sky was overcast, and a gray drizzle was falling. It was flood-time on the Yukon. The ice was gone, and the river was up in the town. Back and forth on the main street, in canoes and poling-boats, passed the people that never rested. Often he saw these boats turn aside from the street and enter the flooded square that marked the Barracks' parade-ground. Sometimes they disappeared beneath him, and he heard them jar against the house-logs and their occupants scramble in through the window. After that came the slush of water against men's legs as they waded across the lower room and mounted the stairs. Then they appeared in the doorway, with doffed hats and dripping seaboots, and added themselves to the waiting crowd.

And while they centred their looks on him, and in grim anticipation enjoyed the penalty he was to pay, Imber looked at them,
and mused on their ways, and on their Law that never slept, but
went on unceasing, in good times and bad, in flood and famine,
through trouble and terror and death, and which would go on
unceasing, it seemed to him, to the end of time.

A man rapped sharply on a table, and the conversation droned
away into silence. Imber looked at the man. He seemed one in
authority, yet Imber divined the square-browed man who sat by
a desk farther back to be the one chief over them all and over the
man who had rapped. Another man by the same table uprose and
began to read aloud from many fine sheets of paper. At the top
of each sheet he cleared his throat, at the bottom moistened his
fingers. Imber did not understand his speech, but the others did,
and he knew that it made them angry. Sometimes it made them
very angry, and once a man cursed him, in single syllables, stinging and tense, till a man at the table rapped him to silence.

For an interminable period the man read. His monotonous,
sing-song utterance lured Imber to dreaming, and he was dreaming deeply when the man ceased. A voice spoke to him in his own
Whitefish tongue, and he roused up, without surprise, to look
upon the face of his sister's son, a young man who had wandered
away years agone to make his dwelling with the whites.

"Thou dost not remember me," he said by way of greeting.

"Nay," Imber answered. "Thou art Howkan who went away.
Thy mother be dead."

"She was an old woman," said Howkan.

But Imber did not hear, and Howkan, with hand upon his
shoulder, roused him again.

"I shall speak to thee what the man has spoken, which is the
tale of the troubles thou hast done and which thou hast told, O
fool, to the Captain Alexander. And thou shalt understand and
say if it be true talk or talk not true. It is so commanded."

Howkan had fallen among the mission folk and been taught
by them to read and write. In his hands he held the many fine
sheets from which the man had read aloud, and which had been
taken down by a clerk when Imber first made confession, through
the mouth of Jimmy, to Captain Alexander. Howkan began to

read. Imber listened for a space, when a wonderment rose up in his face and he broke in abruptly.

"That be my talk, Howkan. Yet from thy lips it comes when thy ears have not heard."

Howkan smirked with self-appreciation. His hair was parted in the middle. "Nay, from the paper it comes, O Imber. Never have my ears heard. From the paper it comes, through my eyes, into my head, and out of my mouth to thee. Thus it comes."

"Thus it comes? It be there in the paper?" Imber's voice sank in whisperful awe as he crackled the sheets 'twixt thumb and finger and stared at the charactery scrawled thereon. "It be a great medicine, Howkan, and thou art a worker of wonders."

"It be nothing, it be nothing," the young man responded carelessly and pridefully. He read at hazard from the document: "*In that year, before the break of the ice, came an old man, and a boy who was lame of one foot. These also did I kill, and the old man made much noise—*"

"It be true," Imber interrupted breathlessly. "He made much noise and would not die for a long time. But how dost thou know, Howkan? The chief man of the white men told thee, mayhap? No one beheld me, and him alone have I told."

Howkan shook his head with impatience. "Have I not told thee it be there in the paper, O fool?"

Imber stared hard at the ink-scrawled surface. "As the hunter looks upon the snow and says, Here but yesterday there passed a rabbit; and here by the willow scrub it stood and listened, and heard, and was afraid; and here it turned upon its trail; and here it went with great swiftness, leaping wide; and here, with greater swiftness and wider leapings, came a lynx; and here, where the claws cut deep into the snow, the lynx made a very great leap; and here it struck, with the rabbit under and rolling belly up; and here leads off the trail of the lynx alone, and there is no more rabbit,—as the hunter looks upon the markings of the snow and says thus and so and here, dost thou, too, look upon the paper and say thus and so and here be the things old Imber hath done?"

"Even so," said Howkan. "And now do thou listen, and keep thy woman's tongue between thy teeth till thou art called upon for speech."

Thereafter, and for a long time, Howkan read to him the confession, and Imber remained musing and silent. At the end, he said:

"It be my talk, and true talk, but I am grown old, Howkan, and forgotten things come back to me which were well for the head man there to know. First, there was the man who came over the Ice Mountains, with cunning traps made of iron, who sought the beaver of the Whitefish. Him I slew. And there were three men seeking gold on the Whitefish long ago. Them also I slew, and left them to the wolverines. And at the Five Fingers there was a man with a raft and much meat."

At the moments when Imber paused to remember, Howkan translated and a clerk reduced to writing. The courtroom listened stolidly to each unadorned little tragedy, till Imber told of a red-haired man whose eyes were crossed and whom he had killed with a remarkably long shot.

"Hell," said a man in the forefront of the onlookers. He said it soulfully and sorrowfully. He was red-haired. "Hell," he repeated. "That was my brother Bill." And at regular intervals throughout the session, his solemn "Hell" was heard in the courtroom; nor did his comrades check him, nor did the man at the table rap him to order.

Imber's head drooped once more, and his eyes went dull, as though a film rose up and covered them from the world. And he dreamed as only age can dream upon the colossal futility of youth.

Later, Howkan roused him again, saying: "Stand up, O Imber. It be commanded that thou tellest why you did these troubles, and slew these people, and at the end journeyed here seeking the Law."

Imber rose feebly to his feet and swayed back and forth. He began to speak in a low and faintly rumbling voice, but Howkan interrupted him.

"This old man, he is damn crazy," he said in English to the square-browed man. "His talk is foolish and like that of a child."

"We will hear his talk which is like that of a child," said the square-browed man. "And we will hear it, word for word, as he speaks it. Do you understand?"

Howkan understood, and Imber's eyes flashed, for he had witnessed the play between his sister's son and the man in authority. And then began the story, the epic of a bronze patriot which might well itself be wrought into bronze for the generations un-born. The crowd fell strangely silent, and the square-browed judge leaned head on hand and pondered his soul and the soul of his race. Only was heard the deep tones of Imber, rhythmically alternating with the shrill voice of the interpreter, and now and again, like the bell of the Lord, the wondering and meditative "Hell" of the red-haired man.

"I am Imber of the Whitefish people." So ran the interpretation of Howkan, whose inherent barbarism gripped hold of him, and who lost his mission culture and veneered civilization as he caught the savage ring and rhythm of old Imber's tale. "My father was Otsbaok, a strong man. The land was warm with sunshine and gladness when I was a boy. The people did not hunger after strange things, nor hearken to new voices, and the ways of their fathers were their ways. The women found favor in the eyes of the young men, and the young men looked upon them with con-tent. Babes hung at the breasts of the women, and they were heavy-hipped with increase of the tribe. Men were men in those days. In peace and plenty, and in war and famine, they were men.

"At that time there was more fish in the water than now, and more meat in the forest. Our dogs were wolves, warm with thick hides and hard to the frost and storm. And as with our dogs so with us, for we were likewise hard to the frost and storm. And when the Pellys came into our land we slew them and were slain. For we were men, we Whitefish, and our fathers and our fathers' fathers had fought against the Pellys and determined the bounds of the land.

"As I say, with our dogs, so with us. And one day came the first white man. He dragged himself, so, on hand and knee, in the snow. And his skin was stretched tight, and his bones were sharp beneath. Never was such a man, we thought, and we wondered of what strange tribe he was, and of its land. And he was weak, most weak, like a little child, so that we gave him a place by the fire, and warm furs to lie upon, and we gave him food as little children are given food.

"And with him was a dog, large as three of our dogs, and very

weak. The hair of this dog was short, and not warm, and the tail
was frozen so that the end fell off. And this strange dog we fed,
and bedded by the fire, and fought from it our dogs, which else
would have killed him. And what of the moose meat and the sun-
dried salmon, the man and dog took strength to themselves; and
what of the strength they became big and unafraid. And the man
spoke loud words and laughed at the old men and young men,
and looked boldly upon the maidens. And the dog fought with
our dogs, and for all of his short hair and softness slew three of
them in one day.

"When we asked the man concerning his people, he said, 'I
have many brothers,' and laughed in a way that was not good.
And when he was in his full strength he went away, and with him
went Noda, daughter to the chief. First, after that, was one of our
bitches brought to pup. And never was there such a breed of
dogs,—big-headed, thick-jawed, and short-haired, and helpless.
Well do I remember my father, Otsbaok, a strong man. His face
was black with anger at such helplessness, and he took a stone,
so, and so, and there was no more helplessness. And two summers
after that came Noda back to us with a man-child in the hollow
of her arm.

"And that was the beginning. Came a second white man, with
short-haired dogs, which he left behind him when he went. And
with him went six of our strongest dogs, for which, in trade, he
had given Koo-So-Tee, my mother's brother, a wonderful pistol
that fired with great swiftness six times. And Koo-So-Tee was
very big, what of the pistol, and laughed at our bows and arrows.
'Woman's things,' he called them, and went forth against the bald-
face grizzly, with the pistol in his hand. Now it be known that it
is not good to hunt the bald-face with a pistol, but how were we
to know? and how was Koo-So-Tee to know? So he went against
the bald-face, very brave, and fired the pistol with great swiftness
six times; and the bald-face but grunted and broke in his breast
like it were an egg, and like honey from a bee's nest dripped the
brains of Koo-So-Tee upon the ground. He was a good hunter,
and there was no one to bring meat to his squaw and children.
And we were bitter, and we said, 'That which for the white men

is well, is for us not well.' And this be true. There be many white men and fat, but their ways have made us few and lean.

"Came the third white man, with great wealth of all manner of wonderful foods and things. And twenty of our strongest dogs he took from us in trade. Also, what of presents and great promises, ten of our young hunters did he take with him on a journey which fared no man knew where. It is said they died in the snow of the Ice Mountains where man has never been, or in the Hills of Silence which are beyond the edge of the earth. Be that as it may, dogs and young hunters were seen never again by the Whitefish people.

"And more white men came with the years, and ever, with pay and presents, they led the young men away with them. And sometimes the young men came back with strange tales of dangers and toils in the lands beyond the Pellys, and sometimes they did not come back. And we said: 'If they be unafraid of life, these white men, it is because they have many lives; but we be few by the Whitefish, and the young men shall go away no more.' But the young men did go away; and the young women went also; and we were very wroth.

"It be true, we ate flour, and salt pork, and drank tea which was a great delight; only, when we could not get tea, it was very bad and we became short of speech and quick of anger. So we grew to hunger for the things the white men brought in trade. Trade! trade! all the time was it trade! One winter we sold our meat for clocks that would not go, and watches with broken guts, and files worn smooth, and pistols without cartridges and worthless. And then came famine, and we were without meat, and two score died ere the break of spring.

" 'Now are we grown weak,' we said; 'and the Pellys will fall upon us, and our bounds be overthrown.' But as it fared with us, so had it fared with the Pellys, and they were too weak to come against us.

"My father, Otsbaok, a strong man, was now old and very wise. And he spoke to the chief, saying: 'Behold, our dogs be worthless. No longer are they thick-furred and strong, and they die in the frost and harness. Let us go into the village and kill them, saving only the wolf ones, and these let us tie out in the night that they may mate with the wild wolves of the forest. Thus shall we have dogs warm and strong again.'

"And his word was harkened to, and we Whitefish became known for our dogs, which were the best in the land. But known we were not for ourselves. The best of our young men and women had gone away with the white men to wander on trail and river to far places. And the young women came back old and broken, as Noda had come, or they came not at all. And the young men came back to sit by our fires for a time, full of ill speech and rough ways, drinking evil drinks and gambling through long nights and days, with a great unrest always in their hearts, till the call of the white men came to them and they went away again to the unknown places. And they were without honor and respect, jeering the old-time customs and laughing in the faces of chief and shamans.

"As I say, we were become a weak breed, we Whitefish. We sold our warm skins and furs for tobacco and whiskey and thin cotton things that left us shivering in the cold. And the coughing sickness came upon us, and men and women coughed and sweated through the long nights, and the hunters on trail spat blood upon the snow. And now one, and now another, bled swiftly from the mouth and died. And the women bore few children, and those they bore were weak and given to sickness. And other sicknesses came to us from the white men, the like of which we had never known and could not understand. Smallpox, likewise measles, have I heard these sicknesses named, and we died of them as die the salmon in the still eddies when in the fall their eggs are spawned and there is no longer need for them to live.

"And yet, and here be the strangeness of it, the white men come as the breath of death; all their ways lead to death, their nostrils are filled with it; and yet they do not die. Theirs the whiskey, and tobacco, and short-haired dogs; theirs the many sicknesses, the smallpox and measles, the coughing and mouth-bleeding; theirs the white skin, and softness to the frost and storm; and theirs the pistols that shoot six times very swift and are worthless. And yet they grow fat on their many ills, and prosper, and lay a heavy hand over all the world and tread mightily upon its peoples. And their women, too, are soft as little babes, most breakable and never broken, the mothers of men. And out of all this softness, and sickness, and weakness, come strength, and power, and authority. They be gods, or devils, as the case may be. I do not know. What do I know, I, old Imber of the White-fish? Only do I know that they are past understanding, these white men, far-wanderers and fighters over the earth that they be.

"As I say, the meat in the forest became less and less. It be true, the white man's gun is most excellent and kills a long way off; but of what worth the gun, when there is no meat to kill? When I was a boy on the Whitefish there was moose on every hill, and each year came the caribou uncountable. But now the hunter may take the trail ten days and not one moose gladden his eyes, while the caribou uncountable come no more at all. Small worth the gun, I say, killing a long way off, when there be nothing to kill.

"And I, Imber, pondered upon these things, watching the while the Whitefish, and the Pellys, and all the tribes of the land, per-ishing as perished the meat of the forest. Long I pondered. I talked with the shamans and the old men who were wise. I went apart that the sounds of the village might not disturb me, and I ate no meat so that my belly should not press upon me and make me slow of eye and ear. I sat long and sleepless in the forest, wide-eyed for the sign, my ears patient and keen for the word that was to come. And I wandered alone in the blackness of night to the river bank, where was wind-moaning and sobbing of water, and where I sought wisdom from the ghosts of old shamans in the trees and dead and gone.

"And in the end, as in a vision, came to me the short-haired and detestable dogs, and the way seemed plain. By the wisdom of Otsbaok, my father and a strong man, had the blood of our own wolf-dogs been kept clean, wherefore had they remained warm of hide and strong in the harness. So I returned to my village and made oration to the men. 'This be a tribe, these white men,' I said. 'A very large tribe, and doubtless there is no longer meat in their land, and they are come among us to make a new land for them-selves. But they weaken us, and we die. They are a very hungry folk. Already has our meat gone from us, and it were well, if we would live, that we deal by them as we have dealt by their dogs.'

"And further oration I made, counselling fight. And the men of the Whitefish listened, and some said one thing, and some another, and some spoke of other and worthless things, and no man made brave talk of deeds and war. But while the young men were weak as water and afraid, I watched that the old men sat silent, and that in their eyes fires came and went. And later, when the village slept and no one knew, I drew the old men away into the forest and made more talk. And now we were agreed, and we remembered the good young days, and the free land, and the times of plenty, and the gladness and sunshine; and we called ourselves brothers, and swore great secrecy, and a mighty oath to cleanse the land of the evil breed that had come upon it. It be plain we were fools, but how were we to know, we old men of the Whitefish?

"And to hearten the others, I did the first deed. I kept guard upon the Yukon till the first canoe came down. In it were two white men, and when I stood upright upon the bank and raised my hand they changed their course and drove in to me. And as the man in the bow lifted his head, so, that he might know wherefore I wanted him, my arrow sang through the air straight to his throat, and he knew. The second man, who held paddle in the stern, had his rifle half to his shoulder when the first of my three spear-casts smote him.

" 'These be the first,' I said, when the old men had gathered to me. 'Later we will bind together all the old men of all the tribes, and after that the young men who remain strong, and the work will become easy.'

"And then the two dead white men we cast into the river. And of the canoe, which was a very good canoe, we made a fire, and a fire, also, of the things within the canoe. But first we looked at the things, and they were pouches of leather which we cut open with our knives. And inside these pouches were many papers, like that from which thou hast read, O Howkan, with markings on them which we marvelled at and could not understand. Now, I am become wise, and I know them for the speech of men as thou hast told me."

A whisper and buzz went around the courtroom when Howkan finished interpreting the affair of the canoe, and one man's voice spoke up: "That was the lost '91 mail, Peter James and Delaney bringing it in and last spoken at Le Barge by Matthews going out." The clerk scratched steadily away, and another paragraph was added to the history of the North.

"There be little more," Imber went on slowly. "It be there on the paper, the things we did. We were old men, and we did not understand. Even I, Imber, do not now understand. Secretly we slew, and continued to slay, for with our years we were crafty and we had learned the swiftness of going without haste. When white men came among us with black looks and rough words, and took away six of the young men with irons binding them helpless, we knew we must slay wider and farther. And one by one we old men departed up river and down to the unknown lands. It was a brave thing. Old we were, and unafraid, but the fear of far places is a terrible fear to men who are old.

"So we slew, without haste and craftily. On the Chilcoot and in the Delta we slew, from the passes to the sea, wherever the white men camped or broke their trails. It be true, they died, but it was without worth. Ever did they come over the mountains, ever did they grow and grow, while we, being old, became less and less. I remember, by the Caribou Crossing, the camp of a white man. He was a very little white man, and three of the old men came upon him in his sleep. And the next day I came upon the four of them. The white man alone still breathed, and there was breath in him to curse me once and well before he died.

"And so it went, now one old man, and now another. Sometimes the word reached us long after of how they died, and sometimes it did not reach us. And the old men of the other tribes were weak and afraid, and would not join with us. As I say, one by one, till I alone was left. I am Imber, of the Whitefish people. My father was Otsbaok, a strong man. There are no Whitefish now. Of the old men I am the last. The young men and young women are gone away, some to live with the Pellys, some with the Salmons, and more with the white men. I am very old, and very tired, and it being vain fighting the Law, as thou sayest, Howkan, I am come seeking the Law."

"O Imber, thou art indeed a fool," said Howkan.

But Imber was dreaming. The square-browed judge likewise dreamed, and all his race rose up before him in a mighty phantasmagoria—his steel-shod, mail-clad race, the lawgiver and world-maker among the families of men. He saw it dawn red-flickering across the dark forests and sullen seas; he saw it blaze, bloody and red, to full and triumphant noon; and down the shaded slope he saw the blood-red sands dropping into night. And through it all he observed the Law, pitiless and potent, ever unswerving and ever ordaining, greater than the motes of men who fulfilled it or were crushed by it, even as it was greater than he, his heart speaking for softness.

The Story of Jees Uck

There have been renunciations, and renunciations. But, in its essence, renunciation is ever the same. And the paradox of it is that men and women forego the dearest thing in the world for something dearer. It was never otherwise. Thus it was when Abel brought of the firstlings of his flock and of the fat thereof. The firstlings and the fat thereof were to him the dearest things in the world; yet he gave them over that he might be on good terms with God. So it was with Abraham when he prepared to offer up his son Isaac on a stone. Isaac was very dear to him; but God, in incomprehensible ways, was yet dearer. It may be that Abraham feared the Lord. But whether that be true or not, it has since been determined by a few billion people that he loved the Lord and desired to serve Him.

And since it has been determined that love is service, and since to renounce is to serve, then Jees Uck, who was merely a woman of a swart-skinned breed, loved with a great love. She was unversed in history, having learned to read only the signs of weather and of game; so she had never heard of Abel, nor of Abraham; nor, having escaped the good sisters at Holy Cross, had she been told the story of Ruth, the Moabitess, who renounced her very God for the sake of a stranger woman from a strange land. Jees Uck had learned only one way of renouncing, and that was with a club as the dynamic factor, in much the same manner as a dog is made to renounce a stolen marrow-bone. Yet, when the time came, she proved herself capable of rising to the height of the fair-faced royal races and of renouncing in right regal fashion.

So this is the story of Jees Uck, which is also the story of Neil Bonner, and Kitty Bonner, and a couple of Neil Bonner's progeny. Jees Uck was of a swart-skinned breed, it is true, but she was not an Indian; nor was she an Eskimo; nor even an Innuit. Going backward into mouth tradition, there appears the figure of one Skolkz, a Toyaat Indian of the Yukon, who journeyed down in his youth to the Great Delta where dwell the Innuits, and where he forgathered with a woman remembered as Olillie. Now the woman Olillie had been bred from an Eskimo mother by an Innuit man. And from Skolkz and Olillie came Halie, who was one-half Toyaat Indian, one-quarter Innuit, and one-quarter Eskimo. And Halie was the grandmother of Jees Uck.

Now Halie, in whom three stocks had been bastardized, who cherished no prejudice against further admixture, mated with a Russian fur trader called Shpack, also known in his time as the Big Fat. Shpack is herein classed Russian for lack of a more adequate term; for Shpack's father, a Slavonic convict from the Lower Provinces, had escaped from the quick-silver mines into Northern Siberia, where he knew Zimba, who was a woman of the Deer People and who became the mother of Shpack, who became the grandfather of Jees Uck.

Now had not Shpack been captured in his boyhood by the Sea People, who fringe the rim of the Arctic Sea with their misery, he would not have become the grandfather of Jees Uck and there would be no story at all. But he *was* captured by the Sea People, from whom he escaped to Kamchatka, and thence, on a Norwegian whale-ship, to the Baltic. Not long after that he turned up in St. Petersburg, and the years were not many till he went drifting east over the same weary road his father had measured with blood and groans a half-century before. But Shpack was a free man, in the employ of the great Russian Fur Company. And in that employ he fared farther and farther east, until he crossed Bering Sea into Russian America; and at Pastolik, which is hard by the Great Delta of the Yukon, became the husband of Halie, who was the grandmother of Jees Uck. Out of this union came the woman-child, Tukesan.

Shpack, under the orders of the company, made a canoe voyage of a few hundred miles up the Yukon to the post of Nulato. With him he took Halie and the babe Tukesan. This was in 1850, and in 1850 it was that the river Indians fell upon Nulato and wiped it from the face of the earth. And that was the end of Shpack and Halie. On that terrible night Tukesan disappeared. To this day the Toyaats aver they had no hand in the trouble; but, be that as it may, the fact remains that the babe Tukesan grew up among them.

Tukesan was married successively to two Toyaat brothers, to

both of whom she was barren. Because of this, other women shook their heads, and no third Toyaat man could be found to dare matrimony with the childless widow. But at this time, many hundred miles above, at Fort Yukon, was a man, Spike O'Brien. Fort Yukon was a Hudson Bay Company post, and Spike O'Brien one of the company's servants. He was a good servant, but he achieved an opinion that the service was bad, and in the course of time vindicated that opinion by deserting. It was a year's journey, by the chain of posts, back to York Factory on Hudson's Bay. Further, being company posts, he knew he could not evade the company's clutches. Nothing remained but to go down the Yukon. It was true no white man had ever gone down the Yukon, and no white man knew whether the Yukon emptied into the Arctic Ocean or Bering Sea; but Spike O'Brien was a Celt, and the promise of danger was a lure he had ever followed.

A few weeks later, somewhat battered, rather famished, and about dead with river-fever, he drove the nose of his canoe into the earth bank by the village of the Toyaats and promptly fainted away. While getting his strength back, in the weeks that followed, he looked upon Tukesan and found her good. Like the father of Shpack, who lived to a ripe old age among the Siberian Deer People, Spike O'Brien might have left his aged bones with the Toyaats. But romance gripped his heart-strings and would not let him stay. As he had journeyed from York Factory to Fort Yukon, so, first among men, might he journey from Fort Yukon to the sea and win the honor of being the first man to make the North-west Passage by land. So he departed down the river, won the honor, and was unannaled and unsung. In after years he ran a sailors' boarding-house in San Francisco, where he became esteemed a most remarkable liar by virtue of the gospel truths he told. But a child was born to Tukesan, who had been childless. And this child was Jees Uck. Her lineage has been traced at length to show that she was neither Indian, nor Eskimo, nor Innuit, nor much of anything else; also to show what waifs of the generations we are, all of us, and the strange meanderings of the seed from which we spring.

What with the vagrant blood in her and the heritage compounded of many races, Jees Uck developed a wonderful young beauty. Bizarre, perhaps, it was, and Oriental enough to puzzle any passing ethnologist. A lithe and slender grace characterized her. Beyond a quickened lilt to the imagination, the contribution of the Celt was in no wise apparent. It might possibly have put the warm blood under her skin, which made her face less swart and her body fairer; but that, in turn, might have come from Shpack, the Big Fat, who inherited the color of his Slavonic father. And, finally, she had great, blazing black eyes—the half-caste eye, round, full-orbed, and sensuous, which marks the collision of the dark races with the light. Also, the white blood in her, combined with her knowledge that it was in her, made her, in a way, ambitious. Otherwise, by upbringing and in outlook on life, she was wholly and utterly a Toyaat Indian.

One winter, when she was a young woman, Neil Bonner came into her life. But he came into her life, as he had come into the country, somewhat reluctantly. In fact, it was very much against his will, coming into the country. Between a father who clipped coupons and cultivated roses, and a mother who loved the social round, Neil Bonner had gone rather wild. He was not vicious, but a man with meat in his belly and without work in the world has to expend his energy somehow, and Neil Bonner was such a man. And he expended his energy in such fashion and to such extent that when the inevitable climax came, his father, Neil Bonner, senior, crawled out of his roses in a panic and looked on his son with a wondering eye. Then he hied himself away to a crony of kindred pursuits, with whom he was wont to confer over coupons and roses, and between the two the destiny of young Neil Bonner was made manifest. He must go away, on probation, to live down his harmless follies in order that he might live up to their own excellent standard.

This determined upon, a young Neil a little repentant and a great deal ashamed, the rest was easy. The cronies were heavy stockholders in the P. C. Company. The P. C. Company owned fleets of river-steamers and ocean-going craft, and, in addition to farming the sea, exploited a hundred thousand square miles or so of the land that, on the maps of geographers, usually occupies the white spaces. So the P. C. Company sent young Neil Bonner north, where the white spaces are, to do its work and to learn to be good like his father. "Five years of simplicity, close to the soil and far from temptation, will make a man of him," said old Neil Bonner, and forthwith crawled back among his roses. Young Neil set his jaw, pitched his chin at the proper angle, and went to work. As an underling he did his work well and gained the commendation of his superiors. Not that he delighted in the work, but that it was the one thing that prevented him from going mad.

The first year he wished he was dead. The second year he cursed God. The third year he was divided between the two emotions, and in the confusion quarrelled with a man in authority. He had the best of the quarrel, though the man in authority had the last word,—a word that sent Neil Bonner into an exile that made his old billet appear as paradise. But he went without a whimper, for the North had succeeded in making him into a man.

Here and there, on the white spaces on the map, little circlets like the letter "o" are to be found, and, appended to these circlet, on one side or the other, are names such as "Fort Hamilton," "Yanana Station," "Twenty Mile," thus leading one to imagine that the white spaces are plentifully besprinkled with towns and villages. But it is a vain imagining. Twenty Mile, which is very like the rest of the posts, is a log building the size of a corner grocery with rooms to let upstairs. A long-legged cache on stilts may be found in the back yard; also a couple of outhouses. The back yard is unfenced, and extends to the sky-line and an unascertainable bit beyond. There are no other houses in sight, though the Toyaats sometimes pitch a winter camp a mile or two down the Yukon. And this is Twenty Mile, one tentacle of the many-tentacled P. C. Company. Here the agent, with an assistant, barters with the Indians for their furs, and does an erratic trade on a gold-dust basis with the wandering miners. Here, also, the agent and his assistant yearn all winter for the spring, and when the spring comes, camp blasphemously on the roof while the Yukon washes out the establishment. And here, also, in the fourth year of his sojourn in the land, came Neil Bonner to take charge.

He had displaced no agent; for the man that previously ran the post had made away with himself; "because of the rigors of the place," said the assistant, who still remained; though the Toyaats, by their fires, had another version. The assistant was a shrunken-shouldered, hollow-chested man, with a cadaverous face and cavernous cheeks that his sparse black beard could not hide. He coughed much, as though consumption gripped his lungs, while his eyes had that mad, fevered light common to consumptives in the last stage. Pentley was his name,—Amos Pentley,—and Bonner did not like him, though he felt a pity for the forlorn and hopeless devil. They did not get along together, these two men who, of all men, should have been on good terms in the face of the cold and silence and darkness of the long winter.

In the end, Bonner concluded that Amos was partly demented, and left him alone, doing all the work himself except the cooking. Even then, Amos had nothing but bitter looks and an undisguised hatred for him. This was a great loss to Bonner; for the smiling face of one of his own kind, the cheery word, the sympathy of comradeship shared with misfortune—these things meant much; and the winter was yet young when he began to realize the added reasons, with such an assistant, that the previous agent had found to impel his own hand against his life.

It was very lonely at Twenty Mile. The bleak vastness stretched away on every side to the horizon. The snow, which was really frost, flung its mantle over the land and buried everything in the silence of death. For days it was clear and cold, the thermometer steadily recording forty to fifty degrees below zero. Then a change came over the face of things. What little moisture had oozed into the atmosphere gathered into dull gray, formless clouds; it became quite warm, the thermometer rising to twenty below; and the moisture fell out of the sky in hard frost-granules that hissed like dry sugar or driving sand when kicked underfoot. After that it became clear and cold again, until enough moisture had gathered to blanket the earth from the cold of outer space. That was all. Nothing happened. No storms, no churning waters and threshing forests, nothing but the machine-like precipitation of accumulated moisture. Possibly the most notable thing that occurred through the weary weeks was the gliding of the temperature up to the unprecedented height of fifteen below. To atone for this, outer space smote the earth with its cold till the mercury froze and the spirit thermometer remained more than seventy below for a fortnight, when it burst. There was no telling how much colder it was after that. Another occurrence, monotonous in its regularity, was the lengthening of the nights, till day became a mere blink of light between the darknesses.

Neil Bonner was a social animal. The very follies for which he was doing penance had been bred of his excessive sociability. And here, in the fourth year of his exile, he found himself in company—which were to travesty the word—with a morose and speechless creature in whose sombre eyes smouldered a hatred as bitter as it was unwarranted. And Bonner, to whom speech and fellowship were as the breath of life, went about as a ghost might go, tantalized by the gregarious revelries of some former life. In the day his lips were compressed, his face stern; but in the night he clenched his hands, rolled about in his blankets, and cried aloud like a little child. And he would remember a certain man in authority and curse him through the long hours. Also, he cursed God. But God understands. He cannot find it in His heart to blame weak mortals who blaspheme in Alaska.

And here, to the post of Twenty Mile, came Jees Uck, to trade for flour and bacon, and beads, and bright scarlet cloths for her fancy work. And further, and unwittingly, she came to the post of Twenty Mile to make a lonely man more lonely, make him reach out empty arms in his sleep. For Neil Bonner was only a man. When she first came into the store, he looked at her long, as a thirsty man may look at a flowing well. And she, with the heritage bequeathed her by Spike O'Brien, imagined daringly and smiled up into his eyes, not as the swart-skinned peoples should smile at the royal races, but as a woman smiles at a man. The thing was inevitable; only, he did not see it, and fought against her as fiercely and passionately as he was drawn toward her. And she? She was Jees Uck, by upbringing wholly and utterly a Toyaat Indian woman.

She came often to the post to trade. And often she sat by the big wood stove and chatted in broken English with Neil Bonner. And he came to look for her coming; and on the days she did not come he was worried and restless. Sometimes he stopped to think, and then she was met coldly, with a reserve that perplexed and piqued her, and which, she was convinced, was not sincere. But more often he did not dare to think, and then all went well and there were smiles and laughter. And Amos Pentley, gasping like a stranded catfish, his hollow cough a-reek with the grave, looked upon it all and grinned. He, who loved life, could not live, and it rankled his soul that others should be able to live. Wherefore he hated Bonner, who was so very much alive and into whose eyes sprang joy at the sight of Jees Uck. As for Amos, the very thought of the girl was sufficient to send his blood pounding up into a hemorrhage.

Jees Uck, whose mind was simple, who thought elementally and was unused to weighing life in its subtler quantities, read Amos Pentley like a book. She warned Bonner, openly and bluntly, in few words; but the complexities of higher existence confused the situation to him, and he laughed at her evident anxiety. To him, Amos was a poor, miserable devil, tottering desperately into the grave. And Bonner, who had suffered much, found it easy to forgive greatly.

But one morning, during a bitter snap, he got up from the breakfast table and went into the store. Jees Uck was already there, rosy from the trail, to buy a sack of flour. A few minutes later, he was out in the snow lashing the flour on her sled. As he bent over he noticed a stiffness in his neck and felt a premonition of impending physical misfortune. And as he put the last half-hitch into the lashing and attempted to straighten up, a quick spasm seized him and he sank into the snow. Tense and quivering, head jerked back, limbs extended, back arched and mouth twisted and distorted, he appeared as though being racked limb from limb. Without cry or sound, Jees Uck was in the snow beside him; but he clutched both her wrists spasmodically, and as long as the convulsion endured she was helpless. In a few moments the spasm relaxed and he was left weak and fainting, his forehead beaded with sweat, his lips flecked with foam.

"Quick!" he muttered, in a strange, hoarse voice. "Quick! Inside!"

He started to crawl on hands and knees, but she raised him up, and, supported by her young arm, he made faster progress. As he entered the store the spasm seized him again, and his body writhed irresistibly away from her and rolled and curled on the floor. Amos Pentley came and looked on with curious eyes.

"Oh, Amos!" she cried in an agony of apprehension and help-lessness, "him die, you think?" But Amos shrugged his shoulders and continued to look on.

Bonner's body went slack, the tense muscles easing down and an expression of relief coming into his face. "Quick!" he gritted between his teeth, his mouth twisting with the on-coming of the next spasm and with his effort to control it. "Quick, Jees Uck! The medicine! Never mind! Drag me!"

She knew where the medicine-chest stood, at the rear of the room, beyond the stove, and thither, by the legs, she dragged the struggling man. As the spasm passed, he began, very faint and very sick, to overhaul the chest. He had seen dogs die exhibiting symptoms similar to his own, and he knew what should be done. He held up a vial of chloral hydrate, but his fingers were too weak and nerveless to draw the cork. This Jees Uck did for him, while he was plunged into another convulsion. As he came out of it he found the open bottle proffered him and looked into the great black eyes of the woman and read what men have always read in the Mate-woman's eyes. Taking a full dose of the stuff, he sank back until another spasm had passed. Then he raised himself limply on his elbow.

"Listen, Jees Uck!" he said very slowly, as though aware of the necessity for haste and yet afraid to hasten. "Do what I say. Stay by my side, but do not touch me. I must be very quiet, but you must not go away." His jaw began to set and his face to quiver and distort with the forerunning pangs, but he gulped and struggled to master them. "Do not go away. And do not let Amos go away. Understand! Amos must stay right here."

She nodded her head, and he passed off into the first of many convulsions, which gradually diminished in force and frequency. Jees Uck hung over him, remembering his injunction and not dar-ing to touch him. Once Amos grew restless and made as though to go into the kitchen; but a quick blaze from her eyes quelled him, and after that, save for his labored breathing and charnel cough, he was very quiet.

Bonner slept. The blink of light that marked the day disap-peared. Amos, followed about by the woman's eyes, lighted the kerosene lamps. Evening came on. Through the north window the heavens were emblazoned with an auroral display, which flamed and flared and died down into blackness. Some time after that, Neil Bonner roused. First he looked to see that Amos was still there, then smiled at Jees Uck and pulled himself up. Every muscle was stiff and sore, and he smiled ruefully, pressing and prodding himself as if to ascertain the extent of the ravage. Then his face went stern and businesslike.

"Jees Uck," he said, "take a candle. Go into the kitchen. There is food on the table—biscuits and beans and bacon; also, coffee in the pot on the stove. Bring it here on the counter. Also, bring tumblers and water and whiskey, which you will find on the top shelf of the locker. Do not forget the whiskey."

Having swallowed a stiff glass of the whiskey, he went carefully through the medicine chest, now and again putting aside, with definite purpose, certain bottles and vials. Then he set to work on the food, attempting a crude analysis. He had not been unused to the laboratory in his college days and was possessed of sufficient imagination to achieve results with his limited materials. The condition of tetanus, which had marked his paroxysms, simplified matters, and he made but one test. The coffee yielded nothing; nor did the beans. To the biscuits he devoted the utmost care. Amos, who knew nothing of chemistry, looked on with steady curiosity. But Jees Uck, who had boundless faith in the white man's wisdom, and especially in Neil Bonner's wisdom, and who not only knew nothing but knew that she knew nothing, watched his face rather than his hands.

Step by step he eliminated possibilities, until he came to the final test. He was using a thin medicine vial for a tube, and this he held between him and the light, watching the slow precipitation of a salt through the solution contained in the tube. He said nothing, but he saw what he had expected to see. And Jees Uck, her eyes riveted on his face, saw something, too,—something that made her spring like a tigress upon Amos and with splendid suppleness and strength bend his body back across her knee. Her knife was out of its sheath and uplifted, glinting in the lamplight. Amos was snarling; but Bonner intervened ere the blade could fall.

"That's a good girl, Jees Uck. But never mind. Let him go!"

She dropped the man obediently, though with protest writ large on her face; and his body thudded to the floor. Bonner nudged him with his moccasined foot.

"Get up, Amos!" he commanded. "You've got to pack an outfit yet to-night and hit the trail."

"You don't mean to say—" Amos blurted savagely.

"I mean to say that you tried to kill me," Neil went on in cold, even tones. "I mean to say that you killed Birdsall, for all the company believes he killed himself. You used strychnine in my case. God knows with what you fixed him. Now I can't hang you. You're too near dead, as it is. But Twenty Mile is too small for the pair of us, and you've got to mush. It's two hundred miles to Holy Cross. You can make it if you're careful not to overexert. I 'll give you grub, a sled, and three dogs. You'll be as safe as if you were in jail, for you can't get out of the country. And I'll give you one chance. You're almost dead. Very well. I shall send no word to the company until the spring. In the meantime, the thing for you to do is to die. Now, *mush!*"

"You go to bed!" Jees Uck insisted, when Amos had churned away into the night toward Holy Cross. "You sick man yet, Neil."

"And you're a good girl, Jees Uck," he answered. "And here's my hand on it. But you must go home."

"You don't like me," she said simply.

He smiled, helped her on with her *parka*, and led her to the door. "Only too well, Jees Uck," he said softly; "only too well."

After that the pall of the Arctic night fell deeper and blacker on the land. Neil Bonner discovered that he had failed to put proper valuation upon even the sullen face of the murderous and death-stricken Amos. It became very lonely at Twenty Mile. "For the love of God, Prentiss, send me a man," he wrote to the agent at Fort Hamilton, three hundred miles up river. Six weeks later the Indian messenger brought back a reply. It was characteristic: "Hell. Both feet frozen. Need him myself—Prentiss."

To make matters worse, most of the Toyaats were in the back country on the flanks of a caribou herd, and Jees Uck was with them. Removing to a distance seemed to bring her closer than ever, and Neil Bonner found himself picturing her, day by day, in camp and on trail. It is not good to be alone. Often he went out of the quiet store, bare-headed and frantic, and shook his fist at the blink of day that came over the southern sky-line. And on still, cold nights he left his bed and stumbled into the frost, where he assaulted the silence at the top of his lungs, as though it were some tangible, sentient thing that he might arouse; or he shouted at the sleeping dogs till they howled and howled again. One shaggy brute he brought into the post, playing that it was the new man sent by Prentiss. He strove to make it sleep decently under blankets at night and to sit at table and eat as a man should; but the beast, mere domesticated wolf that it was, rebelled, and sought out dark corners and snarled and bit him in the leg, and was finally beaten and driven forth.

Then the trick of personification seized upon Neil Bonner and mastered him. All the forces of his environment metamorphosed into living, breathing entities and came to live with him. He recreated the primitive pantheon; reared an altar to the sun and burned candle fat and bacon grease thereon; and in the unfenced yard, by the long-legged cache, made a frost devil, which he was wont to make faces at and mock when the mercury oozed down into the bulb. All this in play, of course. He said it to himself that it was in play, and repeated it over and over to make sure, unaware that madness is ever prone to express itself in make-believe and play.

One midwinter day, Father Champreau, a Jesuit missionary, pulled into Twenty Mile. Bonner fell upon him and dragged him into the post, and clung to him and wept, until the priest wept with him from sheer compassion. Then Bonner became madly hilarious and made lavish entertainment, swearing valiantly that his guest should not depart. But Father Champreau was pressing to Salt Water on urgent business for his order, and pulled out next morning, with Bonner's blood threatened on his head.

And the threat was in a fair way toward realization, when the Toyaats returned from their long hunt to the winter camp. They had many furs, and there was much trading and stir at Twenty Mile. Also, Jees Uck came to buy beads and scarlet cloths and things, and Bonner began to find himself again. He fought for a week against her. Then the end came one night when she rose to leave. She had not forgotten her repulse, and the pride that drove Spike O'Brien on to complete the Northwest Passage by land was her pride.

"I go now," she said; "good night, Neil."

But he came up behind her. "Nay, it is not well," he said.

And as she turned her face toward his with a sudden joyful flash, he bent forward, slowly and gravely, as it were a sacred thing, and kissed her on the lips. The Toyaats had never taught her the meaning of a kiss upon the lips, but she understood and was glad.

With the coming of Jees Uck, at once things brightened up. She was regal in her happiness, a source of unending delight. The elemental workings of her mind and her naive little ways made an immense sum of pleasurable surprise to the overcivilized man that had stooped to catch her up. Not alone was she solace to his loneliness, but her primitiveness rejuvenated his jaded mind. It was as though, after long wandering, he had returned to pillow his head in the lap of Mother Earth. In short, in Jees Uck he found the youth of the world—the youth and the strength and the joy.

And to fill the full round of his need, and that they might not see overmuch of each other, there arrived at Twenty Mile one Sandy MacPherson, as companionable a man as ever whistled along the trail or raised a ballad by a camp-fire. A Jesuit priest had run into his camp, a couple of hundred miles up the Yukon, in the nick of time to say a last word over the body of Sandy's partner. And on departing, the priest had said, "My son, you will be lonely now." And Sandy had bowed his head brokenly. "At Twenty Mile," the priest added, "there is a lonely man. You have need of each other, my son."

So it was that Sandy became a welcome third at the post, brother to the man and woman that resided there. He took Bonner moose-hunting and wolf-trapping; and, in return, Bonner resurrected a battered and way-worn volume and made him friends with Shakespeare, till Sandy declaimed iambic pentameters to his sled-dogs whenever they waxed mutinous. And of the long evenings they played cribbage and talked and disagreed about the universe, the while Jees Uck rocked matronly in an easy-chair and darned their moccasins and socks.

Spring came. The sun shot up out of the south. The land exchanged its austere robes for the garb of a smiling wanton. Everywhere light laughed and life invited. The days stretched out their balmy length and the nights passed from blinks of darkness to no darkness at all. The river bared its bosom, and snorting steamboats challenged the wilderness. There were stir and bustle, new faces, and fresh facts. An assistant arrived at Twenty Mile, and Sandy MacPherson wandered off with a bunch of prospectors to invade the Koyokuk country. And there were newspapers and magazines and letters for Neil Bonner. And Jees Uck looked on in worriment, for she knew his kindred talked with him across the world.

Without much shock, it came to him that his father was dead. There was a sweet letter of forgiveness, dictated in his last hours. There were official letters from the company, graciously ordering him to turn the post over to the assistant and permitting him to depart at his earliest pleasure. A long, legal affair from the lawyers informed him of interminable lists of stocks and bonds, real estate, rents, and chattels that were his by his father's will. And a dainty bit of stationery, sealed and monogrammed, implored dear Neil's return to his heart-broken and loving mother.

Neil Bonner did some swift thinking, and when the *Yukon Belle* coughed in to the bank on her way down to Bering Sea, he departed—departed with the ancient lie of quick return young and blithe on his lips.

"I'll come back, dear Jees Uck, before the first snow flies," he promised her, between the last kisses at the gang-plank.

And not only did he promise, but, like the majority of men under the same circumstances, he really meant it. To John Thompson, the new agent, he gave orders for the extension of unlimited credit to his wife, Jees Uck. Also, with his last look from the deck of the *Yukon Belle*, he saw a dozen men at work rearing the logs that were to make the most comfortable house along a thousand miles of river front—the house of Jees Uck, and likewise the house of Neil Bonner—ere the first flurry of snow. For he fully and fondly meant to come back. Jees Uck was dear to him, and, further, a golden future awaited the North. With his father's money he intended to verify that future. An ambitious dream allured him. With his four years of experience, and aided by the friendly cooperation of the P. C. Company, he would return to become the Rhodes of Alaska. And he would return, fast as steam could drive, as soon as he had put into shape the affairs of his father, whom he had never known, and comforted his mother, whom he had forgotten.

There was much ado when Neil Bonner came back from the Arctic. The fires were lighted and the fleshpots slung, and he took of it all and called it good. Not only was he bronzed and creased, but he was a new man under his skin, with a grip on things and a seriousness and control. His old companions were amazed when he declined to hit up the pace in the good old way, while his father's crony rubbed hands gleefully, and became an authority upon the reclamation of wayward and idle youth.

For four years Neil Bonner's mind had lain fallow. Little that was new had been added to it, but it had undergone a process of selection. It had, so to say, been purged of the trivial and superfluous. He had lived quick years, down in the world; and, up in the wilds, time had been given him to organize the confused mass of his experiences. His superficial standards had been flung to the winds and new standards erected on deeper and broader generalizations. Concerning civilization, he had gone away with one set of values, had returned with another set of values. Aided, also, by the earth smells in his nostrils and the earth sights in his eyes, he laid hold of the inner significance of civilization, beholding with clear vision its futilities and powers. It was a simple little philosophy he evolved. Clean living was the way to grace. Duty performed was sanctification. One must live clean and do his duty in order that he might work. Work was salvation. And to work toward life abundant, and more abundant, was to be in line with the scheme of things and the will of God.

Primarily, he was of the city. And his fresh earth grip and virile conception of humanity gave him a finer sense of civilization and endeared civilization to him. Day by day the people of the city clung closer to him and the world loomed more colossal. And, day by day, Alaska grew more remote and less real. And then he met Kitty Sharon—a woman of his own flesh and blood and kind;

a woman who put her hand into his hand and drew him to her, till he forgot the day and hour and the time of the year the first snow flies on the Yukon.

Jees Uck moved into her grand log-house and dreamed away three golden summer months. Then came the autumn, post-haste before the down rush of winter. The air grew thin and sharp, the days thin and short. The river ran sluggishly, and skin ice formed in the quiet eddies. All migratory life departed south, and silence fell upon the land. The first snow flurries came, and the last homing steamboat bucked desperately into the running mush ice. Then came the hard ice, solid cakes and sheets, till the Yukon ran level with its banks. And when all this ceased the river stood still and the blinking days lost themselves in the darkness.

John Thompson, the new agent, laughed; but Jees Uck had faith in the mischances of sea and river. Neil Bonner might be frozen in anywhere between Chilkoot Pass and St. Michael's, for the last travellers of the year are always caught by the ice, when they exchange boat for sled and dash on through the long hours behind the flying dogs.

But no flying dogs came up the trail, nor down the trail, to Twenty Mile. And John Thompson told Jees Uck, with a certain gladness ill concealed, that Bonner would never come back again. Also, and brutally, he suggested his own eligibility. Jees Uck laughed in his face and went back to her grand log-house. But when midwinter came, when hope dies down and life is at its lowest ebb, Jees Uck found she had no credit at the store. This was Thompson's doing, and he rubbed his hands, and walked up and down, and came to his door and looked up at Jees Uck's house, and waited. And he continued to wait. She sold her dog-team to a party of miners and paid cash for her food. And when Thompson refused to honor even her coin, Toyaat Indians made her purchases, and sledded them up to her house in the dark.

In February the first post came in over the ice, and John Thompson read in the society column of a five months' old paper of the marriage of Neil Bonner and Kitty Sharon. Jees Uck held the door ajar and him outside while he imparted the information; and, when he had done, laughed pridefully and did not believe. In March, and all alone, she gave birth to a man-child, a brave bit of new life at which she marvelled. And at that hour, a year later, Neil Bonner sat by another bed, marvelling at another bit of new life that had fared into the world.

The snow went off the ground and the ice broke out of the Yukon. The sun journeyed north, and journeyed south again; and, the money from the dogs being spent, Jees Uck went back to her own people. Oche Ish, a shrewd hunter, proposed to kill the meat for her and her babe, and catch the salmon, if she would marry him. And Imego and Hah Yo and Wy Nooch, husky young hunters all, made similar proposals. But she elected to live alone and seek her own meat and fish. She sewed moccasins and *parkas* and mittens—warm, serviceable things, and pleasing to the eye, withal, what of the ornamental hairtufts and bead work. These she sold to the miners, who were drifting faster into the land each year. And not only did she win food that was good and plentiful, but she laid money by, and one day took passage on the *Yukon Belle* down the river.

At St. Michael's she washed dishes in the kitchen of the post. The servants of the company wondered at the remarkable woman with the remarkable child, though they asked no questions and she vouchsafed nothing. But just before Bering Sea closed in for the year, she bought a passage south on a strayed sealing schooner. That winter she cooked for Captain Markheim's household at Unalaska, and in the spring continued south to Sitka on a whiskey sloop. Later, she appeared at Metlakahtla, which is near to St. Mary's on the end of the Pan-Handle, where she worked in the cannery through the salmon season. When autumn came and the Siwash fishermen prepared to return to Puget Sound, she embarked with a couple of families in a big cedar canoe; and with them she threaded the hazardous chaos of the Alaskan and Canadian coasts, till the Straits of Juan de Fuca were passed and she led her boy by the hand up the hard pave of Seattle.

There she met Sandy MacPherson, on a windy corner, very much surprised and, when he had heard her story, very wroth—not so wroth as he might have been, had he known of Kitty Sharon; but of her Jees Uck breathed no word, for she had never believed. Sandy, who read commonplace and sordid desertion into the circumstance, strove to dissuade her from her trip to San Francisco, where Neil Bonner was supposed to live when he was at home. And, having striven, he made her comfortable, bought her tickets and saw her off, the while smiling in her face and muttering "damshame" into his beard.

With roar and rumble, through daylight and dark, swaying and lurching between the dawns, soaring into the winter snows and sinking to summer valleys, skirting depths, leaping chasms, piercing mountains, Jees Uck and her boy were hurled south. But she had no fear of the iron stallion; nor was she stunned by this masterful civilization of Neil Bonner's people. It seemed, rather, that she saw with greater clearness the wonder that a man of such godlike race had held her in his arms. The screaming medley of San Francisco, with its restless shipping, belching factories, and thundering traffic, did not confuse her; instead, she comprehended swiftly the pitiful sordidness of Twenty Mile and the skin-lodged Toyaat village. And she looked down at the boy that clutched her hand and wondered that she had borne him by such a man.

She paid the hack-driver five prices and went up the stone steps to Neil Bonner's front door. A slant-eyed Japanese parleyed with her for a fruitless space, then led her inside and disappeared. She remained in the hall, which to her simple fancy seemed to be the guest room—the show-place wherein were arrayed all the household treasures with the frank purpose of parade and dazzlement. The walls and ceiling were of oiled and panelled redwood. The floor was more glassy than glare ice, and she sought standing place on one of the great skins that gave a sense of security to the polished surface. A huge fireplace—an extravagant fireplace, she deemed it—yawned in the farther wall. A flood of light, mellowed by stained glass, fell across the room, and from the far end came the white gleam of a marble figure.

This much she saw, and more, when the slant-eyed servant led the way past another room—of which she caught a fleeting glance—and into a third, both of which dimmed the brave show of the entrance hall. And to her eyes the great house seemed to hold out a promise of endless similar rooms. There was such length and breadth to them, and the ceilings were so far away! For the first time since her advent into the white man's civilization, a feeling of awe laid hold of her. Neil, her Neil, lived in this house, breathed the air of it, and lay down at night and slept! It was beautiful, all this that she saw, and it pleased her; but she felt, also, the wisdom and mastery behind. It was the concrete expression of power in terms of beauty, and it was the power that she unerringly divined.

And then came a woman, queenly tall, crowned with a glory of hair that was like a golden sun. She seemed to come toward Jees Uck as a ripple of music across still water; her sweeping garment itself a song, her body playing rhythmically beneath. Jees Uck was herself a man compeller. There were Oche Ish and Imego and Hah Yo and Wy Nooch, to say nothing of Neil Bonner and John Thompson and other white men that had looked upon her and felt her power. But she gazed upon the wide blue eyes and rose-white skin of this woman that advanced to meet her, and she measured her with woman's eyes looking through man's eyes; and as a man compeller she felt herself diminish and grow insignificant before this radiant and flashing creature.

"You wish to see my husband?" the woman asked; and Jees Uck gasped at the liquid silver of a voice that had never sounded harsh cries at snarling wolf dogs, nor moulded itself to a guttural speech, nor toughened in storm and frost and camp smoke.

"No," Jees Uck answered slowly and gropingly, in order that she might do justice to her English. "I come to see Neil Bonner."

"He is my husband," the woman laughed.

Then it was true! John Thompson had not lied that bleak February day, when she laughed pridefully and shut the door in his face. As once she had thrown Amos Pentley across her knee and ripped her knife into the air, so now she felt impelled to spring upon this woman and bear her back and down, and tear the life out of her fair body. But Jees Uck was thinking quickly and gave no sign, and Kitty Bonner little dreamed how intimately she had for an instant been related with sudden death.

Jees Uck nodded her head that she understood, and Kitty Bonner explained that Neil was expected at any moment. Then they sat down on ridiculously comfortable chairs, and Kitty sought to entertain her strange visitor, and Jees Uck strove to help her.

"You knew my husband in the North?" Kitty asked, once.

"Sure. I wash um clothes," Jees Uck had answered, her English abruptly beginning to grow atrocious.

"And this is your boy? I have a little girl."

Kitty caused her daughter to be brought, and while the children, after their manner, struck an acquaintance, the mothers indulged in the talk of mothers and drank tea from cups so fragile that Jees Uck feared lest hers should crumble to pieces between her fingers. Never had she seen such cups, so delicate and dainty. In her mind she compared them with the woman who poured the tea, and there uprose in contrast the gourds and pannikins of the Toyaat village and the clumsy mugs of Twenty Mile, to which she likened herself. And in such fashion and such terms the problem presented itself. She was beaten. There was a woman other than herself better fitted to bear and upbring Neil Bonner's children. Just as his people exceeded her people, so did his womenkind exceed her. They were the man compellers, as their men were the world compellers. She looked at the rose-white tenderness of Kitty Bonner's skin and remembered the sun-beat on her own face. Likewise she looked from brown hand to white—the one, workworn and hardened by whip handle and paddle, the other as guiltless of toil and soft as a newborn babe's. And, for all the obvious softness and apparent weakness, Jees Uck looked into the blue eyes and saw the mastery she had seen in Neil Bonner's eyes and in the eyes of Neil Bonner's people.

"Why, it's Jees Uck!" Neil Bonner said, when he entered. He said it calmly, with even a ring of joyful cordiality, coming over to her and shaking both her hands, but looking into her eyes with a worry in his own that she understood.

"Hello, Neil!" she said. "You look much good."

"Fine, fine, Jees Uck," he answered heartily, though secretly studying Kitty for some sign of what had passed between the two. Yet he knew his wife too well to expect, even though the worst had passed, such a sign.

"Well, I can't say how glad I am to see you," he went on. "What's happened? Did you strike a mine? And when did you get in?"

"Oo-a, I get in to-day," she replied, her voice instinctively seeking its guttural parts. "I no strike it, Neil. You know Cap'n Markheim, Unalaska? I cook, his house, long time. No spend money. Bime-by, plenty. Pretty good, I think, go down and see White Man's Land. Very fine, White Man's Land, very fine," she added. Her English puzzled him, for Sandy and he had sought, constantly, to better her speech, and she had proved an apt pupil. Now it seemed that she had sunk back into her race. Her face was guileless, stolidly guileless, giving no cue. Kitty's untroubled brow likewise baffled him. What had happened? How much had been said? and how much guessed?

While he wrestled with these questions and while Jees Uck wrestled with her problem—never had he looked so wonderful and great—a silence fell.

"To think that you knew my husband in Alaska!" Kitty said softly.

Knew him! Jees Uck could not forbear a glance at the boy she had borne him, and his eyes followed hers mechanically to the window where played the two children. An iron band seemed to tighten across his forehead. His knees went weak and his heart leaped up and pounded like a fist against his breast. His boy! He had never dreamed it!

Little Kitty Bonner, fairylike in gauzy lawn, with pinkest of cheeks and bluest of dancing eyes, arms outstretched and lips puckered in invitation, was striving to kiss the boy. And the boy, lean and lithe, sunbeaten and browned, skin-clad and in hair-fringed and hair-tufted *muclucs* that showed the wear of the sea and rough work, coolly withstood her advances, his body straight and stiff with the peculiar erectness common to children of savage people. A stranger in a strange land, unabashed and unafraid, he appeared more like an untamed animal, silent and watchful, his black eyes flashing from face to face, quiet so long as quiet endured, but prepared to spring and fight and tear and scratch for life, at the first sign of danger.

The contrast between boy and girl was striking, but not pitiful. There was too much strength in the boy for that, waif that he was of the generations of Shpack, Spike O'Brien, and Bonner. In his features, clean cut as a cameo and almost classic in their severity, there were the power and achievement of his father, and his grandfather, and the one known as the Big Fat, who was captured by the Sea People and escaped to Kamchatka.

Neil Bonner fought his emotion down, swallowed it down, and choked over it, though his face smiled with good humor and the joy with which one meets a friend.

"Your boy, eh, Jees Uck?" he said. And then turning to Kitty: "Handsome fellow! He'll do something with those two hands of his in this our world."

Kitty nodded concurrence. "What is your name?" she asked.

The young savage flashed his quick eyes upon her and dwelt over her for a space, seeking out, as it were, the motive beneath the question.

"Neil," he answered deliberately when the scrutiny had satisfied him.

"Injun talk," Jees Uck interposed, glibly manufacturing languages on the spur of the moment. "Him Injun talk, *nee-al,* all the same 'cracker.' Him baby, him like cracker; him cry for cracker. Him say, '*Nee-al, nee-al,*' all time him say, '*Nee-al.*' Then I say that um name. So um name all time Nee-al."

Never did sound more blessed fall upon Neil Bonner's ear than that lie from Jees Uck's lips. It was the cue, and he knew there was reason for Kitty's untroubled brow.

"And his father?" Kitty asked. "He must be a fine man."

"Oo-a, yes," was the reply. "Um father fine man. Sure!"

"Did you know him, Neil?" queried Kitty.

"Know him? Most intimately," Neil answered, and harked back to dreary Twenty Mile and the man alone in the silence with his thoughts.

And here might well end the story of Jees Uck, but for the crown she put upon her renunciation. When she returned to the North to dwell in her grand log-house, John Thompson found that the P. C. Company could make a shift somehow to carry on its business without his aid. Also, the new agent and the succeeding agents received instructions that the woman Jees Uck should be given whatsoever goods and grub she desired, in whatsoever quantities she ordered, and that no charge should be placed upon the books. Further, the company paid yearly to the woman Jees Uck a pension of five thousand dollars.

When he had attained suitable age, Father Champreau laid hands upon the boy, and the time was not long when Jees Uck received letters regularly from the Jesuit college in Maryland. Later on these letters came from Italy, and still later from France. And in the end there returned to Alaska one Father Neil, a man mighty for good in the land, who loved his mother and who ultimately went into a wider field and rose to high authority in the order.

Jees Uck was a young woman when she went back into the North, and men still looked upon her and yearned. But she lived straight, and no breath was ever raised save in commendation. She stayed for a while with the good sisters at Holy Cross, where she learned to read and write and became versed in practical medicine and surgery. After that she returned to her grand log-house and gathered about her the young girls of the Toyaat village, to show them the way of their feet in the world. It is neither Protestant nor Catholic, this school in the house built by Neil Bonner for Jees Uck, his wife; but the missionaries of all the sects look upon it with equal favor. The latchstring is always out, and tired prospectors and trail-weary men turn aside from the flowing river or frozen trail to rest there for a space and be warm by her fire. And, down in the States, Kitty Bonner is pleased at the interest her husband takes in Alaskan education and the large sums he devotes to that purpose; and, though she often smiles and chaffs, deep down and secretly she is but the prouder of him.

Love of Life

"This out of all will remain—
They have lived and have tossed:
So much of the game will be gain,
Though the gold of the dice has been lost."

They limped painfully down the bank, and once the foremost of the two men staggered among the rough-strewn rocks. They were tired and weak, and their faces had the drawn expression of patience which comes of hardship long endured. They were heavily burdened with blanket packs which were strapped to their shoulders. Head-straps, passing across the forehead, helped support these packs. Each man carried a rifle. They walked in a stooped posture, the shoulders well forward, the head still farther forward, the eyes bent upon the ground.

"I wish we had just about two of them cartridges that's layin' in that cache of ourn," said the second man.

His voice was utterly and drearily expressionless. He spoke without enthusiasm; and the first man, limping into the milky stream that foamed over the rocks, vouchsafed no reply.

The other man followed at his heels. They did not remove their foot-gear, though the water was icy cold—so cold that their ankles ached and their feet went numb. In places the water dashed against their knees, and both men staggered for footing.

The man who followed slipped on a smooth boulder, nearly fell, but recovered himself with a violent effort, at the same time uttering a sharp exclamation of pain. He seemed faint and dizzy and put out his free hand while he reeled, as though seeking support against the air. When he had steadied himself he stepped forward, but reeled again and nearly fell. Then he stood still and looked at the other man, who had never turned his head.

The man stood still for fully a minute, as though debating with himself. Then he called out:

"I say, Bill, I've sprained my ankle."

Bill staggered on through the milky water. He did not look around. The man watched him go, and though his face was expressionless as ever, his eyes were like the eyes of a wounded deer.

The other man limped up the farther bank and continued straight on without looking back. The man in the stream watched him. His lips trembled a little, so that the rough thatch of brown hair which covered them was visibly agitated. His tongue even strayed out to moisten them.

"Bill!" he cried out.

It was the pleading cry of a strong man in distress, but Bill's head did not turn. The man watched him go, limping grotesquely and lurching forward with stammering gait up the slow slope toward the soft sky-line of the low-lying hill. He watched him go till he passed over the crest and disappeared. Then he turned his gaze and slowly took in the circle of the world that remained to him now that Bill was gone.

Near the horizon the sun was smouldering dimly, almost obscured by formless mists and vapors, which gave an impression of mass and density without outline or tangibility. The man pulled out his watch, the while resting his weight on one leg. It was four o'clock, and as the season was near the last of July or first of August,—he did not know the precise date within a week or two,—he knew that the sun roughly marked the northwest. He looked to the south and knew that somewhere beyond those bleak hills lay the Great Bear Lake; also, he knew that in that direction the Arctic Circle cut its forbidding way across the Canadian Barrens. This stream in which he stood was a feeder to the Coppermine River, which in turn flowed north and emptied into Coronation Gulf and the Arctic Ocean. He had never been there, but he had seen it, once, on a Hudson Bay Company chart.

Again his gaze completed the circle of the world about him. It was not a heartening spectacle. Everywhere was soft sky-line. The hills were all low-lying. There were no trees, no shrubs, no grasses—naught but a tremendous and terrible desolation that sent fear swiftly dawning into his eyes.

"Bill!" he whispered, once and twice; "Bill!"

He cowered in the midst of the milky water, as though the vastness were pressing in upon him with overwhelming force, brutally crushing him with its complacent awfulness. He began to shake as with an ague-fit, till the gun fell from his hand with a splash. This served to rouse him. He fought with his fear and pulled himself together, groping in the water and recovering the weapon. He hitched his pack farther over on his left shoulder, so as to take a portion of its weight from off the injured ankle. Then he proceeded, slowly and carefully, wincing with pain, to the bank.

He did not stop. With a desperation that was madness, unmindful of the pain, he hurried up the slope to the crest of the hill over which his comrade had disappeared—more grotesque and comical by far than that limping, jerking comrade. But at the crest he saw a shallow valley, empty of life. He fought with his fear again, overcame it, hitched the pack still farther over on his left shoulder, and lurched on down the slope.

The bottom of the valley was soggy with water, which the thick moss held, spongelike, close to the surface. This water squirted out from under his feet at every step, and each time he lifted a foot the action culminated in a sucking sound as the wet moss reluctantly released its grip. He picked his way from muskeg to muskeg, and followed the other man's footsteps along and across the rocky ledges which thrust like islets through the sea of moss.

Though alone, he was not lost. Farther on he knew he would come to where dead spruce and fir, very small and weazened, bordered the shore of a little lake, the *titchin-nichilie*, in the tongue of the country, the "land of little sticks." And into that lake flowed a small stream, the water of which was not milky. There was rush-grass on that stream—this he remembered well—but no timber, and he would follow it till its first trickle ceased at a divide. He would cross this divide to the first trickle of another stream, flowing to the west, which he would follow until it emptied into the river Dease, and here he would find a cache under an upturned canoe and piled over with many rocks. And in this cache would be ammunition for his empty gun, fish-hooks and lines, a small net—all the utilities for the killing and snaring of food. Also, he would find flour,—not much,—a piece of bacon, and some beans.

Bill would be waiting for him there, and they would paddle away south down the Dease to the Great Bear Lake. And south across the lake they would go, ever south, till they gained the Mackenzie. And south, still south, they would go, while the winter raced vainly after them, and the ice formed in the eddies, and the days grew chill and crisp, south to some warm Hudson Bay Company post, where timber grew tall and generous and there was grub without end.

These were the thoughts of the man as he strove onward. But hard as he strove with his body, he strove equally hard with his mind, trying to think that Bill had not deserted him, that Bill would surely wait for him at the cache. He was compelled to think this thought, or else there would not be any use to strive, and he would have lain down and died. And as the dim ball of the sun sank slowly into the northwest he covered every inch—and many times—of his and Bill's flight south before the downcoming winter. And he conned the grub of the cache and the grub of the Hudson Bay Company post over and over again. He had not eaten for two days; for a far longer time he had not had all he wanted to eat. Often he stooped and picked pale muskeg berries, put them into his mouth, and chewed and swallowed them. A muskeg berry is a bit of seed enclosed in a bit of water. In the mouth the water melts away and the seed chews sharp and bitter. The man knew there was no nourishment in the berries, but he chewed them patiently with a hope greater than knowledge and defying experience.

At nine o'clock he stubbed his toe on a rocky ledge, and from sheer weariness and weakness staggered and fell. He lay for some time, without movement, on his side. Then he slipped out of the pack-straps and clumsily dragged himself into a sitting posture. It was not yet dark, and in the lingering twilight he groped about among the rocks for shreds of dry moss. When he had gathered a heap he built a fire,—a smouldering, smudgy fire,—and put a tin pot of water on to boil.

He unwrapped his pack and the first thing he did was to count his matches. There were sixty-seven. He counted them three times to make sure. He divided them into several portions, wrapping them in oil paper, disposing of one bunch in his empty tobacco pouch, of another bunch in the inside band of his battered hat, of a third bunch under his shirt on the chest. This accomplished, a panic came upon him, and he unwrapped them all and counted them again. There were still sixty-seven.

He dried his wet foot-gear by the fire. The moccasins were in soggy shreds. The blanket socks were worn through in places, and his feet were raw and bleeding. His ankle was throbbing, and he gave it an examination. It had swollen to the size of his knee. He tore a long strip from one of his two blankets and bound the ankle tightly. He tore other strips and bound them about his feet to serve for both moccasins and socks. Then he drank the pot of water, steaming hot, wound his watch, and crawled between his blankets.

He slept like a dead man. The brief darkness around midnight came and went. The sun arose in the northeast—at least the day dawned in that quarter, for the sun was hidden by gray clouds.

At six o'clock he awoke, quietly lying on his back. He gazed straight up into the gray sky and knew that he was hungry. As he rolled over on his elbow he was startled by a loud snort, and saw a bull caribou regarding him with alert curiosity. The animal was not more than fifty feet away, and instantly into the man's mind leaped the vision and the savor of a caribou steak sizzling and frying over a fire. Mechanically he reached for the empty gun, drew a bead, and pulled the trigger. The bull snorted and leaped away, his hoofs rattling and clattering as he fled across the ledges.

The man cursed and flung the empty gun from him. He groaned aloud as he started to drag himself to his feet. It was a slow and arduous task. His joints were like rusty hinges. They worked harshly in their sockets, with much friction, and each bending or unbending was accomplished only through a sheer exertion of will. When he finally gained his feet, another minute or so was consumed in straightening up, so that he could stand erect as a man should stand.

He crawled up a small knoll and surveyed the prospect. There were no trees, no bushes, nothing but a gray sea of moss scarcely diversified by gray rocks, gray lakelets, and gray streamlets. The sky was gray. There was no sun nor hint of sun. He had no idea of north, and he had forgotten the way he had come to this spot the night before. But he was not lost. He knew that. Soon he would come to the land of the little sticks. He felt that it lay off to the left somewhere, not far—possibly just over the next low hill.

He went back to put his pack into shape for travelling. He assured himself of the existence of his three separate parcels of matches, though he did not stop to count them. But he did linger, debating, over a squat moose-hide sack. It was not large. He could hide it under his two hands. He knew that it weighed fifteen pounds,—as much as all the rest of the pack,—and it worried him. He finally set it to one side and proceeded to roll the pack. He paused to gaze at the squat moose-hide sack. He picked it up hastily with a defiant glance about him, as though the desolation were trying to rob him of it; and when he rose to his feet to stagger on into the day, it was included in the pack on his back.

He bore away to the left, stopping now and again to eat muskeg berries. His ankle had stiffened, his limp was more pronounced, but the pain of it was as nothing compared with the pain of his stomach. The hunger pangs were sharp. They gnawed and gnawed until he could not keep his mind steady on the course he must pursue to gain the land of little sticks. The muskeg berries did not allay this gnawing, while they made his tongue and the roof of his mouth sore with their irritating bite.

He came upon a valley where rock ptarmigan rose on whirring wings from the ledges and muskegs. Ker—ker—ker was the cry they made. He threw stones at them, but could not hit them. He placed his pack on the ground and stalked them as a cat stalks a sparrow. The sharp rocks cut through his pants' legs till his knees left a trail of blood; but the hurt was lost in the hurt of his hunger. He squirmed over the wet moss, saturating his clothes and chilling his body; but he was not aware of it, so great was his fever for food. And always the ptarmigan rose, whirring, before him, till their ker—ker—ker became a mock to him, and he cursed them and cried aloud at them with their own cry.

Once he crawled upon one that must have been asleep. He did not see it till it shot up in his face from its rocky nook. He made a clutch as startled as was the rise of the ptarmigan, and there remained in his hand three tail-feathers. As he watched its flight he hated it, as though it had done him some terrible wrong. Then he returned and shouldered his pack.

As the day wore along he came into valleys or swales where game was more plentiful. A band of caribou passed by, twenty and odd animals, tantalizingly within rifle range. He felt a wild desire to run after them, a certitude that he could run them down. A black fox came toward him, carrying a ptarmigan in his mouth. The man shouted. It was a fearful cry, but the fox, leaping away in fright, did not drop the ptarmigan.

Late in the afternoon he followed a stream, milky with lime, which ran through sparse patches of rush-grass. Grasping these rushes firmly near the root, he pulled up what resembled a young onion-sprout no larger than a shingle-nail. It was tender, and his teeth sank into it with a crunch that promised deliciously of food. But its fibers were tough. It was composed of stringy filaments saturated with water, like the berries, and devoid of nourishment. He threw off his pack and went into the rush-grass on hands and knees, crunching and munching, like some bovine creature.

He was very weary and often wished to rest—to lie down and sleep; but he was continually driven on—not so much by his desire to gain the land of little sticks as by his hunger. He searched little ponds for frogs and dug up the earth with his nails for worms, though he knew in spite that neither frogs nor worms existed so far north.

He looked into every pool of water vainly, until, as the long twilight came on, he discovered a solitary fish, the size of a minnow, in such a pool. He plunged his arm in up to the shoulder, but it eluded him. He reached for it with both hands and stirred up the milky mud at the bottom. In his excitement he fell in, wetting himself to the waist. Then the water was too muddy to admit of his seeing the fish, and he was compelled to wait until the sediment had settled.

The pursuit was renewed, till the water was again muddied. But he could not wait. He unstrapped the tin bucket and began to bale the pool. He baled wildly at first, splashing himself and flinging the water so short a distance that it ran back into the pool. He worked more carefully, striving to be cool, though his heart was pounding against his chest and his hands were trembling. At the end of half an hour the pool was nearly dry. Not a cupful of water remained. And there was no fish. He found a hidden crevice among the stones through which it had escaped to the adjoining and larger pool—a pool which he could not empty in a night and a day. Had he known of the crevice, he could have closed it with a rock at the beginning and the fish would have been his.

Thus he thought, and crumpled up and sank down upon the wet earth. At first he cried softly to himself, then he cried loudly to the pitiless desolation that ringed him around; and for a long time after he was shaken by great dry sobs.

He built a fire and warmed himself by drinking quarts of hot water, and made camp on a rocky ledge in the same fashion he had the night before. The last thing he did was to see that his matches were dry and to wind his watch. The blankets were wet and clammy. His ankle pulsed with pain. But he knew only that he was hungry, and through his restless sleep he dreamed of feasts and banquets and of food served and spread in all imaginable ways.

He awoke chilled and sick. There was no sun. The gray of earth and sky had become deeper, more profound. A raw wind was blowing, and the first flurries of snow were whitening the hilltops. The air about him thickened and grew white while he made a fire and boiled more water. It was wet snow, half rain, and the flakes were large and soggy. At first they melted as soon as they came in contact with the earth, but ever more fell, covering the ground, putting out the fire, spoiling his supply of moss-fuel.

This was a signal for him to strap on his pack and stumble onward, he knew not where. He was not concerned with the land of little sticks, nor with Bill and the cache under the upturned canoe by the river Dease. He was mastered by the verb "to eat." He was hunger-mad. He took no heed of the course he pursued, so long as that course led him through the swale bottoms. He felt his way through the wet snow to the watery muskeg berries, and went by feel as he pulled up the rush-grass by the roots. But it was tasteless stuff and did not satisfy. He found a weed that tasted sour and he ate all he could find of it, which was not much, for it was a creeping growth, easily hidden under the several inches of snow.

He had no fire that night, nor hot water, and crawled under his blanket to sleep the broken hunger-sleep. The snow turned into a cold rain. He awakened many times to feel it falling on his upturned face. Day came—a gray day and no sun. It had ceased raining. The keenness of his hunger had departed. Sensibility, as far as concerned the yearning for food, had been exhausted. There was a dull, heavy ache in his stomach, but it did not bother him so much. He was more rational, and once more he was chiefly interested in the land of little sticks and the cache by the river Dease.

He ripped the remnant of one of his blankets into strips and bound his bleeding feet. Also, he recinched the injured ankle and prepared himself for a day of travel. When he came to his pack, he paused long over the squat moose-hide sack, but in the end it went with him.

The snow had melted under the rain, and only the hilltops showed white. The sun came out, and he succeeded in locating the points of the compass, though he knew now that he was lost. Perhaps, in his previous days' wanderings, he had edged away too far to the left. He now bore off to the right to counteract the possible deviation from his true course.

Though the hunger pangs were no longer so exquisite, he realized that he was weak. He was compelled to pause for frequent rests, when he attacked the muskeg berries and rush-grass patches. His tongue felt dry and large, as though covered with a fine hairy growth, and it tasted bitter in his mouth. His heart gave him a great deal of trouble. When he had travelled a few minutes it would begin a remorseless thump, thump, thump, and then leap up and away in a painful flutter of beats that choked him and made him go faint and dizzy.

In the middle of the day he found two minnows in a large pool. It was impossible to bale it, but he was calmer now and managed to catch them in his tin bucket. They were no longer than his little finger, but he was not particularly hungry. The dull ache in his stomach had been growing duller and fainter. It seemed almost that his stomach was dozing. He ate the fish raw, masticating with painstaking care, for the eating was an act of pure reason. While he had no desire to eat, he knew that he must eat to live.

In the evening he caught three more minnows, eating two and saving the third for breakfast. The sun had dried stray shreds of moss, and he was able to warm himself with hot water. He had not covered more than ten miles that day; and the next day, travelling whenever his heart permitted him, he covered no more than five miles. But his stomach did not give him the slightest uneasiness. It had gone to sleep. He was in a strange country, too, and the caribou were growing more plentiful, also the wolves. Often their yelps drifted across the desolation, and once he saw three of them slinking away before his path.

Another night; and in the morning, being more rational, he untied the leather string that fastened the squat moose-hide sack. From its open mouth poured a yellow stream of coarse gold-dust and nuggets. He roughly divided the gold in halves, caching one half on a prominent ledge, wrapped in a piece of blanket, and returning the other half to the sack. He also began to use strips of the one remaining blanket for his feet. He still clung to his gun, for there were cartridges in that cache by the river Dease.

This was a day of fog, and this day hunger awoke in him again. He was very weak and was afflicted with a giddiness which at times blinded him. It was no uncommon thing now for him to stumble and fall; and stumbling once, he fell squarely into a ptarmigan nest. There were four newly hatched chicks, a day old— little specks of pulsating life no more than a mouthful; and he ate them ravenously, thrusting them alive into his mouth and crunching them like egg-shells between his teeth. The mother ptarmigan beat about him with great outcry. He used his gun as a club with which to knock her over, but she dodged out of reach. He threw stones at her and with one chance shot broke a wing. Then she fluttered away, running, trailing the broken wing, with him in pursuit.

The little chicks had no more than whetted his appetite. He hopped and bobbed clumsily along on his injured ankle, throwing stones and screaming hoarsely at times; at other times hopping and bobbing silently along, picking himself up grimly and patiently when he fell, or rubbing his eyes with his hand when the giddiness threatened to overpower him.

The chase led him across swampy ground in the bottom of the valley, and he came upon footprints in the soggy moss. They were not his own—he could see that. They must be Bill's. But he could not stop, for the mother ptarmigan was running on. He would catch her first, then he would return and investigate.

He exhausted the mother ptarmigan; but he exhausted himself. She lay panting on her side. He lay panting on his side, a dozen feet away, unable to crawl to her. And as he recovered she recovered, fluttering out of reach as his hungry hand went out to her. The chase was resumed. Night settled down and she escaped. He stumbled from weakness and pitched head foremost on his face, cutting his cheek, his pack upon his back. He did not move for a long while; then he rolled over on his side, wound his watch, and lay there until morning.

Another day of fog. Half of his last blanket had gone into foot-wrappings. He failed to pick up Bill's trail. It did not matter. His hunger was driving him too compellingly—only—only he wondered if Bill, too, were lost. By midday the irk of his pack became too oppressive. Again he divided the gold, this time merely spilling half of it on the ground. In the afternoon he threw the rest of it away, there remaining to him only the half-blanket, the tin bucket, and the rifle.

An hallucination began to trouble him. He felt confident that one cartridge remained to him. It was in the chamber of the rifle and he had overlooked it. On the other hand, he knew all the time that the chamber was empty. But the hallucination persisted. He fought it off for hours, then threw his rifle open and was confronted with emptiness. The disappointment was as bitter as though he had really expected to find the cartridge.

He plodded on for half an hour, when the hallucination arose again. Again he fought it, and still it persisted, till for very relief he opened his rifle to unconvince himself. At times his mind wandered farther afield, and he plodded on, a mere automaton, strange conceits and whimsicalities gnawing at his brain like worms. But these excursions out of the real were of brief duration, for ever the pangs of the hunger-bite called him back. He was jerked back abruptly once from such an excursion by a sight that caused him nearly to faint. He reeled and swayed, doddering like a drunken man to keep from falling. Before him stood a horse. A horse! He could not believe his eyes. A thick mist was in them, intershot with sparkling points of light. He rubbed his eyes savagely to clear his vision, and beheld, not a horse, but a great brown bear. The animal was studying him with bellicose curiosity.

The man had brought his gun halfway to his shoulder before he realized. He lowered it and drew his hunting-knife from its beaded sheath at his hip. Before him was meat and life. He ran his thumb along the edge of his knife. It was sharp. The point was sharp. He would fling himself upon the bear and kill it. But his heart began its warning thump, thump, thump. Then followed the wild upward leap and tattoo of flutters, the pressing as of an iron band about his forehead, the creeping of the dizziness into his brain.

His desperate courage was evicted by a great surge of fear. In his weakness, what if the animal attacked him? He drew himself up to his most imposing stature, gripping the knife and staring hard at the bear. The bear advanced clumsily a couple of steps, reared up, and gave vent to a tentative growl. If the man ran, he would run after him; but the man did not run. He was animated now with the courage of fear. He, too, growled, savagely, terribly, voicing the fear that is to life germane and that lies twisted about life's deepest roots.

The bear edged away to one side, growling menacingly, himself appalled by this mysterious creature that appeared upright and unafraid. But the man did not move. He stood like a statue till the danger was past, when he yielded to a fit of trembling and sank down into the wet moss.

He pulled himself together and went on, afraid now in a new way. It was not the fear that he should die passively from lack of food, but that he should be destroyed violently before starvation had exhausted the last particle of the endeavor in him that made toward surviving. There were the wolves. Back and forth across the desolation drifted their howls, weaving the very air into a fabric of menace that was so tangible that he found himself, arms in the air, pressing it back from him as it might be the walls of a wind-blown tent.

Now and again the wolves, in packs of two and three, crossed his path. But they sheered clear of him. They were not in sufficient numbers, and besides they were hunting the caribou, which did not battle, while this strange creature that walked erect might scratch and bite.

In the late afternoon he came upon scattered bones where the wolves had made a kill. The débris had been a caribou calf an hour before, squawking and running and very much alive. He contemplated the bones, clean-picked and polished, pink with the cell-life in them which had not yet died. Could it possibly be that he might be that ere the day was done! Such was life, eh? A vain and fleeting thing. It was only life that pained. There was no hurt in death. To die was to sleep. It meant cessation, rest. Then why was he not content to die?

But he did not moralize long. He was squatting in the moss, a bone in his mouth, sucking at the shreds of life that still dyed it faintly pink. The sweet meaty taste, thin and elusive almost as a memory, maddened him. He closed his jaws on the bones and crunched. Sometimes it was the bone that broke, sometimes his teeth. Then he crushed the bones between rocks, pounded them to a pulp, and swallowed them. He pounded his fingers, too, in his haste, and yet found a moment in which to feel surprise at the fact that his fingers did not hurt much when caught under the descending rock.

Came frightful days of snow and rain. He did not know when he made camp, when he broke camp. He travelled in the night as much as in the day. He rested wherever he fell, crawled on whenever the dying life in him flickered up and burned less dimly. He, as a man, no longer strove. It was the life in him, unwilling to die, that drove him on. He did not suffer. His nerves had become blunted, numb, while his mind was filled with weird visions and delicious dreams.

But ever he sucked and chewed on the crushed bones of the caribou calf, the least remnants of which he had gathered up and carried with him. He crossed no more hills or divides, but auto-

matically followed a large stream which flowed through a wide
and shallow valley. He did not see this stream nor this valley. He
saw nothing save visions. Soul and body walked or crawled side
by side, yet apart, so slender was the thread that bound them.

He awoke in his right mind, lying on his back on a rocky ledge.
The sun was shining bright and warm. Afar off he heard the
squawking of caribou calves. He was aware of vague memories of
rain and wind and snow, but whether he had been beaten by the
storm for two days or two weeks he did not know.

For some time he lay without movement, the genial sunshine
pouring upon him and saturating his miserable body with its
warmth. A fine day, he thought. Perhaps he could manage to
locate himself. By a painful effort he rolled over on his side. Below
him flowed a wide and sluggish river. Its unfamiliarity puzzled
him. Slowly he followed it with his eyes, winding in wide sweeps
among the bleak, bare hills, bleaker and barer and lower-lying
than any hills he had yet encountered. Slowly, deliberately, without excitement or more than the most casual interest, he followed
the course of the strange stream toward the sky-line and saw it
emptying into a bright and shining sea. He was still unexcited.
Most unusual, he thought, a vision or a mirage—more likely a
vision, a trick of his disordered mind. He was confirmed in this
by sight of a ship lying at anchor in the midst of the shining sea.
He closed his eyes for a while, then opened them. Strange how
the vision persisted! Yet not strange. He knew there were no seas
or ships in the heart of the barren lands, just as he had known
there was no cartridge in the empty rifle.

He heard a snuffle behind him—a half-choking gasp or cough.
Very slowly, because of his exceeding weakness and stiffness, he
rolled over on his other side. He could see nothing near at hand,
but he waited patiently. Again came the snuffle and cough, and
outlined between two jagged rocks not a score of feet away he
made out the gray head of a wolf. The sharp ears were not pricked
so sharply as he had seen them on other wolves; the eyes were
bleared and bloodshot, the head seemed to droop limply and for-
lornly. The animal blinked continually in the sunshine. It seemed
sick. As he looked it snuffled and coughed again.

This, at least, was real, he thought, and turned on the other side so that he might see the reality of the world which had been veiled from him before by the vision. But the sea still shone in the distance and the ship was plainly discernible. Was it reality, after all? He closed his eyes for a long while and thought, and then it came to him. He had been making north by east, away from the Dease Divide and into the Coppermine Valley. This wide and sluggish river was the Coppermine. That shining sea was the Arctic Ocean. That ship was a whaler, strayed east, far east, from the mouth of the Mackenzie, and it was lying at anchor in Coronation Gulf. He remembered the Hudson Bay Company chart he had seen long ago, and it was all clear and reasonable to him.

He sat up and turned his attention to immediate affairs. He had worn through the blanket-wrappings, and his feet were shapeless lumps of raw meat. His last blanket was gone. Rifle and knife were both missing. He had lost his hat somewhere, with the bunch of matches in the band, but the matches against his chest were safe and dry inside the tobacco pouch and oil paper. He looked at his watch. It marked eleven o'clock and was still running. Evidently he had kept it wound.

He was calm and collected. Though extremely weak, he had no sensation of pain. He was not hungry. The thought of food was not even pleasant to him, and whatever he did was done by his reason alone. He ripped off his pants' legs to the knees and bound them about his feet. Somehow he had succeeded in retaining the tin bucket. He would have some hot water before he began what he foresaw was to be a terrible journey to the ship.

His movements were slow. He shook as with a palsy. When he started to collect dry moss, he found he could not rise to his feet. He tried again and again, then contented himself with crawling about on hands and knees. Once he crawled near to the sick wolf. The animal dragged itself reluctantly out of his way, licking its chops with a tongue which seemed hardly to have the strength to curl. The man noticed that the tongue was not the customary healthy red. It was a yellowish brown and seemed coated with a rough and half-dry mucus.

After he had drunk a quart of hot water the man found he was able to stand, and even to walk as well as a dying man might be supposed to walk. Every minute or so he was compelled to rest. His steps were feeble and uncertain, just as the wolf's that trailed him were feeble and uncertain; and that night, when the shining sea was blotted out by blackness, he knew he was nearer to it by no more than four miles.

Throughout the night he heard the cough of the sick wolf, and now and then the squawking of the caribou calves. There was life all around him, but it was strong life, very much alive and well, and he knew the sick wolf clung to the sick man's trail in the hope that the man would die first. In the morning, on opening his eyes, he beheld it regarding him with a wistful and hungry stare. It stood crouched, with tail between its legs, like a miserable and woe-begone dog. It shivered in the chill morning wind, and grinned dispiritedly when the man spoke to it in a voice that achieved no more than a hoarse whisper.

The sun rose brightly, and all morning the man tottered and fell toward the ship on the shining sea. The weather was perfect. It was the brief Indian Summer of the high latitudes. It might last a week. To-morrow or next day it might be gone.

In the afternoon the man came upon a trail. It was of another man, who did not walk, but who dragged himself on all fours. The man thought it might be Bill, but he thought in a dull, un-interested way. He had no curiosity. In fact, sensation and emotion had left him. He was no longer susceptible to pain. Stomach and nerves had gone to sleep. Yet the life that was in him drove him on. He was very weary, but it refused to die. It was because it refused to die that he still ate muskeg berries and minnows, drank his hot water, and kept a wary eye on the sick wolf.

He followed the trail of the other man who dragged himself along, and soon came to the end of it—a few fresh-picked bones where the soggy moss was marked by the foot-pads of many wolves. He saw a squat moose-hide sack, mate to his own, which had been torn by sharp teeth. He picked it up, though its weight was almost too much for his feeble fingers. Bill had carried it to the last. Ha! ha! He would have the laugh on Bill. He would survive and carry it to the ship in the shining sea. His mirth was hoarse and ghastly, like a raven's croak, and the sick wolf joined

him, howling lugubriously. The man ceased suddenly. How could
he have the laugh on Bill if that were Bill; if those bones, so pinky-
white and clean, were Bill?

He turned away. Well, Bill had deserted him; but he would not
take the gold, nor would he suck Bill's bones. Bill would have,
though, had it been the other way around, he mused as he staggered on.

He came to a pool of water. Stooping over in quest of minnows, he jerked his head back as though he had been stung. He
had caught sight of his reflected face. So horrible was it that sensibility awoke long enough to be shocked. There were three minnows in the pool, which was too large to drain; and after several
ineffectual attempts to catch them in the tin bucket he forbore.
He was afraid, because of his great weakness, that he might fall
in and drown. It was for this reason that he did not trust himself
to the river astride one of the many drift-logs which lined its sand-
spits.

That day he decreased the distance between him and the ship
by three miles; the next day by two—for he was crawling now as
Bill had crawled; and the end of the fifth day found the ship still
seven miles away and him unable to make even a mile a day. Still
the Indian Summer held on, and he continued to crawl and faint,
turn and turn about; and ever the sick wolf coughed and wheezed
at his heels. His knees had become raw meat like his feet, and
though he padded them with the shirt from his back it was a red
track he left behind him on the moss and stones. Once, glancing
back, he saw the wolf licking hungrily his bleeding trail, and he
saw sharply what his own end might be—unless—unless he could
get the wolf. Then began as grim a tragedy of existence as was
ever played—a sick man that crawled, a sick wolf that limped,
two creatures dragging their dying carcasses across the desolation
and hunting each other's lives.

Had it been a well wolf, it would not have mattered so much
to the man; but the thought of going to feed the maw of that
loathsome and all but dead thing was repugnant to him. He was
finicky. His mind had begun to wander again, and to be perplexed
by hallucinations, while his lucid intervals grew rarer and shorter.

He was awakened once from a faint by a wheeze close in his

ear. The wolf leaped lamely back, losing its footing and falling in its weakness. It was ludicrous, but he was not amused. Nor was he even afraid. He was too far gone for that. But his mind was for the moment clear, and he lay and considered. The ship was no more than four miles away. He could see it quite distinctly when he rubbed the mists out of his eyes, and he could see the white sail of a small boat cutting the water of the shining sea. But he could never crawl those four miles. He knew that, and was very calm in the knowledge. He knew that he could not crawl half a mile. And yet he wanted to live. It was unreasonable that he should die after all he had undergone. Fate asked too much of him. And, dying, he declined to die. It was stark madness, perhaps, but in the very grip of Death he defied Death and refused to die.

He closed his eyes and composed himself with infinite precaution. He steeled himself to keep above the suffocating languor that lapped like a rising tide through all the wells of his being. It was very like a sea, this deadly languor, that rose and rose and drowned his consciousness bit by bit. Sometimes he was all but submerged, swimming through oblivion with a faltering stroke; and again, by some strange alchemy of soul, he would find another shred of will and strike out more strongly.

Without movement he lay on his back, and he could hear, slowly drawing near and nearer, the wheezing intake and output of the sick wolf's breath. It drew closer, ever closer, through an infinitude of time, and he did not move. It was at his ear. The harsh dry tongue grated like sandpaper against his cheek. His hands shot out—or at least he willed them to shoot out. The fingers were curved like talons, but they closed on empty air. Swiftness and certitude require strength, and the man had not this strength.

The patience of the wolf was terrible. The man's patience was no less terrible. For half a day he lay motionless, fighting off unconsciousness and waiting for the thing that was to feed upon him and upon which he wished to feed. Sometimes the languid sea rose over him and he dreamed long dreams; but ever through it all, waking and dreaming, he waited for the wheezing breath and the harsh caress of the tongue.

He did not hear the breath, and he slipped slowly from some dream to the feel of the tongue along his hand. He waited. The fangs pressed softly; the pressure increased; the wolf was exerting its last strength in an effort to sink teeth in the food for which it had waited so long. But the man had waited long, and the lacerated hand closed on the jaw. Slowly, while the wolf struggled feebly and the hand clutched feebly, the other hand crept across to a grip. Five minutes later the whole weight of the man's body was on top of the wolf. The hands had not sufficient strength to choke the wolf, but the face of the man was pressed close to the throat of the wolf and the mouth of the man was full of hair. At the end of half an hour the man was aware of a warm trickle in his throat. It was not pleasant. It was like molten lead being forced into his stomach, and it was forced by his will alone. Later the man rolled over on his back and slept.

There were some members of a scientific expedition on the whale-ship *Bedford*. From the deck they remarked a strange object on the shore. It was moving down the beach toward the water. They were unable to classify it, and, being scientific men, they climbed into the whale-boat alongside and went ashore to see. And they saw something that was alive but which could hardly be called a man. It was blind, unconscious. It squirmed along the ground like some monstrous worm. Most of its efforts were ineffectual, but it was persistent, and it writhed and twisted and went ahead perhaps a score of feet an hour.

Three weeks afterward the man lay in a bunk on the whale-ship *Bedford*, and with tears streaming down his wasted cheeks told who he was and what he had undergone. He also babbled incoherently of his mother, of sunny Southern California, and a home among the orange groves and flowers.

The days were not many after that when he sat at table with the scientific men and ship's officers. He gloated over the spectacle of so much food, watching it anxiously as it went into the mouths of others. With the disappearance of each mouthful an expression of deep regret came into his eyes. He was quite sane, yet he hated those men at mealtime. He was haunted by a fear that the food would not last. He inquired of the cook, the cabin-boy, the captain, concerning the food stores. They reassured him countless times; but he could not believe them, and pried cunningly about the lazarette to see with his own eyes.

It was noticed that the man was getting fat. He grew stouter with each day. The scientific men shook their heads and theorized. They limited the man at his meals, but still his girth increased and he swelled prodigiously under his shirt.

The sailors grinned. They knew. And when the scientific men set a watch on the man, they knew too. They saw him slouch for'ard after breakfast, and, like a mendicant, with outstretched palm, accost a sailor. The sailor grinned and passed him a fragment of sea biscuit. He clutched it avariciously, looked at it as a miser looks at gold, and thrust it into his shirt bosom. Similar were the donations from other grinning sailors.

The scientific men were discreet. They let him alone. But they privily examined his bunk. It was lined with hardtack; the mattress was stuffed with hardtack; every nook and cranny was filled with hardtack. Yet he was sane. He was taking precautions against another possible famine—that was all. He would recover from it, the scientific men said; and he did, ere the *Bedford*'s anchor rumbled down in San Francisco Bay.

The Sun-Dog Trail

Sitka Charley smoked his pipe and gazed thoughtfully at the *Police Gazette* illustration on the wall. For half an hour he had been steadily regarding it, and for half an hour I had been slyly watching him. Something was going on in that mind of his, and, whatever it was, I knew it was well worth knowing. He had lived life, and seen things, and performed that prodigy of prodigies, namely, the turning of his back upon his own people, and, in so far as it was possible for an Indian, becoming a white man even in his mental processes. As he phrased it himself, he had come into the warm, sat among us, by our fires, and become one of us. He had never learned to read nor write, but his vocabulary was remarkable, and more remarkable still was the completeness with which he had assumed the white man's point of view, the white man's attitude toward things.

We had struck this deserted cabin after a hard day on trail. The dogs had been fed, the supper dishes washed, the beds made, and we were now enjoying that most delicious hour that comes each day, and but once each day, on the Alaskan trail, the hour when nothing intervenes between the tired body and bed save the smoking of the evening pipe. Some former denizen of the cabin had decorated its walls with illustrations torn from magazines and newspapers, and it was these illustrations that had held Sitka Charley's attention from the moment of our arrival two hours before. He had studied them intently, ranging from one to another and back again, and I could see that there was uncertainty in his mind, and bepuzzlement.

"Well?" I finally broke the silence.

He took the pipe from his mouth and said simply, "I do not understand."

He smoked on again, and again removed the pipe, using it to point at the *Police Gazette* illustration.

"That picture—what does it mean? I do not understand."

I looked at the picture. A man, with a preposterously wicked face, his right hand pressed dramatically to his heart, was falling backward to the floor. Confronting him, with a face that was a composite of destroying angel and Adonis, was a man holding a smoking revolver.

"One man is killing the other man," I said, aware of a distinct bepuzzlement of my own and of failure to explain.

"Why?" asked Sitka Charley.

"I do not know," I confessed.

"That picture is all end," he said. "It has no beginning."

"It is life," I said.

"Life has beginning," he objected.

I was silenced for the moment, while his eyes wandered on to an adjoining decoration, a photographic reproduction of somebody's "Leda and the Swan."

"That picture," he said, "has no beginning. It has no end. I do not understand pictures."

"Look at that picture," I commanded, pointing to a third decoration. "It means something. Tell me what it means to you."

He studied it for several minutes.

"The little girl is sick," he said finally. "That is the doctor looking at her. They have been up all night—see, the oil is low in the lamp, the first morning light is coming in at the window. It is a great sickness; maybe she will die, that is why the doctor looks so hard. That is the mother. It is a great sickness, because the mother's head is on the table and she is crying."

"How do you know she is crying?" I interrupted. "You cannot see her face. Perhaps she is asleep."

Sitka Charley looked at me in swift surprise, then back at the picture. It was evident that he had not reasoned the impression.

"Perhaps she is asleep," he repeated. He studied it closely. "No, she is not asleep. The shoulders show that she is not asleep. I have seen the shoulders of a woman who cried. The mother is crying. It is a very great sickness."

"And now you understand the picture," I cried.

He shook his head, and asked, "The little girl—does it die?"

It was my turn for silence.

"Does it die?" he reiterated. "You are a painter-man. Maybe you know."

"No, I do not know," I confessed.

"It is not life," he delivered himself dogmatically. "In life little girl die or get well. Something happen in life. In picture nothing happen. No, I do not understand pictures."

His disappointment was patent. It was his desire to understand all things that white men understand, and here, in this matter, he failed. I felt, also, that there was challenge in his attitude. He was bent upon compelling me to show him the wisdom of pictures. Besides, he had remarkable powers of visualization. I had long since learned this. He visualized everything. He saw life in pictures, felt life in pictures, generalized life in pictures; and yet he did not understand pictures when seen through other men's eyes and expressed by those men with color and line upon canvas.

"Pictures are bits of life," I said. "We paint life as we see it. For instance, Charley, you are coming along the trail. It is night. You see a cabin. The window is lighted. You look through the window for one second, or for two seconds, you see something, and you go on your way. You saw maybe a man writing a letter. You saw something without beginning or end. Nothing happened. Yet it was a bit of life you saw. You remember it afterward. It is like a picture in your memory. The window is the frame of the picture."

I could see that he was interested, and I knew that as I spoke he had looked through the window and seen the man writing the letter.

"There is a picture you have painted that I understand," he said. "It is a true picture. It has much meaning. It is in your cabin at Dawson. It is a faro table. There are men playing. It is a large game. The limit is off."

"How do you know the limit is off?" I broke in excitedly, for here was where my work could be tried out on an unbiassed judge who knew life only, and not art, and who was a sheer master of reality. Also, I was very proud of that particular piece of work. I had named it "The Last Turn," and I believed it to be one of the best things I had ever done.

"There are no chips on the table," Sitka Charley explained. "The men are playing with markers. That means the roof is the limit. One man play yellow markers—maybe one yellow marker worth one thousand dollars, maybe two thousand dollars. One man play red markers. Maybe they are worth five hundred dollars, maybe one thousand dollars. It is a very big game. Everybody play very high, up to the roof. How do I know? You make the dealer with blood little bit warm in face." (I was delighted.) "The lookout, you make him lean forward in his chair. Why he lean forward? Why his face very much quiet? Why his eyes very much bright? Why dealer warm with blood a little bit in the face? Why all men very quiet?—the man with yellow markers? the man with white markers? the man with red markers? Why nobody talk? Because very much money. Because last turn."

"How do you know it is the last turn?" I asked.

"The king is coppered, the seven is played open," he answered. "Nobody bet on other cards. Other cards all gone. Everybody one mind. Everybody play king to lose, seven to win. Maybe bank lose twenty thousand dollars, maybe bank win. Yes, that picture I understand."

"Yet you do not know the end!" I cried triumphantly. "It is the last turn, but the cards are not yet turned. In the picture they will never be turned. Nobody will ever know who wins nor who loses."

"And the men will sit there and never talk," he said, wonder and awe growing in his face. "And the lookout will lean forward, and the blood will be warm in the face of the dealer. It is a strange thing. Always will they sit there, always; and the cards will never be turned."

"It is a picture," I said. "It is life. You have seen things like it yourself."

He looked at me and pondered, then said, very slowly: "No, as you say, there is no end to it. Nobody will ever know the end. Yet is it a true thing. I have seen it. It is life."

For a long time he smoked on in silence, weighing the pictorial wisdom of the white man and verifying it by the facts of life. He nodded his head several times, and grunted once or twice. Then he knocked the ashes from his pipe, carefully refilled it, and, after a thoughtful pause, lighted it again.

"Then have I, too, seen many pictures of life," he began; "pictures not painted, but seen with the eyes. I have looked at them like through the window at the man writing the letter. I have seen many pieces of life, without beginning, without end, without understanding."

With a sudden change of position he turned his eyes full upon me and regarded me thoughtfully.

"Look you," he said; "you are a painter-man. How would you paint this which I saw, a picture without beginning, the ending of which I do not understand, a piece of life with the northern lights for a candle and Alaska for a frame."

"It is a large canvas," I murmured.

But he ignored me, for the picture he had in mind was before his eyes and he was seeing it.

"There are many names for this picture," he said. "But in the picture there are many sun-dogs, and it comes into my mind to call it 'The Sun-Dog Trail.' It was a long time ago, seven years ago, the fall of '97, when I saw the woman first time. At Lake Linderman I had one canoe, very good Peterborough canoe. I came over Chilcoot Pass with two thousand letters for Dawson. I was letter carrier. Everybody rush to Klondike at that time. Many people on trail. Many people chop down trees and make boats. Last water, snow in the air, snow on the ground, ice on the lake, on the river ice in the eddies. Every day more snow, more ice. Maybe one day, maybe three days, maybe six days, any day maybe freeze-up come, then no more water, all ice, everybody walk, Dawson six hundred miles, long time walk. Boat go very quick. Everybody want to go boat. Everybody say, 'Charley, two hundred dollars you take me in canoe,' 'Charley, three hundred dollars,' 'Charley, four hundred dollars.' I say no, all the time I say no. I am letter carrier.

"In morning I get to Lake Linderman. I walk all night and am much tired. I cook breakfast, I eat, then I sleep on the beach three hours. I wake up. It is ten o'clock. Snow is falling. There is wind, much wind that blows fair. Also, there is a woman who sits in the snow alongside. She is white woman, she is young, very pretty, maybe she is twenty years old, maybe twenty-five years old. She look at me. I look at her. She is very tired. She is no dance-woman. I see that right away. She is good woman, and she is very tired.

" 'You are Sitka Charley,' she says. I get up quick and roll blankets so snow does not get inside. 'I go to Dawson,' she says. 'I go in your canoe—how much?'

"I do not want anybody in my canoe. I do not like to say no. So I say, 'One thousand dollars.' Just for fun I say it, so woman cannot come with me, much better than say no. She look at me very hard, then she says, 'When you start?' I say right away. Then she says all right, she will give me one thousand dollars.

"What can I say? I do not want the woman, yet have I given my word that for one thousand dollars she can come. I am surprised. Maybe she make fun, too, so I say, 'Let me see thousand dollars.' And that woman, that young woman, all alone on the trail, there in the snow, she take out one thousand dollars, in greenbacks, and she put them in my hand. I look at money, I look at her. What can I say? I say, 'No, my canoe very small. There is no room for outfit.' She laugh. She says, 'I am great traveller. This is my outfit. She kick one small pack in the snow. It is two fur robes, canvas outside, some woman's clothes inside. I pick it up. Maybe thirty-five pounds. I am surprised. She take it away from me. She says, 'Come, let us start.' She carries pack into canoe. What can I say? I put my blankets into canoe. We start.

"And that is the way I saw the woman first time. The wind was fair. I put up small sail. The canoe went very fast, it flew like a bird over the high waves. The woman was much afraid. 'What for you come Klondike much afraid?' I ask. She laugh at me, a hard laugh, but she is still much afraid. Also is she very tired. I run canoe through rapids to Lake Bennett. Water very bad, and woman cry out because she is afraid. We go down Lake Bennett, snow, ice, wind like a gale, but woman is very tired and go to sleep.

"That night we make camp at Windy Arm. Woman sit by fire and eat supper. I look at her. She is pretty. She fix hair. There is much hair, and it is brown, also sometimes it is like gold in the firelight, when she turn her head, so, and flashes come from it like golden fire. The eyes are large and brown, sometimes warm like a candle behind a curtain, sometimes very hard and bright like broken ice when sun shines upon it. When she smile—how can I say?—when she smile I know white man like to kiss her, just like that, when she smile. She never do hard work. Her hands are soft, like baby's hand. She is soft all over, like baby. She is not thin, but round like baby; her arm, her leg, her muscles, all soft and round like baby. Her waist is small, and when she stand up, when she walk, or move her head or arm, it is—I do not know the word—but it is nice to look at, like—maybe I say she is built on lines like the lines of a good canoe, just like that, and when she move she is like the movement of the good canoe sliding through still water or leaping through water when it is white and fast and angry. It is very good to see.

"Why does she come into Klondike, all alone, with plenty of money? I do not know. Next day I ask her. She laugh and says: 'Sitka Charley, that is none of your business. I give you one thousand dollars take me to Dawson. That only is your business.' Next day after that I ask her what is her name. She laugh, then she says, 'Mary Jones, that is my name.' I do not know her name, but I know all the time that Mary Jones is not her name.

"It is very cold in canoe, and because of cold sometimes she not feel good. Sometimes she feel good and she sing. Her voice is like a silver bell, and I feel good all over like when I go into church at Holy Cross Mission, and when she sing I feel strong and paddle like hell. Then she laugh and says, 'You think we get to Dawson before freeze-up, Charley?' Sometimes she sit in canoe and is thinking far away, her eyes like that, all empty. She does not see Sitka Charley, nor the ice, nor the snow. She is far away. Very often she is like that, thinking far away. Sometimes, when she is thinking far away, her face is not good to see. It looks like a face that is angry, like the face of one man when he want to kill another man.

"Last day to Dawson very bad. Shore-ice in all the eddies, mush-ice in the stream. I cannot paddle. The canoe freeze to ice. I cannot get to shore. There is much danger. All the time we go down Yukon in the ice. That night there is much noise of ice. Then ice stop, canoe stop, everything stop. 'Let us go to shore,' the woman says. I say no, better wait. By and by, everything start down-stream again. There is much snow. I cannot see. At eleven o'clock at night, everything stop. At one o'clock everything start again. At three o'clock everything stop. Canoe is smashed like eggshell, but is on top of ice and cannot sink. I hear dogs howling. We wait. We sleep. By and by morning come. There is no more snow. It is the freeze-up, and there is Dawson. Canoe smash and stop right at Dawson. Sitka Charley has come in with two thousand letters on very last water.

"The woman rent a cabin on the hill, and for one week I see her no more. Then, one day, she come to me. 'Charley,' she says, 'how do you like to work for me? You drive dogs, make camp, travel with me.' I say that I make too much money carrying letters. She says, 'Charley, I will pay you more money.' I tell her that pick-and-shovel man get fifteen dollars a day in the mines. She says, 'That is four hundred and fifty dollars a month.' And I say, 'Sitka Charley is no pick-and-shovel man.' Then she says, 'I understand, Charley. I will give you seven hundred and fifty dollars each month.' It is a good price, and I go to work for her. I buy for her dogs and sled. We travel up Klondike, up Bonanza and Eldorado, over to Indian River, to Sulphur Creek, to Dominion, back across divide to Gold Bottom and to Too Much Gold, and back to Dawson. All the time she look for something, I do not know what. I am puzzled. 'What thing you look for?' I ask. She laugh. 'You look for gold?' I ask. She laugh. Then she says, 'That is none of your business, Charley.' And after that I never ask any more.

"She has a small revolver which she carries in her belt. Sometimes, on trail, she makes practice with revolver. I laugh. 'What for you laugh, Charley?' she ask. 'What for you play with that?' I say. 'It is no good. It is too small. It is for a child, a little plaything.' When we get back to Dawson she ask me to buy good revolver for her. I buy a Colt's 44. It is very heavy, but she carry it in her belt all the time.

"At Dawson comes the man. Which way he come I do not know. Only do I know he is che-cha-quo—what you call tenderfoot. His hands are soft, just like hers. He never do hard work. He is soft all over. At first I think maybe he is her husband. But he is too young. Also, they make two beds at night. He is maybe twenty years old. His eyes blue, his hair yellow, he has a little mustache which is yellow. His name is John Jones. Maybe he is her brother. I do not know. I ask questions no more. Only I think his name not John Jones. Other people call him Mr. Girvan. I do not think that is his name. I do not think her name is Miss Girvan, which other people call her. I think nobody know their names.

"One night I am asleep at Dawson. He wake me up. He says, 'Get the dogs ready; we start.' No more do I ask questions, so I get the dogs ready and we start. We go down the Yukon. It is night-time, it is November, and it is very cold—sixty-five below. She is soft. He is soft. The cold bites. They get tired. They cry under their breaths to themselves. By and by I say better we stop and make camp. But they say that they will go on. Three times I say better to make camp and rest, but each time they say they will go on. After that I say nothing. All the time, day after day, is it that way. They are very soft. They get stiff and sore. They do not under-stand moccasins, and their feet hurt very much. They limp, they stagger like drunken people, they cry under their breaths; and all the time they say, 'On! on! We will go on!'

"They are like crazy people. All the time do they go on, and on. Why do they go on? I do not know. Only do they go on. What are they after? I do not know. They are not after gold. There is no stampede. Besides, they spend plenty of money. But I ask questions no more. I, too, go on and on, because I am strong on the trail and because I am greatly paid.

"We make Circle City. That for which they look is not there. I think now that we will rest, and rest the dogs. But we do not rest, not for one day do we rest. 'Come,' says the woman to the man, 'let us go on.' And we go on. We leave the Yukon. We cross the divide to the west and swing down into the Tanana Country. There are new diggings there. But that for which they look is not there, and we take the back trail to Circle City.

"It is a hard journey. December is most gone. The days are short. It is very cold. One morning it is seventy below zero. 'Bet-ter that we do not travel to-day,' I say, 'else will the frost be unwarmed in the breathing and bite all the edges of our lungs. After that we will have bad cough, and maybe next spring will come pneumonia.' But they are *che-cha-quo*. They do not under-stand the trail. They are like dead people they are so tired, but they say, 'Let us go on.' We go on. The frost bites their lungs, and they get the dry cough. They cough till the tears run down

their cheeks. When bacon is frying they must run away from the
fire and cough half an hour in the snow. They freeze their cheeks
a little bit, so that the skin turns black and is very sore. Also, the
man freezes his thumb till the end is like to come off, and he must
wear a large thumb on his mitten to keep it warm. And sometimes,
when the frost bites hard and the thumb is very cold, he must
take off the mitten and put the hand between his legs next to the
skin, so that the thumb may get warm again.

"We limp into Circle City, and even I, Sitka Charley, am tired.
It is Christmas Eve. I dance, drink, make a good time, for to-
morrow is Christmas Day and we will rest. But no. It is five
o'clock in the morning—Christmas morning. I am two hours
asleep. The man stand by my bed. 'Come, Charley,' he says, 'harness the dogs. We start.'

"Have I not said that I ask questions no more? They pay me
seven hundred and fifty dollars each month. They are my masters.
I am their man. If they say, 'Charley, come, let us start for hell,' I
will harness the dogs, and snap the whip, and start for hell. So
I harness the dogs, and we start down the Yukon. Where do we
go? They do not say. Only do they say, 'On! on! We will go on!'

"They are very weary. They have travelled many hundreds of
miles, and they do not understand the way of the trail. Besides,
their cough is very bad—the dry cough that makes strong men
swear and weak men cry. But they go on. Every day they go on.
Never do they rest the dogs. Always do they buy new dogs. At
every camp, at every post, at every Indian village, do they cut out
the tired dogs and put in fresh dogs. They have much money,
money without end, and like water they spend it. They are crazy?
Sometimes I think so, for there is a devil in them that drives them
on and on, always on. What is it that they try to find? It is not
gold. Never do they dig in the ground. I think a long time. Then
I think it is a man they try to find. But what man? Never do we
see the man. Yet are they like wolves on the trail of the kill. But
they are funny wolves, soft wolves, baby wolves who do not understand the way of the trail. They cry aloud in their sleep at
night. In their sleep they moan and groan with the pain of their
weariness. And in the day, as they stagger along the trail, they cry
under their breaths. They are funny wolves.

"We pass Fort Yukon. We pass Fort Hamilton. We pass Minook. January has come and nearly gone. The days are very short. At nine o'clock comes daylight. At three o'clock comes night. And it is cold. And even I, Sitka Charley, am tired. Will we go on forever this way without end? I do not know. But always do I look along the trail for that which they try to find. There are few people on the trail. Sometimes we travel one hundred miles and never see a sign of life. It is very quiet. There is no sound. Sometimes it snows, and we are like wandering ghosts. Sometimes it is clear, and at midday the sun looks at us for a moment over the hills to the south. The northern lights flame in the sky, and the sun-dogs dance, and the air is filled with frost-dust.

"I am Sitka Charley, a strong man. I was born on the trail, and all my days have I lived on the trail. And yet have these two baby wolves made me very tired. I am lean, like a starved cat, and I am glad of my bed at night, and in the morning am I greatly weary. Yet ever are we hitting the trail in the dark before daylight, and still on the trail does the dark after nightfall find us. These two baby wolves! If I am lean like a starved cat, they are lean like cats that have never eaten and have died. Their eyes are sunk deep in their heads, bright sometimes as with fever, dim and cloudy sometimes like the eyes of the dead. Their cheeks are hollow like caves in a cliff. Also are their cheeks black and raw from many freezings. Sometimes it is the woman in the morning who says, 'I cannot get up. I cannot move. Let me die.' And it is the man who stands beside her and says, 'Come, let us go on.' And they go on. And sometimes it is the man who cannot get up, and the woman says, 'Come, let us go on.' But the one thing they do, and always do, is to go on. Always do they go on.

"Sometimes, at the trading posts, the man and woman get letters. I do not know what is in the letters. But it is the scent that they follow, these letters themselves are the scent. One time an Indian gives them a letter. I talk with him privately. He says it is a man with one eye who gives him the letter, a man who travels fast down the Yukon. That is all. But I know that the baby wolves are after the man with the one eye.

"It is February, and we have travelled fifteen hundred miles. We are getting near Bering Sea, and there are storms and blizzards.

The going is hard. We come to Anvig. I do not know, but I think sure they get a letter at Anvig, for they are much excited, and they say, 'Come, hurry, let us go on.' But I say we must buy grub, and they say we must travel light and fast. Also, they say that we can get grub at Charley McKeon's cabin. Then do I know that they take the big cut-off, for it is there that Charley McKeon lives where the Black Rock stands by the trail.

"Before we start, I talk maybe two minutes with the priest at Anvig. Yes, there is a man with one eye who has gone by and who travels fast." And I know that for which they look is the man with the one eye. We leave Anvig with little grub, and travel light and fast. There are three fresh dogs bought in Anvig, and we travel very fast. The man and woman are like mad. We start earlier in the morning, we travel later at night. I look sometimes to see them die, these two baby wolves, but they will not die. They go on and on. When the dry cough take hold of them hard, they hold their hands against their stomach and double up in the snow, and cough, and cough, and cough. They cannot walk, they cannot talk. Maybe for ten minutes they cough, maybe for half an hour, and then they straighten up, the tears from the coughing frozen on their faces, and the words they say are, 'Come, let us go on.'

"Even I, Sitka Charley, am greatly weary, and I think seven hundred and fifty dollars is a cheap price for the labor I do. We take the big cut-off, and the trail is fresh. The baby wolves have their noses down to the trail, and they say, 'Hurry!' All the time do they say, 'Hurry! Faster! Faster!' It is hard on the dogs. We have not much food and we cannot give them enough to eat, and they grow weak. Also, they must work hard. The woman has true sorrow for them, and often, because of them, the tears are in her eyes. But the devil in her that drives her on will not let her stop and rest the dogs.

"And then we come upon the man with the one eye. He is in the snow by the trail, and his leg is broken. Because of the leg he has made a poor camp, and has been lying on his blankets for three days and keeping a fire going. When we find him he is swearing. He swears like hell. Never have I heard a man swear like that man. I am glad. Now that they have found that for which they look, we will have rest. But the woman says, 'Let us start. Hurry!'

"I am surprised. But the man with the one eye says, 'Never mind me. Give me your grub. You will get more grub at McKeon's cabin to-morrow. Send McKeon back for me. But do you go on.' Here is another wolf, an old wolf, and he, too, thinks but the one thought, to go on. So we give him our grub, which is not much, and we chop wood for his fire, and we take his strongest dogs and go on. We left the man with one eye there in the snow, and he died there in the snow, for McKeon never went back for him. And who that man was, and why he came to be there, I do not know. But I think he was greatly paid by the man and the woman, like me, to do their work for them.

"That day and that night we had nothing to eat, and all next day we travelled fast, and we were weak with hunger. Then we came to the Black Rock, which rose five hundred feet above the trail. It was at the end of the day. Darkness was coming, and we could not find the cabin of McKeon. We slept hungry, and in the morning looked for the cabin. It was not there, which was a strange thing, for everybody knew that McKeon lived in a cabin at Black Rock. We were near to the coast, where the wind blows hard and there is much snow. Everywhere there were small hills of snow where the wind had piled it up. I have a thought, and I dig in one and another of the hills of snow. Soon I find the walls of the cabin, and I dig down to the door. I go inside. McKeon is dead. Maybe two or three weeks he is dead. A sickness had come upon him so that he could not leave the cabin. The wind and the snow had covered the cabin. He had eaten his grub and died. I looked for his cache, but there was no grub in it.

" 'Let us go on,' said the woman. Her eyes were hungry, and her hand was upon her heart, as with the hurt of something inside. She bent back and forth like a tree in the wind as she stood there. 'Yes, let us go on,' said the man. His voice was hollow, like the *klonk* of an old raven, and he was hunger-mad. His eyes were like live coals of fire, and as his body rocked to and fro, so rocked his soul inside. And I, too, said, 'Let us go on.' For that one thought, laid upon me like a lash for every mile of fifteen hundred miles, had burned itself into my soul, and I think that I, too, was mad. Besides, we could only go on, for there was no grub. And we went on, giving no thought to the man with the one eye in the snow.

"There is little travel on the big cut-off. Sometimes two or three months and nobody goes by. The snow had covered the trail, and there was no sign that men had ever come or gone that way. All day the wind blew and the snow fell, and all day we travelled, while our stomachs gnawed their desire and our bodies grew weaker with every step they took. Then the woman began to fall. Then the man. I did not fall, but my feet were heavy and I caught my toes and stumbled many times.

"That night is the end of February. I kill three ptarmigan with the woman's revolver, and we are made somewhat strong again. But the dogs have nothing to eat. They try to eat their harness, which is of leather and walrus-hide, and I must fight them off with a club and hang all the harness in a tree. And all night they howl and fight around that tree. But we do not mind. We sleep like dead people, and in the morning get up like dead people out of their graves and go on along the trail.

"That morning is the 1st of March, and on that morning I see the first sign of that after which the baby wolves are in search. It is clear weather, and cold. The sun stay longer in the sky, and there are sun-dogs flashing on either side, and the air is bright with frost-dust. The snow falls no more upon the trail, and I see the fresh sign of dogs and sled. There is one man with that outfit, and I see in the snow that he is not strong. He, too, has not enough to eat. The young wolves see the fresh sign, too, and they are much excited. 'Hurry!' they say. All the time they say, 'Hurry! Faster, Charley, faster!'

"We make hurry very slow. All the time the man and the woman fall down. When they try to ride on sled the dogs are too weak, and the dogs fall down. Besides, it is so cold that if they ride on the sled they will freeze. It is very easy for a hungry man to freeze. When the woman fall down, the man help her up. Sometimes the woman help the man up. By and by both fall down and cannot get up, and I must help them up all the time, else they will not get up and will die there in the snow. This is very hard work, for I am greatly weary, and as well I must drive the dogs, and the man and woman are very heavy with no strength in their bodies. So, by and by, I, too, fall down in the snow, and there is no one to help me up. I must get up by myself. And always do I get up by myself, and help them up, and make the dogs go on.

"That night I get one ptarmigan, and we are very hungry. And that night the man says to me, 'What time start to-morrow, Charley?' It is like the voice of a ghost. I say, 'All the time you make start at five o'clock.' 'To-morrow,' he says, 'we will start at three o'clock.' I laugh in great bitterness, and I say, 'You are dead man.' And he says, 'To-morrow we will start at three o'clock.'

"And we start at three o'clock, for I am their man, and that which they say is to be done, I do. It is clear and cold, and there is no wind. When daylight comes we can see a long way off. And it is very quiet. We can hear no sound but the beat of our hearts, and in the silence that is a very loud sound. We are like sleep-walkers, and we walk in dreams until we fall down; and then we know we must get up, and we see the trail once more and hear the beating of our hearts. Sometimes, when I am walking in dreams this way, I have strange thoughts. Why does Sitka Charley live? I ask myself. Why does Sitka Charley work hard, and go hungry, and have all this pain? For seven hundred and fifty dollars a month, I make the answer, and I know it is a foolish answer. Also is it a true answer. And after that never again do I care for money. For that day a large wisdom came to me. There was a great light, and I saw clear, and I knew that it was not for money that a man must live, but for a happiness that no man can give, or buy, or sell, and that is beyond all value of all money in the world.

"In the morning we come upon the last-night camp of the man who is before us. It is a poor camp, the kind a man makes who is hungry and without strength. On the snow there are pieces of blanket and of canvas, and I know what has happened. His dogs have eaten their harness, and he has made new harness out of his blankets. The man and woman stare hard at what is to be seen, and as I look at them my back feels the chill as of a cold wind against the skin. Their eyes are toil-mad and hunger-mad, and burn like fire deep in their heads. Their faces are like the faces of people who have died of hunger, and their cheeks are black with the dead flesh of many freezings. 'Let us go on,' says the man. But the woman coughs and falls in the snow. It is the dry cough where the frost has bitten the lungs. For a long time she coughs, then like a woman crawling out of her grave she crawls to her feet. The tears are ice upon her cheeks, and her breath makes a noise as it comes and goes, and she says, 'Let us go on.'

"We go on. And we walk in dreams through the silence. And every time we walk is a dream and we are without pain; and every time we fall down is an awakening, and we see the snow and the mountains and the fresh trail of the man who is before us, and we know all our pain again. We come to where we can see a long way over the snow, and that for which they look is before them. A mile away there are black spots upon the snow. The black spots move. My eyes are dim, and I must stiffen my soul to see. And I see one man with dogs and a sled. The baby wolves see, too. They can no longer talk, but they whisper, 'On, on. Let us hurry!'

"And they fall down, but they go on. The man who is before us, his blanket harness breaks often, and he must stop and mend it. Our harness is good, for I have hung it in trees each night. At eleven o'clock the man is half a mile away. At one o'clock he is a quarter of a mile away. He is very weak. We see him fall down many times in the snow. One of his dogs can no longer travel, and he cuts it out of the harness. But he does not kill it. I kill it with the axe as I go by, as I kill one of my dogs which loses its legs and can travel no more.

"Now we are three hundred yards away. We go very slow. Maybe in two, three hours we go one mile. We do not walk. All the time we fall down. We stand up and stagger two steps, maybe three steps, then we fall down again. And all the time I must help up the man and woman. Sometimes they rise to their knees and fall forward, maybe four or five times before they can get to their feet again and stagger two or three steps and fall. But always do they fall forward. Standing or kneeling, always do they fall forward, gaining on the trail each time by the length of their bodies.

"Sometimes they crawl on hands and knees like animals that live in the forest. We go like snails, like snails that are dying we go so slow. And yet we go faster than the man who is before us. For he, too, falls all the time, and there is no Sitka Charley to lift him up. Now he is two hundred yards away. After a long time he is one hundred yards away.

"It is a funny sight. I want to laugh out loud, Ha! ha! just like that, it is so funny. It is a race of dead men and dead dogs. It is like in a dream when you have a nightmare and run away very fast for your life and go very slow. The man who is with me is mad. The woman is mad. I am mad. All the world is mad, and I want to laugh, it is so funny.

"The stranger-man who is before us leaves his dogs behind and goes on alone across the snow. After a long time we come to the dogs. They lie helpless in the snow, their harness of blanket and canvas on them, the sled behind them, and as we pass them they whine to us and cry like babies that are hungry.

"Then we, too, leave our dogs and go on alone across the snow. The man and the woman are nearly gone, and they moan and groan and sob, but they go on. I, too, go on. I have but one thought. It is to come up to the stranger-man. Then it is that I shall rest, and not until then shall I rest, and it seems that I must lie down and sleep for a thousand years, I am so tired.

"The stranger-man is fifty yards away, all alone in the white snow. He falls and crawls, staggers, and falls and crawls again. He is like an animal that is sore wounded and trying to run from the hunter. By and by he crawls on hands and knees. He no longer stands up. And the man and woman no longer stand up. They, too, crawl after him on hands and knees. But I stand up. Sometimes I fall, but always do I stand up again.

"It is a strange thing to see. All about is the snow and the silence, and through it crawl the man and the woman, and the stranger-man who goes before. On either side the sun are sundogs, so that there are three suns in the sky. The frost-dust is like the dust of diamonds, and all the air is filled with it. Now the woman coughs, and lies still in the snow until the fit has passed, when she crawls on again. Now the man looks ahead, and he is blear-eyed as with old age and must rub his eyes so that he can see the stranger-man. And now the stranger-man looks back over his shoulder. And Sitka Charley, standing upright, maybe falls down and stands upright again.

"After a long time the stranger-man crawls no more. He stands slowly upon his feet and rocks back and forth. Also does he take off one mitten and wait with revolver in his hand, rocking back and forth as he waits. His face is skin and bones and frozen black. It is a hungry face. The eyes are deep-sunk in his head, and the lips are snarling. The man and woman, too, get upon their feet and they go toward him very slowly. And all about is the snow and the silence. And in the sky are three suns, and all the air is flashing with the dust of diamonds.

"And thus it was that I, Sitka Charley, saw the baby wolves make their kill. No word is spoken. Only does the stranger-man snarl with his hungry face. Also does he rock to and fro, his shoulders drooping, his knees bent, and his legs wide apart so that he does not fall down. The man and woman stop maybe fifty feet away. Their legs, too, are wide apart so that they do not fall down, and their bodies rock to and fro. The stranger-man is very weak. His arm shakes, so that when he shoots at the man his bullet strikes in the snow. The man cannot take off his mitten. The stranger-man shoots at him again, and this time the bullet goes by in the air. Then the man takes the mitten in his teeth and pulls it off. But his hand is frozen and he cannot hold the revolver, and it falls in the snow. I look at the woman. Her mitten is off, and the big Colt's revolver is in her hand. Three times she shoot, quick, just like that. The hungry face of the stranger-man is still snarling as he falls forward into the snow.

"They do not look at the dead man. 'Let us go on,' they say. And we go on. But now that they have found that for which they look, they are like dead. The last strength has gone out of them. They can stand no more upon their feet. They will not crawl, but desire only to close their eyes and sleep. I see not far away a place for camp. I kick them. I have my dog-whip, and I give them the lash of it. They cry aloud, but they crawl. And they do crawl to the place for camp. I build fire so that they will not freeze. Then I go back for sled. Also, I kill the dogs of the stranger-man so that we may have food and not die. I put the man and woman in blankets and they sleep. Sometimes I wake them and give them little bit of food. They are not awake, but they take the food. The woman sleep one day and a half. Then she wake up and go to sleep again. The man sleep two days and wake up and go to sleep again. After that we go down to the coast at St. Michaels. And when the ice goes out of Bering Sea, the man and woman go away on a steamship. But first they pay me my seven hundred and fifty dollars a month. Also, they make me a present of one thousand dollars. And that was the year that Sitka Charley gave much money to the Mission at Holy Cross."

"But why did they kill the man?" I asked.

Sitka Charley delayed reply until he had lighted his pipe. He glanced at the *Police Gazette* illustration and nodded his head at it familiarly. Then he said, speaking slowly and ponderingly:

"I have thought much. I do not know. It is something that happened. It is a picture I remember. It is like looking in at the window and seeing the man writing a letter. They came into my life and they went out of my life, and the picture is as I have said, without beginning, the end without understanding."

"You have painted many pictures in the telling," I said.

"Ay," he nodded his head. "But they were without beginning and without end."

"The last picture of all had an end," I said.

"Ay," he answered. "But what end?"

"It was a piece of life," I said.

"Ay," he answered. "It was a piece of life."

To Build a Fire

Day had broken cold and gray, exceedingly cold and gray, when the man turned aside from the main Yukon trail and climbed the high earth-bank, where a dim and little-travelled trail led eastward through the fat spruce timberland. It was a steep bank, and he paused for breath at the top, excusing the act to himself by looking at his watch. It was nine o'clock. There was no sun nor hint of sun, though there was not a cloud in the sky. It was a clear day, and yet there seemed an intangible pall over the face of things, a subtle gloom that made the day dark, and that was due to the absence of sun. This fact did not worry the man. He was used to the lack of sun. It had been days since he had seen the sun, and he knew that a few more days must pass before that cheerful orb, due south, would just peep above the sky-line and dip immediately from view.

The man flung a look back along the way he had come. The Yukon lay a mile wide and hidden under three feet of ice. On top of this ice were as many feet of snow. It was all pure white, rolling in gentle undulations where the ice-jams of the freeze-up had formed. North and south, as far as his eye could see, it was unbroken white, save for a dark hair-line that curved and twisted from around the spruce-covered island to the south, and that curved and twisted away into the north, where it disappeared behind another spruce-covered island. This dark hair-line was the trail—the main trail—that led south five hundred miles to the Chilcoot Pass, Dyea, and salt water; and that led north seventy miles to Dawson, and still on to the north a thousand miles to Nulato, and finally to St. Michael on Bering Sea, a thousand miles and half a thousand more.

But all this—the mysterious, far-reaching hair-line trail, the absence of sun from the sky, the tremendous cold, and the strangeness and weirdness of it all—made no impression on the man. It was not because he was long used to it. He was a newcomer in the land, a *chechaquo*, and this was his first winter. The trouble with him was that he was without imagination. He was quick and alert in the things of life, but only in the things, and not in the significances. Fifty degrees below zero meant eighty-odd degrees of frost. Such fact impressed him as being cold and uncomfortable, and that was all. It did not lead him to meditate upon his frailty as a creature of temperature, and upon man's frailty in general, able only to live within certain narrow limits of heat and cold; and from there on it did not lead him to the conjectural field of immortality and man's place in the universe. Fifty degrees below zero stood for a bite of frost that hurt and that must be guarded against by the use of mittens, ear-flaps, warm moccasins, and thick socks. Fifty degrees below zero was to him just precisely fifty degrees below zero. That there should be anything more to it than that was a thought that never entered his head.

As he turned to go on, he spat speculatively. There was a sharp, explosive crackle that startled him. He spat again. And again, in the air, before it could fall to the snow, the spittle crackled. He knew that at fifty below spittle crackled on the snow, but this spittle had crackled in the air. Undoubtedly it was colder than fifty below—how much colder he did not know. But the temperature did not matter. He was bound for the old claim on the left fork of Henderson Creek, where the boys were already. They had come over across the divide from the Indian Creek country, while he had come the roundabout way to take a look at the possibilities of getting out logs in the spring from the islands in the Yukon. He would be in to camp by six o'clock; a bit after dark, it was true, but the boys would be there, a fire would be going, and a hot supper would be ready. As for lunch, he pressed his hand against the protruding bundle under his jacket. It was also under his shirt, wrapped up in a handkerchief and lying against the naked skin. It was the only way to keep the biscuits from freezing. He smiled agreeably to himself as he thought of those biscuits, each cut open and sopped in bacon grease, and each enclosing a generous slice of fried bacon.

He plunged in among the big spruce trees. The trail was faint. A foot of snow had fallen since the last sled had passed over, and he was glad he was without a sled, travelling light. In fact, he carried nothing but the lunch wrapped in the handkerchief. He was surprised, however, at the cold. It certainly was cold, he concluded, as he rubbed his numb nose and cheek-bones with his mittened hand. He was a warm-whiskered man, but the hair on his face did not protect the high cheek-bones and the eager nose that thrust itself aggressively into the frosty air.

At the man's heels trotted a dog, a big native husky, the proper wolf-dog, gray-coated and without any visible or temperamental difference from its brother, the wild wolf. The animal was depressed by the tremendous cold. It knew that it was no time for travelling. Its instinct told it a truer tale than was told to the man by the man's judgment. In reality, it was not merely colder than fifty below zero; it was colder than sixty below, than seventy below. It was seventy-five below zero. Since the freezing-point is thirty-two above zero, it meant that one hundred and seven degrees of frost obtained. The dog did not know anything about thermometers. Possibly in its brain there was no sharp consciousness of a condition of very cold such as was in the man's brain. But the brute had its instinct. It experienced a vague but menacing apprehension that subdued it and made it slink along at the man's heels, and that made it question eagerly every unwonted movement of the man as if expecting him to go into camp or to seek shelter somewhere and build a fire. The dog had learned fire, and it wanted fire, or else to burrow under the snow and cuddle its warmth away from the air.

The frozen moisture of its breathing had settled on its fur in a fine powder of frost, and especially were its jowls, muzzle, and eyelashes whitened by its crystalled breath. The man's red beard and mustache were likewise frosted, but more solidly, the deposit taking the form of ice and increasing with every warm, moist breath he exhaled. Also, the man was chewing tobacco, and the muzzle of ice held his lips so rigidly that he was unable to clear his chin when he expelled the juice. The result was that a crystal beard of the color and solidity of amber was increasing its length on his chin. If he fell down it would shatter itself, like glass, into brittle fragments. But he did not mind the appendage. It was the penalty all tobacco-chewers paid in that country, and he had been out before in two cold snaps. They had not been so cold as this, he knew, but by the spirit thermometer at Sixty Mile he knew they had been registered at fifty below and at fifty-five.

He held on through the level stretch of woods for several miles, crossed a wide flat of nigger-heads, and dropped down a bank to the frozen bed of a small stream. This was Henderson Creek, and he knew he was ten miles from the forks. He looked at his watch. It was ten o'clock. He was making four miles an hour, and he calculated that he would arrive at the forks at half-past twelve. He decided to celebrate that event by eating his lunch there.

The dog dropped in again at his heels, with a tail drooping discouragement, as the man swung along the creek-bed. The furrow of the old sled-trail was plainly visible, but a dozen inches of snow covered the marks of the last runners. In a month no man had come up or down that silent creek. The man held steadily on. He was not much given to thinking, and just then particularly he had nothing to think about save that he would eat lunch at the forks and that at six o'clock he would be in camp with the boys. There was nobody to talk to; and, had there been, speech would have been impossible because of the ice-muzzle on his mouth. So he continued monotonously to chew tobacco and to increase the length of his amber beard.

Once in a while the thought reiterated itself that it was very cold and that he had never experienced such cold. As he walked along he rubbed his cheek-bones and nose with the back of his mittened hand. He did this automatically, now and again changing hands. But rub as he would, the instant he stopped his cheek-bones went numb, and the following instant the end of his nose went numb. He was sure to frost his cheeks; he knew that, and experienced a pang of regret that he had not devised a nose-strap of the sort Bud wore in cold snaps. Such a strap passed across the cheeks, as well, and saved them. But it did n't matter much, after all. What were frosted cheeks? A bit painful, that was all; they were never serious.

Empty as the man's mind was of thoughts, he was keenly observant, and he noticed the changes in the creek, the curves and bends and timber-jams, and always he sharply noted where he placed his feet. Once, coming around a bend, he shied abruptly, like a startled horse, curved away from the place where he had been walking, and retreated several paces back along the trail. The creek he knew was frozen clear to the bottom,—no creek could contain water in that arctic winter,—but he knew also that there were springs that bubbled out from the hillsides and ran along under the snow and on top the ice of the creek. He knew that the coldest snaps never froze these springs, and he knew likewise their danger. They were traps. They hid pools of water under the snow that might be three inches deep, or three feet. Sometimes a skin of ice half an inch thick covered them, and in turn was covered by the snow. Sometimes there were alternate layers of water and ice-skin, so that when one broke through he kept on breaking through for a while, sometimes wetting himself to the waist.

That was why he had shied in such panic. He had felt the give under his feet and heard the crackle of a snow-hidden ice-skin. And to get his feet wet in such a temperature meant trouble and danger. At the very least it meant delay, for he would be forced to stop and build a fire, and under its protection to bare his feet while he dried his socks and moccasins. He stood and studied the creek-bed and its banks, and decided that the flow of water came from the right. He reflected awhile, rubbing his nose and cheeks, then skirted to the left, stepping gingerly and testing the footing for each step. Once clear of the danger, he took a fresh chew of tobacco and swung along at his four-mile gait.

In the course of the next two hours he came upon several similar traps. Usually the snow above the hidden pools had a sunken, candied appearance that advertised the danger. Once again, however, he had a close call; and once, suspecting danger, he compelled the dog to go on in front. The dog did not want to go. It hung back until the man shoved it forward, and then it went quickly across the white, unbroken surface. Suddenly it broke through, floundered to one side, and got away to firmer footing. It had wet its forefeet and legs, and almost immediately the water that clung to it turned to ice. It made quick efforts to lick the ice off its legs, then dropped down in the snow and began to bite out the ice that had formed between the toes. This was a matter of instinct. To permit the ice to remain would mean sore feet. It did not know this. It merely obeyed the mysterious prompting that arose from the deep crypts of its being. But the man knew, having achieved a judgment on the subject, and he removed the mitten from his right hand and helped tear out the ice-particles. He did not expose his fingers more than a minute, and was astonished at the swift numbness that smote them. It certainly was cold. He pulled on the mitten hastily, and beat the hand savagely across his chest.

At twelve o'clock the day was at its brightest. Yet the sun was too far south on its winter journey to clear the horizon. The bulge of the earth intervened between it and Henderson Creek, where the man walked under a clear sky at noon and cast no shadow. At half-past twelve, to the minute, he arrived at the forks of the creek. He was pleased at the speed he had made. If he kept it up, he would certainly be with the boys by six. He unbuttoned his jacket and shirt and drew forth his lunch. The action consumed no more than a quarter of a minute, yet in that brief moment the numbness laid hold of the exposed fingers. He did not put the mitten on, but, instead, struck the fingers a dozen sharp smashes against his leg. Then he sat down on a snow-covered log to eat. The sting that followed upon the striking of his fingers against his leg ceased so quickly that he was startled. He had had no chance to take a bite of biscuit. He struck the fingers repeatedly and returned them to the mitten, baring the other hand for the purpose of eating. He tried to take a mouthful, but the ice-muzzle prevented. He had forgotten to build a fire and thaw out. He chuckled at his foolishness, and as he chuckled he noted the numbness creeping into the exposed fingers. Also, he noted that the stinging which had first come to his toes when he sat down was already passing away. He wondered whether the toes were warm or numb. He moved them inside the moccasins and decided that they were numb.

He pulled the mitten on hurriedly and stood up. He was a bit frightened. He stamped up and down until the stinging returned into the feet. It certainly was cold, was his thought. That man from Sulphur Creek had spoken the truth when telling how cold it sometimes got in the country. And he had laughed at him at the time! That showed one must not be too sure of things. There was no mistake about it, it *was* cold. He strode up and down, stamping his feet and threshing his arms, until reassured by the returning warmth. Then he got out matches and proceeded to make a fire. From the undergrowth, where high water of the previous spring had lodged a supply of seasoned twigs, he got his fire-wood. Working carefully from a small beginning, he soon had a roaring fire, over which he thawed the ice from his face and in the protection of which he ate his biscuits. For the moment the cold of space was outwitted. The dog took satisfaction in the fire, stretching out close enough for warmth and far enough away to escape being singed.

When the man had finished, he filled his pipe and took his comfortable time over a smoke. Then he pulled on his mittens, settled the ear-flaps of his cap firmly about his ears, and took the creek trail up the left fork. The dog was disappointed and yearned back toward the fire. This man did not know cold. Possibly all the generations of his ancestry had been ignorant of cold, of real cold, of cold one hundred and seven degrees below freezing-point. But the dog knew; all its ancestry knew, and it had inherited the knowledge. And it knew that it was not good to walk abroad in such fearful cold. It was the time to lie snug in a hole in the snow and wait for a curtain of cloud to be drawn across the face of outer space whence this cold came. On the other hand, there was no keen intimacy between the dog and the man. The one was the toil-slave of the other, and the only caresses it had ever received were the caresses of the whip-lash and of harsh and menacing throat-sounds that threatened the whip-lash. So the dog made no effort to communicate its apprehension to the man. It was not concerned in the welfare of the man; it was for its own sake that it yearned back toward the fire. But the man whistled, and spoke to it with the sound of whip-lashes, and the dog swung in at the man's heels and followed after.

The man took a chew of tobacco and proceeded to start a new amber beard. Also, his moist breath quickly powdered with white his mustache, eyebrows, and lashes. There did not seem to be so many springs on the left fork of the Henderson, and for half an hour the man saw no signs of any. And then it happened. At a place where there were no signs, where the soft, unbroken snow seemed to advertise solidity beneath, the man broke through. It was not deep. He wet himself halfway to the knees before he floundered out to the firm crust.

He was angry, and cursed his luck aloud. He had hoped to get into camp with the boys at six o'clock, and this would delay him an hour, for he would have to build a fire and dry out his footgear. This was imperative at that low temperature—he knew that much; and he turned aside to the bank, which he climbed. On top, tangled in the underbrush about the trunks of several small spruce trees, was a high-water deposit of dry fire-wood—sticks and twigs, principally, but also larger portions of seasoned branches and fine, dry, last-year's grasses. He threw down several large pieces on top of the snow. This served for a foundation and prevented the young flame from drowning itself in the snow it otherwise would melt. The flame he got by touching a match to a small shred of birch-bark that he took from his pocket. This burned even more readily than paper. Placing it on the foundation, he fed the young flame with wisps of dry grass and with the tiniest dry twigs.

He worked slowly and carefully, keenly aware of his danger. Gradually, as the flame grew stronger, he increased the size of the twigs with which he fed it. He squatted in the snow, pulling the twigs out from their entanglement in the brush and feeding directly to the flame. He knew there must be no failure. When it is seventy-five below zero, a man must not fail in his first attempt to build a fire—that is, if his feet are wet. If his feet are dry, and he fails, he can run along the trail for half a mile and restore his circulation. But the circulation of wet and freezing feet cannot be restored by running when it is seventy-five below. No matter how fast he runs, the wet feet will freeze the harder.

All this the man knew. The old-timer on Sulphur Creek had told him about it the previous fall, and now he was appreciating the advice. Already all sensation had gone out of his feet. To build the fire he had been forced to remove his mittens, and the fingers had quickly gone numb. His pace of four miles an hour had kept his heart pumping blood to the surface of his body and to all the extremities. But the instant he stopped, the action of the pump eased down. The cold of space smote the unprotected tip of the planet, and he, being on that unprotected tip, received the full force of the blow. The blood of his body recoiled before it. The blood was alive, like the dog, and like the dog it wanted to hide away and cover itself up from the fearful cold. So long as he walked four miles an hour, he pumped that blood, willy-nilly, to the surface; but now it ebbed away and sank down into the recesses of his body. The extremities were the first to feel its absence. His wet feet froze the faster, and his exposed fingers numbed the faster, though they had not yet begun to freeze. Nose and cheeks were already freezing, while the skin of all his body chilled as it lost its blood.

But he was safe. Toes and nose and cheeks would be only touched by the frost, for the fire was beginning to burn with strength. He was feeding it with twigs the size of his finger. In another minute he would be able to feed it with branches the size of his wrist, and then he could remove his wet foot-gear, and, while it dried, he could keep his naked feet warm by the fire, rubbing them at first, of course, with snow. The fire was a success. He was safe. He remembered the advice of the old-timer on Sulphur Creek, and smiled. The old-timer had been very serious in laying down the law that no man must travel alone in the Klondike after fifty below. Well, here he was; he had had the accident; he was alone; and he had saved himself. Those old-timers were rather womanish, some of them, he thought. All a man had to do was to keep his head, and he was all right. Any man who was a man could travel alone. But it was surprising, the rapidity with which his cheeks and nose were freezing. And he had not thought his fingers could go lifeless in so short a time. Lifeless they were, for he could scarcely make them move together to grip a twig, and they seemed remote from his body and from him. When he touched a twig, he had to look and see whether or not he had hold of it. The wires were pretty well down between him and his finger-ends.

All of which counted for little. There was the fire, snapping and crackling and promising life with every dancing flame. He started to untie his moccasins. They were coated with ice; the thick German socks were like sheaths of iron halfway to the knees; and the moccasin strings were like rods of steel all twisted and knotted as by some conflagration. For a moment he tugged with his numb fingers, then, realizing the folly of it, he drew his sheath-knife.

But before he could cut the strings, it happened. It was his own fault or, rather, his mistake. He should not have built the fire under the spruce tree. He should have built it in the open. But it had been easier to pull the twigs from the brush and drop them directly on the fire. Now the tree under which he had done this carried a weight of snow on its boughs. No wind had blown for weeks, and each bough was fully freighted. Each time he had pulled a twig he had communicated a slight agitation to the tree —an imperceptible agitation, so far as he was concerned, but an agitation sufficient to bring about the disaster. High up in the tree one bough capsized its load of snow. This fell on the boughs beneath, capsizing them. This process continued, spreading out and involving the whole tree. It grew like an avalanche, and it descended without warning upon the man and the fire, and the fire was blotted out! Where it had burned was a mantle of fresh and disordered snow.

The man was shocked. It was as though he had just heard his own sentence of death. For a moment he sat and stared at the spot where the fire had been. Then he grew very calm. Perhaps the old-timer on Sulphur Creek was right. If he had only had a trail-mate he would have been in no danger now. The trail-mate could have built the fire. Well, it was up to him to build the fire over again, and this second time there must be no failure. Even if he succeeded, he would most likely lose some toes. His feet must be badly frozen by now, and there would be some time before the second fire was ready.

Such were his thoughts, but he did not sit and think them. He was busy all the time they were passing through his mind. He made a new foundation for a fire, this time in the open, where no treacherous tree could blot it out. Next, he gathered dry grasses and tiny twigs from the high-water flotsam. He could not bring his fingers together to pull them out, but he was able to gather them by the handful. In this way he got many rotten twigs and bits of green moss that were undesirable, but it was the best he could do. He worked methodically, even collecting an armful of the larger branches to be used later when the fire gathered strength. And all the while the dog sat and watched him, a certain yearning wistfulness in its eyes, for it looked upon him as the fire-provider, and the fire was slow in coming.

When all was ready, the man reached in his pocket for a second piece of birch-bark. He knew the bark was there, and, though he could not feel it with his fingers, he could hear its crisp rustling as he fumbled for it. Try as he would, he could not clutch hold of it. And all the time, in his consciousness, was the knowledge that each instant his feet were freezing. This thought tended to put him in a panic, but he fought against it and kept calm. He pulled on his mittens with his teeth, and threshed his arms back and forth, beating his hands with all his might against his sides. He did this sitting down, and he stood up to do it; and all the while the dog sat in the snow, its wolf-brush of a tail curled around warmly over its forefeet, its sharp wolf-ears pricked forward intently as it watched the man. And the man, as he beat and threshed with his arms and hands, felt a great surge of envy as he regarded the creature that was warm and secure in its natural covering.

After a time he was aware of the first faraway signals of sensation in his beaten fingers. The faint tingling grew stronger till it evolved into a stinging ache that was excruciating, but which the man hailed with satisfaction. He stripped the mitten from his right hand and fetched forth the birch-bark. The exposed fingers were quickly going numb again. Next he brought out his bunch of sulphur matches. But the tremendous cold had already driven the life out of his fingers. In his effort to separate one match from the others, the whole bunch fell in the snow. He tried to pick it out of the snow, but failed. The dead fingers could neither touch nor clutch. He was very careful. He drove the thought of his freezing feet, and nose, and cheeks, out of his mind, devoting his whole soul to the matches. He watched, using the sense of vision in place of that of touch, and when he saw his fingers on each side the bunch, he closed them—that is, he willed to close them, for the wires were down, and the fingers did not obey. He pulled the mitten on the right hand, and beat it fiercely against his knee. Then, with both mittened hands, he scooped the bunch of matches, along with much snow, into his lap. Yet he was no better off.

After some manipulation he managed to get the bunch between the heels of his mittened hands. In this fashion he carried it to his mouth. The ice crackled and snapped when by a violent effort he opened his mouth. He drew the lower jaw in, curled the upper lip out of the way, and scraped the bunch with his upper teeth in order to separate a match. He succeeded in getting one, which he dropped on his lap. He was no better off. He could not pick it up. Then he devised a way. He picked it up in his teeth and scratched it on his leg. Twenty times he scratched before he succeeded in lighting it. As it flamed he held it with his teeth to the birch-bark. But the burning brimstone went up his nostrils and into his lungs, causing him to cough spasmodically. The match fell into the snow and went out.

The old-timer on Sulphur Creek was right, he thought in the moment of controlled despair that ensued: after fifty below, a man should travel with a partner. He beat his hands, but failed in exciting any sensation. Suddenly he bared both hands, removing the mittens with his teeth. He caught the whole bunch between the heels of his hands. His arm-muscles not being frozen enabled him to press the hand-heels tightly against the matches. Then he scratched the bunch along his leg. It flared into flame, seventy sulphur matches at once! There was no wind to blow them out. He kept his head to one side to escape the strangling fumes, and held the blazing bunch to the birch-bark. As he so held it, he became aware of sensation in his hand. His flesh was burning. He could smell it. Deep down below the surface he could feel it. The sensation developed into pain that grew acute. And still he endured it, holding the flame of the matches clumsily to the bark that would not light readily because his own burning hands were in the way, absorbing most of the flame.

At last, when he could endure no more, he jerked his hands apart. The blazing matches fell sizzling into the snow, but the birch-bark was alight. He began laying dry grasses and the tiniest twigs on the flame. He could not pick and choose, for he had to lift the fuel between the heels of his hands. Small pieces of rotten wood and green moss clung to the twigs, and he bit them off as well as he could with his teeth. He cherished the flame carefully and awkwardly. It meant life, and it must not perish. The withdrawal of blood from the surface of his body now made him begin to shiver, and he grew more awkward. A large piece of green moss fell squarely on the little fire. He tried to poke it out with his fingers, but his shivering frame made him poke too far, and he disrupted the nucleus of the little fire, the burning grasses and tiny twigs separating and scattering. He tried to poke them together again, but in spite of the tenseness of the effort, his shivering got away with him, and the twigs were hopelessly scattered. Each twig gushed a puff of smoke and went out. The fire-provider had failed. As he looked apathetically about him, his eyes chanced on the dog, sitting across the ruins of the fire from him, in the snow, making restless, hunching movements, slightly lifting one forefoot and then the other, shifting its weight back and forth on them with wistful eagerness.

The sight of the dog put a wild idea into his head. He remembered the tale of the man, caught in a blizzard, who killed a steer and crawled inside the carcass, and so was saved. He would kill the dog and bury his hands in the warm body until the numbness went out of them. Then he could build another fire. He spoke to the dog, calling it to him; but in his voice was a strange note of fear that frightened the animal, who had never known the man to speak in such way before. Something was the matter, and its suspicious nature sensed danger—it knew not what danger, but somewhere, somehow, in its brain arose an apprehension of the man. It flattened its ears down at the sound of the man's voice, and its restless, hunching movements and the liftings and shiftings of its forefeet became more pronounced; but it would not come to the man. He got on his hands and knees and crawled toward the dog. This unusual posture again excited suspicion, and the animal sidled mincingly away.

The man sat up in the snow for a moment and struggled for calmness. Then he pulled on his mittens, by means of his teeth, and got upon his feet. He glanced down at first in order to assure himself that he was really standing up, for the absence of sensation in his feet left him unrelated to the earth. His erect position in itself started to drive the webs of suspicion from the dog's mind; and when he spoke peremptorily, with the sound of whip-lashes in his voice, the dog rendered its customary allegiance and came to him. As it came within reaching distance, the man lost his control. His arms flashed out to the dog, and he experienced genuine surprise when he discovered that his hands could not clutch, that there was neither bend nor feeling in the fingers. He had forgotten for the moment that they were frozen and that they were freezing more and more. All this happened quickly, and before the animal could get away, he encircled its body with his arms. He sat down in the snow, and in this fashion held the dog, while it snarled and whined and struggled.

But it was all he could do, hold its body encircled in his arms and sit there. He realized that he could not kill the dog. There was no way to do it. With his helpess hands he could neither draw nor hold his sheath-knife nor throttle the animal. He released it, and it plunged wildly away, with tail between its legs, and still snarling. It halted forty feet away and surveyed him curiously, with ears sharply pricked forward. The man looked down at his hands in order to locate them, and found them hanging on the ends of his arms. It struck him as curious that one should have to use his eyes in order to find out where his hands were. He began threshing his arms back and forth, beating the mittened hands against his sides. He did this for five minutes, violently, and his heart pumped enough blood up to the surface to put a stop to his shivering. But no sensation was aroused in the hands. He had an impression that they hung like weights on the ends of his arms, but when he tried to run the impression down, he could not find it.

A certain fear of death, dull and oppressive, came to him. This fear quickly became poignant as he realized that it was no longer a mere matter of freezing his fingers and toes, or of losing his hands and feet, but that it was a matter of life and death with the chances against him. This threw him into a panic, and he turned and ran up the creek-bed along the old, dim trail. The dog joined in behind and kept up with him. He ran blindly, without intention, in fear such as he had never known in his life. Slowly, as he ploughed and floundered through the snow, he began to see things again,—the banks of the creek, the old timber-jams, the leafless aspens, and the sky. The running made him feel better. He did not shiver. Maybe, if he ran on, his feet would thaw out; and, anyway, if he ran far enough, he would reach camp and the boys. Without doubt he would lose some fingers and toes and some of his face; but the boys would take care of him, and save the rest of him when he got there. And at the same time there was another thought in his mind that said he would never get to the camp and the boys; that it was too many miles away, that the freezing had too great a start on him, and that he would soon be stiff and dead. This thought he kept in the background and refused to consider. Sometimes it pushed itself forward and demanded to be heard, but he thrust it back and strove to think of other things.

It struck him as curious that he could run at all on feet so frozen that he could not feel them when they struck the earth and took the weight of his body. He seemed to himself to skim along above the surface, and to have no connection with the earth. Somewhere he had once seen a winged Mercury, and he wondered if Mercury felt as he felt when skimming over the earth.

His theory of running until he reached camp and the boys had one flaw in it: he lacked the endurance. Several times he stumbled, and finally he tottered, crumpled up, and fell. When he tried to rise, he failed. He must sit and rest, he decided, and next time he would merely walk and keep on going. As he sat and regained his breath, he noted that he was feeling quite warm and comfortable. He was not shivering, and it even seemed that a warm glow had come to his chest and trunk. And yet, when he touched his nose or cheeks, there was no sensation. Running would not thaw them out. Nor would it thaw out his hands and feet. Then the thought came to him that the frozen portions of his body must be extending. He tried to keep this thought down, to forget it, to think of something else; he was aware of the panicky feeling that it caused, and he was afraid of the panic. But the thought asserted itself, and persisted, until it produced a vision of his body totally frozen. This was too much, and he made another wild run along the trail. Once he slowed down to a walk, but the thought of the freezing extending itself made him run again.

And all the time the dog ran with him, at his heels. When he fell down a second time, it curled its tail over its forefeet and sat in front of him, facing him, curiously eager and intent. The warmth and security of the animal angered him, and he cursed it till it flattened down its ears appeasingly. This time the shivering came more quickly upon the man. He was losing in his battle with the frost. It was creeping into his body from all sides. The thought of it drove him on, but he ran no more than a hundred feet, when he staggered and pitched headlong. It was his last panic. When he had recovered his breath and control, he sat up and entertained in his mind the conception of meeting death with dignity. However, the conception did not come to him in such terms. His idea of it was that he had been making a fool of himself, running around like a chicken with its head cut off—such was the simile that occurred to him. Well, he was bound to freeze anyway, and he might as well take it decently. With this new-found peace of mind came the first glimmerings of drowsiness. A good idea, he thought, to sleep off to death. It was like taking an anæsthetic. Freezing was not so bad as people thought. There were lots worse ways to die.

He pictured the boys finding his body next day. Suddenly he found himself with them, coming along the trail and looking for himself. And, still with them, he came around a turn in the trail and found himself lying in the snow. He did not belong with himself any more, for even then he was out of himself, standing with the boys and looking at himself in the snow. It certainly was cold, was his thought. When he got back to the States he could tell the folks what real cold was. He drifted on from this to a vision of the old-timer on Sulphur Creek. He could see him quite clearly, warm and comfortable, and smoking a pipe.

"You were right, old hoss; you were right," the man mumbled to the old-timer of Sulphur Creek.

Then the man drowsed off into what seemed to him the most comfortable and satisfying sleep he had ever known. The dog sat facing him and waiting. The brief day drew to a close in a long, slow twilight. There were no signs of a fire to be made, and, besides, never in the dog's experience had it known a man to sit like that in the snow and make no fire. As the twilight drew on, its eager yearning for the fire mastered it, and with a great lifting and shifting of forefeet, it whined softly, then flattened its ears down in anticipation of being chidden by the man. But the man remained silent. Later, the dog whined loudly. And still later it crept close to the man and caught the scent of death. This made the animal bristle and back away. A little longer it delayed, howling under the stars that leaped and danced and shone brightly in the cold sky. Then it turned and trotted up the trail in the direction of the camp it knew, where were the other food-providers and fire-providers.

EXPLANATORY NOTES

Jack London's references to specific towns and geographical features in Alaska and the Canadian Yukon are for the most part highly accurate in these stories. Given my own emphasis on treating London's Northland as an abstract symbolic terrain, I have refrained from glossing particular locations, which can easily be identified by consulting any detailed map of the Yukon Territory.

"The White Silence"

2 [Epworth] The Epworth League was a Methodist youth organization founded in 1889.

3 [gee-pole] A steering mechanism attached to the front right runner of the dog sled.

7 [bench claim] Title for a piece of mining property issued by a judge or law court.

"The Son of the Wolf"

19 [Jelchs, the Raven] In the mythology of the Indians of Upper Tanana in northern Alaska (where this story takes place), as well as Northwest Coast tribes such as the Tlingit, the totemic figure of the Raven plays the role of Transformer or Creator. One Tlingit creation myth in particular recounts how a spirit called Yehlh, appearing in the form of a Raven, released the sun and gave fire and light to the earth.

"In a Far Country"

28 [*voyageur*] A person who transported goods and men by boat during the Canadian fur trade.

32 [Yukon stove-pipe] The Yukon stove was a portable contraption that was for used for cooking as well as heating.

33 [to clip his coupons] The practice by which owners of stock routinely redeemed their corporate dividends.

34 [slush-lamp] A primitive lamp usually made of a tin can which used bacon grease instead of oil.

37   [Caliban] The savage, deformed slave of the exiled Duke Prospero in Shakepeare's *The Tempest*.

"To the Man on Trail"

43   [Lochinvar] The hero of a ballad in Sir Walter Scott's *Marmion*, who runs away with another lover just as she is about to be married to someone else.

49   [P. C. store] The store of a trading company (presumably the Alaska Commercial Company), which often served as a bank for its customers.

50   [Captain Constantine] Beginning in 1895, Inspector Charles Constantine was the chief land agent, collector of customs, as well as the leader of the Northwest Mounted Police in the Yukon District.

51   [jumps the limit, and drops the whole sack] Instead of purchasing a claim in Dawson City for Westondale, Castrell gambles away the entire sum.

"The Wisdom of the Trail"

58   [Factor] The principal financial agent of a trading company.

"An Odyssey of the North"

61   [Yukon stove] See note 32.

61   [*voyageurs*] See note 28.

61   [Wolseley] In 1884–1885 Garnet Joseph Wolseley headed the British military campaign along the Nile River to the city of Khartoum.

61   [Louis Reil (sic)] In 1869–1870 and in 1885 Louis Riel unsuccessfully led Frenchmen, Indians, and half-breeds to fight for their cultural and political rights by rebelling against British rule in the Northwest Territories.

62   [*coureurs du bois*] An unlicensed French or French-Indian fur trader or trapper.

62   [*bois brules*] Literally, burnt wood, Canadian term for French-Indian half-breeds.

67   [a king of Eldorado] A miner who has struck it rich in the Klondike's Eldorado Creek, named after the mythic New World land of limitless gold.

69   [quartz . . . placer] Quartz gold is embedded in rocks, usually a

more substantial source than placer gold, which is gold mixed in with sand or gravel.

70   [slush-lamp] See note 34.

73   [oomiak] Same as umaik, a large, open boat made of skins used by Eskimos for transporting goods.

90   [Constantine] See note 50.

"The God of His Fathers"
94   [Chief Factor] See note 58.

"Siwash"
106   [Yukon stove] See note 32.

"Grit of Women"
121   [Sulphur Creek stampede] One important site of the early rush to the Klondike gold fields.

124   [factor's] See note 58.

128   [sun-dogs] Colloquial for parhelions, bright, colored spots of light sometimes seen in conjunction with a solar halo.

"The Law of Life"
147   [bald-face] A type of grizzly bear.

"The Death of Ligoun"
162   [bald-face] See note 147.

"The League of the Old Men"
187   [time of the captains] During the early stages of settlement, the Yukon was under paramilitary control by the officers of the Northwest Mounted Police, before a governor was assigned to oversee the region. The Yukon was not officially declared a Territory of the Canadian Dominion until 1898. As the story opens Old Imber is waiting for trial in the Barracks headquarters of the Mounted Police.

189   [Eldorado king's sombrero] See note 67.

"The Story of Jees Uck"
206   [clipped coupons] See note 33.

217   [Rhodes of Alaska] Cecil J. Rhodes (1853–1902), financier and

colonial administrator who helped develop South Africa under British rule.

"The Sun-Dog Trail"

246 [title] See note 128.

247 ["Leda and the Swan"] Leading to the birth of Helen of Troy, this mythic rape between the woman Leda and the god Zeus (disguised as a swan) was the subject of numerous fin-de-siècle paintings.

254 [stampede] See note 121.

"To Build a Fire"

268 [niggerheads] dark bunches of vegetation spotting the Yukon landscape.

273 [wires were pretty well down] A metaphor taken from telegraph transmission to explain the man's loss of control over his body.

APPENDIX

This is the order of stories as published in Jack London's first three collected Northland volumes, followed parenthetically by places and dates of initial periodical publication.

The Son of the Wolf: Tales of the Far North. Houghton, Mifflin and Co., Boston, April 1900.

"The White Silence" (*Overland Monthly* 33 [February 1899]).
"The Son of the Wolf" (*Overland Monthly* 33 [April 1899]).
"The Men of Forty-Mile" (*Overland Monthly* 33 [May 1899]).
"In a Far Country" (*Overland Monthly,* 33 [June 1899]).
"To the Man on Trail" (*Overland Monthly* 33 [January 1899]).
"The Priestly Prerogative" (*Overland Monthly* 34 [July 1899]).
"The Wisdom of the Trail" (*Overland Monthly* 34 [December 1899]).
"The Wife of a King" (*Overland Monthly* 34 [August 1899]).
"An Odyssey of the North" (*Atlantic Monthly* 85 [January 1900]).

The God of His Fathers & Other Stories. McClure, Phillips and Co., New York, May 1901.

"The God of His Fathers" (*McClure's* 17 [May 1901]).
"The Great Interrogation" (*Ainslee's Magazine* 6 [December 1900]).
"Which Make Men Remember" (published as "Uri Bram's God" in *San Francisco Examiner, Sunday Examiner Magazine,* June 24, 1900).
"Siwash" (*Ainslee's Magazine* 7 [March 1901]).
"The Man with the Gash" (*McClure's* 15 [September 1900]).
"Jan, the Unrepentant" (*Outing* 36 [August 1900]).
"Grit of Women" (*McClure's* 15 [August 1900]).
"Where the Trail Forks" (*Outing* 37 [December 1900]).

"A Daughter of the Aurora" (*San Francisco Wave*, December 24, 1899).

"At the Rainbow's End" (*Pittsburgh Leader*, March 24, 1901).

"The Scorn of Women" (*Overland Monthly* 37 [May 1901]).

Children of the Frost. The Macmillan Co., New York, September 1902.

"In the Forests of the North" (*Pearson's Magazine* 14 [September 1902]).

"The Law of Life" (*McClure's* 16 [March 1901]).

"Nam-Bok the Unveracious" (published as "Nam-Bok, the Liar" in *Ainslee's Magazine* 10 [August 1902]).

"The Master of Mystery" (*Out West* 17 [September 1902]).

"The Sunlanders" (no periodical publication).

"The Sickness of Lone Chief" (*Out West* 17 [October 1902]).

"Keesh, the Son of Keesh" (published as "Keesh, Son of Keesh" in *Ainslee's Magazine* 8 [January 1902]).

"The Death of Ligoun" (no periodical publication).

"Li Wan, the Fair" (published as "Li-Wan, the Fair" in *Atlantic Monthly* 90 [August 1902]).

"The League of the Old Men" (*Brandur Magazine* 1 [October 4, 1902]).

Publication dates and places for the remaining stories in this present edition are as follows:

The Faith of Men. The Macmillan Co., New York, 1904.

"The Story of Jees Uck" (*Smart Set* 8 [September 1902]).

Love of Life and Other Stories. The Macmillan Co., New York, 1907.

"Love of Life" (*McClure's* 26 [December 1905]).

"The Sun-Dog Trail" (*Harper's* 112 [December 1905]).

Lost Face. The Macmillan Co., New York, 1910.

"To Build a Fire" (*The Century Magazine* 76 [August 1908]).